TWELVE MONTHS

JIM BUTCHER

TWELVE MONTHS

A NOVEL OF THE DRESDEN FILES

ACE
NEW YORK

ACE
Published by Berkley
An imprint of Penguin Random House LLC
1745 Broadway, New York, NY 10019
penguinrandomhouse.com

Library of Congress Cataloging-in-Publication Data

Names: Butcher, Jim, 1971- author
Title: Twelve months : a novel of the Dresden files / Jim Butcher.
Description: New York : ACE, [2026] | Series: The Dresden files
Identifiers: LCCN 2025030089 (print) | LCCN 2025030090 (ebook) |
ISBN 9780593199336 (hardcover) | ISBN 9780593199350 (ebook)
Subjects: LCSH: Dresden, Harry (Fictitious character)--Fiction |
Wizards--Fiction | LCGFT: Fantasy fiction | Novels | Fiction
Classification: LCC PS3602.U85 T94 2026 (print) | LCC PS3602.U85 (ebook)
LC record available at https://lccn.loc.gov/2025030089
LC ebook record available at https://lccn.loc.gov/2025030090

Printed in the United States of America
1st Printing

The authorized representative in the EU for product safety and compliance is
Penguin Random House Ireland, Morrison Chambers, 32 Nassau Street,
Dublin D02 YH68, Ireland, https://eu-contact.penguin.ie.

For the people who helped me through a very bad year.
You know who you are. Thank you.

TWELVE MONTHS

Chapter
One

Pain is a fire.

That's true for all of the people, some of the time. If you've never had to stand in that fire, be patient: Your turn is coming.

Whether the pain is physical or purely mental doesn't really matter—it turns out that your brain reacts to it the same way, lighting up many of the same centers of perception. Some brainy types in lab coats proved that one fairly recently. The suffering from a broken heart is similar to that from a gunshot wound, in terms of how our minds react over the long term.

It all hurts.

When you have to live with that hurt, with that pain, when there's no way to turn it off or get away from it, you start to make adjustments. Your choices in how you deal with your pain determine the course of your recovery. That's why people who go through a difficult ordeal sometimes come out stronger, and sometimes they come out broken—but they always come out . . .

Changed.

Pain is a fire.

I opened my eyes so I could stop seeing Murphy's cold, dead face.

Her lips, turning blue.

"Murph?" I mumbled, looking around.

But I was alone.

I checked my windup Mickey Mouse alarm clock. Three thirty a.m.

That meant I had slept fifteen minutes longer than I had the night before. Almost one hour and thirty minutes of rest.

Progress.

It had been somewhere around three weeks since Karrin Murphy died and a big bite of the city got stomped flat. Three weeks since Chicago had lost tens of thousands of innocent lives, seen a million people displaced from their homes, and had its infrastructure wrecked by an EMP—an energetic magical pulse. Three weeks since I had seen young wizards I had helped train, friends, die before their enemies. Three weeks since I had been cast out from the White Council of Wizardry entirely.

Three weeks since the battle with Ethniu had announced to an entire metroplex of poor innocent normies that the things under the bed and hiding in the closet weren't just in their imaginations anymore.

The alarm was set for five a.m. Which gave me about ninety minutes of my own time when no one with a kind, concerned expression was watching me.

Alone time.

I let the pain have me. Replayed old memories of those who were gone. Relived the most hideous moments of the battle, and of battles past.

I don't win them all.

I cried. I cried and I screamed into my pillow until my stomach muscles were sore and my throat ached. In the snug, lonely little chamber in the basement of the castle, with stone walls a foot thick, no one was going to hear me.

That used up maybe thirty minutes. Then I sort of sank into a stupor, staring while tears came steadily.

When the alarm rang, I started putting myself back together as best I could. I got up and washed my face and brushed my teeth. I went through a stretching routine that the ignorant would call yoga. I made the bed.

I still had a broken arm. The gunshot wound in my calf had closed and healed up nicely. My ankle wasn't swollen anymore. Those didn't really trouble me. None of the physical injuries did.

The real pain was all in my head.

That's why the routine was important. Fires are all chaos. Putting them out requires the imposition of order, and getting your head back into order means routine. I didn't feel like doing any of the standard morning things—mostly I wanted to lie there and hurt. But that wasn't the same thing as healing.

There would be time to let myself bleed again tomorrow.

And there were people who needed me.

So I followed the routine, trusting that the pain would slowly grow less. It hadn't, that I could tell, but it would.

I kept telling myself that. Out loud. I'd been devastated before. I'd healed before.

I just needed time.

I got dressed in exercise clothes and shambled out into the castle's early morning. Pain focuses the mind wonderfully—since you can't really think about very much else. I went to the kitchen to make myself eat some breakfast, get the morning report, and then I would hit the gym for a couple of hours.

Squats focus the mind wonderfully, too.

Will Borden was waiting for me in the kitchen. He looked like a statue of Hercules at three-quarters scale, maybe a little under five and a half feet of heavy muscle. He wore jeans, a button-down shirt, and a blazer, all tailored to fit someone of his unusual proportions, and his eyes were thick with sleep. Will had been living in guest quarters in the castle (which was to say on an air mattress in a dank stone chamber) and had taken some time off from being a successful engineering consultant to serve as my de facto castellan.

"Harry," Will said with a yawn and passed over a cup of steaming coffee, black.

I felt seen.

I picked up the coffee, mumbled something that could have been a curse or a greeting under my breath, and drank liquid morning for a minute or two. Will did the same. The castle's commercial kitchen was huge, all stainless steel and polished concrete. It was also empty, for the time being.

In a bit, the volunteer cooks from the Ordo Lebes would come in and start preparing a meal for me and my staff (Will). They'd also cook for the refugees from the neighborhood, folks whose homes had burned and who had been unable to find another place to stay—about thirty people total in a few different families.

Then there were a half dozen Knights of the Bean, all single men who had survived the battle and had nowhere else to go.

Oh, and a couple of kids who had been homeless already. The streets were a hell of a lot worse than they'd ever been, and child services were swamped. So I did what I could.

I told them all they could stay with me until they got back on their feet. Most of them were sleeping on air mattresses and camp rolls, but they had a roof, which was better than a lot of the town was doing. I could imagine how horrified the stuffier members of the White Council of Wizardry would be at my opening up my home like this. If I'd been a community activist or a cult leader instead of a wizard, I'd have been off to a great start.

But for the moment, Will and I had the place to ourselves—except for the occasional rustle and whisper of one of the Little Folk, my personal bodyguards, who were always on hand when I was outside my private chambers.

The Little Folk had stopped a bombing attempt by parties unknown a week before. The bad guys had sent gremlins. Maybe I should have put out a hit on Joe Dante.

"Okay. What's today, Will?" I mumbled.

"Back day, so get a few extra carbs," the brawny young man advised me.

I got out some oatmeal, eggs, bacon, and fruit. Started making breakfast for us. Second breakfast would come after the workout.

"After that?" I asked.

Will checked his list. He said something, and then said it again more slowly, and then said, "Harry?"

I looked up from where I'd been folding eggs for a few moments and remembering the blood draining from Murphy's face. "Sorry."

He gave me a lopsided smile. "'S'okay. I said you have a meeting with Michael at noon. He's done roughing in the residential chambers upstairs and wants to talk about how you want to arrange things in the main hall."

I grunted. "Anything else?"

Will consulted his checklist. "No—you wanted this afternoon left open to get ready, remember?"

I frowned, got out some pans, lit the gas stove, and started cooking in earnest. I honestly couldn't recall what he was talking about and reminded myself not to beat me up over it. I wasn't firing on all cylinders for an excellent reason.

I just needed time.

"Ready for what?" I asked him.

"Um," Will said, frowning. "Your first date with Ms. Raith. It's tonight."

My cylinders did a slow turn. "Ah," I said. "Right."

Lara Raith was the power behind, above, under, around, and everywhere else except on the throne in the White Court of vampires. She'd had enough clout, a few years ago, to get the US Navy to send a ship to support yours truly after the Battle of Chichén Itzá, and word had it that she hadn't slowed down since. Apparently, on the internet she was in pictures with a lot of people in big money. And big tech. And big pharma. And big oil. And big politics.

I wouldn't say that they were helpless against her charms, but only because I didn't want to be that lame guy observing the obvious out loud. When Lara crooked a finger, a lot of people came running. They couldn't help it. She was the next best thing to a succubus, and I wasn't sure even one of them could have been more dangerous.

And here I was, engaged to her.

We hadn't been on a date or anything, unless you counted the fights we'd had beside (and against) each other. Given my record with women, I honestly wasn't sure which column to put them in. We were, however, to be married in just under a year, by decree of my boss, the Queen of Air and Darkness.

I mean, I know politics makes strange bedfellows, but this was ridiculous.

I realized that I'd been sitting in my room and staring blankly at the wall for about twenty minutes while I went over all these thoughts. My brain just wouldn't get moving. Maybe I needed caffeine. I took another five minutes to think about that and was interrupted by a knock at my door.

"Hmm," I said, with no particular emphasis.

"Harry, it's me," said Molly. "I'm coming in. All right?"

"Hmm," I agreed.

The door opened, and a tall young woman came into the room. She was wearing dark blue leather pants that didn't creak and a purplish drapey top that showed off her collarbones. She looked like she'd skipped a lot of meals, her blue eyes were sharp, and her long hair, silver-blond, hung down to her lower back. Molly liked changing her appearance a lot.

She took one glance at me and winced. "Oh, for the love of . . . Harry, are you all right?"

"Fine," I said. "Just . . . you know."

"Let's assume I don't," she said quietly, and came to sit on the bed beside me. She generated subtle tension by doing it. I noted it and let it go right on by. Just as I always had.

"Hey," she said. Then a few seconds later she said, with gentle emphasis, "Hey."

I blinked and looked up at her. "Oh right. Sorry. I haven't been sleeping so well."

"I know," she said.

"How's that?" I asked.

"I feel it when you dream. You haven't done much of that. None of it is very friendly."

Molly was the Winter Lady, a genuine faerie princess. She'd been simply mortal once, but that time was past. Now she carried Power, and a lot of it, and she had responsibilities I wasn't sure I understood completely. Power was a dangerous thing to hand to anyone. It makes people more of what they already are. So far, Molly had been more focused and more disciplined, but there were times when I wondered how much of her was still that person I'd known since she was a kid, and how much of her was the Winter Lady.

She took my hand and held it in both of hers, and I felt some tension I hadn't sensed ease out of me. Today, at least, she was just Molly.

"Look, maybe I can get this delayed for a while," she said.

"Get what delayed?"

"Your date with Lara?" she reminded me gently.

"Right, right." I shook my head. "Mab seemed pretty insistent last time she came by."

"You're in no shape for it," she said.

"I'm fine," I said. "I mean the arm has a ways to go, but other than that."

Her hand squeezed mine. "Harry, come on."

I closed my eyes and bowed my head. "I just keep seeing her die, Molls."

She put an arm around my shoulders and pulled me toward her.

I leaned in. She felt warm and kind, and part of me whispered that I didn't deserve such comforts after all the things I'd done wrong.

That's what pain sounds like when it talks to you.

I don't know when I started crying, but I did it in stillness, without sobbing. Just tears.

"Christ," I said. "I'm tired of this."

"I know, Harry," she said. "I know. But I need to know where your head is."

"It's on your shoulder," I said.

She bumped my leg with her knee. "I'm serious." She was quiet for a moment. Then she said, "Once upon a time, there was an apprentice wizard. Her mentor was kind, but sometimes rash, and determined never to let an innocent be harmed."

"I don't think I've heard this one," I said.

"Shut up, wiseass," Molly said absently. "I'm telling a story. The apprentice learned from her mentor and made mistakes and tried to make up for them. Until one day, her mentor was shot and killed."

"The end?" I guessed.

She put a thumb in my trapezius muscle, the one I'd twinged in the gym that morning, and dug into it absently. It felt amazing and I shut up. "She blamed herself for his death. And she went out and made all manner of unwise choices. She got involved with dark powers. And she did some dark things." Molly paused to think. "And the whole time, she kept thinking to herself that it couldn't really get any worse, and if it did she'd probably earned it."

"Thanks for cheering me up."

She let out a soft snort through her nose. "Harry. I'm just saying. I've been to a place kind of like where you are now. Before I expose you to Lara Raith, I need to know that you don't think you deserve horrible things for what happened."

I was silent for a long time.

Because I'd thought about it.

When one of the White Court feeds on you . . . it feels good. Nothing else feels as good. Nothing else matters.

Nothing hurts.

The thought of letting Lara take a nibble of me was like standing with my toes on the edge of a cliff. I could wiggle them and feel the little pebbles falling out from under them and think to myself, *What if?*

Lara had once offered me surcease. Leaned in and whispered the word, like an invocation. It had haunted me ever since.

But never more than now.

I closed my eyes. And I thought of the one thing that protected me from that delicious, probably poisonous promise.

Maggie. My daughter.

She was at that age where I'd been starting to outline awkward but necessary talks with her about biology and such. She wasn't quite there yet, but the time was coming. I had her lined up for school at St. Mark's Academy for the Gifted and Talented, and my dog, Mouse, was going with her. She liked to snuggle up next to me for the second movie at a drive-in, and almost always fell asleep with her head on my chest before it was over.

I thought of the trust and love implied in her sleepy, heavy warmth. And, like always, I took a step back from the cliff.

"I'm not planning on drinking Lara's Kool-Aid," I said quietly.

Molly lifted her head, lifted my chin with her fingertips, and peered at my expression closely. "You're sure?"

"I'm . . ." I sighed. "I'm hurting. I just need time. I'll get through this."

Her beautiful features looked uncertain and worried.

"I'm sorry Mab is making you . . . you know." I grimaced. "Plan everything."

Her mouth quirked in a sardonic smile. "Yeah. Well. I'm just worried about you." She took in a deep breath. "If Lara tries to use her come-hither on you, she's breaking the agreement for the first outing. Winter's people will be nearby. All you have to do is say the word, and they'll be there."

"If she can't use her mojo on me," I said, "why are you so worried?"

"Because she's charming, manipulative, extremely intelligent, and she's forgotten more about seduction than most will ever know," Molly said. "Plus, she's a woman. And history suggests you don't deal well with those."

"Hey," I said. Then I scowled. "Yeah. Well. It's just coffee. Right?"

"This time," she said. "But I need your head in it, okay? Focused."

I took a deep breath, closed my eyes, and willed my thoughts to clear.

It was possible that they reduced their opacity. Slightly.

I just needed time.

And I wasn't going to get it.

"Okay," I said. "Let's do this."

Chapter Two

Chicago was closed for remodeling.

The Eye of Balor, a magical superweapon currently residing deep under my very own private spooky island of Demonreach in Lake Michigan, had inflicted the equivalent of a massive electromagnetic pulse on the whole town.

Anything with a microchip in it was history. Pretty much anything that did anything with electricity was history. Light bulbs, automobiles, televisions, radios, streetlights—and generators and batteries—all had been rendered into inert junk. Massive numbers of circuit boards, capacitors, chips, filaments, and all other manner of electronic equipment had to be replaced, and the country quite simply didn't have enough parts to get the job done.

Less than a month after the pulse, Chicago was back in the dark ages, with a curfew of eight o'clock, and candles and chemical glow sticks provided most of the light after sundown. Emergency priority had been given to police and utility services, and they were working around the clock to get things up and running again, but Chicago being Chicago, that meant that the Gold Coast was starting to slowly light up again and most of the rest of the city got real wary at night.

All the dead automobiles were gradually being towed away, but there were so many of them that they'd had trouble finding places to store them until they could be repaired, if they ever got enough parts to get the job done—assuming you weren't one of the unlucky ones whose cars got smashed out of the way by heavy military equipment rumbling through the pulse zone to combat "the terrorists" who had inflicted it on the good citizenry.

"The terrorists" was how everyone was talking about it on TV, Bob the Skull had reported to me. That's how Ethniu's attack on Chicago was being interpreted by the mortal world: as a terrorist attack. One that had leveled skyscrapers and left eight million people with medieval levels of technology.

The smell was becoming medieval, too. The sewers mostly didn't require much in the way of electronics to function, but the treatment plants did, and so did the pumps that filled the water towers. For the most part, bathing had become something you did with bottled water, if you didn't have access to your own nineteenth-century tech.

The only reliable way to get around town at the moment was on motorcycles that had been brought out after the pulse (since you never knew which streets would be blocked by stalled cars) or bicycles, or walking. Some of the main roads had been cleared enough to let military and FEMA support vehicles in, but in most of the town it was blind chance whether or not any given street was open.

The federal government had responded with a massive effort to go to the aid of the citizens of Chicago, and to give them credit, most people seemed to have enough bottled water—but food was tight and getting tighter. A city the size of Chicago needs its roads like a living animal needs its arteries. Despite a massive outpouring of help from the rest of the nation (everyone from the NAACP to the Red Cross was collecting canned goods and sending them our way), the real problem was that it was hard to ship food into the city, hard to do business, hard to transport things around town, hard to carry the food up the stairs to apartments.

Things were getting tense.

A million people had been displaced from their homes, either in buildings that had been destroyed or in the neighboring buildings that had been flooded with dust and smashed and damaged by debris. A large but unknown number of citizens had simply been killed in the battle, mostly as collateral damage. Thousands, if not tens of thousands, more were dying for lack of advanced medical care caused by a combination of an overloaded system, no power, and greatly curtailed communications. Millions were trying to flee the city for areas that still had electricity and clean water and plumbing, causing even more problems along the choked roads.

Those who stayed were mostly the stubborn, the foolish, the well-prepared, those too old to flee, or those tied down with small children who couldn't chance walking them out of the disaster zone.

Oh. And predators.

Wolves get fat in winter.

Chicago's version of that metaphorical winter was always summertime, when it got warm enough for the violence to escalate. It was hard to get local news, what with nothing working, but word from the few friendly faces I still had in the police department was that murders and violent crime had gone up a hell of a lot more than expected. They thought. The police were having trouble even keeping track of how much violence was going on—the chaos was a giant flashing neon opportunity sign for anyone who wanted vengeance on anyone else to go out and take it.

After all, guns still worked.

I came out the doors of the castle wearing my long black leather duster and a black baseball cap over my shaggy hair. A couple of the Knights of the Bean were on guard outside the place, shotguns that would normally have been anathema in Chicago in hand, and they nodded to me in passing. I wore jeans and motorcycle boots and a black T-shirt with white lettering that read WHINE LATER. SUCK IT UP NOW, because I respected the Stoics.

This was a date, so I wasn't carrying my staff, or an assault rifle or a rocket launcher, but my blasting rod was tied to its thong inside my duster; my shield bracelet was ready.

If I needed more than that to survive a coffee date, I was kind of screwed anyway.

Outside, a carriage was waiting for me, a slim little glossy black number behind a glossy black horse. I knew the fae driving it, one of the Sidhe wearing a red driving cap. The Redcap didn't even glance at me as he waited in the driver's seat—his unnaturally bright eyes were scanning everything in sight all at once, somehow, his body tense and ready for action.

I didn't speak to him, either, or show any discomfort. You don't show weakness to the Winter Fae. They get ideas.

I stomped over to the carriage and got up into it, and a second later the "horse" (I didn't believe for a second that it was a natural horse, and a quick probe with my wizard's senses told me it was just something, maybe a Black Dog, glamoured to look like one) took off at a trot and soon we were moving, clippety-clop down the streets of a modern city.

A lot of people were out walking. Not many jobs were still functioning, but cold storage of food had vanished, so everyone had to get out for a lot of things most every day. That meant either walking a long way or standing in a long line, or both, so simply procuring victuals had become a full-time job for many. They kept mostly to the sidewalks by pure habit, but a lot of kids and young people were using the streets, and the few cars that were moving around them proved to be no faster than my own conveyance.

The city was weirdly silent. No one was talking much. People stayed in tight groups or defended the space around them with body language and glares. I got a lot of glowers as the carriage went down the street. I even heard someone mutter my name to a companion. *That's Harry Dresden. Wizard.*

The looks I got weren't friendly ones.

The government might have been trying to convince people that terrorists had hit the city, but the people who were actually there knew how full of crap the government was. They'd seen mythic armies smashing into one another, seen monsters tearing people apart, seen giants and ogres and elves and twisted things with no names go screaming into battle with their own eyes. They'd seen their neighbors run down and killed. Their homes smashed and burned.

They knew the supernatural world had come to their town and gutted it.

And I was the town wizard. The guy in the phone book. A known quantity of weird. The fact that I'd been fighting to keep the town safe wouldn't matter much in the aftermath, not to people who were as hurt and scared and shocked and tired as I was. I understood. And I just didn't have the energy to be angry about it.

Well. No one threw any rocks at me. At least that was something.

The carriage took about forty minutes to make a trip that had taken ten a month ago, and wound up outside of McAnally's Pub.

There was a crowd gathered in the parking lot, where a sort of impromptu market of walled plastic canopies and tents had popped up. I recognized a lot of the faces from the local supernatural community. There were several of the larger and rougher types from our crowd hanging around conspicuously, returning the glares of passersby with level looks, while the rest of the magical crowd conducted business, doing some with cash and some by barter.

A lot of enclaves like this one had sprung up around the city, where neighbors or other like-minded folk had gathered together, forted up, and posted guards. Wolves like easy targets. If they had a choice between going at an organized group and going at isolated individuals, they went for the loners.

At the same time my carriage was pulling up, there was a shining white and silver cart drawn by a pair of muscular security guys who wore light jackets, even on a simmering July evening on bicycles, coming down the street from the other direction. The black carriage and the white cart stopped opposite each other next to the little parking lot, and the not-horse and the Redcap traded steady looks with the two security guys, who dismounted and braced to attention.

I got out of the carriage, while Lara got out of her white cart.

Lara Raith cut a stunning figure, like always. She was a woman who looked like a magnificent thirty, though I knew she was at least a century old. She wore black riding boots, blue jeans that she made look amazing, and a simple white T-shirt that was dating out of its class, like me. Her raven-dark hair was pulled back into a ponytail that fell past her shoulders, and silver glinted at her pale throat and upon her ears. She smiled and nodded at the nearest people in the crowd outside of the pub.

They smiled back, even if they did it nervously.

I knew how they felt.

Lara's summer-sky-blue eyes fell on me, and her smile widened as she walked toward me. I went forward to meet her about halfway between our guards.

"Harry," she said, and extended her hand.

"Hey, Lara," I said. I took her cool fingers in mine, and my body's engines revved, somewhere in the background. They weren't important. I bowed over her hand, almost brushing her fingers with my lips, but not quite. Then I stepped forward, capturing her hand under my arm, and she fell into step beside me smoothly as we approached the pub. The sun cast our shadows out in front of us, hers slim and straight, and mine long, wide, and looming.

I felt her fingers tighten slightly on my duster's sleeve and stroke it thoughtfully. "Isn't that terribly hot?" she asked.

"Yes," I said.

She looked up at me for a moment, lips pursed, began to say something, and then seemed to think better of it. She fell quiet, nodding to those we passed like a queen.

I suppose she was one, of sorts.

We went down the steps to the sunken entrance. I opened the door, and we went into McAnally's.

It was my favorite pub. The thirteen ceiling fans spread throughout the barroom were still now. Thirteen wooden columns carved with figures from the Grimm fairy tales, the unvarnished ones, supported a fairly low ceiling. Thirteen stools stood along the winding bar, and thirteen tables were spread throughout the room. The layout of the place was intended to disperse and disrupt negative magical energies, and it had always felt like being home. Behind the bar, Mac himself was tending to a woodstove and a charcoal grill, both being vented by battery-powered fans blowing up into their hoods. The bar and all the tables but one were filled, and that one in the far corner, set a bit away from everyone else.

"Look at all the witnesses," I muttered.

"Depending on how it goes, I suppose they could always be innocent bystanders," Lara said, the corner of her mouth quirked.

"Heh," I said, a little surge of something that wasn't quite so heavy flickering through my chest. I walked her to the table, nodding to a couple of folks I knew, studying a lot of faces I didn't. The alliance between the White Court of vampires and the Winter Court of the Fae was big news. The marriage I'd been threatened with was a part of that alliance. I think it was mostly a PR thing. That was the whole reason for the series of dates Mab had required—we were showing the flag for the new alliance.

I held out a chair for Lara, got her settled, then took off my duster, looking around the room for any potential hostile gazes. Jokes aside, I didn't have any illusions about innocent bystanders. The proper people to witness Lara and me together had been carefully curated—and some of them would probably be representing beings who didn't like me very much.

A lot of eyes dropped as my gaze swept around the room.

Damn. What did my face look like?

"Mac," Lara called. "Coffee?"

"Ungh," Mac said agreeably, without looking back. An old wooden sign hanging up behind the bar read, in plain lettering, **TIPS APPRE-CIATED**. It was an artifact I'd stolen from the vault of Lord Hades himself. The working of its power was so subtle that I would never have felt it if I hadn't known what to look for, but it was doing its job. Things would be peaceful here.

"You look like hell," Lara said frankly.

"No," I said. "I've been there. Looks different than this."

"Worse?" she said. "Or better?"

"Oh, way better," I said, and told the corners of my mouth to turn up a little.

She studied my face carefully. "You haven't been sleeping, have you?"

"It's all been so exciting," I said in a dull tone.

"It must be difficult to be in Chicago," she said. "Have you considered leaving for a while?"

I arched an eyebrow at her.

Her mouth quirked at the corner again. "No. Of course not."

"A lot of people got a lot more hurt than I did," I said. "I'm looking out for some of them."

"Are you?" Lara asked. She put her hands flat on the table and chose her words carefully. "I know you want to. You're a protector. That's who you are. But you clearly aren't your usual self."

"I'll be fine."

"Harry," she said. "I know that when you see people with empty cups, it's your instinct to fill them." She studied my face. "Can you do that if your own cup is empty?"

I was quiet for a long moment.

"Coffee up," Mac said from across the room.

I pushed myself slowly to my feet, walked across the room, got the two cups, and carried them, and fixings, back to Lara.

I put my cup down in front of me and set hers gently in front of her. I sat down, took the cup in both hands, lifted it to my mouth, and inhaled. Glorious. Plain old coffee-flavored coffee.

"I have to try," I said.

"No, you don't," Lara said. "There are plenty of people who aren't trying."

"Yeah," I said. "That's why I have to try."

She added cream to her coffee, and broke and emptied a plastic stick of honey into it. She stirred it gently, without clinking. Every movement was precise and orderly and controlled and beautiful. It would have been very, very easy to watch her and not think about anything else.

"Let me help you," she said.

"Help me with what?"

"Let me help you protect them," she said. "What do your people need?"

I sipped my coffee slowly and set it back down just as carefully.

In my experience, you always have to get really, really careful when the monsters offer to help.

I wanted to tell her to go jump in the lake. That was my first, angry reaction.

But that wouldn't have done my people any good.

"Beds," I said quietly. "They're sleeping on foam pads and air mattresses. They're surviving. I want them to live."

"What else?" she asked.

"A doctor. Antibiotics. A supply of insulin. I've got a diabetic who is running low, and there's none to be found. Some kind of painkiller. There's not many of those, either, and I've got casualties from the battle. They only get enough to get a little sleep and spend their awake time . . . making do."

She nodded, and I could see her taking mental notes. "Anything else?"

"More hours in the day," I said wearily. "I need more time."

"Oh," she said gently. "Yes. I know that one. When I have a solution, I'll let you know."

I nodded. We both took a sip of coffee, and she studied my features carefully, without speaking. She didn't seem uncomfortable in the silence. There was an aura of patience around her that I'd only really felt among older, much older, beings.

"I've tried to track Justine," I said finally.

Justine was my brother Thomas's woman, had been since I'd known him. She was carrying his child and had been possessed by a spiritual entity that had blackmailed him into attempting an assassination on Etri, king of the svartalves. He'd barely survived it, and now he was stuck in stasis out on my spooky island—and Justine was missing.

Lara frowned. "Oh?"

I nodded. "The thing possessing her destroyed anything easy that I might have used to do it. Hair, nail clippings, that kind of thing. It was very thorough."

"Then how did you manage an attempt?"

"Goodman Grey swiped a lock of her hair just in case. Sent it to me with my invoice."

Lara smiled faintly. "The man is nefariously professional."

"I used the lock," I said. "But she must have shaved her head. I barely latched onto anything, and it was a long way off. I think she's in Europe."

"That agrees with what I've been able to find out," Lara agreed. "She's been sighted in Romania." She swallowed. "How is Thomas?"

Thomas was her half brother, the same as he was mine, though through different parents. "I went out to the island two days ago. He's still . . . asleep. What he went through was bad enough that his mind isn't ready to deal with it yet. He's safe, and his body is healing. The island is keeping his Hunger from doing him any further harm."

Lara exhaled. "Like a medically induced coma."

I nodded tiredly. "Yeah. Exactly like that. I've been doing some research, trying to figure out how to keep his Hunger from starting in on him again. It's . . . slow work."

Lara's expression looked gently pained. "I believe it."

I'd spoken more words all at once in the past few moments than I had in the previous week. I felt exhausted. I fell into silence again as we sipped coffee. Again, that patient stillness just radiated out from her. The rest of my dander that had been riled up settled down, and I just felt sad and weary.

"Why?" I asked her, moments later.

"Why help you?" she asked.

I grunted in the affirmative.

She took a moment to consider her answer. "I could tell you it was because I simply want to help you, but you wouldn't believe that. You'd consider it a manipulation. I could tell you that it was because it would look good for the alliance, and that would be the truth. But it also wouldn't be the whole truth, and you'd sense that. I could tell you that it's because the possibility exists that I might be feeding on you in the future, and I don't want to poison myself with so much pain and despair, and there would be a certain amount of truth in that. I could tell you it was because you are effectively holding my brother prisoner, as well as keeping him from dying, and I want to put you at your ease, and that would be part of the truth as well. And I could tell you that it's clear that you are recovering from brutal losses in the battle, and that I need you operating to the fullness of your abilities to save my brother, and that also would contain truth." She shook her head. "There are always dangers to cultivating the kind of reputation I have made for myself. The answer is, 'it's complicated,' Harry. But among all the pressures and crosscurrents of interest, I do want to help you."

"Yeah. But why?" I asked.

She smiled faintly. "Why do *you* want to help them?"

"Because I can," I said. "Because it's right."

"I would take it as a personal favor if you would consider this possibility," she said.

"What?"

She met my dark eyes with her very blue ones for a daring moment. "That, just occasionally," she said, "I think so, too."

Chapter
Three

Lara walked with her hand on my arm as we went back to our waiting carriages. The shadows were getting longer as the sun went down.

"So," she said. "Next month?"

"Sure," I said. "My people will get with your people."

She sighed. "Yes, I suppose so." We stopped and she took her hand back, studying my face. "Fill your cup, Harry. Whatever it is that gives you yourself. Do more of it."

"I'll get by," I said.

"Getting by is surviving," she said. "I thought you wanted to live."

"Can't always get what you want," I said. "Ask you something?"

"I suppose."

"What's with your eyes?" I asked.

She tilted her head, her deep blue eyes narrowing. "How so?"

"They've been blue all day," I said. "I've seen them grey. Silver sometimes. Sometimes white."

"Ah," she said. She seemed to consider it for a moment and then said, "When you see that, you're seeing my Hunger peeking out."

"You ate before our date," I said.

"Sometimes three is a crowd."

"So, when your eyes get lighter, I need to worry."

Her expression was unreadable for a moment. Then she said, "We both do. May I ask a question in reply?"

"Seems fair."

"Why won't you meet my eyes for more than a second?"

"Bad things can happen when a wizard does that," I said. "It's called a soulgaze. I see you as you are."

"That seems like it would be an advantage."

One side of my mouth pulled up bitterly.

Murphy was gone by the time I'd decided to try it with her.

"Not really," I said. "You'd get to see me back."

"Would that be so terrible?"

"People have screamed and fainted," I said.

Lara tilted her head. I looked at her eyes long enough to see the wheels spinning, then lengthened my gaze past her. "Now. That is fascinating. Good night, Dresden."

I watched her go to her cart, which her bodyguards had turned around while we were inside. The Redcap had done the same with my carriage.

The two sets of guards tried not to show that they were watching the others too much. I got into the black carriage so that it rocked on its springs and slumped back into the seat. I pulled the brim of my cap down, folded my arms, and told the Redcap, "Drive."

Perhaps wisely, he didn't say a word to me. He clucked to the not-horse, and clip-clop we went down the clearing streets. The shadows were cooling off the streets as the sun went into the west, and people who remained outside had the look of those in a hurry to get somewhere safe.

Body removal had been a problem. Most of the people who died in the open had been collected by now, but there simply wasn't the time or space to deal with them all. There were mass graves being dug somewhere out west of town, but the dead didn't have priority over bringing in supplies for the living, so the faintest taint of death was in the air almost anywhere you went. They kept finding remains in the wreckage of buildings, in nooks and crannies where people had crawled off to die.

The first two weeks had been positively ghoulish.

Now it was just a fact.

The carriage passed into some deep shadow that gathered beneath some tall buildings, and when it came out into the next column of setting sunlight, the seat next to me was occupied.

Mab, the Queen of Air and Darkness, ruler of the Winter Court, sat primly in the seat next to me, dressed in white pants, silvery heels, and a winter-blue blouse. She wore a broad-brimmed summer hat and black plastic sunglasses that reflected the colors of sunset in a deep blue and purple spectrum. She was beautiful like few beings I had ever seen, and her lips were rich and soft-looking and the color of frozen mulberries.

The air around her was chill. It was like sitting next to an open re-frigerator.

The Redcap turned enough to touch the brim of his cap and incline his head to her, then went back to driving.

"Barely adequate, my Knight," Mab said in a calm, cool voice.

I didn't move or react. "Gee. And here I was, longing for your ap-proval."

She didn't move her head, but the weight of her gaze on me was pal-pable nonetheless. "Time is fleeting," she said. "We have little to spare in preparation. This alliance is part of that preparation."

"For what?" I asked.

One corner of her mouth twisted. "The next great conflict. The vampire wields a great deal of power among the mortals. That influence will be critical to my efforts. You must secure her . . . cooperation. By whatever means necessary."

"Lara likes girls, too. Go seduce her yourself."

"There are days when you say inane things," Mab said. "And then there are days when you run your mouth and remind me how utterly young and witless you can be. I have a Knight for a reason, fool."

"I'm not looking to get myself an addiction on top of my other prob-lems," I said. "And the way I am right now, I don't think I'd be particularly healthy for Lara, either."

"Mmmm," Mab said, nodding her chin once. "True. You are currently more useless than you have generally proven in the past."

The way she said "useless" made me shift uncomfortably in my seat.

"You are not irreplaceable," she reminded me in a quiet voice.

"I'm not invincible, either," I replied in a dull tone. "I went to war just like you wanted me to. There's a cost for that."

"Perhaps it was too high to be borne," she suggested in a very lovely, very poisonous voice.

I glowered at her from beneath the brim of my cap. "Perhaps I let Ethniu out and you can dance with her again," I said. "Perhaps if anything happens to me, that's already set up with Demonreach. Perhaps that's the real reason I went out there before this first date."

Mab's face turned slowly toward me. She stared for a long moment.

"Finally," she said. "You are at least learning something, my Knight." She turned back to face front and was silent for a moment more. "You will give yourself to Ms. Raith. If not now, then later. But it will happen."

I let out a light breath through my nose.

"Time will tell," Mab said smoothly. "Meanwhile, you have another task."

"Oh?"

She nodded. "King Etri of the Svartalves knows that you have somehow concealed Thomas Raith from him," Mab said. "He has demanded that I give him your head in compensation for the loss of Raith."

I swallowed. "Oh?"

"You will mend fences with Etri," Mab said. "In the conflict that is coming, the svartalves are necessary allies. They are my armory, and thanks to your actions, they refuse to speak to me or my court, or to the allies I have chosen for the fight, much less arm any of us. That will not do. Fix it."

"How the hell am I supposed to do that?" I asked her. "Etri is old-school. Thomas killed one of his closest henchmen. Even assuming Etri is willing to bargain, he'll want a life in recompense."

"Then provide it," Mab said in a soft, sharply edged tone. "This matter falls upon you. Rectify the situation."

"Or what?"

"There is no 'or what.' You will do it. This task is more necessary and needful than anything you are capable of imagining. If I must seize your mind and walk you like a puppet through negotiation and give you over to Etri's service in repayment for the life-debt, I will do so." She regarded me over the rims of her glasses, her eyes a poisonous shade of green. "Or some other life connected to yours."

The dull void of emotions I felt thanks to my essential weariness vanished in a sudden boiling flash of rage.

"Did you," I asked very quietly, "just threaten my daughter?"

"There would be a certain amount of justice in it," Mab said. "Blood for blood."

"You try it," I said, "and I will empty Demonreach's cells and give every single one of the things in it your address."

Mab let out a low laugh. It was cold and it was cruel. "You would unleash a black tide upon humanity itself, should you do that." She settled back into her own seat, relaxed and confident. "Do not assume you can predict the outcome of such an act. Far better for both of us and for tens of millions of your precious mortals that we work in tandem with one another."

I ground my teeth. "Even if I wanted to pacify Etri," I said, "I'd have no idea how to go about it."

"I have great confidence in your base cunning and ingenuity," Mab replied. "You will think of something. Or else." She pushed her sunglasses back up on her nose. "That," she added, "was a threat."

"Okay," I said. "So you want me to addict myself to the personification of heroin, and pull off a major diplomatic coup between supernatural nations at the same time."

"Yes," Mab said, her tone very, very faintly exasperated. "At any point did I stutter?"

"If you did, I might have missed it," I said. "I wasn't listening as closely as I usually do."

Mab pressed her luscious lips together and shook her head. "I suggest, Sir Knight," she said, "that you pull yourself together as quickly as possible. I know you suffered loss. But there is no time to waste upon your mourning."

"It doesn't work like that for mortals, Mab," I said quietly. "It hurts until you're done hurting. You heal as fast as you heal. I just need time."

"You haven't been exactly mortal in quite a while, my Knight," Mab said in a low, firm tone. "There are too many lives at stake for you to fall to the ground weeping. And not even I can readily summon extra seconds from the void. There *is* no time. Get up and fight. Or I will find someone who can."

The carriage passed into another deep, cool shadow, and when it came back out into the bloody sunset shafts of light again, I was alone.

God, I felt tired.

"Pick up the pace," I growled at the Redcap.

He didn't speak to me. But he nodded and flicked the reins, and the not-horse began to trot faster.

I closed my eyes and summoned images of my daughter to raise like a shield against nihilistic despair. Honestly, I wasn't sure I cared enough about me to work all that hard to keep myself alive.

Maggie was a different story.

She needed her father.

How the hell was I going to handle this one?

Chapter
Four

Three days later, I'd finished my workout in the bare-essentials gym on the second floor of the castle, and Will and I were talking with the parents of the families currently staying with me—four couples and a harried single mother whose husband had gone missing during the fighting and hadn't turned up. Two of the families had sick kids who weren't getting better like they should have. The single mother was the one with a diabetic child. All of them were worried.

Three of my Knights of the Bean were loitering in the great hall at a folding card table, playing listless hands of poker using M&M's as chips. I'd have joined them, but when I did, I spent most of my time eating my bets.

Will was doing most of the talking, while I nodded and made the occasional monosyllabic comment, and at precisely eight o'clock, someone started pounding on the castle's great door.

The reaction was instantaneous. Will came to his feet, whipped off his T-shirt in a single smooth movement, and rippled into the form of a lean, terrible timber wolf who stepped calmly out of his sweatpants. The Knights of the Bean rose, taking up weapons—shotguns and a high-powered deer rifle, in this case. The parents acted a beat later, rising and hurrying back out of the great hall toward their chambers, doubtless to round up their kids.

I glanced back over my shoulder until the civilians were out of the way. Then I put down my cup of coffee, rose deliberately, and started for the door, taking up my staff as I walked, passing into the entry hall.

The front doors of the castle were great double doors twice as high as the average Joe. We opened both doors whenever the troops needed to sally out, which was never, and the rest of the time we used the smaller door that was built into one of the big ones. The knocking was coming from the small door, and I shot the bolt without preamble, calling enough power into my staff to set the runes carved into it ablaze with green-gold light and to fill the air with the faint scent of woodsmoke.

Then I faced the door and called, "What's the password?"

The knocking stopped.

There was a silent moment, and then a scratching sound beneath the larger doors. With a little difficulty, someone managed to wiggle a small vellum envelope beneath the door.

I picked it up, testing it with my wizard's senses, but there wasn't anything to it but paper. I mean, I suppose someone could have put anthrax in it or something, but when I opened it carefully there wasn't any powder or anything. Just a note:

Harry,

What you asked for and a little more.

—Lara

I scanned the note and then held it down at eye level for Will, who let out a suspicious growl.

"I know," I said. "It's weirding me out a little, too. Stand ready."

The Knights of the Bean fanned out and covered the doorway from several angles. I just hoped none of them would shoot me in the back. They had hearts of solid oak, and they'd stood to fight when Chicago needed them, but they weren't professionals.

I waited until they were in position and opened the door.

"Hi!" boomed a large, cheerful-looking woman on the other side. "I'm Bear!"

I blinked for a moment.

When I said she was a large woman, I meant larger than me. Seven feet tall if she was an inch. She wasn't any kind of lean, mean fighting machine, either. She probably weighed around four hundred, and that was before you added in the heavy canvas sling bag she had on her shoulder, the rifle cases under one arm, and the scaled-up, stuffed-full ruck she had on her back. She was pretty and round-cheeked, with forest-green eyes and dark brown hair pulled into a braid as thick as my forearm, and her smile was absolutely radiant. She wore comfortable jeans and a battered old black biker jacket over a golden T-shirt.

"I like it when they answer their own door," she said. "You're the *seidrmadr*, huh?"

"Uh," I said, looking up at her. That was not an angle to which I was accustomed. "I'm Dresden."

She tilted her head back over her shoulder. "I come bearing beds, meds, and a doc," she said. "Plus me."

I leaned my head out enough to look past her, though I had to stand on tiptoe to do it. Sure enough, on the street outside was a trio of little workhorse four-wheelers, each of them hauling a trailer big enough to handle several mattresses. I recognized Lara's head of security, a guy named Riley, at the head of the column. He was helping a middle-aged woman carrying a satchel with a red cross on it off the back of one of the four-wheelers.

"Plus you?" I asked, feeling somewhat bewildered. "Oh wait. *Seidrmadr.* You're a Valkyrie."

Bear clapped my shoulder, and several things in her ruck and bags clanked. "Buddy," she said, "I'm *the* Valkyrie. And I'm here to protect your skinny ass. Invite me in."

"Hah," I said. "How do I know you're who you say you are?"

Bear scowled at me, nodding. "Careful. That's smart. Well, Riley over there will vouch for me. Freydis told me to tell you a seven is better than any man has done since Hastings and to call her if you want to share a bottle. And here." She stuffed her free hand into her jacket pocket, pulled out a heavily folded sheaf of papers, and thrust them at me.

I took it and unfolded it as best as I could. It had what appeared to be barbecue sauce stains on it, but the paper was on familiar letterhead. Monoc Securities. I scanned the contract, between said corporation and Lara Raith.

". . . whose sole duty will be to protect the person and home of Harry Dresden, wizard, currently residing in the city of Chicago . . ." I muttered. "Term of service of not less than five years."

I practically choked upon reading that. I'd looked into what it might take to hire one myself, and Valkyries cost way more than a guy with a couple of gym socks full of mystery diamonds could afford.

"You want, call One-Eye," Bear said affably. "He'll tell you what I look like."

I stared at her for a moment and said, "Will. Watch her."

"Hey, a werewolf, excellent," Bear said, her smile widening. She fell a pace back from the door. "Good to see you got a lick of sense, *sei-drmadr*. Make this job a lot easier. I'll wait. I get paid the same either way. And it ain't like I'm getting any older."

I strode away, back down into the guts of the castle, past my chambers, and opened the door in the floor that led down to my repaired and recoalescing laboratory, the only thing standing from my original home in Mrs. Spunkelcrief's rooming house. It was little more than five levels of wire shelving around three walls and a long worktable in the middle, with a little space for a writing desk and a fire-ruined copper summoning circle built into the floor at one end of the table.

But it was home.

I could breathe here.

"Bob," I called, letting my impatience show in my voice.

A blue streak of light suddenly appeared on the white paint of the concrete wall. It swept around the room to the old shelf where an ancient human skull rested, nestled among a pile of paperback romances. The skull's eye sockets kindled to life with glowing red-gold embers a moment later, and it burbled, "You have but to call and I am here!"

"I noticed." I sighed. The spirit of intellect that lived in the skull was an old friend and confidant, or at least a mostly faithful assistant. When I had moved into the castle, it had become clear that the building had been constructed with a great many magical systems built into it—but it had to have a spirit to run it, a genius constructi, if you will. Bob had taken to the place as gleefully as a fourteen-year-old who'd been given the keys to a monster truck. He could inhabit the stones of the castle as easily as he could his own skull, and he'd been positively bouncy ever since.

"Look, I know you get satellite and radio and television signals now," I began.

"And internet!" Bob burbled. "Do you wanna watch *Lord of the Rings* again?"

"You're never going to convince me that Arwen was actually wearing lingerie the whole film," I said soberly. "You edited."

"Well," Bob said sullenly. "Just be glad it wasn't Gimli."

"I need to speak to Vadderung," I said.

Bob whistled. "Harry. You don't just call up One-Eye himself."

"Good God," I said. "We're not summoning him. I've got more sense than that."

"Do you, though?"

"I need to confirm that the Valkyrie at the front door is who she says she is," I said.

"Oh, easy, then," Bob said brightly. "That's a corporate thing. I'll just call his office."

"Thank you," I said. "Please do."

"Riiiinnnng," Bob said. "Riiiinnnng!"

There was a clicking sound from the skull, and a woman's cold, calm voice said, "Monoc Securities, Mister Vadderung's office. Who may I say is calling?"

"This is Harry Dresden, wizard," I said.

"Oh," she said, her tone clearly disappointed.

"Please let him know I need a moment of his time," I said.

"I am skeptical of that," she replied, and suddenly Muzak started playing. I never knew Wagner could be Muzaked.

"Dresden," came a deep, resonant voice a minute later. "I take it Bear has arrived."

"Yeah, Andrea the Giant in a motorcycle jacket, green eyes," I said.

"That's the one," Vadderung said with a low chuckle. "Ms. Raith seems somewhat determined to ensure your safety. Bear is my best."

"Huh," I said. "You read her contract?"

"Negotiated it myself," Vadderung said. "Bear is practically family."

"So this is on the level?" I asked.

"As far as I can tell," Vadderung replied. "You have my word."

"Okay," I said. "Uh. Thanks, I guess. That's all I needed."

"Make sure she gets enough to eat," Vadderung suggested, "or you'll regret it." And then he hung up.

I blinked. "I have to feed her?"

"Whoa!" Bob exclaimed. "Harry, you've got a Valkyrie bodyguard!" His eyes flicked toward the front doors of the castle, as if he had no trouble gazing through the earth and stone between the two points. "A big one! Wow!"

For a second, I wished it could have been a little one.

About five feet tall and blond would do.

I closed my eyes.

"Harry!" Bob said, in a tone that suggested he'd already said it several times.

I blinked my eyes open to find Bob's glowing presence in the wall nearest my head.

"You okay, boss?"

I scowled and said, "I'm getting tired of people asking me that."

"Well," Bob said, "stop checking out in the middle of conversations, maybe."

I grunted. "Thanks, Bob. We'll do movies later tonight."

I went back upstairs to the front doors and found Bear sitting on the rifle cases, her face tilted up to the sun. She looked down and opened her eyes as I approached, and then stood up.

"Okay, wizard," she said. "We in business?"

"We're in business," I said. "Come in. We'll find you quarters."

"You'll put me in a room next to yours," she said cheerfully, scooping up her gear again. She must have been carrying a couple hundred pounds of stuff. She slung it around like a kid with a book bag. Then she turned, put her thumb and forefinger in her mouth, and let out an earsplitting whistle. "Hey, Riley! Let's unload this stuff! Doc, you're with me."

She stepped back as I pulled some bolts and opened one of the main doors to make room for the men carrying mattresses in, and a second later, Bear came stomping in, with a few extra stomps as if testing the firmness of the flagstones beneath her feet.

"Oh, hell yeah," she said. "Proper fortress spells here. You got a nice setup, wizard. Doc, come here. This is Harry Dresden. Harry, this is Doctor Lacalle."

The middle-aged woman with the shoulder bag nodded firmly at me. "Ms. Raith tells me you have sick children here."

"Yeah," I said quietly. "We do."

She gave me a professional smile and a nod. "Well then," she said. "Let's see how we can help them."

Chapter Five

A couple of days later, I was wrapping up back day in the gym, finishing off by running the rack of mismatched dumbbells with bent-over rows, starting at hundred pounders and moving down in five-pound increments without stopping between sets. My form wasn't fantastic, but it didn't need to be—this one was about endurance. Will was up on the third floor of the castle, working with Michael Carpenter and his people on getting the living quarters made livable.

I had gotten down to thirty pounders when Bear came stomping into the gym. "Hey. Boss."

"Hnghf," I gasped. I finished the set with the thirties and shifted immediately to twenty-fives.

"There's this stocky little bald dude with a seriously spooky vibe standing in the entry hall with a kid, maybe twenty. Says he knows you and needs to talk."

"Mort?" I groaned. My lats were on fire. "Mort Lindquist?"

"Yeah, I think," Bear said.

"Almost . . . nnnngh . . . done."

"Yeah, those twenty-fives are doing you dirty, Mighty Mouse."

"Bite . . . mmmmngh . . . me."

"You're all bone. Be like eating sparrow wings."

I had a snappy comeback, honest I did, but I didn't have enough breath to give it to her. So I worked until my body was too full of exhaustion for me to notice my mind and heart, and when I finished the last set with a pair of fives, I had to use hip action to get them back up onto the damned rack.

Bear tossed me a worn but clean towel, and I mopped at my face with it, the chill of the castle, a steady fifty-five degrees, even in the heat of summer, settling over my sweat-soaked body almost instantly. It felt fantastic. By the time I looked up, Bear was handing me a canteen full of cold water, and I drank down half of it before I said, "Thanks."

"I been to the bad place a few times," she said. "Seen a lot of men there. Tough fight?"

I thought of the sound of falling buildings and the sight of smashed baby carriages. Then the direct psychic exposure to the mind-ripping hatred of a Titan. "Little bit. Memories."

"Those are burdens," she said, her voice serious. "Lot of times, they never get any lighter."

"Yeah," I said. "So I'll get bigger."

The Valkyrie gave me an approving nod. "You hang in there, string bean," she said. "You're on the right road. Hey, what's the kitchen making for lunch?"

I went down to my office, which had been a rather large cleaning supply closet a few weeks before. Now it had room for a small desk with a chair, a couple of filing cabinets, and one chair for a visitor. I finished the rest of the canteen of water on the way, and in a few minutes Bear appeared with Mort Lindquist.

Mort was only a little taller than Will, and his thickness had more to do with age than muscle. His usually bald head had grown out some stubble, and his eyes looked sunken and tired. He wore his black suit and black shirt, but they hung a little loose on him. Well. Pretty much everyone in town except Bear was getting thinner.

Mort had a young man with him, and I recognized Fitz immediately from my days being mostly dead. He'd grown maybe three inches in that time, and filled out with more muscle. He had sort of reddish hair and came from a heritage more mixed than a barrel of bar nuts. He, too, wore black, though with him it was black jeans and a black hoodie, so that he looked a bit like the shadow Morty might cast behind him from a low-angle light.

Fitz had been a street kid. No parents. Mixed up with bad company in his day. I knew he'd been hanging around with Mort in the years since, but there was something about him that reminded me of a feral cat. He stood with a kind of constant, restless wariness, with one eye always on the door, showing about as much trust in his safety as a plate of cookies in a kindergarten.

I leaned across the desk to shake hands with both of them, and Fitz said, "Finally I can put a face to the voice."

"Heh," I said. "I heard you'd taken up with Mort as an apprentice ectomancer," I said.

Fitz glanced back and forth between me and Mort uncertainly.

"Yeah," Mort said. "About that." He took a deep breath. "Harry, you know I don't screw around with the White Council. There are seriously scary people there."

The White Council of Wizardry had kicked me out on my ass in the aftermath of the battle. Apparently they found a rogue wizard with his own city-killing Titan in a Poké Ball a little intimidating. They were not notable for their kindness and tolerance.

"Yeah, I've got to watch my step with them myself these days," I said. "What have they got to do with your visit?"

Mort hooked a thumb over his shoulder at Fitz as he sat down. "The kid bloomed."

I tilted my head and studied them both. Fitz's talent had been minor and erratic at best, the last I checked. "In ectomancy?"

Mort shook his head slowly. "In everything. I think he's Council material."

I settled back in my seat and let out a low whistle. "That so, kid?"

Fitz shrugged uncomfortably. "Things just kept getting easier. And during the battle, things went nuts and there was this old couple running away from this Uruk-hai-looking thing and I"—he waved a hand vaguely—"set it on fire."

I stared at the kid for a moment. "Did you."

"I worked with him, best I could," Mort added, nodding. "Showed him what I knew, but I pretty much only deal in spirits, Harry. The kid can access all the elements, and he gets stronger every day. I don't know much, and what I do know tells me that he could get out of control fast. He needs guidance from someone with real experience, before . . ."

Mort let it hang, but I knew where his thoughts were going. The Wardens of the White Council spent a whole hell of a lot of their time hunting down rogue wizards. Unfortunately, a lot of those rogues were kids whose talent had gone out of control and hurt or killed somebody.

"I hear you," I said tiredly. I shook my head. "Look. I'm not much these days."

"I heard," Mort said quietly. "My condolences. She was a remarkable woman. I saw her shade once . . ." He studied me closely for a moment and frowned. "Harry, look. I don't have the tools he needs to get his gift under control. You do. Otherwise, I have to go to the Wardens and ask for their help."

"Neither of us wants that." I sighed. "And I guess I owe him a favor or two, don't I?"

"Seems like that," Mort said seriously.

"How about it, Fitz?" I asked him. "I can show you how to not hurt anyone. That what you want?"

The young man grimaced. He looked between me and the door warily. Then he said, "No."

I traded a look with Mort. "Go on," I said.

"My whole life I've . . . been on my own. In the system. In the street. Even in the gang." He lifted his chin a little and said, "I used to think I'd be dead by the time I hit twenty. Now there's this whole new world. I . . . I want to see how far I can go."

I exhaled through my nose. "That's a very different kind of request, Fitz. If the White Council finds out I've taken you on as an apprentice, that could get real violent, real fast."

"I don't want to cause you any trouble," he said quietly. "But . . . I've seen what the White Council does to people."

"Oh, they're definitely a freight train of dicks," I said. "But they know their business. I'm not exactly in good odor with them right now. They hear I'm training you up, that could go bad for both of us."

"Oh," Fitz said, frowning and looking down. "I didn't realize."

"Well, you'd best start realizing things," I said. "Especially if you're going to be working with me."

"You'll do it?" Fitz asked, his face brightening.

"Not yet," I said in my grumpiest wizard voice. "You're going to have to think about this one. Sleep on it. Mort, you know how the White Council operates. Answer his questions. Give him some perspective." I looked back at Fitz. "Kid, once upon a time you did me a real solid. So, if you have a long talk with Mort and you still want it, yeah. I'll train you."

Fitz blinked several times and then his face brightened. "Thank you!"

I held up a hand. "Lesson one. Too soon. Wait a few years to see if you owe me thanks or a punch in the nose. Sometimes it can be hard to tell."

"I . . . Okay. Yeah, okay, right," Fitz said.

"Go on, kid," Mort drawled to Fitz. "I need to talk to him alone for a minute."

"Sure," Fitz said, nodding, clearly elated. He stepped out of the office, and I heard his light footsteps heading down the hallway toward the stairs up.

"I'm not sure you're doing the kid a favor here, Mort," I said, once he was gone.

"Me?" Mort asked.

I waved a hand. "I'm not sure I am, either. My outcome record with apprentices isn't exactly sunny."

"Look. I've met a bunch of White Council assholes," Mort said. "You're the only one of them I know who ever seemed to give a damn about people. You were me, which would you choose?" He looked over his shoulder and his face became troubled. "He's a good kid, Harry. I mean, he walks around like a cat at a dog convention. He ain't got much in the way of trust. And there's something chewing at him he won't talk about, not even after all the time he's worked with me. But he's kind. Gentle. You should see him handling the shades of children. Helping them on their way."

"They're all good kids," I said quietly. *Even you, Harry, once upon a time.*

"Yeah, but I've seen what the Council does to them." Mort shook his head. "I think the kid is at a crossroads. He could go either way. I'll take my chances with you."

I wasn't sure I had it in me to be the kind of stable presence an emergent wizard needed to help him embrace his power effectively and wisely.

But I was sure I didn't have it in me to turn him away.

I'd been Fitz once.

"You think I can help him?" I asked.

Mort blew out a breath. "I think you have a shot. Better than me, anyway. Sure as hell better than those pricks on the Council. If you can get him to open up with you, I think it could go a long way."

And if I couldn't, it could go a long way, too. And I wasn't in the best of shape.

But I had to try.

"Okay," I said. "Have him show up with a couple of changes of clothes and as many books as he wants."

"Thank you," Mort said quietly.

I nodded. "How about you?" I asked him. "How's your side of town?"

Mort shook his head. "Business is . . . booming, I suppose. I've spent the past couple of weeks sorting through crowds of newborn shades. The Eye of Balor killed a lot of people and left a much higher percentage of shades than natural deaths."

I sighed. "I hadn't thought about that one. But it makes sense. What's happening?"

Mort shrugged. "They're confused as hell. A lot of them don't even have a proper grave yet. They have to go back to their corpses to get away from the sun. That doesn't bode well for their sanity. I've been sending in tips to Lieutenant Stallings about where there are bodies that still haven't been found, but . . . Jesus, Harry, the death rate in town has tripled or quadrupled at least."

"Killings?" I asked.

"Some of them," he said. "But a lot more are just people dying of things that could have been recovered from if the town hadn't been blown to hell. Heart attacks, accidents, illnesses. I've got an old crystal radio, so I can get some of the news, but nobody has any real idea of what's happening in the city. Until we get communications back up, everyone's on their own."

I sighed and rubbed at my head. "Halloween is going to be the spooky season for real this year."

"Most likely," he said, nodding. "Me and Fitz been doing our best, but there's only two of us—and now it will just be me."

"It's not just you," I said quietly. "We're all in this train wreck together."

Mort gave me a cynical tilt of his head. "You don't get out of the castle much, do you?"

"Not for a few days," I said.

"There are groups forming," he said. "Some of them have been going after people they think are connected to the supernatural. Showing up at night. Harassing them. Tagging their apartments and homes."

"Violence?" I asked.

"Not yet. But we're getting there."

I exhaled slowly.

I should probably start paying more attention to things outside of my routine. But the very thought sent quavers running through my belly that might have sent the shade of my breakfast spewing from my mouth.

When I looked up at Mort, he was watching me with a troubled expression.

Hell's bells.

He wanted me to tell him what to do.

My breakfast struggled to manifest into the physical world. I didn't want to do this. I wanted to stick to my routine. To grieve. To heal.

I just needed time.

Instead, I spoke. "Talk to Artemis Bock," I said. "His bookstore is still a hub for our people. Ask him to start gathering information on what's going on. Before you do that, head for the kitchen. The Ordo Lebes is there. They've coordinated on establishing protection for the community before. They'll be some of the best folks to figure out what can be done now." I nodded. "After that, I want you to keep doing what you do, and keep me informed. If things get really bad in the ghostly way, maybe we can put together some kind of ritual to keep things under wraps."

"What about McAnally's?" Mort asked.

"There's a market set up in the parking lot," I said. "Mostly our people. Good place for information. But Mac wants his place peaceful and neutral. He wants in, he'll let us know."

Mort closed his eyes for a moment and took a deep breath. "Yeah. Okay. Makes sense."

I'd just been making it up as I went along. But I supposed there was no need to burden Mort with that. "Sure," I said. "I'll . . . uh, I'll expect you to go over the risks with Fitz. But we both know he'll want to do it. Tomorrow. Six a.m."

"That early?"

"Might as well start the way I mean to continue," I said.

"He'll be here." Mort rose to leave but paused by the door. "Harry . . . thank you. You do a lot that people don't see. I know what that's like. So thank you."

I felt responsibility piling up on my shoulders like lead weights.

But I nodded at him and said, "Sure, Mort. You're welcome."

Chapter
Six

August came with furious heat that year. It did bad things to the city. The smell of death was everywhere, even if it was fainter than it had been. It hung about at the very edges of perception, a ghost that reminded everyone of that horrible midsummer night of the battle. Trash had piled up, too. There was simply too much of it to be moved through the limited access of the streets. That smell dominated the air, along with effluvia from sewers that had been clogged by the debris of destroyed buildings.

More people had moved out of town, maybe half of them. It made the streets eerily empty. At night, no one went outside. Ghouls had been drawn to the vast stench of death, and they haunted the night even in places where they would never have dreamed of coming out before. It was to be expected at any tragedy large enough. They wiggled into ruins and ate corpses—and probably made some new ones.

Inside the castle, it wasn't too bad. The heavy stones kept out the heat. Only some of the rooms had windows, and we kept those curtained.

"Three more minutes of push-ups," I said to Fitz. "And keep reading."

The kid was dressed in gym shorts and sneakers, like me, as we worked out in the castle's upper dining hall, which had been converted into a gym. I'd had Fitz doing a lot of calisthenics when he expressed skepticism about lifting weights. I was working the heavy bag, building up the arm that had been broken and just gotten out of its cast. I was taking the opportunity to charge up my kinetic energy rings, each of the magical tools storing back a little energy every time I threw a punch.

"I'm . . . sweating . . . on the pages . . ." Fitz gasped, laboring to keep his body straight and his arms pushing and contracting.

"You want to be a major-league wizard, it's going to mean being able to concentrate even when you're out of breath and your arms hurt," I said, throwing steady combos at the bag. I alternated left-side and right-side combinations, shifting my feet so that the punches were coming up from my legs and hips. "You want to do every other letter of the alphabet instead?"

"I read . . . this one . . . five times . . . already . . ." Fitz complained.

"*Elementary Magic* is all about the fundamentals," I said. "Fundamentals, fundamentals, fundamentals. Just like professional ball. The greats are always working on their basic skills."

I slammed several blows into the heavy bag that made it jump and rattle on its chain. I hadn't ever punched it off the chain like Captain America, and I hadn't ever broken a bag open, but my knuckles had lost their share of skin, even inside the wraps.

My hands didn't hurt. The mantle of the Winter Knight saw to that.

Thinking about the people I'd lost did.

Karrin.

Susan.

Wild Bill.

Yukie Yoshimo.

I threw punches until I ran out of wind and then let my arms drop. I stood there with my head bowed, breathing hard, sweat running down me. The bag kept swinging on its chain for a good minute.

I looked up to see Fitz staring at me.

"Jesus," he said.

"Better it comes out here than when I'm using magic," I told him seriously. "Almost every major obstacle to being a wizard comes down to a lack of emotional control. Learning to manage your feelings isn't optional."

"Yeah, yeah," Fitz said. "Just set them aside."

I blinked for a moment, grabbed a towel, and rubbed my head and upper body with it. "Not really," I said. "There's times when you need to do that—when the pressure is on and you're working on emergency time. When seconds count. You can stuff them down for a bit and come back to them later. That's normal. But it isn't enough. Stuffing things down comes back to gut you at the damnedest times. You gotta learn how to manage your feelings over years, not just suppress them in the short term. You start wielding power at White Council levels, you're going to be around a while. Means taking your mental health damned seriously."

He sat up from the book, breathing hard himself. "Is that why you push so hard in the gym?"

"It's one reason," I said. "Moving your body around is good for your head. And practicing something that requires discipline does a lot of positive things for you, too." I nodded at a threadbare cushion in the corner. "Meditation time, kid."

"Aw, Harry," Fitz complained. "It's boring."

"Boring is fine," I said. "Boring is good. Gives your head time to sort things out. Go breathe and think about why you might need that someday."

Fitz heaved an enormous sigh. But he slouched over to the cushion, settled himself cross-legged on it, sat up straight, rested his palms on his knees, and closed his eyes.

He was covered in sweat and would start to chill a little in only a moment or two, but that was routine now. Learning how to control the body's instinctive reactions was a good warm-up to learning to control powerful magical energies.

Boot steps came thumping confidently up the stairs to the gym and Bear's voice preceded her down the hallway. "*Seidrmadr*, we got company."

I hung the towel over my shoulders and frowned at her.

"The Wardens are paying you a visit," she said. Her voice was calm, but she was cleaning her nails with a short, hook-pointed knife while she spoke.

"Today?" I demanded. "Damn."

"Get used to it," she said. "Always something interfering with date night, in my experience."

"Hah hah," I said in a flat tone. "Fitz, give it forty-five minutes, then take the back stairway down to the kitchen. I'll meet you there."

My new apprentice nodded once without speaking or opening his eyes. Good. He was learning things.

I threw on my discarded T-shirt, got a fresh towel and did my hair again, then raked my fingers back through it and followed Bear down the stairs to the great hall.

Two grey-cloaked Wardens were waiting for me there. One of them was Carlos Ramirez, solid and stiff with his cane held in both hands and his silver saber at his side. His arm was still set in its cast from where the Black Court elder had shattered his forearm. He looked exhausted, like he had during the war with the Red Court, solid with muscle yet with his skin stretched tighter over his bones than it should have been. He'd lost weight over the past month. He looked . . .

Older.

Hell. I couldn't throw any stones at him on that score. I was shedding weight despite my best efforts to keep eating. He'd lost some of the same people I had during the battle. He turned to me as I regarded him and gave me a sober nod. I returned it.

The second Warden was a young woman, about five four and petite, but muscled like the ballet dancer she had been before her talent had emerged and she'd been claimed by the White Council. She had pale, stark features, white-blond hair that fell to her lower back in a straight, neat cut, and almost invisible eyebrows, and wore her dark suit, grey cloak, and silver court sword with an air of practicality.

"Ilyana," I said. "Long time no see. I thought you were still in China with Ancient Mai."

She regarded me the way one might something both dangerous and disgusting, like one of those big Komodo lizards with the poisonous, gangrenous drool. She pressed her lips together in disapproval and shook her head once. "A great many things have changed since you were cast from the White Council, Harry Dresden. It would save us all time and trouble if you would confess to your misdeeds and accompany us back to Edinburgh."

I mopped a bit more sweat from my face. Even the White Council shouldn't have found out about Fitz already, unless someone in the castle was an informer. Pleasant thought, and maybe something I should expect to happen sooner or later. But if they thought I was violating my parole, they sure as hell wouldn't have sent only two people to arrest me. So it stood to reason that Ilyana was on a fishing trip.

"I'm famous for that," I drawled. "Saving the Council time and trouble. Hey, Carlos."

"Harry," he said casually. "You'll have to excuse Ilyana. She grew up in the Morgan school."

Ilyana made a disgusted sound and turned away impatiently. "This is a waste of time. He's going to cross the line sooner or later."

"All the better to get him used to being visited then, isn't it," Ramirez said amiably. "If you're unable to perform your duties with a modicum of objectivity, Warden, I'll be happy to ask Captain Luccio to find a different position for you."

"I am fine," Ilyana snapped. She turned to me. "Have you had any contact with any member of the White Council?"

"No," I said calmly. "I've been taking in the sweet Chicago summer. Didn't you notice?"

That seemed to rattle her cage a little. Ilyana glanced toward the nearest wall, her expression disturbed. Sure, as a young Warden, she'd seen some things. But even a month later, the remnants of the Battle of Chicago were horrific. I tried to avoid going out into them.

"There have been many members of the substandard magical community visiting," she said stiffly.

"There's a lot of people hurting," I said. "A lot of people scared. A lot of people hungry. A lot of people without shelter. We're helping each other out."

"Is that your plan?" she demanded. "To obligate them to you and subvert them for your own ends?"

"Okey dokey." I sighed. "I'm pretty sure I'm not going to stand in my own damned home and take this from anyone. Ilyana, you're running at about a nine on the psycho scale. If you want this to stay friendly, I'd like you to dial it down to maybe a six."

Ilyana's hand went to her sword. "You heard him," she said to Carlos. "He threatened us."

Ramirez put his hand over Ilyana's, preventing her from drawing the enchanted blade, and gave me a half-weary, half-exasperated look. "Dresden, for the love of God."

I held up my hands guilelessly. "You heard her, Carlos. I'm out. I don't have to be a team player anymore."

"My God," Ramirez said, blowing out a breath. "You actually think you were a team player."

I waggled a hand. "Relatively, sure."

He shook his head. "We're going to be coming by once a month or so. We won't be announcing ourselves. I'll expect you to make time to talk to us when we do."

"Warlock protocol," I noted.

"That's how it is," Ramirez said. "Though with a couple of notable exceptions"—he glanced at Ilyana—"not even the Wardens think you're going to be getting up to any mischief for a while."

"Heh," I said. "Yeah. You know me, Carlos."

"I did once," he said.

I nodded. I paused to visibly consider. Then I looked up, smiled pleasantly, and told him, "No."

He went still.

"What?" Ilyana asked, disbelievingly.

"No," I repeated calmly. "See, I'm not just some schmuck you can kick around like a wounded dog. I'm not some random two-bit talent that has to roll over for you. This isn't Council territory. It's Winter. I'm the Winter Knight. This is my home, rightfully won at arms. You want to visit me, Carlos, fine. You call ahead. Like a proper guest."

There was a long silence.

"You *dare*—" Ilyana began.

Ramirez silenced her with a look.

She fumed.

Carlos turned slowly to me and spoke softly. "What are you doing, Harry?"

"It's called establishing boundaries," I said. "It's healthy. You should read up."

"Take him now!" Ilyana snapped to Ramirez.

"We're standing in Merlin's fortress," Ramirez told her, "and its capabilities are not in our control. Dresden is one of the top ten or twenty most powerful wizards on the planet. And he's facing us with a Valkyrie backing him up. Even if it was the right procedure to follow, it would be suicide."

"I'd probably just throw you out the first time," I said. "But you wouldn't be welcome back. The White Council can show basic courtesy and respect. I'll be happy to do the same. But I'm not the Council's whipping boy anymore, Warden Ramirez. And we're not going to pretend that I am."

Carlos thumped his cane down a couple of times, thoughtfully. "Suppose the Council decides to take issue with this decision, Harry?"

"You can send someone to Mab," I suggested. "Someone expendable. Once you tell her you want to humiliate her by abusing her chosen champion, she's going to react predictably."

"Arrogant fool," Ilyana snarled.

"Get out," Carlos said quietly to her. "Right now."

Ilyana shot him a look from ice-cold blue eyes that could have curdled milk. Maybe literally. Then she turned and walked stiffly out of the great hall and back to the entry hall.

Ramirez watched her go and then said, quietly, "She had a twin sister. Went warlock, bad. Then the warlock sister set Ilyana up to take the fall with the Council. Luccio worked out what happened just before the sword fell." He shook his head. "Ilyana's got a lot of feelings and she doesn't have much forgiveness in her for anyone who comes close to crossing the line."

"Do you?" I asked.

Ramirez bobbed his head slightly to one side. "I've lost a lot of illusions lately."

"Yeah," I said wearily.

We were quiet for a moment.

"You going to play ball here, Harry?" he asked me.

"Start with showing some respect," I said without heat. "I'll try to do the same."

"I can work with that," Ramirez said. "Maybe. See where it takes us. The Merlin won't like it."

"I'm going to lose sleep over that thought," I said. "The Merlin not liking something."

Ramirez smiled briefly. "He denied expenditure of Council resources to recover Wild Bill's and Yoshimo's bodies."

Wild Bill Meyers and Yukie Yoshimo had been turned by Black Court vampires during the Battle of Chicago. They weren't themselves anymore. They were undead things with our friends' stolen faces and memories, under the thrall of the most powerful Black Courters left on the planet. Their sacrifice and discipline and talents had been taken and would be used for malevolent purposes by some truly epic monsters, and even through my constant fog of personal pain, I felt slow anger rising.

"He's not going to help lay them to rest," I said quietly.

Ramirez's eyes looked sunken. "Says it isn't time." He took a deep breath. "So here's how it is. I'm not your junior anymore, either, Harry. So if I'm going to work with you, you're going to work with me. When we're both ready, we track them down. We settle things. You and me. Like you said."

He looked up at me, his gaze searching.

I nodded slowly. "We'll find them. We'll bring them home. And settle up with Drakul and his people. Just like I said."

Ramirez offered me his hand.

I crossed to him and shook it.

Chapter

Seven

"What did you do to the *Water Beetle*?" I complained.

Molly and I had just gotten out of a Winter Court stretch limousine. The waterfront roads hadn't been busy when the EMP had gone off, and they had been cleared quickly so that supplies being shipped in via Lake Michigan could be distributed more efficiently. I'd had to walk several blocks to meet the limo, and I'd gotten mildly motion sick riding in the back of the thing, but it had air-conditioning. The summer noon was brutally hot, possibly as a result of the interaction of Summer and Winter power over the city back in June.

"Oh, come on, Harry," Molly said, a faint smile on her face. "Can't you just say 'thank you' and enjoy it?"

"Hmph," I said, and folded my arms.

My old fishing tub, the *Water Beetle*, was almost a clone of the *Orca* in the movie *Jaws*. It wasn't a terribly sexy vessel, but it had been practical, serviceable, and comfortable—at least until Justine had stolen it, torn open its belly on rocks, and sunk it in three feet of water.

Molly's people had salvaged the *Water Beetle* and given it a makeover.

The hull had been cleaned up and repainted in clean white. Brass and stainless steel fittings and fastenings had been polished and shone in the summer sun. Smudged and dirty old glass windows had been switched out with mirror-tinted replacements.

It looked brand-new.

"Belowdecks is still like it was, right?" I asked.

Molly laughed. "Harry, it was sunk. We had to replace a lot. And it's not as if you've been terribly communicative lately, so you don't get to complain when I do something nice for you."

"This is still America," I said. "I can complain about anything I want, no matter how irrational."

"It's still practical," Molly said soothingly. "For God's sake, Harry. It's just clean. We can't have you taking a visiting head of state out in an old waterlogged rust bucket." She brushed silver hair back from her eyes and studied my expression for a moment.

"What?" I asked her uncertainly.

"Harry," she said quietly, "it's okay for you to have some good things in your life. You know that, right? It's okay for things to get better sometimes."

I looked back at the city. At the skyline. It had gaps in it, as unsettling and ugly as broken and missing teeth. Part of that was on me. When I had struck down the Red Court, years ago, it had created the instability that had let the Fomor get ideas about asserting power. The city had been attacked as a result.

Molly watched me, her blue eyes intent, as if reading my thoughts. "You're feeling bad because you've got a new house and a new boat when so many people have so little."

"I'm feeling bad because I'm part of the *reason* they have so little," I countered.

"That's partly true," Molly said. She came over and put a hand on my shoulder. "But if you hadn't been here to defend Chicago, there wouldn't *be* any buildings left, Harry. And hundreds of thousands more people would have died. I was there. I saw it."

"Couldn't have happened without me," I said.

"Or me," she said. "Or Vadderung. Or Mab. Or Titania. Or a lot of other people." She shook her head. "You've always been kind of arrogant about some things, Harry. But claiming responsibility for something this big crosses a line somewhere. Maybe it becomes hubris." She squeezed my shoulder. "Stop torturing yourself. Please. You aren't the only one who gets hurt when you do it."

I frowned and glanced at her.

She smiled mostly with her eyes and held up both hands placatingly. "Maybe just consider the idea that you did the best you could in a bad situation that nobody could have managed perfectly. And maybe take that anger you're feeling toward yourself and direct it where it rightly belongs—with Ethniu and the Fomor. You know. The ones who actually destroyed the town and murdered people."

"There are always predators, Molls," I said quietly. "They always make the same choices. It's up to us to make the ones that keep them from hurting anyone."

"Hubris, Harry," she said gently. "It's not given to us to stop every bad thing that happens to anyone, anywhere. That's not how it works. We don't have that kind of power."

"If not us," I said, "who?"

"Maybe nobody," Molly said. "Maybe there's just power and choice and consequence."

"There's more," I said. I stared at the clean white lines of the *Water Beetle.* "There has to be."

"Harry," she said. "You're a dear friend. I love you. I want you to be strong and happy." She shook her head. "But right now, you're taking the weight of the whole world on your shoulders because you feel guilty about Karrin's death, and you want to punish yourself. I grew up Catholic. I know the look."

"What do you recommend?" I asked. "Confession?"

She thought for a moment before answering. "Eventually," she said carefully, "you'll find more balance. It's hard to see very far past the end of your own nose when you're in a lot of pain. You need to take care of yourself. You need to heal." She exhaled through her nose. "Are you ready for today?"

I grunted. "Lara tries anything, I'll dunk her in the lake until she calms down. I don't think there will be an issue. Last time she tried something on the island, I sat her down pretty hard."

"When she tried to kill you, you mean. And you still played nice."

"You got a problem with that?" I asked her, genuinely curious.

"If it had been a man who had crossed that line, I think you'd have killed him," Molly said.

My thoughts went unbidden to Detective Lieutenant Rudolph. The man responsible for Karrin's death. It had taken two Knights of the Cross to keep me from murdering him. The burn on my arm ached and smoldered, the only real, unfiltered physical pain I'd felt since I'd taken up the mantle of the Winter Knight.

I thought of a number of Fomor soldiers who had been about to kill a bunch of the people who had risen up to defend Chicago. The enemy troops had all been male. I'd incinerated them.

"You don't think about women the same way you think about men," Molly said. "That's partly because you see yourself as a protector. As a knight in shining armor."

"Point of order," I said. "I am in fact a Knight."

Molly waved a hand, a little impatiently. "I'm serious, Harry. Tactically speaking, there's no difference. Lara could kill you. So could Sarissa. So could Gard. So could I. It's fucking foolish of you not to protect yourself with the same amount of prejudice just because the threat has breasts."

"She tries something again," I said, "you want me to kill her? The functioning head of the White Court?"

"I didn't say that," Molly said. "As Winter Lady, I can't. But as Molly Carpenter, your friend, I worry about you." She squinted out at the lake. "I still don't think you should be alone with her, away from support, for that long."

"She needs proof of life for Thomas," I said. "Can't blame her for that. And Demonreach isn't a vacation spot."

Molly nodded stiffly. "I have been commanded," she said, as though the words were being forced out of her with the end of a sharp stick, "to advise you to make this entire matter simpler by allowing her to seduce you."

I grunted. "Last thing Maggie needs, her father an addict."

She blew out a breath through her nose and relaxed a little. "You're not wrong. They're here."

I looked up as Lara's classic silver limo pulled into the waterfront lot, looking like something out of the Golden Age of Hollywood. She got out wearing a white sundress with matching sandals, a broad black woven hat, and black sunglasses, and carrying a no-kidding pic-a-nick basket.

I was all Biffed-out, too: white leisure shorts, a winter-blue polo shirt, and grey boat shoes. Together, we'd look like a couple in a vacation commercial, except for all my scars.

"Molls," I said quietly. "I'm sorry Mab is making you do this. Arrange everything."

Molly had been unrequited by me for a long time.

She smiled faintly and said, "I'm sorry she's making you do it, too."

"I know you're busy with your duties. But we need to talk privately," I said.

Her expression went opaque. "Not really possible," she said. "She has my ear."

We were talking about Queen Mab, of course.

"I'll look into it," I said. "Maybe there's something."

Molly squared off on me, her face hardening. "Harry," she said. "Believe me. There isn't. I'm doing everything I can. Not want to. Can." She grimaced. "Sometimes getting more power means accepting more limits. This is one of those." Her expression softened. "I'm sorry. But she's focused on this. You'll have to find someone else."

I felt a little shock of pain go through me. I'd assumed that Molly would be my confidant as much as anyone could.

I could read her expression at my reaction. She didn't like it any better than I did.

Which meant that she was being watched very, very closely.

Or worse, being kept on a very short leash. Mab could command beings of her Court, and they obeyed, period. Her word was literally law to them. It was entirely possible that Mab had laid down the law on Molly, maybe even forbidden her to speak about it.

I could just let myself be hurt by the fact that she wasn't available to support me in the same way she had been in the past. Or I could accept that she was in a different place, and still doing whatever she could within the boundaries of what had been imposed on her.

Hell. That described me pretty well, too.

Maybe I just had to trust her. Sometimes friendships, especially long ones, get to places like that. She'd do what she could, when she could, because that's who Molly was.

I gave her a lopsided smile and said, "We do what we can."

She matched me, her eyes sad, and nodded. "That's right."

Lara came walking up, looking as delicious as she always did. The dress showed off her shoulders and neck. She smiled warmly at me and then at Molly. "Harry. Lady Molly. My, the boat cleans up very nicely." She looked over her shoulder at the security guys who had gotten out of the front of the limo and were watching her the same way Maggie's dog, Mouse, did when she went into the bathroom by herself. "Everyone advised me not to go out there with you alone, you know."

"You bring a knife this time?" I asked.

Lara laughed. "Should I have?"

"Knife is often handy," I mused. "Shall we?"

I traded a slow nod with Molly, offered Lara my arm, and we walked down to the boat together. Her hand was cool on my burned forearm. Even the light pressure made the burn from Sir Butters's holy sword, *Fidelacchius*, ache.

Lara noticed me frowning down at my arm and asked quietly, "Is something wrong?"

"You're not being burned when you touch me," I noted quietly. I held her hand to give her a point of balance as she went up the short ramp to the boat's deck. "I've been with someone who loved me." I cleared my throat. "Reasonably recently. In fact, the night of the battle, you got blistered. But you're not getting scorched. Why not?"

She thought about it for a moment before answering. "Likely because I've fed my Hunger and I'm keeping it well in check," she replied. "Like last time. If I allowed it to try to influence you or feed from you, that's when the burns happen." She frowned down at my arm. "That's not healing like the rest of your injuries from the battle, is it?"

"Holy sword," I said shortly, coming aboard. "Some kind of divine thing, I think. Isn't bad."

"I . . . see," she said. "Can I help you cast off?"

"Get the ropes aft," I said, heading to the bow.

We unmoored the *Water Beetle* and I climbed the ladder to the second steering wheel atop the wheelhouse, while Lara went up to the front of the boat and draped herself attractively across the new bench seating that had been installed there. The engine started with a smooth rumble. I checked the fuel and oil indicators and we pulled slowly out of dock, out of the marina, and onto Lake Michigan.

Michigan is a cold-water lake. Though the sun beat down on us, the spray the boat began to kick up as I turned it into the wind leeched the worst of the heat out of the air. Lara took her hat off and let her head fall back to bare her throat to the light.

My instincts told me to lock the wheel, go down to her, and see if her throat would feel as soft against my lips as it looked like it would. Supported by the primal power of the Winter mantle, my instincts spoke very loudly—but I'd been working out so hard earlier in the morning precisely to give them less weight in my decision-making process, and I ignored them.

Lara was playing polite and cautious with me. I was doing the same with her. As long as that balance was maintained, things would remain convivial.

If it started slipping, I wasn't sure what would happen.

She seemed to feel my gaze on her. Her head tilted, and she opened her eyes though she didn't look directly at me.

I wondered if she was thinking along the same lines I was.

Perhaps it would be wisest not to find out.

We cleared the markers close to shore and I opened up the throttle, setting course for Demonreach.

Chapter
Eight

Lara watched me carefully and calmly once we got to the island. It was a short hike to the ruined lighthouse at the island's summit and the little cottage built at its base, and I felt her eyes on me the whole way.

"It's interesting," she said.

"What?" I asked.

"You never look down here," she said. "You're normally very aware where you put your feet."

I glanced over my shoulder at her without slowing down. "You have feet as big as mine, you get used to looking out for other people's toes."

"You do," Lara countered. "Not everyone would. There is no shortage of people who enjoy stepping on toes."

"I don't have to be those people," I said. "I just have to be me."

"Yes," she said. "Fascinating."

I frowned at her.

"To see someone with so much power use it so carefully," she clarified. "It is unusual to see it in a person of your . . ."

"Idealism?" I suggested. "Clumsiness? Trauma?"

She smiled. "Youth."

"Ah. Well. I started early," I said. I slung the backpack I'd found in the *Water Beetle*'s cabin off of my shoulder, opened it, and took out a pair of white training shoes in Lara's size. "Here. There're socks in one of them."

She accepted the shoes and frowned at me.

"We're taking the stairs," I said casually.

Lara arched an eyebrow. "How many stairs?" she asked.

I beamed at her.

It took the better part of an hour to go down the spiral staircase into the earth and reach the caverns beneath Demonreach.

"How you doing?" I asked, most of the way down.

"Do you want the polite answer?" Lara replied.

I paused and glanced back up at her. I didn't let my eyes linger over-long on her legs because I liked them more than was good for me. "Maybe we should decide right now just to be direct and honest with each other."

"Something wizards are famous for," she said wryly.

"Something vampires are famous for," I replied calmly. "We both suck at it by nature. So maybe we learn how. It's probably something that's good to have as an option."

"All right," she said. "No. This place is terrifying. I've had night-mares of it for weeks."

"It isn't for me," I said, frowning. "I . . ."

Something sent a slow shiver down my spine. I stopped talking and stared up the long shaft toward the distant light of the entrance to the staircase, in the base of the lighthouse.

Lara tensed. "What is it?"

"I . . ." I closed my eyes for a second. The spirit of the island was connected with me in ways I still didn't understand as much as I wished I could. It shared its awareness with me. Simply put, when I was here, I knew things. Just knew things. There was no chain of consequence to it, no logical progression. There was simply awareness. Another shiver went down my spine as I felt a sudden coolness, the way you might when a cloud suddenly blocks the sun on a glaring hot day.

"I'm not sure," I said finally. "There's something. I can't tell what."

"I thought you . . . basically were a god here," Lara said.

"Yeah. Well. I'm new at it."

I was suddenly aware that Lara was afraid. Her heart rate was up. She was trembling very slightly, though she hid it quite well from my mortal senses. The hairs on the back of her neck were standing straight up. The chemical scent of fear rose from her skin, though my physical nose didn't get any of it. I simply knew.

"Hey," I said, more gently. "I know this place doesn't come off as friendly to outsiders. But you aren't in any danger here."

"If I had to pick a single word to describe you, Dresden," she said, without heat, "it would be *dangerous.*"

"I'd have thought it would be *funny,*" I said.

Her lips quirked at one corner. "I might go as far as *amusing.*" She shook her head. "I believe that you generally mean well. But everywhere you go, things fall apart."

I looked quickly back down the stairwell. "That's me. Rough beast."

"You've read Yeats," she said.

"I used to read a lot," I said, very quietly. "The Red Court burned down my old life. Before all of this. Before Mab. My books went with it."

"Which was your favorite?" she asked.

"You can't pick a favorite," I said. "They're books. They're pieces of someone's mind and soul. They're almost friends." I started back down the stairs again. "Sometimes a poet speaks best to what's happening to you. Sometimes it's a philosopher. Sometimes it's a storyteller. Lately, I've been thinking of Kipling a lot."

I felt Lara's gaze on me intently. Her fear was fading. "'If you can meet with Triumph and Disaster and treat those two imposters just the same . . .'"

I smiled thinly. "Something like that. Yes."

"Men are rare," she said quietly. "I'm in a position to know."

"Maybe it's the circles you run in," I said.

Something self-mocking came into her voice. "I've run in a great many circles."

"Hah," I said. "I know that feeling." We reached the bottom of the staircase, and I turned to her. "We're going to start walking past a lot of crystals soon," I said. "Some of them are as big as a house. Don't touch any of them."

She tilted her head. "Why not?"

"Sometimes, if you do, the things inside make mental contact," I said. "It would be unpleasant."

She folded her hands beneath her armpits, frowning. "I see. Is that how you expect me to speak to Thomas?"

"I don't know if he'll be coherent enough for speech," I said quietly. "I've checked on him a few times. He's still asleep. He's been provided with physical nutrients. The damage to his body has been healing. But at something close to human speed."

She nodded. "His Hunger. Did you do something to it?"

I shook my head. "They aren't really separable. It's in stasis. You were right to liken it to a medical coma. When I wake Thomas up, I think his Hunger will wake up, too. I don't know what will happen to him then."

"It seems to me that he's effectively in a cage with a hungry predator," she said. "I should think it would start devouring him."

I grimaced and bowed my head. "Yeah. Well. I'll take steps if I have to."

From very far away, something echoed through the dank, cool air. A cry, or shriek. It was answered by dozens of muffled sounds that shuddered through the walls of earth and stone. Some ululating. Some were basso moans. Some were smothered howls. All of them were alien and weird and full of rage and pain.

"Empty night," Lara gasped. She pressed her arms closer against her torso, and her blue eyes flickered with lighter shades. "What was that?"

"I think . . ." I closed my eyes and communed with the island. "I think something is flying overhead. Over Demonreach."

"Are we in danger?" Lara asked.

I looked back at her and said, "There's a Titan down here, and other things, some of them maybe worse. If something tries to give us a hard time, I'll bottle it and put it on the shelf right next to them."

Lara held very still and then smiled slowly. "Dangerous."

"You're not wrong," I said. "This way."

I took her to the seventh tunnel of thirteen underneath the island. It was the quietest area of the supernatural prison, where I'd spent the most time. It was simply an enormous round shaft going down at a slight angle, and every few yards there was a large green crystal or a cluster of them.

Some were about the size of a coffin. Others were as big as a house. The crystals put off a faint, constant luminescence—which showed a dark, ambiguous form inside each crystalline outcrop.

"What are they?" Lara asked me in a subdued voice, as we passed a crystalline tomb that contained something the size of a whale. She kept herself well clear of all of them.

"I only know some of them," I said. "The . . . inventory system, I suppose, lists each resident, but the only way to know even a little about them is to touch on their essence, which I suspect is very bad for the average human mind. I only go through a handful at a time. Figure it will take me nine or ten decades to be familiar with everything I've got locked up."

"Is . . . is the Titan in here?"

"She's in thirteen," I said. "The worst things are." I paused and looked at Lara. "Not many people know what this place is. Imagine a hundred Ethnius, all loose at once."

Lara looked very reserved and a little sick. "You could do that?"

"God, no," I said. "I mean, I suppose I technically could. But it would take someone who is a bigger fool than me to try it. The things in here would probably eat me first if I turned them loose. Until I'm more familiar with this place, I'm going to assume that everything in here is here for a damned good reason." I pointed at a crystal as we passed. "That one is this giant blob thing covered in eyes and mouths that devours sanity. It's responsible for half a dozen mass hysterias. That one next to it is like a cross between a Komodo dragon and a giant beetle. It wants to poison all the fresh water on the planet with a disease in its saliva that would turn everyone into lizards. That little one there is a lizard-bat that feeds on newborn babies. I've got half a dozen of those shapeshifting things"—I rode out a flash of ugly mental imagery—"we fought at your place that one time in minimum security upstairs. These are the quiet ones."

Lara stared at me as we approached a coffin-sized crystal.

"Okay," I said to the air as I touched the crystal. "Stand this up vertical with his feet down, please."

The rock beneath the crystal coffin groaned and grumbled and began to change shape. The crystal rumbled and rotated up to the vertical, and I could see the humanoid form inside. I touched the crystal and . . .

. . . and felt a great, weary sadness. Quiet yearning. Bittersweet pain. My half brother.

Thomas.

I felt my breath catch and forced myself to keep breathing evenly. There was this empty pit inside me where all my recent pain and loss lived, and I felt an urge to hurl myself into it, but I held off. That was the point of all the meditation I'd been doing—to give me some measure of ability to keep functioning even when my body and my heart wanted me to collapse screaming.

Sometimes that happened to me at night, late.

I'd just start screaming. I'd scream and I wouldn't be able to stop until I'd screamed myself out. Until I was breathing too hard to keep doing it, until my throat hurt, until my jaws ached from forcing my mouth open too wide.

Bear said it happened pretty regularly to folks who had gone to war. That I should roll with it.

I wanted to start screaming. But instead, I took a slow, measured breath as I had thousands of times over recent weeks, and murmured, "Here he is. Hang on . . ."

I focused on the crystal and the energies flowing through it. The entire island was mine to command. Normally, I'd have seen the personification of the genius loci of the place, Alfred, by now, but he hadn't shown himself. After Alfred had wrestled Ethniu into a cell, he'd been exhausted, and was apparently still resting. So I felt my way through the spells binding the crystal casket on my own and found the one that would let us talk to my brother.

I opened my eyes and found myself looking at a ghostly image of Thomas, superimposed over the shadowy form within the crystal. He was a man just a shade away from six feet in height, pale and beautiful as a statue. The image's long black hair was curling and textured like Lara's, and his eyes were closed.

"Hey," I said gently. "Thomas. Can you hear me, man?"

The image blinked its eyes open slowly. It looked around blindly for a moment and then licked its lips. A voice, somehow sounding as if it was coming from twenty feet away, and not right in front of me, croaked out, "Harry? Is that you?"

Lara inhaled sharply.

"Yeah, man. It's me."

"Am I dead?"

I closed my eyes and leaned my forehead against the crystal. "No, man. You're in stasis until we can figure out how to help you."

"Who is we?" Thomas asked. "Is Justine with you? Harry, it's not her. She's been possessed. You can't trust her."

"No, no," I said. "It's not Justine."

Lara reached out her hand and touched the crystal. "Brother mine," she said gently.

Thomas's image closed his eyes for a moment, his expression pained. "Sister mine."

"Your Hunger," Lara said gently. "Are you all right?"

Thomas was silent for a moment before he said, "It's . . . stirring." He grimaced. "It's still . . . still chewing on me."

"I know," Lara said, her voice compassionate. "Thomas, if we release you and feed it immediately, you might recover."

"Hah," he said, his tone glum. "You know where I stand on this."

"I could make it a command," Lara almost whispered.

"Don't you dare," Thomas snapped. "Harry, don't you listen to her."

I held up a hand to Lara and asked Thomas, "What is she talking about doing?"

"If I try to feed my Hunger when it's like this, it's going to rip the life right out of someone," Thomas said quietly. "Or several someones. And after that . . ." His expression became ashamed. "After that, I'd go wild for a time."

"Taking a life that way," Lara explained to me, "is physically, psychically, and psychologically rewarding on a level that is difficult to convey. Thomas, myself, and several other of my most enlightened siblings make it a point to avoid doing so. The following high can last for weeks and . . ."

"And makes you want to take more hits," I said.

Lara nodded.

"So you're suggesting feeding him a bunch of women who he'll certainly kill?" I asked.

"In his state, they needn't all be women," Lara said in a practical tone. "In the past, my people executed criminals to sate their Hunger. But that has its own dangers."

"You are what you eat," I murmured.

"Yes," Lara said. "The only people who are safe to devour are the ones who least deserve any such thing."

"I'm not going to do that, Lara," Thomas said. "Don't make me."

I frowned at her. "You could do that?"

She shrugged an elegant shoulder. "His Hunger is an animal I know well how to handle. Yes."

"No one is eating anyone just yet," I said firmly. "Thomas, I'm on it. I'm going to find a way to get you out of there safely."

"Okay," Thomas said, his image's expression pained and relieved at the same time. "Okay. Hey, how long have I been out?"

"It's August," I said quietly.

"Oh God," he said. "Justine. The baby."

Justine was Thomas's woman. Or had been, before she'd been possessed by an enemy spirit known as Nemesis. The spirit had influenced Justine to become pregnant and then used the lives of Justine and the unborn child to leverage Thomas into trying to assassinate the king of the svartalves, Etri. Thomas had missed the king but taken the life of Etri's bodyguard and friend.

What a mess.

"We're looking for them," I assured him quietly.

"The baby would be due in the spring," Thomas said. "Harry, you've got to find her. Lara, the child is the blood of Raith. You owe it your protection."

"I know what I owe our House," Lara said, her voice thick with compassion. "Harry, can you feel that?"

I closed my eyes and paid attention. I could feel Thomas's sadness and confusion and frustration—and under it, something else, something hectic and directionless and uncontrolled, building steadily, the way a seizure or panic attack might.

"That's his Hunger," Lara said. "It's rousing itself up to keep attacking him."

I took my hand off the crystal and said, "There. You've talked to him. Is that satisfactory, that it's him and he's still alive?"

She mirrored me, her expression weary. "The first thing he did was start babbling about Justine. Of course it's Thomas."

I nodded and put my hand back on the crystal. "Listen, man, I've got to get you back to sleep before you start getting torn up again. You're going to be okay."

"Don't worry about me," he said, the image's face creasing with concern. "Find Justine! Find the baby!"

I wanted to start screaming.

But instead, I said, "I'm working on it, man. I promise."

His image smiled faintly. "Yeah. Okay, man. Lara, you're on it, too?"

"Absolutely," she said. "We will find them."

"Okay," Thomas said. His image's expression broke, tears spilling down his face. "Okay. God. I know I screwed up, Harry. But the thing had Justine. It had the baby. It said if I told anyone that it would kill them both. It just stopped her heart right in front of me . . ."

"Easy," I said. "Easy. I get it, man. I get it."

When the bad guys had taken my Maggie, I would have done anything to keep her safe. I had, in fact, done unthinkable things for her sake. I was still living with the consequences. Even if I got Thomas out, he'd still be living with his. The svartalves did not forget those who had either helped or harmed them.

"God," he said. "I'm so tired. I'm so damned tired, Harry."

"Get some rest," I said gently. "I'll be back as soon as I can figure something out."

His image nodded, sagging.

I focused on the crystal, and the image faded. It went back to glowing green stillness. Thomas's sense of unease and incipient panic faded, the sense of his presence retreating, until it was just sadness and regret again.

I took my hand down from the casket slowly.

"I raised him, you know," Lara said quietly. "His mother wisely fled. And Father couldn't be bothered, of course." She shook her head. "I took care of him. Fed him. Taught him to . . . be."

I turned to look at her. Her crystal-blue eyes looked vibrant against the red that had come into her sclera with what looked like the beginning of tears.

"Thomas told me what pregnancy with one of your kind is like," I said quietly. "You can't have children of your own, can you?"

"I have Thomas," she said quietly. "I will save him. If my way is the only way, I will save him. I don't care what it costs. He will recover himself in time."

"Seems like I have something to say about that," I said.

And suddenly I was facing Lara Raith. The creature who had subverted command of the White Court of vampires. The being whose influence extended throughout the mortal world to a degree that was frankly scary to contemplate. She was cold and beautiful, and her presence was suddenly a thing that I could feel with every inch of my skin, that sent the hairs on my neck crawling about, warning me that a dangerous predator was very, very close.

"There are some places," she said finally, "where it is foolish for anyone to stand. Between a mother and her child is one of the most wellknown. Thomas is mine in a way that no one else ever will be, Dresden. I think it would be best for both of us to concentrate on the goals we have in common."

"Don't try to make me bring innocent people out here," I said. "It's not going to happen."

Lara's blue eyes became drowning deep and the timbre of her voice slid into something lower, slower, more sensual. "I can ask," she said slowly, her voice like honey for my ears, "very . . . very . . . sweetly. Don't make me say pretty please, Harry."

Approximately seventy percent of me wanted to tackle her to the floor and go primal on an immediate basis.

Maybe twenty percent of me wanted to start screaming.

The tithe of me that was left made my body turn on one heel and start walking toward the exit before anything bad (or really, really bad) could happen.

"Let's go," I said, and could hear how harsh my voice sounded. "Before choices get made. We both want to help him. That's the main thing."

I heard her quietly begin following me back to the stairs.

"He's family," she said. "It's the only thing."

Chapter Nine

Lara Raith is old-school," Bear said. "I like that."

"Says the Chooser of the Slain," I noted wryly. "You're not exactly the latest fad." I caught the basketball the kids staying at the castle were playing with as it sailed through outstretched arms. I'd secured a portable hoop and set it up in the main hall. Fitz was serving as referee.

"Thanks, Harry," Fitz said, holding up his hands.

I hit him with a firm pass. Fitz turned back to the three-on-three. "Okay, guys, way to pass, but, Olivia, you gotta stop throwing those elbows . . ."

Bear watched my interaction with Fitz with approval. "True enough, I suppose," she said.

"How old are you anyway?" I asked.

"Hah," Bear said. "That's a more complicated question than you realize. You're only familiar with the linear-time thing."

"Try me."

"Subjectively, I'm a hell of a lot older than I would be if I told you that I was born before the Messiah."

"Jesus," I said, blinking.

"That's the one," she said, nodding. "I was at the Crucifixion. There was quite a crowd actually."

I stared at her for a second and then said, "Wait . . . capital-C Crucifixion?"

She folded her huge arms, watching the game, and nodded calmly.

I didn't quite know how to respond to that. So I asked, "What was that like?"

"Smelly," she said quietly. "Sad." She glanced at me. "Not for me. I didn't know the man. But the people in his life suffered deeply. You could see it." Her eyes tracked the ball. "The world was a great deal more dangerous then, and in that time and place the Romans were the most dangerous people in it. I know it's quite popular to talk about how awful the world is today, but I've been here for a while. Things are better now in more places than I've ever seen so far."

I nodded toward the kids. "Pretty sure that there are people in town who might argue with that."

She shrugged. "They're playing ball, aren't they? Sure, Chicago took a pounding. But it's still here. I've seen cities where the gutters literally ran with the blood of the slain. Where not one stone remained upon another. On multiple occasions. By the standards of history, your battle was a mild one."

My voice crackled with heat I hadn't felt coming. "It didn't feel very fucking mild at the time."

Bear wasn't ruffled. The big Valkyrie looked somewhere between sad and amused. "You probably don't want to take that tone with me."

"Oh yeah?"

"Oh. Yeah."

I scowled at her and looked back at the game.

"You personally took a historically significant hit during it, *seidrmadr*. I'll give you that. Time has rubbed off the rough edges of death on a civilizational scale. But it will never make losing friends or lovers or family any easier."

I fell quiet at that and folded my arms.

Bear squinted at me. "You go to bed early every night."

"Yeah. So."

"You don't sleep much."

I grunted.

Bear tilted her head, studying me. "Sometimes I hear you talking. Even laughing."

I didn't say anything.

She nodded slowly. "Good for you to talk. Even if it's just to yourself."

"What I do with my personal time is my personal business," I said.

"Of course," she said. We watched the kids play for a couple of minutes, and then she asked, "What was she like?"

"I'll meet you out front at three," I said, and walked away from the game.

I met King Etri at McAnally's.

Mac had cleared the pub out for us and put a table in the middle of the floor with some room around it. Bear sidled up to the bar and nodded to Etri's single bodyguard, a small man in a neat suit who all but vibrated with energy and certainly wasn't human. He bought her the first round. Mac bustled about quietly. He even brought a pair of bottles to our table, so he clearly thought the meeting was an important one.

Etri was wearing his human disguise, svartalf magic making him appear to be a man of less than average height, late forties, with swept-back dark hair, a silvering beard, and piercing black eyes.

"Sir Knight," he said quietly.

"Your Majesty," I responded, and inclined my head briefly. In feudal terms, Etri was a head of state, and I was something like a neighboring landholding knight. He had extended goodwill to meet with me. I took up my bottle, and he his. We clinked and sipped.

Etri closed his eyes for a moment and then turned and lifted the bottle toward Mac. The svartalves respected nothing so much as beautiful craftsmanship, and Mac's brew was unparalleled.

"You wish to negotiate on behalf of Thomas Raith," Etri said.

"That is correct," I said.

Etri nodded. Svartalves have some of the best poker faces around. I got nothing from his face. "Why would you do this?"

"Politics," I half lied. "My new fiancée wishes to protect her brother."

"Mmmm," Etri said. "Understandable. But the matter is clear. Thomas Raith was a trusted guest in my home. He attacked and injured my people. He attempted to murder me. He took the life of a trusted subordinate and friend." Etri shook his head. "This is a violation of the oldest traditions upon the face of this world, treachery, murder, and an insult to both myself and the svartalf kingdom. I cannot be tolerant of this act."

"Let us speak clearly," I said.

Etri nodded his firm approval. "Thomas Raith will answer for the life he took with his own."

"A life for a life," I said.

"Precisely. That is the old way."

I nodded slowly. "There may be mitigating factors."

"Explain."

"There is a spirit I will not name," I said. "A being that works toward chaos and conflict. One who can possess almost anyone and cause them to act against their will."

"No," Etri said calmly. "I know the being of which you speak. Our security measures would have detected any such invasive spirit the moment it crossed our threshold—even that one. You cannot excuse his actions thus."

"Not Raith," I said. "It took his woman and demanded he act or forfeit her life and the life of her unborn child."

Etri leaned back in his seat at that, his expression perhaps, barely, troubled. "Meaning no disrespect, that could be an easily arranged ploy."

"It could be," I said. "It isn't."

"I have no way of knowing that."

I nodded and took a sip of my own beer. "This could be a matter where consciously applied faith might help resolve many difficulties."

"I have given my faith already and paid for it with my friend's life," Etri said, his voice made of cold, cold iron. "We are beyond that."

I nodded slowly. "What if I provided you proof?" I asked.

Etri took a slow drink of his ale, studying me. "In that event," he said, "then the onus of my wrath belongs to a different being."

"And Thomas would be free of reprisal?"

"No," Etri said with slow, granite intonation. "Though he may have been compelled, that does not change the consequence of his actions.

Nor will I permit my nation to be seen as weak." He turned one hand palm up. "However. There might be more latitude as to the nature of the reprisal."

I exhaled slowly. "If it comes to it," I said, "I will fight for him. Winter will be with me. As will Lara Raith."

Etri showed me his teeth. "I am aware of the stakes, wizard. You would not be our first foe. Nor our last."

"Do not misunderstand me," I said. "I point this out only because it benefits us all to find a way forward without such conflict."

"Agreed," King Etri said. "But I did not initiate these events. In the absence of this proof you claim exists, Thomas Raith's life is forfeit. If you wish peace, that is the only way forward."

I had to work to keep from clenching my hands and jaw in frustration.

Etri studied my face for a moment and then relaxed back into his seat. "Understand, wizard, that I know that you swept Raith from custody. I have no evidence to bring before an Accorded judge, of course, but do not think me blind or foolish. I can see how I was manipulated by Lara Raith so that you could free her brother. That became obvious the moment the alliance between Winter and the White Court was made known."

I stared at him and said nothing.

"We have looked for Thomas Raith, of course," Etri said. "There are comparatively few places and beings who might be able to successfully hide him from our agents and our spells. I did not initially think you skilled enough to be one of them. I have since altered that supposition."

The crystal that contained Thomas's physical body was the closest thing to truly impervious I had ever seen, both magically and physically. When Demonreach buttoned something up, it stayed buttoned.

I tilted my head to one side and said nothing.

"Out of respect for Mab, I have reserved my judgment of you, thus far," Etri said. "And wizards meddle. It is what they do."

"Meaning?" I asked.

"Many things are not what they seem. Your conduct in this matter will show me who you are," he said. "If you prove false, you will find yourself my enemy and the enemy of my people. Believe that we will make your life an affliction for the world to see."

I wanted to swallow very, very badly.

"Resolve it with honor," Etri continued, "and you may yet retain our respect. Do you understand?"

"Yeah," I said. "Either I bring you proof that a damned near untraceable and undetectable entity was manipulating events, I hand over Raith to be executed—"

"Tortured and executed," Etri interjected. "We do not take treachery lightly."

"Tortured and executed," I corrected, "or you declare war on me personally. Which Mab is likely to let me handle on my own."

"You have until one year from the day you took Thomas Raith from us. Do you understand?"

"I understand," I said.

Etri's tone gentled. "I take no pleasure in this," he said. "My people are craftsmen. We are content to create, to live, and to let live. But a life was taken from us. It will be answered for. There are no other options." He rose from the table.

I rose to match him and inclined my head.

For a second, Etri looked tired. "We all love. This is understandable. But death is death. I like you, wizard. I would prefer it if you did not make yourself my enemy."

"I would prefer that as well."

Etri nodded firmly. "We cannot control all things. What will be will be." He turned to nod respectfully to McAnally, beckoned his bodyguard, and left. They both took their bottles with them.

Mac watched them go and then nodded approvingly to me. He bent over and came up with a wooden box full of bottles. He grunted and set it down on the bar in front of Bear.

Bear beamed at him, finished her bottle in a long pull, and rose. She took up the box and we walked toward the door.

"You're not going to make my job easy, are you?" she asked.

"That's why you get paid the big bucks." I sighed.

"King Etri," she said, "and his people."

"Yeah?"

"When Asgard was strong," she said, her expression serious, "they wouldn't go to war with the svartalves. There are always more of them than you think. They always have something unexpected in store. And they don't know how to quit. Remember that war is a craft, too. One-Eye learned much from them."

A cold feeling slid through my guts. If they truly were that dangerous, Mab would certainly throw me off the sleigh, rather than expend the resources of her realm on an optional war.

"Do the nigh impossible or die," I said. I finished off my bottle and waved at Mac. "Well. At least this feels familiar. Let's go."

This was turning out to be one hell of a year.

Chapter

Ten

So you gotta find this vampire's girlfriend," Fitz said. "I don't get it. You can't get her hair or something?"

"Already tried," I said. "The thing possessing her cleaned out the apartment before it vanished with her."

I finished hand-driving a screw into the T-brace attached to the cardboard plank on the floor of the castle's gunnery range. The city had pulled our permit for it when they had retracted all the other benefits Marcone had wrested out of them, but no municipal codes existed to address the indoor use of tactical magic.

"Could the White Council help?" Fitz asked.

"They won't," I said.

"Not like the official guys," Fitz said. "I mean more like people you know there. When I was on the streets, we'd never have called the cops for help, right? But I knew a couple that were okay, and sometimes we could talk to them."

"Get that end," I said, and we set up the target. It was a rectangle about five feet tall and three across. I had taken some black paint and sketched in the rough form of a ghoul, complete with googly eyes and cartoon-quality teeth. "If I was going to go to anyone, there's this contractor I know. And the money is right. But he already got a bite of this case during the battle and he doesn't want anything else to do with it." I stood up and walked back to the far end of the shooting range. "It would need to be someone based in mainland Europe, and my contacts there are pretty limited. No one I know there would stick their neck out."

Fitz frowned. "Well. How are you going to find her, then?"

"The spirit world might have answers," I said.

"You don't mean, like, shades, right?"

"Right," I said. "Shades can be a really fantastic resource. But they can also be patchy and weird. I'm talking like voodoo-level stuff here. Entities that exist on a level of power somewhere between the shades of regular people and blue-collar angels."

"So let's get us a Ouija board and go to town."

"Isn't that simple," I said. "Those spirits are dangerous, and they want what they want. Call up the wrong one, get the offering wrong, or ask them the wrong question, and I'll have more troubles, not less."

I didn't want to mention that dealing with spiritual entities was very much a matter of focus, will, and intent, and I was still a wreck. Call up a spirit when you weren't certain of yourself, your boundaries, and your power, and you could wind up just as possessed as Justine currently was.

"If you didn't have any hair, how'd you try tracking her already?" Fitz asked, frowning.

"I had hair, actually. And some of her possessions," I said. "Favorite jewelry, books she liked, that kind of thing." It had actually felt a little creepy, building what amounted to an altar to my brother's woman and using it in a painstakingly slow and careful ritual. "I barely got a reading, and that was only as specific as 'Europe.' There was too much water between us, and I suspect the entity is suppressing her personality full-time."

"That's fu—"

I glanced at him. Fitz was learning mental discipline. I'd had him quit cursing two weeks ago.

"Screwed up," he corrected himself.

I nodded approval. "The vampires are running the mortal circuits," I said. "They've got operatives in the field looking, trying to track her down by purely mortal means." Which wasn't quite true. A White Court vampire had senses to rival those of any predator on earth. If one of them ran across Justine's scent, they could track her like a hound.

"Couldn't you ask, like, an angel?"

"They have really limited avenues to exercise their power," I said. "They only mix it up in human affairs when Hell crosses a line."

"So ask Hell," Fitz said. "On the streets, I knew outfit guys, too."

"They only trade in names," I said. "And they've got all but one of mine already. Last thing I need is to go all Linda Blair." I cleared my throat and gestured down the range. "Okay, kid. Show me what you've got."

"One fire coming up," Fitz said, and lifted his hand.

I caught his wrist. "Fitz," I said. "What happens when there's a fire in a closed room?"

He paused. "Smoke?"

"Air gets burned up, too," I said. "And fire tends to be a little hard on buildings sometimes. Fire's for outdoors and emergencies only." I nodded up toward the ducting mounted on the walls and ceiling. "This place is ventilated for propellant fumes, so we probably wouldn't run out of air. But that also means the fire has what it needs to spread to other fuel."

Fitz frowned. "So what do I do?"

"You've read McCoy. What would he say?" I asked him.

Fitz screwed up his face, thinking. "Long, closed, narrow space. Not really a lot of air to work with. It's dry, so water is out. I've got to use either earth or force."

"Good," I said. "Earth is a hell of a lot harder to use without years and years of practice. You're going to start that, but I've been slinging evocation for a couple of decades and change now, and I don't trust myself to use earth magic in a real fight yet."

"So, force?" he asked hesitantly.

"Yeah," I said. "Force is the least efficient way to translate your will into energy, but also the most flexible and it's the easiest to control. You pick out your word yet?"

"Yeah," he said. "*Forza.*"

I tilted my head and looked at him.

"I figure Italian kinda learned from Latin, only it's not old as sh— as hell," Fitz said. "Like me and you."

"Hah," I said. "Okay. But don't just go around saying the word. Use it only when you use the spell, or you'll wind up burning out things in your brain. Okay?"

"Right," he said.

I nodded at him and stepped back.

Fitz closed his eyes for a few seconds and drew in his breath slowly. I didn't press him to go faster. You don't learn to shoot a gun as fast as you can when you start. You learn to make it go bang while pointing it in the right direction and not getting anyone killed when you do it.

It took him about ten seconds to draw the energy together, making the air around him crackle, and then he opened his eyes, his young face set in dark, intense focus. He held up his right hand, pointed his index finger at the cartoon ghoul, and snarled, *"Forza!"*

Magic lashed downrange in a wave and a cascade of sparks and small shrieking sounds like runaway fireworks. Fitz hadn't been able to focus all the power he'd poured into the spell into pure directed force, and the inefficiency spilled out into other expressions of energy. By the time the invisible wave reached the target, it had dissipated severely. The plyboard plank rocked about half an inch off the floor and then wobbled back down. The cartoon ghoul grinned triumphantly.

Fitz gasped and fell to his hands and knees, his head down. He breathed hard for half a minute, then groaned and fell over onto his side.

I dropped to my heels beside him. "Actually, not that bad," I said to him. "The first time I tried force, I threw myself into a chain-link fence. You could play tic-tac-toe on my back with markers for a week. You paid attention to your McCoy."

Fitz nodded, bringing his breathing back under control. "Use as much force to stabilize yourself as you throw out."

"Correct," I said approvingly, rose, and offered him my hand. "We'll try it again, but we'll try to focus the energy better. This time don't just point your finger. I want you to visualize poking that ghoul in the eye with it as you release the power."

"Wait, I gotta add another layer to all of that?"

"Gets easier with practice," I said. "You've got the mind for this. Use it."

Fitz grimaced down the range, clenched his jaw, and took my hand, rising. "Okay. Why was that so hard? When I set that thing on fire the night of the battle, I just kept running."

"Hell of a lot of power in the air that night," I said. "Made everything easier. And you just threw your instincts into that one, all unconscious thought. You had to piece this one together."

He frowned, panting. "So how come I don't just do it all by instinct?"

"Good way to get killed," I said. "Happens to a lot of untrained practitioners. Things happen when you get upset. Or don't happen when you really need them to. It's better to learn the process, so you have control over when something gets set on fire. That's the whole reason Mort brought you to me. That's the whole point of what we've been learning."

Fitz frowned and chewed over that thought for a moment, and I let him. It was pretty important that he was on board with the concept. "Okay," he said slowly. "Okay. But it gets easier?"

"With practice and greater discipline and the development of your personal will, yes."

"Guess nothing's easy at first, is it?"

"Nothing worthwhile."

He huffed out a laugh. "How come I'm so hungry?"

"You just packed the output of maybe twenty minutes of exercise into about a second of effort," I said. "Your body is trying to catch up. You draw a lot more energy from your body until your will works up to the job. Probably why wizards are generally skinny." I nodded at a backpack in the corner. "Bunch of fruit snacks in there. Go eat some, and we'll try it again."

"Nice," Fitz said with some enthusiasm and seized the pack.

I let him get a few mouthfuls in before I said, "You said you could talk to some folks on the street."

"Sure," he said, munching.

"About what?"

He shrugged a shoulder. "Shelters giving out food. Places to stay in bad storms. Jobs for a little money. Stuff like that."

"Uh-huh," I said. "Who'd you talk to about important things?"

Some of that alley cat wariness came back into his expression. "Like what?"

"Life. The future. Pain. That kind of thing."

He stared at me for a long minute, chewing slowly, his eyes opaque. "You were in the system, huh?"

"Yeah," I said.

"But not the streets," Fitz said quietly. Something haunted went through his eyes. "You mostly don't talk about that stuff."

Then he turned back to the food, eating like a starving animal. Like one that might bite if I got too close.

There was a knock at the range's doorway, and Bear loomed up in it. "Dresden," the Valkyrie said, frowning, "the police are here. They want to talk to you."

Bear had let the officers into the cooler main hall rather than making them wait in the drizzle out on the sidewalk. September had come with considerable rain. The charnel-house stench had begun to fade—though I supposed that might have been all of us just getting used to it. Still. It was probably better for me to choose to believe that the rain was at least beginning to wash the city clean.

According to the news, it was also washing old toxins out of collapsed buildings and into the streets and sewers. But Chicago wasn't built in a day. It wouldn't be repaired in a day, either.

Three uniformed officers I didn't recognize were in the main hall, along with Detective Lieutenant John Stallings of Special Investigations. Stallings was a tall man with greying hair, nearing retirement age. His brown suit hung on him loosely. There were dark bags under his eyes. The officers with him looked tense, though many observers probably wouldn't have noticed. The hall was otherwise empty, though I suspected the Knights of the Bean would be hanging out in adjacent rooms.

I walked over to Stallings and shook his hand.

"Harry," he said. "How you holding up?"

"Just trying to keep some people sheltered and fed," I said. I looked at the uniformed officers. "You here to pick someone up?"

Stallings waved a hand. "Hell, I don't mind people with rifles keeping things peaceful, given what's out there. We just don't go out with less than four these days. Policy."

"Damn," I said. "That bad?"

He shrugged. "Last two months, we've lost a hundred officers," he said.

I grimaced. "Gangs?"

"Hell," he said. "Gangs are keeping some order at this point. Got a lot of people just snapping. You know?"

"I know the feeling," I said, frowning. "I thought they'd sent in the National Guard to keep the law."

"The Guard is mostly handling all the people who got out of Chicago," he said. "Suburbs are full of tent camps and portable toilets. We've got soldiers around the Gold Coast, the city's landmarks, and such. They bring food into the stadiums where more people are staying. But the law ain't coming back anytime soon to eighty percent of the city."

"Can't you get more Guard brought in?"

Stallings snorted. He walked me a little way from the uniformed officers, out of easy earshot. "Look. The governor is the one in charge of that. And he's assuring everyone that everything is under control."

"Oh," I said. "Politics."

Stallings looked exhausted and furious. "Yeah. News is covering the concerts they're having out in the suburbs, for Chrissake. But they don't let camera crews into town. And there's a reason there ain't no cell service or internet back yet."

"Can't hear all the gunfire over concerts. Hear no evil, see no evil," I said. "People don't get out and talk?"

"Gets chalked up to heebie-jeebies," Stallings said. "Nerve toxin causing hallucinations and paranoia, gotta be sympathetic for such folks, offer them care, keep them safe from self-harm, that kind of bullshit. People learned to keep their mouths shut and be glad they ain't in town anymore."

I burned with shame for my city. For the people still suffering. I felt furious at myself for my weakness. For my inability to do something. And I felt tired, tired of all of it, of the struggle, of the pain, of the suffering.

I wanted to go somewhere dark and cold and wait it out.

But I couldn't do that.

"How can I help?" I asked.

Stallings just looked at me for a second. He closed his eyes briefly. Then he took a breath and opened them again. "There's things on the street at night, making people disappear. Looked into it. We're talking maybe a thousand victims in the last month that we know about. Mostly the very old and the very young."

"Ghouls," I spat quietly. "There's always been a few. But all this death and chaos have drawn them like flies."

Special Investigations, in normal times, had the job of explaining away supernatural weirdness. Stallings and the other men and women on the team knew about ghouls and other common threats from the preternatural side of the street.

"Well," he said, glancing back at the uniformed officers and lowering his voice, "there's too many of them for SI to handle alone. And if you try explaining what's really going on to regular cops, you get suspended and sent for a heebie-jeebies evaluation. They don't let you come back until you've 'stopped hallucinating.'"

"Tell them it's a cult on PCP and HBGB," I said. "That they watched too many monster movies and became what they feared in order to escape it, yada yada."

"That ain't gonna keep uniforms from getting torn to pieces," Stallings said seriously.

"That's the PCP angle," I said. "Tell them they need to carry shotguns loaded with slugs. That nothing short of that will stop them."

"Christ," Stallings muttered. "Ghouls are tough."

"Get tougher," I said quietly. "I don't see much choice."

"Don't know if that's going to fly with city hall." Stallings sighed. "Governor's got them by the balls." His voice was too flat and tired to be called "pleading." "I had hoped you could do something."

"I'm just one guy," I said.

"Bullshit," Stallings said.

I exhaled slowly. Then I said, "When's the last time you had a hot meal?"

"What's a meal?" Stallings said.

I nodded. "Bear," I called.

The Valkyrie walked over to me.

"These men need some hot food. Ask the ladies in the kitchen to help?"

Bear nodded affably, smiled down at Stallings, and lumbered out.

Stallings watched her go and shook his head. "Jesus, Dresden. You starting a wrestling league?"

"Look," I said. "I can't easily explain to you how much bad stuff is coming down on my side of the street. I'm stretched pretty thin. I don't know what I can do. But I'll try."

"Holy Christ," Stallings said, sniffing. "Is that beef?"

"And potatoes. Get you and your guys some food," I said. "I'll look into it and do what I can."

Chapter
Eleven

September continued to smolder. There had been fires in Canada, and sunset had filled the crippled city with an orange haze.

Bear was training half a dozen Knights of the Bean on the roof of the castle, where several wrestling mats had been tossed down. Will was working with them, and so was Fitz, at my suggestion. Bear was teaching them pankration—an ancient Greek style of martial arts that basically amounted to boxing plus wrestling plus kicking plus the dirtiest fighting tricks of human history.

Bear had learned in Sparta, so she was what you might call a pure source. She'd started giving me solo lessons about a week before, and I had a mouse under one eye and bruises all over my torso to show for it. Spartan pankration wasn't exactly something you did for recreation, and the boys were taking their bruises learning.

I was with Michael Carpenter at the grill, making burgers and dogs.

"They think you're getting better, don't they?" Michael said calmly. He opened the cooler and got out a couple of chilled bottles of Mac's pale. He opened them and passed me one.

"I'm functioning better," I said. "I handled a case for this tutoring service. There was an evil hag and a spirit bear and explosions and everything."

Michael grunted. He was a man in his fifties, tall and hale, with artistically grizzled hair and beard. He was half-covered in drywall dust. Several of his crew had joined in on the pankration lessons along with my guys. He was my friend.

"That's not the same thing as you dealing with what happened to you," he said quietly.

"I'm moving on," I said shortly. I flipped a burger and it sizzled. "Isn't that what I'm supposed to do?"

He clinked my bottle with his and said, "Drink."

I remembered and did.

He mirrored me and said, "I know you want to be there for people, Harry," he said. "That's who you are. But if you don't get yourself squared away, you're not going to be able to provide for anyone."

"How's Maggie?" I asked him.

He grimaced. He studied my face for a moment and visibly decided to relent. "She wishes you'd visit more. Charity formed a soccer league for the local kids, and they take over the street every afternoon. She's playing goalkeeper. She lost her last baby tooth."

"Did you—" I began.

"Collected it, ground it to dust, scattered it," Michael said, his voice soothing. "I remember."

I nodded slowly, relaxing.

"We're having dinner on Sunday," he said. "I'll expect you to be there."

"I have some things going on here," I said, gesturing toward the training mats. Will caught Fitz in a throw and slammed the young man down onto the mat with a thump that made everyone stop and look for a second.

Michael smiled with his eyes. "I'm guarding and feeding your daughter while the city bleeds," he said. "You'll be there. It will be good for you."

"We'll see," I said grumpily.

But we both knew better.

"Good," he said. "Get up and walk, son," he called to Fitz. "It'll bring your wind back faster." He studied the burgers for a moment and said, "Like them rare, huh?"

"Leaves the most nutrition in them," I said.

"Makes my stomach hurt," he said. "Be more patient with a couple."
I obliged.

"You could talk to me about it, you know," Michael said. "I'm here most days."

"You're working on getting the castle ready to keep people safe and warm this winter."

"Try me," he said.

"Okay," I said. I started flipping a burger for each bullet point, the meat sizzling. "Vampire queen is threatening to be nice to me. My boss wants me to sleep with her and turn myself into a junkie. King Etri wants me to do the impossible or he hounds me to death. Thomas is dying and won't save himself unless he can do it with a clear conscience. Justine and her baby are still missing. The Black Court has the remains of my friends and is using them for God knows what. The White Council thinks I'm Voldemort and I'm doing stuff to make them sure of it if I get caught. SI wants me to help them stop ghouls from taking about thirty people a night." I slapped the last few burgers over harder, making flames leap up from the charcoal. "There's probably more that I'm forgetting."

"That's what's happening," Michael said gently. "I want you to tell me what's wrong."

I glowered at him and took a drink from my bottle as viciously as I knew how. "What do you want to hear, man?" I asked him in a dull monotone. "You want to hear how I can only sleep two or three hours a night? You want to hear how I can't concentrate? Can barely do magic? You want to hear how the Winter mantle is chewing at me night and day and telling me to take advantage of the chaos, go out and conquer and pillage? How I keep waking up from nightmares about turning people into briquettes? How this stupid burn on my arm hasn't healed? How every time I close my eyes I keep seeing how weird and pale her face looked when she was bleeding out?"

He watched me, his eyes pained, listening.

"I don't taste anything I eat," I said. "I move around and exercise and I meditate and I listen to good advice and it doesn't do a damned thing. When I'm alone at night, I cry. I cry until it hurts. And when I can't cry anymore, it isn't better. It still hurts. It's still all built up inside me. My stomach hurts. All the time." I looked out at the city, at nothing in particular. "Sometimes I start screaming and I can't stop. Nothing sounds good. Nothing looks good. Nothing feels good. Nothing tastes good. Nothing smells good. It's all grey."

"And?" he said gently.

I was quiet for a long moment. "And I miss her, man."

He exhaled slowly.

"Go ahead," I said, an edge coming into my voice. "Tell me how to make it all better."

"You can't," he said gently.

I eyed him.

"Not yet," he said. "It is going to take time, Harry. Time to heal. Time for the good things you're doing to help you get your balance again."

I scoffed and rolled some dogs across the grill.

"I know," he said. "You don't believe it yourself. Not yet. But you will, in time."

"You don't know that," I said shortly.

"Of course not," he said. "How could I?" He smiled at me again. "But I have faith."

"Oh," I said. "Faith."

"I don't always make the right choices, Harry," he said. "I don't always know the right thing to do. But I do know that I have put my faith in you many times over the years of our friendship. And I have never once regretted doing so." He reached out and took the wooden handle of the turner out of my hands and started expertly flicking burgers onto waiting buns. "You walk in a world of shadows, Harry. But you've always carried your own light. Your path has turned dark and winding, and you aren't sure where you are at the moment. But you'll find your way. When it's time. When you're ready."

I closed my eyes.

"There's a little girl who is waiting for you," he said. "She keeps a little light in her window at night, you know. In case you come to see her and need it to find your way."

Something in my chest cracked.

"She does?" I whispered.

"She has faith, too," Michael said. I felt his hand settle on my shoulder and squeeze gently. "Sunday," he said firmly. "Dinner with my family. And yours."

Maggie.

Right.

There could be a world of things happening. But I had to remember why I was doing what I was doing. Building a home. Building back a man who could be her father. Building a place where she could be safe and loved.

The world had dealt me horrible wounds.

It was up to me to make them right again.

For her.

Maybe even for me.

It took me a couple of tries to say, "Well. If it will get you off my back."

"That's more like it." He rumbled out a chuckle and called out, "Bear! Quit beating them and let them eat!"

The Valkyrie laughed and came over to be first in line for the food. Bear ate and drank like the crew of a Viking longship, and filled up the first of what would be two or three plates with enthusiasm. The men who'd been learning from her came off the mats in high spirits, talking and laughing, to collect food and bottles of ale of their own.

For a minute, I just . . . opened myself to it. To the camaraderie. The friendly talk and laughter. Will was deep in a conversation with Fitz, explaining how he'd defeated him. They smelled of sweat and sawdust and propellant and gun-cleaning solvent. For a moment, I set aside all the things that had happened to me, all the bad things I felt in my body, all the terrible memories, and just felt the vibe.

Pleasant exhaustion. High spirits. Hunger. Good food. Excellent beer. Some bruises and scrapes and no hard feelings about them.

I felt as much as heard the footsteps coming up behind me.

I turned to find a middle-aged Latino man, stocky and unremarkable, with silver streaks at his temples and a smile on his face. "Mister Dresden," he said.

I recognized him—the father of one of the families who was staying with me. "Oh, uh. Mister Jiminez, right?"

"Matias," he said easily. "Do you have a moment?"

"Sure," I said.

"My daughter, Elena," he said. His accent was pretty thick, but there was no hesitation to his speech. "She was sick. You got her a doctor."

"Oh," I said. "Yes."

"I have come to thank you," he said. "There are many people in this city who struggle. They cannot take care of anyone else. You have opened your home to us. This is a very big thing. I wanted you to know that we are grateful. We will do whatever we can to return your kindness."

"Oh," I said. "Sure."

"Okay," he said, nodding at me. "It took time for me to get the words. But thank you. You did not have to do this."

"Yes," I said. "I did."

He tilted his head and studied me for a moment and then smiled. He looked at Michael and nodded toward me. "Good man there."

Michael passed Matias a bottle. "Yes. He is."

Something loosened in my stomach.

"You know what?" I said. "I'm hungry."

Michael made me a burger. We didn't have much to go on them—just the buns we'd thawed along with the frozen patties and dogs. Some ketchup. Some mustard.

But I decided I could take a brief time-out from all the bad things around me.

And the food was delicious.

Bear gave Michael a look of decided approval as she chewed.

"Will," I said, licking my fingers.

"Yes, Harry?" he said, looking up at me.

"Get in touch with Carter LaChaise," I said.

"Who's that?"

"King of the Ghouls, more or less," I said casually. "Tell him that he's going to have a talk with me."

Chapter
Twelve

October came, still warmer than it should have been. The days were blazing hot, though the nights came with the chilly promise of winter. The city cleaned the dead cars from the street in front of the castle, and we started seeing occasional traffic. They'd gotten about half of the L lines repaired and one could occasionally hear the rumble of trains, unusually loud in the quiet of the wounded metropolis.

The castle had settled into an evening routine—training on the roof with Bear from early evening until sundown, then board games and music in the great hall. Matias played a twelve-string guitar at a semiprofessional level, and he would settle down by the fire and start playing from the time the sun went down until his wife called him to bed. The ladies had a knitting circle going, though they called it crochet. I wasn't sure of the difference. I did learn to crochet a little, enough to make a red-and-blue scarf for Maggie for the coming holidays. It was an incredibly repetitive and soothing task, and when I did it I found my stomach settling for a while. Plus, I liked making things.

Bear and I folded up the mats and put them into waterproof storage boxes that lived on the roof now, one night after practice.

"So how was Sunday dinner?" she asked.

"You were there," I said. Bear at the Carpenters' table had been a sight to see. She made the room look small.

She shrugged, pulling on her enormous black leather jacket against the coming chill. "You should be around the little girl more."

"Maybe you should keep your opinions about Maggie to yourself," I said. "I can get a little touchy about other people making decisions about her."

"I'm not talking about her," Bear said. "I'm talking about you."

I squinted at her. Then grunted, closed the plastic storage box, and locked it. "Okay, I'll bite. Why?"

"She's good for you."

I closed my eyes. It had been hard, at several points, not to start crying when the kid was around. She was just such a tiny thing. And when I was there, she stayed in physical contact with me as much as she could arrange. Sitting on my lap. Holding my hand. She never left the room. Like she just couldn't get enough.

I just . . . gave her all the love I could, while I was there.

And saved feeling terrible about it until it wouldn't spill onto her.

"I can't have her here," I said quietly. "Hell, freaking gremlins tried to blow the place up within three weeks of me moving in."

"The castle's security enchantments are active now," Bear pointed out. "It hasn't happened again. And you have other people's kids here."

"The other kids don't have anywhere else to go, and don't have me for their dad," I said. "My enemies have already shown me that they'll take her from me. Keeping her at a distance keeps her safer. She's got freaking angels protecting her there. And she knows and loves Michael's family. They're good to her."

Bear spread out her hands in acknowledgment of that. "Maybe her dad would be good for her, too."

"They're not quite so broken as me. I'm sure she'd be thrilled to be around when I get the screams," I said. "I need more time."

"Children can be a trial, even at the best of times," Bear said. "But you won't get better by sitting still."

"You don't say that when I'm meditating," I said.

Bear scowled at me.

I smiled. I rarely scored a point on the Valkyrie.

"The roads are mostly clear between here and the Carpenter home now," she said. "Pick a night of the week. Go see her." She turned and picked up her enormous duffel bag. "Work your way up to every day. Start with two."

I frowned and thought about that for a moment.

Poor Maggie. She was so hungry for my attention and affection.

I could only just barely remember what that had been like with my dad.

"Yeah, okay," I said. "Hey. You carry that damned bag everywhere. What's in it?"

"Trouble for bad guys," she said.

"Like what?"

Bear looked at me for a moment. Then she reached into the bag and pulled out a goddamned cannon.

"Hell's bells," I said. "What is *that*?"

She offered it to me. It weighed about as much as a barbell.

"Four-bore," she said.

It had a lever action that I worked. It lowered a block from the barrel, where you'd put a round about the size of a damned can of Red Bull. Just one round, no magazine or anything. "What's it shoot, tank shells?"

Bear reached into the bag and plucked out a cartridge that was indeed absolutely enormous. She handed it over. The bullet was as big around as my eye socket. "What the hell, Bear?"

"Puts a nice big hole in soft targets," she said.

"Like ghouls," I said.

"Just like them," she confirmed. "You want one?"

"Would it tear my arm off?"

"You're a big guy," she said. "Probably not."

I hefted the empty rifle and examined the iron sights. The weapon was just a block of metal barrel and walnut fittings and felt like it could club someone's head completely off if I got a good two-handed swing behind it. "Can we use this on the range downstairs?"

Bear burst out laughing and then said, "Indoors? I wouldn't."

"Well. Maybe we can take it to an outdoor range at some point." I offered it back to her, and she took it calmly, restowing it in the bag. "Everything arranged?"

"He'll be here at midnight," Bear said. "Alone, under guest-right."

"Ballsy bastard," I noted. "Given the last major violation of guest-right happened right here, in this very building."

"You planning to betray him?" Bear asked. "No judgment, I just want to know what to look out for."

I grimaced. "No. Mab would have my teeth."

"Then I imagine things will go smoothly," Bear said. The big woman paused. "You're wearing your coat, right? Just in case I'm wrong."

A chill went down my spine and I looked up.

There might have been a dark shape soaring overhead, in the dark. Without the lights of the city everywhere, it was hard to tell.

"*Seidrmadr?*" Bear asked.

"You see anything up there?"

She squinted up and said, "No."

"Huh," I said. "Okay. Let's get back indoors."

Carter LaChaise showed up at the front doors of the castle precisely at midnight. He was a ghoul, but he looked like a big, beefy man with grizzled muttonchops to his jawline, dressed in a white linen suit and a pink *Miami Vice* shirt, along with gold chains around his neck and rings on every finger. Bear and a couple of Knights of the Bean escorted him into the great hall, where I was sitting at a table.

"Harry Dresden, I do declare," LaChaise said, his deep Southern accent full of bourbon and gumbo. "I cannot imagine what would cause you to invite me to your lovely home."

"LaChaise," I said. I didn't like ghouls. By which I meant I was willing to torture them to death, given a chance and half an excuse. I nodded at the chair across the table from me and swallowed my bile. "Have a seat."

"No," LaChaise said genially. "Not until you've acknowledged your role as host."

I showed him my teeth. "Please. Be my guest."

LaChaise glanced over his shoulder at Bear and the guards and then sauntered to the table. "She's a deluxe-sized morsel, isn't she? Even I couldn't handle that in one sitting."

"Pretty sure you couldn't handle her in any number of sittings," I said.

LaChaise rumbled out a low laugh. "To what do I owe the honor of this invitation?"

"There are ghouls in Chicago," I said.

"Oh my goodness," LaChaise said.

I drummed my fingers on the tabletop once. I left a moment of silence before I said, "They're killing people."

"That does sometimes happen," LaChaise said, nodding sympathetically.

I took a deep breath and said, "It stops. Now."

LaChaise regarded me for a moment, a patently false smile on his lips. "Oh, Sir Dresden. You are, I am very much afraid, proceeding under a false assumption."

"Oh?" I asked. "What's that?"

"I am no more in charge of every ghoul than you are in charge of every wizard, or every fae," he said, grinning broadly. "I am the lord of the LaChaise clan, of course, and a number of varied and sundry tribes that have allied themselves with my house."

I smiled with my mouth only. "I'm supposed to believe the most notorious ghoul in the world can't make something happen if he wants to."

LaChaise put a hand on his chest modestly, beaming—but his eyes were cold. "Why, Sir Dresden. I'm flattered you think so much of one of my kind."

I met his eyes for a long moment and nothing much happened. You've got to have a soul to set off a soulgaze. He was just a thing. A clever, dangerous thing.

"Let me put this another way," I said. "In an attempt to communicate clearly."

"Oh," he purred. "By all means."

"I've just declared this city off-limits to ghouls," I said. "Effective as of sunrise tomorrow. From that point on, any ghoul found within the city limits of Chicago or any of its suburbs will forfeit its life."

LaChaise's gold-old-boy smile faded. "Some of my people call this fine metropolis home."

"Which is fine," I said. "Until sunrise."

"Is this meeting, then, for the purpose of the Winter Court declaring war on my house, Sir Dresden?"

"Nothing so formal," I said, without blinking or moving. "Just me."

LaChaise stared at me for a long moment. Then he smiled slowly, eyed me, and licked his lips. "You feeling up for a scuffle, then, son?"

"If I were you," I said, "I'd be asking myself some questions."

"Such as?"

"I'd be asking just how Ethniu got put in a bottle. And who is holding the bottle. I'd ask where the Eye of Balor wound up. And I'd ask myself how much I'd heard from the Red Court lately."

LaChaise tensed.

I never saw Bear move. One second she was standing there, and the next she had her four-bore leveled, in one massive paw, with its barrel a foot from LaChaise's temple.

"I could call in some assistance, I suppose," I said. "Make it an Accords matter. I'm still on good terms with some of the White Council. The Winter Court would back me. The Wild Hunt would have a ball going ratting. Baron Marcone might take issue with your . . . people . . . operating in his territory. And I have a lot of favors I've built up over the years." I put my hands on the table and leaned a little toward him. "But for you and your scavengers, I won't need them."

LaChaise narrowed his eyes. Then he leaned back in his chair and said, "Someone's ass is getting awfully big for his breeches. You should be careful someone doesn't take a bite out of it."

"Count yourself fortunate I'm being polite," I said. "Until sunrise, you and your people have safe passage out of town. After that, any of them left here are fair game."

His mouth spread out wide, showing me his teeth.

"I believe we understand one another, Sir Dresden. And let me thank you for the invitation to your lovely home. And for being a real peach." He rose slowly from the table, his hands visible, keeping Bear in his peripheral vision. "I'll just see my little old self out."

"Sunrise," I said.

LaChaise backed away several steps from me before turning his back and sauntering back out of the castle.

Bear saw him out and returned to the table.

"You sure about this play?" she asked me. "You're making it a little personal."

"The advantage of going up against ghouls," I said, "is that you can be real certain about everything."

Her frown deepened. "You sure you're ready for something like this?"

I exhaled slowly, stood up, and headed for the stairs down to my chambers. "We'll find out in the morning."

Chapter
Thirteen

I fell back onto the bed, gasping, my heart pounding against my chest.

The gorgeous woman from the party, I hadn't caught her name, collapsed atop me. She was shaking and made soft, gentle sounds on every exhale.

"Oh God," she breathed. "Oh God. Oh God."

"Shhh," I said, and began to run my hand up and down her back soothingly. "Shhh. Get your breath."

A low laugh came from the padded papasan chair just across from the bed, in the shadows of the room. Moonlight came in through the windows and the draping white gauzy curtains. A slim, pale form slithered up out of the chair and prowled lithely across the rich carpet toward me.

"Oh," Lara breathed. She emerged into a beam of moonlight that caressed every unclad, perfect inch of her. Her eyes glowed brilliant silver. She touched my hand gently and then caressed the woman's back, drawing shudders of pleasure from her.

Lara smiled down at me and leaned in for a slow kiss. Part of my brain melted when our lips met, and turned into slow, swirling liquid pleasure, but she didn't let it last for long.

Not yet.

She drew slowly away, smiling down at me, and said, "That was beautiful."

It took me a moment to get enough breath and focus together to say, "It still feels strange."

"It's been a year," Lara teased, gently—but her eyes were like mirrors as she turned to the woman and kissed her with a sudden, sinuous speed that reminded me inevitably of a serpent striking and devouring its prey.

The woman kissed Lara back helplessly, letting out a brief, intense scream—and then melted, her eyes rolling back.

Lara guided her down to the bed, where she lay in a boneless, whimpering heap, jerking breaths in and shivering, her eyes as unfocused and vacant as those of any narcotics addict. The woman made small animal noises.

"Mmmm," Lara purred, licking her lips. Then those silver eyes, swirling with faint whirls of violet and blue, so easy to stare at, turned to meet my gaze. She wasn't afraid of my eyes anymore. She'd gazed upon my soul, and I upon hers, and she wasn't afraid.

For a second, I wondered if I could say the same.

"Delicious little appetizer," Lara murmured. She took my hand and drew me up from the bed. "But it's time for the main course."

"This is a dream," I rasped aloud, and opened my eyes.

I found myself in my chambers in the basement of the castle. There were still a couple of candles burning. I had thrown the covers off me and was covered with sweat and trembling. Mister the cat looked up from the bed I'd made for him halfway up my bookshelf, and blinked his gold-green eyes at me, before arching his back, stretching a little, and settling back down again.

I swung my legs over the side of the bed. My head was pounding ferociously. My neck ached from collapsing with it at an odd angle on the pillow. I'd drunk too much Scotch, and my burning stomach crept around the inside of my torso as if looking for a way out.

On the low table next to the little couch in my room, there was still a Monopoly game set out. The place where I'd been sitting had very few dollars left next to the empty fifth. The empty spot across from me had most of the money and most of the properties.

No one was there.

"It doesn't have to be a dream," said my voice, from the other side of the room.

I twitched and squinted. I stepped out of the shadows. Well. Not me-me. It was that other guy. That other me. He was dressed in black and had a goatee and didn't have as many scars as I knew I would have if I looked in the mirror. He didn't look younger. Just infinitely better preserved.

"The hell was in that bottle?" I muttered.

"Veritas, maybe," said my double. He went across the room and looked down at the Monopoly board, at the little dog and the thimble. "I've never understood why you like to be the thimble."

"It's useful," I said. "And it protects."

The other me snorted quietly.

"We're going insane, aren't we?" I asked.

He studied me soberly for a moment and then said, "We're deciding." He looked at me and shook his head. "There's a future out there, you know."

My heart tried to rip its way out of my chest and crawl over to the Monopoly board. "Fuck the future. I don't want it."

"That's our pain talking," the other me said.

"Our pain?" I demanded.

"I miss her, too," he said. "She was a hero. It felt good to have a hero protecting us."

"Fuck you," I said in a flat, dead tone.

"Self-pity isn't going to accomplish anything. For anyone."

"I'm doing my fucking best. Asshole."

"You know, you don't talk like this to anyone else," the other me pointed out. "Not to Mab. Not to Marcone. You didn't even talk like this to the ghoul. You'll curse at them, but you save the real venom for yourself."

I sat there and thought about that for a moment.

"Just pointing out the obvious," the other me said. He looked around my room. It was a mess. It was most nights. I would put it back together before I went out to face the day. He nodded toward the Monopoly board and said, "That really isn't very healthy."

"Don't care," I told him.

"Obviously." He shook his head. "Look. I know we don't always see eye to eye when it comes to your moral and ethical limitations."

I snorted. "You and everyone else."

He smiled briefly. "But have you even once considered that life with Lara would have its advantages?"

My body was still recalling the proposed advantages. It was uncomfortable. It made me feel ashamed. And other things.

"You shouldn't be ashamed of wanting to live," the other me said. "Of wanting to embrace life."

"Mind your own business," I snapped.

He spread his hands and gave a helpless little roll of his eyes. "Watch Lara more closely," he said. "You haven't been seeing the same things I have."

"Like what?" I demanded.

"Come on," he said. "You know that's not how I work."

"Not interested," I said.

He glanced at my hips and then shrugged. "If you say so."

"Lara is a monster," I said. "And I have a daughter."

"Who needs you, and who will need you for a few more years," he said. "And who then will face the world on her own, like all grown children. You have many tomorrows to think about."

I let out a half-hysterical laugh. "Figure I should cut them short to be with Lara, eh?"

"Thomas and Justine seemed happy together," he said reasonably. "What if you could strike a similar balance?"

"I had the balance I wanted," I snapped.

"Did you?" he asked lightly. "Then why doesn't Lara burn when she touches you?"

The air turned to crystal.

"You were with her," said my other self. "You haven't been with anyone else. If she loved you and you loved her, it should scorch Lara when she touches you. But it doesn't. Don't you think there's some reason why?"

I snarled, surged to my feet, seized the water glass next to the bed, and threw it at the other me.

It shattered against the door to my room.

Two seconds later, Bear slammed my door open, sending the bolt flying across the room as if it hadn't actually been attached to the door and the frame. She was wearing a long white nightshirt that struggled to contain her arms, and her brown hair was down and fell to her waist. She had a knife with a blade as wide as my forearm in her hand that looked as if it could readily chop telephone poles, and her eyes were wide.

She stared at me and then around the room for a moment, her nostrils flared.

We were alone.

I peered at her blearily.

"You all right?" she asked me.

I started to tell her I was fine.

Instead, I said, "What time is it?"

"Witching hour," she said. "Three a.m."

I nodded slowly. Then my stomach rolled and I took a staggering step toward the bathroom. I fell.

Bear stepped over the broken glass and caught me as if I were a child.

"Hey, easy," she said. "Come on. Come on, you should have drunk that water."

She helped me to the bathroom and got me there in time for me to hurl my guts out.

I collapsed to the tile floor shaking when I was done, my throat burning.

I felt weak.

I felt sad.

I felt lost.

I felt hollow.

I felt like tomorrow had stopped existing.

There was only a constant now, a single ongoing, endless hour of pain.

Of loss.

"Dresden," Bear said gently. "Hey."

I opened my eyes.

She towered over me like some kind of vast sailing ship.

Her hand was held out. Her broad face was gentle.

"Come on, *seidrmadr*," she said gently. "You can take my hand."

My arm felt unbearably heavy. But I did it.

Bear hauled me up. I wasn't able to give her any more help. There just wasn't the will inside me. But she took me to the bed. She was careful with me. She took a cold rag to my face and neck. She made me sip some water that had the fizzy sensation of some kind of effervescent antacid. My head pounded abominably. She got me settled into bed about the same time I started shivering. She covered me and started singing.

Her voice was astoundingly melodic, gentle, and precise. I didn't know the language, and the rhythms were strange. It sounded old, old. A song from a world that had been all but forgotten. It sounded steady. Reassuring. Patient. As if she could continue it all night if she needed to.

I thought I was going to cry but I was just too damned tired.

And that was the first time since Murphy died that I slept until dawn.

Chapter

Fourteen

I spent the day hungover, and we went out to hunt ghouls at sundown.

"For the record," Bear said, as we settled down in the shadows of the alley, "you shouldn't be out tonight."

"Your Valkyrie sense is tingling?" I asked grumpily.

Bear squinted at me. I could barely see her face in the darkness of the trash can fires in the encampment across the street. "Dresden," she asked, "have you ever fought an angel of death?"

"No," I said carefully.

"I have," she said. "And here I am. Could be I know a couple things you don't."

I snorted quietly through my nose. "Could be you know everything I don't. Doesn't change that we need to make some ghouls go away."

Bear grunted a reluctant affirmative. "You're hungover. Your head is a mess. Don't try to pretend you're in shape for a fight. You need more time."

"What I need is a good costume for Halloween."

"Dammit, Dresden," she said, poking me in the forehead with one thick finger. "Focus."

"It's just possible I've taken on ghouls once or twice," I said. I rubbed my head. It hurt less than it had the night before. "I'll be fine."

Bear gave me a skeptical look, her whole weight balanced easily as she crouched on her heels and looked back out at the night.

Footsteps sounded on the street outside the alley, and Fitz appeared. He slipped quietly into place beside us and crouched down. The kid looked short and slight, given his company. "I think something's out there," he said quietly. "Hairs on my neck are standing up. The people in the camp are nervous. They told me to move along."

I grunted. We were waiting in an alley near Michigan Avenue, where a lot of the destruction had happened during the battle. The corpses of a number of skyscrapers covered pretty much everything. An encampment of tents, barrels, and various storage boxes of all kinds stood across the street in the shadow of the ruins.

Scavengers had descended upon the ruined buildings in the weeks after the battle. They'd begun as volunteers looking for the remains of the dead, but now they mostly seemed to be taking whatever had survived the destruction. The police had a lot to do. They hadn't gotten around to breaking up the scavenging camps yet. A number of spots like this one had sprung up, and the ghouls had been vanishing people from them for weeks.

The news was calling the scavengers "ghouls" for taking the possessions of the dead. I didn't have strong feelings either way, given what I knew about actual ghouls. People were just people. When things got bad, they did what they needed to do to survive and protect their families. Some of them were in it to make easy money, I supposed. I just didn't feel like I was in a position to pass much in the way of judgment when it came to random people scooping up whatever they could from the ruins of their world.

Monsters *eating* people was a lot less murky. About the time something was making men, women, and children disappear, it was time for some avenging.

"All right, kid," I said. "The campers have any arms?"

"Handguns, most of them," he said. "Nobody wants to carry a rifle climbing around the ruins. Saw a shotgun in someone's tent, but that was it."

Sidearms weren't too much use against ghouls. About as effective as bear spray was for grizzlies. A pistol would discourage them. Mostly.

"Good work, Fitz. You remember the plan?"

"Stay within arm's reach of you," he said dutifully. "Stay under my veil. Warn you if you're about to get flanked. Don't try anything unless there's no other choice."

"There you go," I said. "Got your knife?"

He opened his coat and showed me the heavy blade at his belt. Fitz had lived a tough life. He knew how to use a knife. He stared across the street at the encampment. The kid had lived like those people for years. His expression looked . . . complicated. "What do we do now?"

"We wait," Bear said patiently. "Ghouls will want people to get drunk and sleepy before they come in. Easier targets."

"Settle in, kid," I said. "A lot of the game is like this."

And we waited.

Waiting in the dark and the cold isn't easy. There's a need to get up, to move. Tired muscles want to stretch. Chilled flesh wants to shift and ease. But when you're hunting, stillness is imperative. Movement is the first thing the eye tends to notice, and we didn't want to reveal ourselves to our would-be prey.

The problem, for me, was that sitting and doing nothing left too many thoughts running around my head. That could have gotten me to bad places, so I let my eyes mostly close, slowed my breathing, and focused exclusively on what I could hear, paying more and more and more attention to the sounds around me, Listening.

I overheard conversations in the camp across the street. Most of them happened around the barrel fires, where a dozen men and four women were cooking some pretty basic food, mostly soup. A couple were being carnal in one of the tents, though not loudly enough for the other people in the camp to notice. There was a pub a couple of blocks away that apparently had its doors open, and the distant sound of singing drifted through the air. We might have had a local end of the world, but the Irish just poured another round and made more songs. On the far side of the nearest ruined skyscraper, someone was working with tools, maybe banging something back into shape. In the very far distance, the clang and clatter of a passing freight train echoed through the air.

For a Chicago night, it was really quiet. It was the lack of auto traffic,

I think. The Guard was still limiting who could take the interstates through the city.

I breathed slowly and Listened and waited, until almost an hour after the scavengers had turned in, and when the ghouls came out of their tunnel somewhere in the ruins, I heard the scrape and scuffle of gravel sliding over gravel.

My head snapped up, and Bear glanced at me. Her green eyes gleamed in the shadows, and she nodded slowly.

"What?" Fitz breathed. To my adjusted hearing, his voice was all but a shout.

"They're here," I whispered.

"How many?" Bear asked.

"Few. Less than half a dozen, I think."

Bear nodded slowly.

"Remember," I whispered. "I'm first. You stay in my shadow, Fitz. Bear, you're riding drag."

The Valkyrie reached up and silently withdrew the four-bore from the scabbard on her back. The gun would make as much noise as your average battle tank when she fired it, but on the other hand she could probably club a killer whale unconscious with it without ever pulling the trigger.

I moved out slowly. It was after eleven, and that meant it was very late by the standards of a society that was, at least temporarily, mainly reliant upon daylight to conduct everyday business. The nearest functioning streetlight was blocks away. The light mostly came from barrel fires and spotlights reflecting from the distant Sears Tower, now the Willis Tower, which had become a kind of orienting beacon. Neither did much more than separate the night into dark and very dark, and I slipped across the street with as little noise as I could manage.

Fitz muttered under his breath and I glanced back to see a blurry haze in the air behind me. As far as veils went, the kid wasn't exactly a natural talent, but he'd be damned hard to focus on in the darkness, and it was as safe as I could make him without leaving him back at the castle.

Bear came along behind us, making me sound clumsy by comparison, never mind our mass difference. She moved as lightly as a bird despite her bulk, and mostly I knew she was there because I could smell the gun oil on her cannon until she took a spot behind a dead car on the side of the road, crouching down.

A single guard remained awake in the camp as Fitz and I approached, a tired-looking man in his fifties, holding his hands out to the last still-burning barrel fire, his shotgun leaned against a cooler within arm's reach, and he might as well have left it home. The first ghoul I saw was nothing more than a glassy gleam of light reflected from large eyes less than a foot from the ground as it spider-crawled forward toward the guard.

I lifted my hand and flashed my palm toward Bear.

She dipped a hand into the pocket of her leather biker jacket, produced a pistol with an abnormally thick barrel, and fired a shot. A canister hissed into the air, and within a couple or three seconds, a red flare glared in the air high above the camp.

The guard flinched and then goggled up at the light for a second, and the ghoul came slithering over the ground toward him, its muzzled jaws opening wide in anticipation.

I lifted my clenched right fist, where every finger was covered in a braided metal ring, and triggered all four of them at once.

Enough stored kinetic energy to flip over a parked tractor trailer lashed out, focused on an area about the size of a coffin. I had aimed at the ground just in front of the ghoul, and shattered concrete and dirt flew up in a bone-crushing wave, simply burying the supernatural predator in a couple of tons of earth and stone.

"Arm up!" I shouted toward the guard, and sprinted forward, shifting my wizard's staff from my left hand into my right as three more gleaming sets of eyes appeared in the dimness behind the first and came bounding toward me in rapid quadrupedal motion through the scarlet light of the flare.

I pointed my staff, and more kinetic energy stored in the rune-carved wood lashed out and took the second ghoul in the face with more or less the energy of a medieval battering ram. There was a crushing, crackling sound and a burst of dark fluid and the ghoul went down, arms and legs alike flailing wildly.

Bear's four-bore spoke like the god of thunder, and the third ghoul's torso simply collapsed in on itself in a spray of green-black ichor, followed by that of the fourth ghoul, who had unwittingly stood in a straight line for the Valkyrie's aim. The huge round passed through both horrors, came out the other side, and smashed a portion of still-standing concrete wall behind them into a shower of gravel. The ghouls fell in opposite directions, twitching like crushed bugs.

I straightened from my fighting crouch, eyes raking the shadows created by the overhead flare for more ghostly reflective eyes. I kept tabs on the downed ghouls peripherally. Ghouls were like cockroaches: They didn't die easily, and even when they did, it was messy.

"Harry!" Fitz shouted, and I felt him give me a hard shove in the lower back.

A shotgun bellowed. Pellets went by in the space I'd just occupied, close enough to hear them burring through the air like angry wasps.

I hit the concrete and heard Fitz grunt as he went down next to me. I whipped my head up to see the old sentry toss his double-barrel to one side and drop to all fours, his expression twisting, a feral muzzle erupting from his face, his eyes going wide and glassy, forearms lengthening, hands stretching into talons as he bounded forward over the ground.

Ghouls erupted from every tent in the scavenger camp.

More appeared from the direction of the next camp down the block.

Still more came bounding out of the ruins, ten yards at a time, thirty or forty of them altogether, and absolutely all of them were focused intently and exactly upon me.

I swept the end of my staff at the nearest one, the one who'd been posing as a sentry, reaching out for the hatred I had for ghouls and what they did to innocent people and . . .

. . . nothing happened.

No rage flooded through me. No power kindled inside me. No magic flowed through me into the staff. And when my lips formed the word, *"Fuego,"* absolutely nothing happened. No power.

No fire.
Nothing.
I just felt tired.
"Fitz!" I spat. "Run!"
And twoscore ghouls descended upon me.

Chapter
Fifteen

Fitz took off like a shot, panic shredding his concentration and with it his veil. He flicked a terrified glance back over his shoulder, freckles standing out against a face gone green-white with terror.

Good man. It would let me focus on keeping him alive.

I came to my feet with my staff gripped firmly in hand. Humans don't run faster than ghouls. We just don't. If we both ran, we'd just get hounded down. If I stood and fought, it would give the kid precious time to escape. I opened myself to the power of the Winter mantle and let the cold flood into me. I shouted my defiance, my breath pluming out into visible mist like a fog machine.

The sentry was the first ghoul to get to me. Ghouls are strong and fast, but when they attack, they function like animals—all muscle and power and savage instinct. It makes them predictable, and I caught it under the chin with a two-handed upward sweep that snapped its jaws shut hard enough to send chips of broken teeth flying out of its mouth. The ghoul staggered, and I landed two skull-cracking blows that sent it to the ground.

Then half a dozen more of them came in.

I landed another hit with the staff, managed to duck away from one that came diving at my face, and then one of them got hold of my duster from behind and dragged me down to one knee. Ghouls were animal-strong, pound for pound more powerful than any human, even the Winter Knight, and in the time it took me to try to gain leverage against being pulled down, three more of them piled onto me, dragging me to the ground. My staff was torn from my grip.

Claws came at my face. I threw up my right arm to block them, trusting the enchantments on my duster to protect me. Jaws closed on my left biceps, crushing down on muscle and tendon and bone despite all my spell-armored coat could do. Something wrenched at my ankle, despite my kicking.

More ghouls piled onto me, sheer weight beginning to crush me down, all of them panting and slavering and screaming. Fangs scraped my scalp and jaw, drawing blood, and I realized that the only reason I hadn't already been torn to pieces was that there were simply too many of the damned things, getting in one another's way.

This wasn't standard ghoul operating procedure, I noted idly, my brain whirring smoothly as the Winter mantle blocked out any feeling of physical pain. Ghouls tended to hunt solo, or in small groups unless gathered together by a greater power—and they didn't tend to use thoughtful tactics, like setting up a whole apparent camp of mortals, or sending out a small group of bait to tempt out an opening attack.

I'd been set up. And I should have seen it coming.

Bear had been one hundred percent correct.

I sank my teeth into a muscled forearm and tasted something fetid and disgusting. Something that I could only assume was a scrambling ghoul's ass smashed against my face, and I knew that I was about to die.

Then the ground shook.

A ghoul let out a squealing scream of pure agony and terror. Thunder roared so loudly that the hearing in my right ear vanished into a high-pitched tone. Something splattered across my neck. Some of the weight vanished from my right side, and I found a rock under my fingers, seized it, and smashed maybe ten pounds of concrete against a skull, letting out a scream.

A huge motorcycle boot smashed down on a ghoul's head, flattening it like a melon, sending grotesque liquid everywhere, and I fought with renewed vigor as Bear, her face fixed in a psychotic grin, swung the four-bore in a scything arc with so much power that it might as well have been a sword, simply smashing its way through ghoul bodies as if they'd been so many disgusting piñatas.

Bear stomped and kicked and swung the four-bore, but as strong as she was, she was only one person, and more and more ghouls poured in.

"Get up, Dresden!" she snarled. "Get on your fucking feet!"

I blocked a ghoul's claws with my forearm an inch shy of my throat, but the ghoul that had locked its jaws on my arm ripped my balance away and I went down again.

Bear looked down at me, and her green eyes had become intense, otherworldly, an arc of every color in the spectrum reflected in them.

In an instant that felt like a long minute, the Chooser of the Slain met my gaze, and I felt the soulgaze begin, and *saw* Bear, saw her in an endless haze of battle, saw men and women dying around her, dying in hopeless battle, dying wounded and outnumbered, dying with screams of defiance, or terror, or laughter upon their lips, and in the skies beyond her, I saw formations of winged beings, shining with the wild rainbows, diving toward battlefields across the span of millennia, sweeping down to take fallen warriors to their reward.

And I matched her wild grin, slammed my head into a ghoul's muzzle, and twisted to hammer a blow into the head of the ghoul on my arm, determined to smash the bastard's skull in before the life was ripped out of me. All I could hear was the thunder of my heart, the high-pitched tone in my right ear, the hollow thud of my fist crashing against the ghoul I was taking with me.

What came next was the sound of a horn.

It rang out with a clarity, a purity the likes of which I had never heard. The very air shivered with the clarion sound, and it hit the ghouls like a goddamned truck. As one, the monsters flinched and screamed, raising their talons around their heads, their eyes wide with sudden panic and pain. An instant later there came a sudden gust of cool, clear wind that swept away the stench of the mob of corpse-eating creatures and brought with it another smell entirely.

Propellant.

And gun oil.

A man screamed, "Give it to them, boys!"

And the night went wild with thunder, with flashes of light, with a flood of illumination from dozens of what must have been flashlights. Boots hammered on the pavement. Gunfire passed within three feet of me with ugly zipping sounds, smashing into a ghoul and sending it screaming and running. The ghoul on my arm let go, scrambling to escape, and as it did, I spitefully seized its ankle, screaming, "Bear!"

Gunfire chewed into ghouls all around me, and I stayed low. Four hundred pounds of Bear came down on the ghoul I had grabbed, and Bear wrapped an arm around its skull and, with a brutal twist of her body, tore the monster's head right off its shoulders.

Ghouls fled, but whoever was shooting knew what they were doing. Of a couple of score of them who had come to the fight, maybe half a dozen got back into the ruins and got away.

"Cease fire!" came a clear shout. "Cease fire!"

The gunshots ended with professional discipline. Then there were quieter commands and the sound of dozens of boots coming closer, flashlights sweeping left and right and all around the area.

"Medic!" called a calm male voice, and footsteps hurried over to me.

Daniel Carpenter, eldest son of Michael Carpenter, suddenly crouched down beside me, his handsome face concerned. He'd filled out with even more muscle since I'd seen him last, and he wore a short, thick beard like his father. He was wearing military boots, dark fatigues, and what looked like body armor under a padded, insulated plaid work shirt, and he held a .45-caliber pistol at a low ready, careful to keep the muzzle from fanning anyone. A Celtic cross made out of what looked like high-quality silver bounced against his chest.

"Harry," he said intently, kneeling down beside me. "You're an almighty mess, man. Where are you hit?"

Maybe twenty-five or thirty guys, most of them dressed like Daniel, came out of the night, all of them armed, all of them wearing the same silver Celtic cross as Daniel.

The adrenaline was buzzing through me so hard that the lights hurt like hell, and the shadows were harder to see into than they might have been otherwise. I stared at him for a long second before my body started to understand that the fight was over, and I was alive.

"Uh," I said. "Uh."

But Bear was already hauling me up to a sitting position and going over me. "I told you that you weren't ready for a fight," she said, scowling, "much less going hand to hand with ghouls. Od's bodkin, Dresden, that was the dumbest thing I've ever seen."

Several of the guys with crosses went from ghoul to ghoul holding pistols and canteens. They methodically went from one fallen foe to the next, putting bullets into any of them that were still wriggling, and then poured some fluid out of the canteens that began to smoke and sizzle the second it hit the bodies. A man holding a medical pack hurried up and knelt down beside me.

"Scalp wound," Bear reported to him. "Bleeding pretty good. And some scratches on his jawline. He's going to need those wounds cleaned out as if he got them in a sewer. Maybe a tetanus shot, too."

"Got it," the medic said quietly. "Anything else?"

"I'm sitting right here," I complained. "Probably cuts on my hands. Long time no see, Daniel."

Without moving his eyes from a constant scan of the ruins and the streets around us, Daniel grinned. "How you doing, Harry?"

I spat foulness out of my mouth onto the ground. "Oh, you know. Can't complain. You make some new friends?"

"Hold still," Bear said firmly. She began examining my hands in more minute detail as the medic broke open his pack.

"Something like that," Daniel said. "I'll let him explain it to you."

"Him who?"

"Clear!" came a shout from one end of the street.

"Clear!" came a shout from the other direction.

Daniel nodded and waved a hand back at the dark. "Okay!"

Three men came walking in from the night, and Fitz walked beside them.

One of them was an elderly man in black clothing, a thick winter coat, and a celluloid collar. He moved calmly and carefully, and while he had more wrinkles and less hair than the last time I'd seen him, his eyes were still bright, clear, and robin's-egg blue behind his spectacles. I hadn't seen Father Forthill recently, but the old priest was one of the kinder people I knew.

Next to him was an even more elderly man with a bushy beard. He wore a shawl and a yarmulke and carried what looked like a long, twisting animal horn on a baldric over one shoulder, and I suddenly realized what that horn call had been. It was a shofar, a traditional Jewish instrument.

Bringing up the rear, by virtue of walking while heavily leaning on a cane, was Michael Carpenter in his usual jeans and flannel shirt under his sheepskin jacket. He hitched his way up to us, grinning broadly at me. "Thank God," he said with relief. "I thought we were going to be too late."

I felt myself smile back at him and offered him my hand. "Timing," I said.

We shook and Michael nodded to the other two men. "Harry, you know Father Forthill. This is Rabbi Aaronson."

The medic poured something over my jawline and the area tingled and vanished into the vague staticky sensation I felt now instead of pain, ever since donning the mantle of the Winter Knight. I didn't flinch. "Rabbi," I said. "That's a real shofar, huh?"

"Obviously," the old man said, squinting around skeptically. "And I'm a real rabbi and I forgot how hard they are to blow. My lips are still buzzing like bees. But those ghouls liked it even less, I think. Did anyone bring coffee?"

"I'll make you some at St. Mary's," Forthill assured him.

"Save the day, not even a coffee," Aaronson said. "Typical. Typical."

"What the he . . . heck, Michael?" I asked. I was still shaking from the battle, but my heart rate had begun to come down. "Did you reactivate the Knights Templar or something?"

Michael shook his head. "The Brotherhood of St. Brigid," he said quietly. "It's, ah. A bit of an ad hoc organization, formed when there's a need to battle rampant darkness."

"You didn't expect the church to do nothing in the face of what's happened, did you, Harry?" Forthill asked gently.

"Mostly," I said. "I mean. I know you're feeding and sheltering a lot of people, but I figured that would be it."

Daniel snorted. "Ghouls are hunting women and children in my hometown," he said. "Plenty of us came out to do something about it. And this block is where the most people have gone missing over the past week, so . . ."

"So you figured the same as we did," I said.

"Looks like," Daniel said amiably. "Hey, Fitz, right? You've grown. Good job getting clear when you did."

Fitz looked at me, his expression uncertain, and I nodded. "Yep. That was definitely too hairy a situation to be distracted looking out for anyone else. You listened. Good job."

Fitz exhaled slowly and nodded, frowning. "Yeah, well." He shook Daniel's hand a little uncomfortably. "Hey, man. Glad you were here."

I wasn't too upset that Daniel and the Brotherhood had shown up, either. That had been a much nastier fight than I had expected.

"You realize," Bear said quietly, "that someone tipped them off. Coordinated them. They were all there for you."

"Yeah," I said. "LaChaise, maybe. Upside is, we got a whole bunch of them at once. And enough of them got away to spread the word that we're not kidding around when we say 'get out.' Glass half-full."

"I'm just glad the glass didn't get shattered to sand," she said wryly. Bear rose and let the medic work on me. She eyed Daniel and nodded to him after a long look.

Bear extended her hand. "I'm Bear. It's an honor. Nice to see the Brotherhood in the fight."

Daniel shook her hand and frowned faintly at her. "Valkyrie?"

"Right now, bodyguard," she said and hooked a thumb at me. "Thanks to you and your people."

"Michael," I said, wincing at the smell as the disinfectant went over my skull. "You were going ghoul hunting and you didn't invite me?"

Michael looked amused. "I know it's hard for you to picture it, Harry, but evil often needs to be fought even when you aren't consulted." He considered and then added, "And I might say the very same thing to you."

I snorted. "I didn't know you were forming a militia." The shakes were subsiding slowly. I bowed my head and said, more quietly, "Thank you."

"Thank Daniel," he said firmly. "The only reason I'm here at all is because I was watching the fights with Father Forthill and the rabbi when the Brotherhood came to get them."

"And here we are," Aaronson said grumpily, consulting a pocket watch, "missing the title bout."

"You'll get to see a fight if you keep up the complaining, you goat," Forthill said.

"Not on your best day, Irishman," Aaronson retorted. "I'll turn all four of your cheeks for you if you try it."

Daniel hunkered down next to me, grinning at the two old men. "Point is, Harry," he said. "I heard things were getting bad up here, so I came home to help. A lot of us did." He tilted his head generally at the other men in crosses. "I know I've screwed some things up in the past. But I've been working on being less stupid." He put a hand on my shoulder and squeezed gently.

Exactly like his father had so many times before.

"We're here to help," he said.

Four words. None of them long.

The truly important words never are.

I bowed my head before I started crying.

"Thank you," I told him.

Chapter
Sixteen

I took Maggie trick-or-treating on Halloween.

Michael's neighborhood had been spared many of the problems of the rest of the city—partly because there were a bunch of angels and a Winter Court mayhem team hanging around the block, and partly because it was simply far enough away from the Battle of Chicago's hot spots that it hadn't been covered in semi-toxic dust from collapsing buildings. As a result, the blocks right around the Carpenter place had gone out of their way to try to set up something like a normal Halloween for the kids. Word had gotten out. The place was crowded with children in whatever costumes they'd been able to make or acquire, and with the adults escorting them.

Maggie was the most beautiful child on this or any other planet, on the bottom end of the bell curve for height and weight, and looked a lot younger than she was. She had dark hair and dark eyes like her mother. And me, I suppose.

Maggie had chosen to wear a Princess Leia costume, inherited from Hope Carpenter, the one from the original film. She even had those cinnamon-bun-style rolls of hair made from a wig and clipped into her hair. Mouse, an enormous mound of fluff and muscle with a wagging tail, padded along next to her with a plastic bowl that had been painted to resemble R2-D2's head held onto his noggin with an elastic strap. He also wore a sign around his neck that said **BEEP BOOP BLEEP** in purple ink. He couldn't really see much with the bowl on his head, but he padded along happily next to her, wearing a black nylon working harness with an orange plastic pumpkin hanging from either side of it, each one full of candy and treats.

Harry Carpenter, Michael's youngest, who had grown up with Maggie for a good long while and who was for all practical purposes her brother, wore a Luke Skywalker getup, complete with a glowing blue toy lightsaber that had somehow survived an hour in my presence without shorting out.

It had been a good hour and a half or so, walking the kids around the neighborhood, waiting in lines that formed at every house. There were so many people carrying lights, never mind the various tiki torches, battery-powered lights, and chemical lights the homeowners had put out, that the whole place had a merry, festival air, even as twilight faded from the skies. The Carpenter house was the most lit up of all, and I could see Charity and Michael handing out candy from huge tubs. God knows how they had gotten the candy shipped in, but they'd managed, as had many other houses in the neighborhood.

The air was full of happiness and peace, and it stood out in harsh contrast to recent months. Kids—including the kids staying at the castle—were running and laughing. It did my heart good.

Michael and his house were waging war on the darkness in the best way possible.

"I don't know," Maggie was saying to little Harry (who had begun to shoot up like a weed in recent months, and who was going to be at least as tall as his father). "It just feels weird, you know? All those rich kids."

"You'll be fine," Harry said breezily. "St. Mark's has this awesome computer program; I game with kids from there all the time. And you can take all kinds of cool classes."

Maggie frowned and looked up at me. "Yeah, but living at the school?"

"It's probably like Hogwarts," Harry said.

"It's not Hogwarts," I said firmly. "But there's enough security there that I won't have to worry about you during the week. And I'll visit for dinner, and on the weekends you can either spend time with the Carpenters or come see me at the castle."

"Woof," Mouse said happily.

Maggie smiled at the big dog. "I know. It's just . . . you know. Different."

"Life is all about change, sweetheart," I said gently. "Maybe wait and see how it goes."

"Hey," Harry said, "that's Kenton and his brother. I haven't seen them since summer break. Can I go talk to them, Mister Dresden?"

He always called me that, to prevent confusion. "Sure," I said. "Stay in sight, huh?"

"I will," he said, and ran off to meet a pair of boys about his own age.

"It's a good school," Maggie said with a sigh. "But I won't know anyone there."

"You'll know Mouse," I said. "And you can take Bonnie with you, too. You'll make friends."

Maggie sank one hand into Mouse's fur. "And . . . you know. Next summer? I'll stay with you?"

"Darn tootin', you will," I said firmly.

That won a sunny smile from her, and I felt like I might float out of my shoes as I returned it.

"Happy birthday, Dad," she said.

I leaned way over and kissed the top of her head. "Thanks, punkin."

Bear drove Molly and me to the Raith estate around ten o'clock in an armored limousine. We stopped at the heavily guarded gate, and she passed over our invitation, on fancy white paper inside a silver envelope.

It had been a silent drive. Molly made a convincing Arwen, especially since she had glamoured herself to look exactly like Liv Tyler in the role.

"I'm worried about you," she said finally, as we pulled into the long drive and began to cruise slowly up it, stopping at the rear of a line of cars similar to ours.

"Oh?" I said mildly.

"You got lucky against those ghouls," she said. "Very lucky. Your magic failed you, didn't it?"

"You already know that, or you wouldn't have asked."

She exhaled through her nose. "Why?"

I shook my head. "I just . . . misfired. I don't know."

"It's because of Karrin," she said quietly.

I gave her side-eye and remained silent.

"She died at the hands of that goddamned bottom-feeder, Rudolph," she said, her voice steady and cool. "And somewhere deep inside, you think you deserve to go out the same way."

"That's ridiculous," I said.

"Ghouls are bottom-feeders," she said. "And at one point, someone taught me that magic only works if you think it could and should happen. Somewhere deep down, you thought you had it coming. From the bottom-feeders in our world. Just like her."

"I don't want to talk about this," I said.

"You're going to have to let her go," she said gently.

I didn't answer her.

"Harry," she said gently. "You know I'm right."

Anger and pain flicked through my chest as if she'd hit me with a whip. "So you know what I'm thinking better than I do," I said, voice hard. "You poking around in my head again?"

"Goddammit," she said and turned away. Not before I saw the tears forming.

I closed my eyes. I took a deep breath. I'd been practicing that a lot the past few months. I felt my thoughts slow down, peel away from the pain.

"I'm sorry," I said. "That was a low blow. It won't happen again."

She didn't look back at me.

But she took my hand and squeezed tightly.

I squeezed back. After a moment, I said, "I don't know what to do about it."

"You have to talk about it," she said. "That's the start."

"To you?"

"To someone," she said. "Anyone. Maybe Dad."

I closed my eyes. "That night . . . she wasn't the only one who died. I did, too. Hundreds of times."

That earned me her gaze and a gentle frown.

"If I sleep too long, it happens to me again. Over and over." I swallowed. "Or I dream of her and I wake up and for a minute I don't remember she's . . . she's dead. Then it hits me. And I lose her again."

"Oh. Harry," she said. She closed her eyes. "I've been where you are. Exactly where you are. It's awful." She gestured vaguely. "It's how I became this."

I was quiet for a minute. Then I asked, "How'd you pull out of it?"

"Took time," she said gently. "And I got the person I lost back. I was able to forgive myself."

"Never been very good at that," I said.

"Then learn," she said.

"How?"

She smiled faintly. "Talking to the wrong person in my family. Dad's the expert on forgiveness."

The car pulled up in front of Raith Manor. Bear promptly got out and walked around to the passenger door.

"I'll think about it," I said.

"Do," she said. "We need you back, Harry. And I need to know. Are you going to throw yourself to the lions tonight?"

"Well," I said lightly, "it *is* the third date."

Her lips formed a hard line and she spoke as if the words were being dragged out of her. "Mab instructed me that I was to order you to do so," she said. "Consider yourself so ordered."

I scowled at the manor. "You'd think she'd know how I react to being ordered around by now."

Bear, in her usual biker leathers, opened the door. I got out, my staff and the thick grey robes and cloak making it awkward, and offered Molly my hand, assisting her out as well. My beard slipped, and I hooked it back around my ears a bit more firmly.

"I still think you should have been Gandalf the White," she murmured.

"The original iteration is always better," I said firmly. "Coke. *Star Wars. Red Dawn. Robocop.* Every single Disney animated film."

"*Buffy the Vampire Slayer,*" she countered.

"Hmph," I said, frowning.

And we turned to walk into the lions' den, the White Court Halloween party.

Raith Manor looks like the summer home of one of those nobles the Crown is always worried about but still has to smile at. It's a sprawling place of brick and marble, about an hour north of town, surrounded by its own aged forest. It has multiple driveways, and you wouldn't have to run too many laps of the place to get a good workout. I'd been inside several times, and with the exception of the entry hall, I'd never been in the same room twice.

Red festive lights painted the whole place, giving it a volcanic glow. I'd have had no idea where to go, but the line of limousines stretched out behind our car as Bear pulled away to park, and a steady stream of guests was flowing into the gaping grand double doors of the manor like sacrifices to some dark Vesuvian god.

Laughter and chatter drifted through the air as we entered, and an automated moving spotlight tracked across my face, and suddenly I was standing before a furious, wounded Titan again, the Eye of Balor gathering energy and power and madness into a concentrated burst that would strip the flesh from my bones before blasting them to ash.

I stopped in place, closing my eyes and bowing my head. I leaned on my staff. I smelled the faint scent of woodsmoke and fought to catch my breath.

I felt Molly's cool hand settle on my right wrist.

"Harry," she said gently. "It's okay. It's okay."

I opened one eye a crack. The runes in my staff were glowing with a sullen green-gold light, and I realized that I had drawn power into it, ready to unleash havoc. I straightened, forced my shoulders back, and took a slow, deep breath. In through the nose. Out through the mouth. I did that maybe half a dozen times and slowly relaxed my grip on the staff, while simultaneously releasing the gathered power out into the night air.

"There," she said gently. "There."

"Thanks," I rasped quietly.

"We can stay right here," she said. "I honestly don't care at all if we're late."

"A wizard is never late," I muttered. "He arrives as soon as he's dealt with his PTSD."

She let out a low chuckle and bumped my leg with her hip. "The mantle can help you with that, you know. Kind of . . . keep you frosty."

"Also going to be distracting as hell," I said. "Better to keep a clear head around Lara."

"Okay," she said. "Just . . . look, if you need some cover, or a distraction, just rap the staff on the ground, okay? I'll run interference for you."

I exhaled again slowly and nodded to her. "Thanks, Molls. For . . . getting it."

"I've been there. You've got this."

I nodded and squared my shoulders. Partygoers were going around us down the entry hall, giving us looks as they went by. Not many people were in full costumes. Most of them were in little black dresses with vaguely suggestive masks, or tuxes with a pair of horns, that kind of thing. Amateurs.

I offered Molly my arm, and she slipped her hand through it. Then we proceeded deeper into the house.

Rows of lit candles led us down hallways and staircases to a gallery overlooking a grand mirrored ballroom, where music was already playing, and where couples were already filling the dance floor. The flow of incoming people pooled at the top of the stairs, where a tall man with an excellent resonant basso voice was announcing each arrival by reading names off of invitations. We got in line and went to the top of the stairs leading down to the dance floor.

"Lady Molly, Queen of the Winter Court," read the master of ceremonies. "And Harry Dresden, the Winter Knight."

Spotlights flared abruptly, blinding me for a few seconds, and I muttered grumpily under my breath. Molly squeezed my arm rather tightly, and I could feel the wary tension lining her whole body. But she gave a dazzling smile, inclined her head, and we descended the stairs together.

Waiting at the bottom of the stairs in an all-black tux was a blade-lean redheaded woman with long hair shaved up high on the sides. She gave me a friendly and genuine-enough grin and fetched Molly a polite bow. "Lady Molly," she said. "And everyone's favorite *seidrmadr*. How's it hanging, Dresden? I hear you headbutted some ghouls."

"Bunch of pansies," I said. "Molly, this is Freydis, Lara's security specialist."

"Hello, Freydis," Molly said. "It seems you can't swing a cat without hitting a Valkyrie these days."

She flashed Molly a predatory grin. "We live in interesting times. Lara's asked me to escort you both to her. Follow me, please."

I gestured for her to lead on, and we followed her around the dance floor.

White Court shindigs are . . . not terribly subtle. There weren't a ton of people there who weren't pretty enough to be painted, male or female. The vast majority were terribly young, by which I meant under thirty. I wasn't exactly in spring chicken territory anymore. Everyone was dressed to show off, the dancing like the night before a world war, and everyone was in a party mood. You could smell weed in the air, and there were plenty of other substances being passed around and used in one corner of the ballroom at . . . good grief, at a literal champagne waterfall.

There were plenty of White Court vampires present. You could tell from the white skin, the dark hair, and the hungry silver eyes. They were generally surrounded by mortals, passing them more champagne, or pills, or smoldering rolled cigarettes of God knew what chemicals. I recognized half a dozen I'd encountered in the past—and felt the weight of their eyes settle on me as I went by.

"You'll have to excuse them," Freydis said, smirking. "They're not used to the idea of one of their kind settling on one partner exclusively, much less Lady Lara. You've become singularly interesting to them."

"Mmmm," I said. "Meaning that they score points against her if they can seduce me," I said.

"Something like that," Freydis agreed. "And of course, everyone goes a little hungry before a gathering like this. The better to feast. Here, the alcove."

Freydis led us to an alcove in the wall, screened off by a wall of gently misting fog and a pair of forbidding-looking bodyguards. She nodded at the two men and one of them nodded back, waving us by. We followed Freydis into the fog, past some curtains, and the sound of the music was greatly muted.

"Lady Lara," Freydis said politely. "The Winter Lady and Knight."

Lara swayed out of the mist, dressed as Galadriel from the motion pictures. She'd coordinated with Molly. Of course she made a stunning platinum blonde, in a long gossamer gown, her feet in silver sandals, jewels in her hair and sparkling at her ears and throat. Silver jewelry wound up her wrists and forearms to the elbow. It matched the hungry gleam of her eyes.

"Wow," Molly said, without sarcasm.

"Welcome, Lady Molly," Lara said. She gave her a smile that was just a trace pained. "I know things have been awkward. I hope it won't keep us from establishing a good working relationship."

Molly inclined her head. "I'm sure we have our priorities sorted properly, Lady Lara," she said smoothly.

It didn't get any less awkward.

Lara turned to me and smiled. "All things considered, I would have thought you'd have gone for Gandalf the White. What with mostly dying and so on."

I waggled my chin, a motion greatly exaggerated by the long false beard. "But then I couldn't do this."

"Priorities," Lara said archly, mirth dancing at the corners of her mouth.

A man's groan, soft, of either ecstasy or agony, drifted out from farther in the fog.

Lara smiled faintly. "Some of my younger sisters are here. No sense of patience. Shall we take some champagne for a walk in the garden? I thought we might talk."

Molly, her cheeks faintly pink, nodded firmly. "Excellent."

"Freydis," Lara said.

The Valkyrie vanished at once and came back with flutes of champagne on a silver tray, offering one to each of us.

With Freydis proceeding us, Lara led us out of the alcove, toward one of many doors that opened onto the gardens in the rear of the manor. We were about to duck out of the ballroom when the master of ceremonies' voice suddenly came clear into a quiet space between musical numbers.

"Ladies and gentlemen," he said, his voice somewhat strangled. "Drakul."

Chapter
Seventeen

U h-oh," I said.

Lara's face went from pale to absolutely white.

Molly eyed me and Lara and she looked confused. She straightened and brushed a hand irritably at her face, and the glamour vanished, revealing her own features. "What am I not getting here?"

"He was *invited*?" I demanded of Lara.

"He's always invited," Lara said. "It would be an insult not to. But he never shows up."

"Hello?" Molly said.

"Drakul," I said to her.

She blinked. "Wait. *Dracula?*"

"No," I said. "Dracula is like his spoiled drama-queen kid," I said. "This is the original. During the battle, he took everything River Shoulders *and* Listens-to-Wind could throw at him, everything the crew from the Red Court war could do, then he and his minions killed Chandler, Wild Bill, and Yoshimo and walked away smiling. He's some kind of elder being."

"Jesus," Molly breathed. "Why is he here?"

"Hell if I know," I said, which was more than half true. Drakul had told me that he was starborn and knew I was, too. He seemed to think we had some kind of weird camaraderie as a result, and the fact that I still knew almost nothing about what being starborn meant was beginning to drive me a little nuts.

But there was some kind of connection between us, based on that. He wanted something from me. I just had no idea what it might be.

Drakul paused at the top of the stairway. The shadows around him all seemed . . . darker, somehow, flowing around him like an honor guard. He was a tall man, six and a half feet at least, wearing close-fit black pants and a vest, with a billowing black shirt beneath. He was corpse pale, and shoulder-length black hair was swept back from an epic widow's peak.

Drakul stopped at the top of the stairs. Eyes like black holes raked over the ballroom, unimpressed with the hedonism—and locked on me.

My stomach did a little panicked flip on me. My hand tightened on my staff.

Molly was just staring at him. "Is this . . . a fight?"

"No," Lara said firmly. She swallowed. "No. He's here as a guest. He's one of the reasons the old laws of hospitality exist. He won't violate that. He's here to talk."

"Very true," said a smooth, mellow, accented voice from behind us, and we all whirled to find Drakul simply *there*. One second, he'd been a good thirty yards off. The next he'd been behind us. No flash, no pop of displaced air, no surge of shadows, no telltale vibration of magical energy, nothing. It was like the concept of space simply didn't apply to him.

All three of us twitch-jumped except for Molly and Lara.

He smiled slowly and showed us pointed canines. "Little Lara Raith. You've come a long way, and very quickly. I warned your father about you, you know. In . . . eighteen hundred and ninety-seven, I believe. He never was a good listener."

"Lord Drakul," Lara said, inclining her head slightly. "I confess, this is a delightful surprise."

Drakul smiled warmly, took her hand, and bowed over it. "Please. You've personally done more damage to me than any three supernatural nations through that writer. Call me Vlad."

"Vlad," she said, and her voice was both tense and lower, throatier. "I would have thought you'd be more . . . hostile."

"Nonsense," Drakul said. "The challenge was an unexpected delight. It kept me busy for decades and pruned away the useless baggage from my creations. I am well content with the long-term results. Only fools see such challenges as insults, when they result in so much growth." He brushed his lips over her knuckles and released her gently. Then he turned his attention to Molly. "And the new Winter Lady. Considerably more disciplined and dangerous already than her predecessor. I am told you turned the tide of the battle against the Titan's forces. I am Lord Vlad Drakul, and I am at your service."

Molly extended her hand, a small smile on her lips. "What a pleasure, Lord Drakul. I am Molly Carpenter."

He took her hand and touched it to his lips, his eyes never leaving hers. "The pleasure is mine, I assure you. Welcome to the society of immortals. I look forward to many such meetings, in time."

I wanted to punch the guy already.

Before he even straightened from the bow, Drakul's black eyes flicked over to my face, and whatever he saw there seemed to amuse him.

"And you," he said, looking me up and down. "The mortal who managed to overcome a Titan."

"It was a team effort," I said. "I was just batting cleanup."

Drakul's face went blank for a moment. Evidently, he wasn't up on his baseball parlance.

"Right place, right time," I clarified generously. "Harry Dresden."

"The man I'm here to see," Drakul said.

"Because I fought a Titan?" I asked.

Drakul laughed. It was a warm, genuine sound. "Goodness, no. That certainly makes you interesting, but I always make it a point to survey the rest of the field before the game begins."

Now it was my turn to have a blank face. Dammit. Getting information about whatever large-scale shenanigans were supposed to happen (that I had apparently been cosmically voluntold to be a part of) was harder than stacking marbles in a corner.

Drakul looked faintly disappointed and offered me a consoling smile. "Ah. It has come to my attention that there are members of the White Council seeking my location."

"You killed some of their people," I said. "Took their bodies and talents and turned them into your personal lackeys. My friends."

"Such things happen in war," Drakul said calmly. "Children take it personally." He dipped two fingers into a vest pocket and produced a black card marked with gold-leaf lettering. "Still, such things can be settled in only one way." He offered me the card, his black eyes bottomless and empty. "My location. Please inform whichever passionate fools the White Council boasts this month that they may call upon me at their convenience. I shall be ready. Alternatively, I can make time for a meeting of their choosing. Anytime. Anyplace."

Wow.

No one did that.

No one just dropped an open challenge to wizards of the White Council.

I took the card warily. I checked. There was no evident enchantment about it.

"Why?" I asked him.

He considered me for a breath. "Is it not obvious, wizard?" he asked. "To duel me openly under the Accords would be suicide. You people will clearly take alternative action, as is your pattern—one I respect, if it matters to you. But I would find the entanglements of any resulting war inconvenient, as would the leadership of the other supernatural nations." He nodded toward Molly and Lara. "Children seldom see the advantage in tidying up their messes. I do. So in the interests of order, I extend the invitation, here and now, and hereby waive the protection of the Accords before two witnesses." He leaned a little closer, smiling. "Unless you would rather display a minute scrap of sanity and allow the matter to drop as part of the fortunes of war."

"Show up or shut up, huh?" I asked him.

He considered the phrasing. "Just so."

"I'm not a member of the Council anymore," I said. "But I'll pass the word along."

"Most courteous," Drakul said, bowing slightly. "I do hope you yourself will take a more mature view of what happened, wizard. It would be a shame to be forced to remove you from the board before you are even truly prepared for the great game."

"Oh, I'm well-known for that," I said. "My maturity."

He smiled again, though there was regret in it, and only a hint of fang. "Ah. To each his nature."

I clenched my jaw. "I've talked to a lot of blowhards like you," I said. "I'm still standing. They aren't."

Drakul's eyes wrinkled at the corners. He inhaled through his nose, as though enjoying the scent of a meal that had not yet been served.

"You have never," he said, in a dead voice, "talked to one like me."

Molly gripped my forearm and squeezed, holding me in place.

"Ladies," Drakul said, breaking into a wider smile. He took a step back and bowed elegantly. "A magnificent gathering, but I regret that I must take my leave. Thank you for the courtesy of an invitation."

And, without even a whoosh, he simply wasn't there anymore.

I stood there for a moment, reaching out with my magical senses. But there was no enchantment around me, no hint of a veil or a tear in the veil between the mortal world and the Nevernever. Nothing. Just music and the dancing and laughter of the intoxicated guests.

I exhaled slowly.

"My," Lara said. She lifted her champagne flute to her mouth and took a quick drink. I almost couldn't see her hand trembling.

"Right?" Molly agreed. She adjusted her dress absently.

"He seems like a wimp," I said calmly.

"Careful," Lara said suddenly.

I looked around and saw why she had. Carter LaChaise, wearing a chef's hat and kitchen outfit, which was quite a choice given his mutton-chops, was approaching us, a broad smile on his beefy face. He stopped to lean over and murmur something into the ear of a girl too young for me, much less him, and she turned happy, glassy eyes to him and gave him the kind of smile that was likely to get her killed. He laughed and held up a finger to her as he approached us.

"Well, well," the ghoul said. "If the two of you ladies don't make the most delicious sight."

"Lord LaChaise," Molly said, inclining her head slightly.

"LaChaise," Lara said with a polite nod and no emotion at all in her tone or expression. "So glad you could come."

"I'm not," I said cheerfully, beaming. "Get fucked and die, ghoul."

LaChaise let out a rumbling laugh, answering my smile with one of his own. "I heard what happened the other evening. Mighty big talk for someone dipped in stupid and rolled in lucky, Dresden," he drawled. "Well. That's all right. Every dog has his day."

I narrowed my eyes and took a step toward him.

Molly moved creepy fast, stepping between us, her shoulders pressing sharply back against my ribs. She faced LaChaise, and the temperature of the room abruptly dropped five or ten degrees. "Excuse me, ghoul? Did you just threaten Winter's Knight?"

"Why, Lady Molly," LaChaise said, spreading his fingers on his chest as if clutching pearls. "I am shocked, shocked and *dismayed* that you would think such a thing. Just because a proven racist, openly full of hatred for my people's kind, delivers a public insult and wishes my death upon me at a friendly gathering to which I am an invited guest." His eyes glittered as he shifted them to Lara. "Honestly. Your reputation as a host is excellent, Ms. Raith. I simply cannot believe you stand there silent in the face of such behavior."

Lara's lips pressed together in distaste.

"I am afraid," she said calmly, "that Lord LaChaise has a point, Harry."

"He what?" I asked.

She faced me, her expression remote. "This is indeed a celebration. You are both in fact *guests*. I am in fact the *host* of said gathering. You did indeed wish death upon LaChaise, a verbal statement that, from a *wizard*, is quite reasonably considered more than mere hot air, after which you made an aggressive physical advance upon him. You will kindly control yourself, sir. Or I will insist you leave."

"Give me a break," I said. "You know what this asshole really is. You know he tried to get me killed the other night."

"I do not *know* any such thing," Lara said. "What I *do* know is that you are my *guest*. And I will not be disrespected. Not by you or anyone else. If you cannot control yourself, you will force me to do it for you."

"Well, well, well," LaChaise drawled, wearing a delighted grin. "Looks like we can all see who is going to wear the pants in this relationship."

"Be careful, LaChaise," Lara shot back instantly. "Or I will have you both put off of my property together. At which point any further developments are no longer my concern."

I saw Molly's reflection in one of the mirrors. She had put on one of those smiles that, on anyone else, would have made me question their sanity.

That did more to intimidate the ghoul than anything I had done. LaChaise's expression became uneasy.

"I do apologize for any misunderstandin' that might have come to pass," he murmured. He turned to Lara and put on a big, cheesy smile. "Perhaps we can attribute it all to the drink. I certainly intended no disrespect to my charmin' hostess."

"Of course," Lara said, and her smile could have made one of those "gleam" sound effects from anime cartoons. She lifted her hand and snapped her fingers twice. It took less than three seconds for a pair of White Court vampires to appear.

One of them was Tania, whom I had encountered a few times before, a petite bundle of apparent fun whom I wouldn't have touched with someone else's ten-foot pole, wearing a nurse's outfit that just barely didn't show off anything. I didn't know the other woman's name, but she was tall and well-muscled and her lustrous dark hair was shaved short on the sides, and her ears were pierced through with enough silver to start a mint, wearing a bikini made of scale mail and carrying a plastic sword. They snuggled up on either side of LaChaise.

"Ladies, please show Lord LaChaise a good time," Lara said. "Give him something to sink his teeth into."

"Oh, I couldn't possibly take up their time," LaChaise said, beaming.

"Nonsense," Lara said sweetly.

Tania wrapped the ghoul's muscled arm all the way around her, and Goth Sonia took his other hand and started leading him away, walking in front of him with a lot of really fascinating English on her movements.

"Twit," Lara breathed quietly. Then she turned to me. "I would like to speak to you alone, outside, please," she said, and stalked out of the doors toward the garden.

I exhaled slowly. My body was still convinced I was about to tangle with a ghoul.

Molly turned to me, her face flushed, and said, "Harry. That was stupid. On a couple of levels." She shook her head. "Winter's alliance with Lara is necessary. Do not screw it up." She looked across the ballroom, where Etri, his sister, and several other svartalves, in their disguises as mortals, were just arriving. "Meanwhile, I need to go ask Etri for favors. It's probably best you aren't with me for that in any case."

My heart was racing. Hell's bells, I hated ghouls.

But Molly was right. I was not behaving in a way that was conducive to survival in my current surroundings.

I gripped my staff and took another deep breath. "Yeah," I said. "Yeah. I hear you."

"Not that I'm not tempted to get LaChaise alone somewhere and leave his guts in a pile on the floor," Molly snarled. She closed her eyes for a second, and when they opened again, they were cat pupiled and calm. "Go," she said.

And I went.

Lara hadn't stopped walking while I waited to follow her. I had to hurry to catch up as she headed down a path into the gardens, all trees and seemingly random plants and softly colored lights. I caught up to her, and we were out of immediate sight of the house.

Lara turned to me, her expression as distant as the stars.

I faced her.

"I get that you're hurting," she said quietly. "I get that you have a past with ghouls. I get that they nearly killed you last week." She took a step closer to me. "I even get that you never asked for the arrangement Mab has established to seal our alliance. It's awkward for both of us. I certainly never saw myself as a long-term partner with anyone." She took another step closer and reached up to pull my head down so that she could whisper in my ear. "But if you ever disrespect the peace of my house, or me, ever again, so help me I will knock your teeth out one at a time."

And then she tore off the big false beard and kissed me.

I've been really drunk before.

I've been tranquilized by a number of drugs.

I've been exposed to a couple of kinds of ecstasy of magical origin.

I've even been kissed by a young, weak White Court vampire once. And once by Lara herself.

This was different.

Everything went away.

Cold flowed through me, light and sensation turned to some liquid like honey, flowing out from the kiss and over the whole of my body. The world spun around and around and suddenly there was grass against my back, and every blade of it brought its own starburst of sensation. And Lara . . . Lara was pressed against me, body to body, and every inch of it was a pleasurable sensation like nothing I had ever known, or had words to describe, her lips moving with perfect sensuality against mine, as if she knew exactly the way I had always wanted to be kissed, the way I usually knew where down was.

The Winter mantle rose in pure, primal desire, going wild in my chest, and at the same time overwhelming languor made every movement its own slow-motion ecstasy.

"If I wanted it," she said against my mouth, her voice shaking, "I could simplify everything and make you happy to be that way."

I tried to say something along the lines of *Yes, please,* but Lara's lips had blended my brain with starlight and oceanic desire and delicious paralysis, and I couldn't remember how to make my voice box operate.

"But in the end that won't work," she said. "Not for either of us."

She pushed herself up and away from me, her eyes almost glowing in the night, pulsing with the same light as the stars. She turned her face up to them and closed her eyes. "I have duties tonight. I'm sorry this is hard for you. Good night, Harry."

And her quiet footsteps vanished over the grass.

I lay there trying to focus my eyes. My lips quivered and tingled. My body ached with pleasure that slowly faded away over the next twenty minutes or half an hour.

And that was just from a kiss.

Hell's bells.

I was sitting there trying to recover when Molly and Bear found me an hour later.

"What happened?" Molly asked quietly.

"She threatened me," I said, my voice rough. "Take me home."

Chapter
Eighteen

It was a week into November, and it was after midnight.

"So, what happened after that?" she asked me.

I threw the pair of dice and got a seven. I advanced the thimble seven spaces and paid out the money for Kentucky Avenue.

"I slept for a day and a half," I said quietly.

"But Lara kissed you once before, right?" she asked, amused.

I picked up the dice and held them out. She blew on them and I threw them for her. Six. I advanced the race car that many spaces.

"Hot damn," she said. "I have enough for Park Place."

I dutifully took the money from that side of the board and counted it out, turning over the property card to her side. "Yeah. But not like that. This time Lara was letting me know what she could do."

"Ah," she said. "So?"

I shifted uncomfortably. "So what?"

She smiled faintly. "So how do you feel about it?"

"I don't know," I said. "I think it was bad for me."

"Oh?"

"Anything that feels that good probably is," I said.

"Harry. Are you sure you aren't leaning Catholic?"

I stared at the board and said, "It's not funny."

"It's a little funny," she assured me.

I frowned and didn't move.

"Game's gonna take a while if you don't roll the dice," she said quietly.

I closed my eyes. I was tired. I usually got too sleepy to stay awake around now, but . . .

"You're not drinking tonight," she noted.

"No," I said. "Figured it was time to stop."

"That's a good thing. It never helped me, really."

I took a deep breath.

"Molly thinks I'm trying to kill myself," I said.

There was a long silence.

"What do you think?" she said gently.

"I . . ." I rolled the dice around in my palm, listening to them click. "If I was insane . . . would I know it?"

"When I talked to counselors," she said, "they would usually say that words like *sane* and *insane* weren't very useful."

I put the dice down. Harder than I had to.

"Let's review," she said. "You went out with insufficient precautions against ghouls, failed to use your magic against them when the balloon went up, and then tried to start a fistfight with another ghoul at an Accorded event while under guest-right, delivering what could have been a deadly insult to your host. At a time when everyone is a little paranoid about upholding the old laws because the last one to break them started a fight that might have exposed the supernatural world to mortals."

"Did expose them," I said quietly. "At least in town. And in the smart circles."

"Stop deflecting," she said. "Is that what you did?"

I counted through my Monopoly money slowly. "Yes," I said. "I did that."

"If it wasn't you," she said, "if it was just some random other wizard behaving that way, what would you think about it?"

"I'd think he was insane," I said. "That he was trying to die."

She blew out a slow breath. And just let me sit with that.

"Maybe I deserve it," I said.

"Maybe you aren't the one to decide such things," she replied.

I didn't answer.

"You look tired," she said.

"Stars and stones," I said. "I'm so tired. I've been so tired for so long."

"Harry. You know I enjoy this," she said. "This time together."

I nodded.

Her voice turned quiet and very, very gentle. "And you know it isn't good for you. Night after night."

I ached. And I just wanted to slide out of my chair and fall over and quit.

"It's what I have," I said.

Her tone firmed up. "Bullshit," she said.

I looked up at her sharply.

"You've got Maggie," she said. "You've got the new kid. You've got Will, and Michael, and so many other people, Harry. You need to reach out to them. You need to take care of yourself. You need sleep."

"I can't sleep," I said.

"Oh, do you think maybe, just maybe, the guy who is subconsciously trying to get himself killed by way of self-punishment is denying himself rest for the same reason?"

I frowned at that. "That's helpful. That kind of sarcasm."

She made a dismissive sound. "I'm your friend," she said. "That's never going to change. It means I tell you the truth."

Weariness hit me like a brick. My shoulders sagged.

Her voice changed again, swelling with compassion. "Oh, Harry. Please. If your daughter had been through something like this, would you want to punish her?"

"Of course not," I said automatically.

"Why not?"

"Because she wouldn't deserve . . ." I took a deep breath. "Oh."

"Yeah," she said quietly.

"I'm not . . . I can't see it like that," I said.

"Not yet," she agreed. "But you're getting closer. Maybe you should pretend that you can see it like that. Just for tonight."

"What do you mean?" I asked.

"Go to bed, you half-wit," she said fondly. "Go get in bed and pull up your covers and pretend you're a little girl whose father loves her very much and go to sleep."

"But . . . we didn't finish the game," I whispered.

"Oh, Harry," she said. "There will be other games."

I felt so very tired.

"You're sure?" I asked.

"You go ahead," she said. "I'll watch over you for a while."

I sat still for a moment, the inertia crushing.

Then I got up and slogged over to my bed. I took a moment to take off my clothes and barely made it under the covers and onto my pillow before my eyes crashed shut and refused to open again.

She started humming a quiet tune. I didn't recognize it.

I didn't drift off to sleep so much as plummet there.

And I slept until morning.

Chapter
Nineteen

So how come we do an hour a day, instead of two hours every other day?" Fitz asked, panting.

We were in the gym and had finished up a pretty intense leg day. My knees were complaining at me, but not enough to make me think I'd actually hurt them. I just wasn't as young as I used to be.

"Because getting stronger isn't about just pushing hard," I said. "It's a lot more important to push steady. Come back again and again. Push too hard, you don't have a chance to recover, the muscles don't get to grow, injuries are more likely. It's a tortoise and hare thing."

"Turtles and hair?" Fitz asked. "What the hell?"

"We'll have to cover some Aesop," I said. "Lot of good practical knowledge in there." I tossed him a protein shake in a box and took one for myself.

"Harry," he said. He frowned down at the shake, took a deep breath, then faced me and said, "I'm sorry. I tried to use magic that night. With the ghouls. I kept gathering it, but I couldn't hold it all together. It just . . . slipped right through my fingers."

I shook my head. "It's hard to do it when you have to think your way through every step. It takes time and practice to turn it all into reflex so you can use it under pressure. Most wizards are even older than me before they can do magic smoothly in a fight."

"A lot of the Wardens are younger than you."

"Everyone has different talents," I said. "Things they're good at naturally. The Council recruits Wardens from among the wizards with natural gifts at evocation." I shook my head. "Honestly, in a lot of ways they're the weakest. Evocation gets things done in a hurry, and if you've got to fight there's nothing like it—but it's short-term, and it's got really limited application. Better to be an enchanter, like Ancient Mai. Or a diviner like the Merlin."

"Diviner?"

"Wizard who specializes in getting, using, and disseminating information," I said. "It's where I've worked hardest to shore up my weaknesses as a practitioner. Knowledge is power, kid. Especially for us."

He drank half of his shake and nodded thoughtfully. "Like me with shades. That's where my talent is."

"Prezactly," I said. "I want you to start putting in half an hour at the range after we lift. Only use force and fire for now."

"So almost every day," Fitz said. "'Cause to grow I need regular practice."

"Discipline, discipline, discipline," I said, nodding. "Without discipline, you don't use power. It uses you. You wind up doing things only out of strong emotion, without reason and balance. People get hurt. Most likely yourself."

Bear thumped into the gym. She had moved with a little more bounce and energy ever since the fight with the ghouls. "*Seidrmadr*," she said quietly. "There's trouble. You'd better come down."

"Come on, Fitz," I said. "Let's go deal with some conflict."

I got downstairs and found a delegation from the magical community waiting for me, headed up by Artemis Bock.

Bock was the owner of Bock Ordered Books, a social locus of the city's magical community, and we hadn't always seen eye to eye. He wasn't really anything more than the most minor practitioner imaginable, and that mostly because he had read a lot of books. He was knowledgeable on theory, though, savvy to the magical world, and generally one of those guys the Wardens looked in on now and then. He was comfortably overweight, somewhere in his fifties, wearing jeans and a button-down shirt and a cardigan.

He had a handful of his cronies from the store with him, two of the old salts I sometimes saw playing chess at Mac's—and a young couple who had been through a beating.

"Bock," I said calmly, as I came down the stairs to the grand hall. The kids staying in the castle had half days of school in one of the meeting rooms upstairs, so the place was largely empty except for a couple of the Knights of the Bean who were hanging around on duty, playing cards.

"Dresden," he said brusquely, nodding. "We need to talk."

I gestured at the nearest table and said, "Come on in. Sit down. Fitz, see if the kitchen has any of that hot cider the Ordo made for us left."

"Got it," Fitz said and hurried out.

Bock shepherded the young couple into the seats next to him and settled down across from me.

"Okay," I said. "Introductions?"

"This is Roger and Bess," Bock said quietly. "They're Kin."

Kin was a general term for people who had supernatural beings somewhere a few generations back in their ancestry. Generally speaking, it got applied to people who were pretty much no different from vanilla mortals, except for being a little weird and having family knowledge of the supernatural world, and maybe some of the most minor abilities. You probably know some people who are Kin. Visit any Renaissance fair and you'll see some. Also, those folks with the really good dyed hair, where you can't see any roots growing in? Probably them, too.

Roger was a thin kid, early twenties, glasses, kind of stork-like, with an Adam's apple that extended almost as far as his chin. He had absolutely black hair and nutmeg-colored skin. His lip had been split, and one of his wrists had been sprained or broken and was heavily wrapped. Bess was a tiny moonfaced pale thing, stocky and curvy. Her hair was silver despite her youth, and very long, though tied back in a tail. She wasn't looking up, but her face was heavily bruised and I could see more bruises spreading out toward her collarbones from her shoulders.

"Hi, guys," I said gently. "I'm Harry Dresden."

"We know who you are," Bess said in a whisper.

I looked at Bock. "What happened?"

"Roger and Bess run a little bakery in the bazaar outside Mac's," Bock said. "They had stayed open a little late, and it was after dark when they were packing up."

I eyed the couple. "That so?"

"They said they wanted to buy some food," Roger said. His voice was surprisingly deep for his build. "When Bess opened up her basket, they just took it."

"Roger tried to get the food back," Bess said. "I mean . . . we're trading for everything right now. We can't afford to lose stock. It's how we're getting along."

"Sure," I said, frowning. "What happened?"

"They, uh." Roger swallowed.

Fitz showed up just then with a tray of steaming paper cups. He gave one to me and started passing them out to the guests. Roger and Bess gripped theirs with both hands, as if they needed the warmth. I took a sip of mine. Cider. Excellent. The ladies from the Ordo Lebes had gone out of their way for me and the others in the castle since the battle.

"Take your time," I said to them.

"They called us freaks," Bess said quietly. "And then they beat us with broom handles." She held up one of her arms to show me purple stripes.

I exhaled slowly. "Hell's bells. Do you know them?"

The young couple shook their heads. "And it was dark when they got there. You know how it is at night now."

"We've been getting a lot of that kind of attention," Bock said quietly. "Outside Mac's. At my store. Normies throwing things. Calling people names. Like playground bullies. But it hadn't ever gone to something like this."

"I'm sorry," I said to the young couple. I looked up at Bock. "You go to the police?"

Bock rolled his eyes. "Some of them give us the same kind of looks. You know?"

Chicago had been given a very rude awakening when Ethniu had shown up and begun mowing down skyscrapers, and when monsters from a dozen different mythoses (mythoi?) had shown up and begun hunting down the city's residents. A lot of people had moved out in a massive human wave—some because the town had been wrecked, and some because they had seen horrible things out of make-believe come to life. Those who had stayed had done so because they were tougher than most, or poorer than most, which in many ways was the same thing.

I had been fearing this. People, afraid, tend to band together—draw into tribes. One of the glues that hold tribes together is fear of other tribes. And there was plenty of reason to fear the supernatural and those connected to it these days.

I looked at the wounded kids. If the cops didn't have time to hunt down murdering ghouls, they wouldn't have time to deal with roving bands of bullies, either.

"Look, Dresden," Bock said quietly. "We aren't really here looking for help. We're here because you need to understand why we're going to do what we're about to do."

I frowned at Bock and the committee behind him. "What are you talking about?"

"We're going to take steps," he said in a quiet, firm voice. "Nothing deadly. But we're not going to just let ourselves get beaten, either."

"You mean to use magic," I said quietly.

He nodded.

"The Wardens won't like that," I said.

"They aren't going to know," he said.

"Aren't they?"

He smiled without mirth. "Not from you, at least. Or we'll tell them about Fitz."

Fitz, now standing behind me, made a quiet sound that could have been a growl.

Bock spread his hands. "I'm not looking for trouble with you," he said. "Honestly. But we've all been through too much. What happened to Roger and Bess is going to happen to other people, too, unless we do something about it."

I drummed my fingers on the tabletop twice and then took a long, slow sip of cider, using the time to think.

Working in a group, a circle of low-powered practitioners could be much more effective than any of them operating alone. They could get up to any amount of serious mischief. Especially if they were motivated by fear, they could put together a number of extremely unpleasant hexes or curses, ranging from nightmares to your classic voodoo doll scenario to burning down a building around the curse's subject. That kind of magic wasn't just dangerous—it had a tendency to spiral out of control and result in greater and greater chaos. The Rule of Three wasn't exactly as concrete as one of Newton's laws—but what went around did tend to come around, sooner or later, when magic was involved.

"What you're planning," I said quietly, "it could get out of hand. If it does, it will draw the attention of the Wardens, even if I don't say anything."

"We're willing to take that chance," Bock said seriously.

"It will also piss me off. Personally."

That made the two old salts exchange an unsettled glance.

"We'll take our chances with that, too," Bock said. "Dresden, we can't just do nothing. You know how predators will react to that."

I sighed. He wasn't wrong about that. Once they'd gotten easy pickings, they'd be back for more. I smoothed my hand over my forehead slowly. "Okay. Okay, let's take a step back here," I said. "Look, the problem is, you don't want your people roughed up, yeah?"

"Yes."

"Suppose I send a couple of Knights of the Bean down every night toward evening," I said. "Couple of armed men should discourage gangs of simple street toughs."

"Or encourage them to show up with more weapons," Bock objected.

"Arty," I said quietly. "What you're talking about doing . . . it could get out of hand. Easy. Really easy. It could do bad things to you. I know what I'm talking about here. If you lean into vengeance and slip over the line into black magic, you might never know it when you lose control."

"We can't just stand there," he said.

"No, you can't," I said. "Let me send you some support. This is the right time for us to stand together."

Bock pressed his lips together warily. "We don't have to listen to you," he said. "You don't run this town."

"Of course I don't," I said. "But I've seen a lot more of how bad it can get than any of you have. I'm begging you. Let me send help."

Bock glanced back at his crew. Then looked at Roger and Bess.

The young couple were studying me warily.

"What happens if it doesn't help?" Bock demanded.

"Then we will take more steps," I said. "But we'll do it together."

He exhaled slowly. He looked at least as tired as I felt. Every face in his crew was weary, wary, and determined.

"Okay," he said finally. "We'll try it your way. For now."

"Fitz," I said. "Get me the KotB roster. We'll send people over starting tonight."

Chapter
Twenty

Will defeated my wristlock, kicked the back of my knee hard enough to take my balance, and slammed an elbow into the base of my jaw as I dropped down, hard enough to make me see little birds.

"Point, Will!" Bear drawled, slashing a hand down between us.

I snarled and swiped out an arm in frustration, pushing Will's proffered hand away.

Bear cuffed me across the head calmly, keeping me from getting any of my balance back. "Cool off, Dresden," she said in a hard voice. "Corners, now."

It was a cold, clear evening on the roof of the castle. November could have come in a lot harder and crueler than it had, though everyone was waiting for the Witch of November, a quasi-apocryphal series of storms that often swept in over Lake Michigan, to put in her appearance. Natural gas service had been prioritized by the city, especially to residential areas, and twenty-four-hour construction crews consisting of contractors and volunteers and Army Engineers had been laboring ceaselessly to try to make sure there would be buildings with heat over the winter.

I went to my corner, panting, until my ears stopped ringing. Will had started off his werewolf career as an idealistic kid. He was a warrior now. And I'd asked him to come at me hard. He'd obliged me, whipping me by twenty points to maybe four of my own. My back had been covered in bruises from the throws. I'd taken half a dozen blows, knees, and kicks to the belly in the last hour. He'd mostly left my head alone.

"Good hit, Will," I muttered, waggling my jaw back into place.

"You're thinking all offense, Dresden," Bear said. "You have to think defense at the same time. Everyone you ever fight to the death is undefeated. They are looking to take you apart. You can't rely on all-out offense. Will's smart, balanced, and strong." She awarded Will a deep bow of her head. "That was properly done, warrior."

"Thank you," Will said quietly. I'd bloodied his lip for him earlier and he'd barely noticed. Damn he was quick for someone built as solidly as he was.

Will frowned and lifted his head to the evening wind, his nostrils flaring.

"Who?" I asked him.

Will considered for a moment before nodding slowly. "Ramirez and the Russian," he said.

"Well, good. I can pass along Lord Darkdoom's invitation. Bear," I said, "the kid."

"I'll see to him," the Valkyrie said, and hurried down off the roof.

"Will," I said, "send them up here, would you?"

"You're going to go after those Black Court bastards, aren't you?" Will said.

I exhaled. "Well. Yeah, probably, sooner or later."

"I'm going with you," Will said.

"Will, I'm not going to be able to look out for you," I said.

"I've been giving you an awful lot of my life lately, Harry. Also, hey, where'd you get all those bruises?" he asked. "Look, man. I told Bear what I had in mind. She's been training me before you get up. And in case you didn't notice, I just spent the last hour handing the Winter Knight his ass."

I growled. "Yeah, well."

"You remember that bruise on the cheek you gave me first round?"

"Yeah," I said.

"You see it now?"

I frowned and peered at him in the gathering dark. There was no mark on his face.

"Bruises take about a minute to go away," he said. "Split my lip, it's better in two. And rare meat is freaking ambrosia."

"How?" I asked quietly.

"All the shifting lately," he said. "And since the night of the battle I've . . . I don't know. Felt things differently." He met my eyes. His reflected light, like a wolf's. "A lot of things changed that night."

There had been an insane amount of power flowing through the city the night of the battle, God knew. It had awakened Council-level power in Fitz, after all. It had taken me days to realize how drunk I had been on it for a while. I had unfurled a psychic banner of pure will and used it to make my allies stronger in that heady brew of terror and fury and pure arcane power that had roiled over the city. I knew I had been stronger then, more able to affect the world around me.

Maybe a lot more.

Maybe with more consequence than I had realized.

I broke my gaze with Will before it got any more complicated. Hell's bells, what had I unleashed without knowing?

I extended my wizard's senses toward the other man and felt . . .

. . . kind of threatened, actually.

Will had always been dangerous as a werewolf. But he was changing. I could feel the shift in energy around him. He had gone through the fire, and he'd come out changed. Harder. Stronger.

"I'll think about it," I relented. "Will, I . . . thank you. For your help lately. I know I'm not firing on all cylinders right now. So . . . thank you."

His expression softened. "Hell, man. You've had our backs since we were a bunch of dumb college kids. How can I not be there for you?"

He held up his hand.

We clasped hands, Arnold and Carl Weathers–style.

"Okay," I said. "Send the Wardens up."

Will vanished down the stairs. I grabbed a towel and mopped it over my sweat-soaked hair. I was only wearing basketball shorts. I needed a haircut and a shave. Now that I wasn't moving, the evening's wind should have been sending chills through me, but it just felt refreshing. I stretched a little, sensing the bruises strain across my back, but it only made me feel a little more alive. The Winter mantle made pain a non-factor, and as the season advanced, it became increasingly difficult to ignore the simple animal pleasure of using my body.

Footsteps came up the stairs, light, clicking, and Ilyana the Warden appeared, wearing a lot of close-fit black under her grey cloak. She stepped out onto the rooftop and stared at me for a long moment, pale eyes raking over me.

"Like some kind of animal," she spat quietly, contempt in her tone.

But she was staring at me, and holding herself in a way that if I didn't know better I would have sworn was intentional. The Winter mantle took keen interest in her grace, her slender appeal. Her white-blond hair that would make her easy to see and hunt down in the dark. Her lips were maddeningly full and appealing, even without makeup, even twisted into a sneer.

I tried not to notice, but ever since Lara had planted one on me, my body had suddenly remembered that sex was a thing, and that fact had been annoying me on a regular basis. Never mind how the oncoming cold weather had woken the mantle, as it always did. I could feel it, like a hungry beast prowling around in my chest and my guts and my . . . elsewhere.

"Nice to see you, too, Miss Astinova." I sighed.

"That's Warden Astinova to you."

I showed her my teeth. "Where's Carlos, Warden?"

"He'll be along," she said coldly. She seemed to make up her mind about something and strode quickly toward me, her eyes bright, her body tense.

Part of me sensed a threat. Part of me sensed an opportunity. I could have reacted in a number of ways, but I chose to just arch one eyebrow and give her my disapproving look.

She was maybe a buck fifteen, maybe five foot four. I had her by a hundred and fifty pounds and almost a foot and a half. She stopped short of me.

Then she took a deep breath, stepped forward, and placed her bare hand on my stomach.

I let her.

She stared at me for a moment, frowning. Then shot me a suspicious glare.

"You don't sense any black magic, eh?" I asked her, my voice a low growl. "Go a little higher or a little lower, and this could get unpredictable."

She jerked her hand back as if she'd been burned.

"I don't understand," she said.

"I'm sure you don't," I told her. I started taking steps toward her, and she began to backpedal, her face turning into a grimace of apprehension. I didn't stop until the small of her back bumped up against one of the merlons in the castle's crenelation. "Let me explain something to you, Ilyana," I said quietly. "When you're here, you're here as a guest. If you take liberties touching me again, I'm going to take it as a betrayal of guest-right and throw you off my roof."

"You wouldn't dare," she snapped.

"You've been duly warned about your breach of the ancient laws," I said. "This isn't White Council territory. Walk carefully."

"Or?"

I smiled again, not pleasantly. "One way or another," I said, "it's time for you to get off my roof."

Her eyes narrowed. "I will remind you," she said in a low, hard voice, "that should I ever find you in breach of the Laws of Magic or Council policy, your already-signed death warrant will be withdrawn from suspension and handed over to the Blackstaff. And you will be executed."

"You say that like I haven't been here before," I said. "With someone a hell of a lot scarier than you with his finger on the trigger. And here I stand." I stepped back calmly and gave her a courtly little bow. "Good night, Warden."

The door to the roof opened and Ramirez stepped out, stockier than usual in a winter coat beneath his Warden's cloak. "Ilyana," he said, his voice frosty. "Return to Edinburgh at once."

Her pale eyes flashed and she strode from the roof, to the doorway and down the stairs. She slammed the door behind her.

"Don't suppose she trained with Morgan?" I asked him.

Ramirez walked over to join me at the edge of the roof and looked out over the neighborhood, and past it, to the illuminated towers of the nicer parts of the city. "Early on. Then with Luccio. She"—he paused— "has been shaped by some of the same forces, I think."

"I kind of miss Morgan sometimes," I said.

"So do I. He was a pain in the ass."

"But you always knew where he stood," I said.

"Amen to that."

I went over to the pile of workout clothes I'd slipped out of before starting rounds with Will and found my wallet. I pulled the business card Drakul had given me out of it and handed it to Ramirez.

Carlos held up a hand and muttered a gentle light spell into being. He read the card and looked up at me. "What's this?"

"Drakul's address," I said. "I think he was telling the truth."

Ramirez exhaled slowly. "Tell me."

I did.

He shook his head. "He's given us a legal license to hunt him down."

"Seemed to think it would simplify things for him if we did."

"Cocky bastard."

I shrugged and slipped my shirt on. "Or maybe he's just that good. Guy creeps me."

"Does that change anything?"

"Hell, no," I said. "But . . . I'm not ready. There was a fight. Ghouls. I, uh. Misfired."

Ramirez tilted his head sharply.

"I don't know," I said. "I'm just not . . ."

"You're mourning," he said quietly. "Murphy."

It didn't feel exactly like a knife going into my heart, I think, to hear her name aloud.

"She was good people," he said. "I only knew her a little. But I could tell that much."

"Yeah," I said quietly.

"You blame yourself for her death," he noted.

I shrugged a shoulder. "Maybe."

"You're too quick to take things like that on. Like you did with the twins."

I didn't answer him. The twins were the reason I hated ghouls. Young wizards in training, back at Camp Kaboom. The ghouls hadn't left much.

Neither had I.

"Our world is dangerous," he said. "Even if we could see every possible future, had the time and the knowledge to make the best choice every time, people would still die, Harry."

"Maybe," I said. "God. If I could go back . . ."

"Stars and stones," Ramirez chuckled. "Don't talk about breaking the Sixth Law right in front of a Warden, Dresden. Even I have limits."

I gave him a bleak smile. "If I'd just disarmed that slimy little me-weasel Rudolph." I sighed. "It wasn't even on purpose. He was panicked. Had his finger on the trigger. His gun went off."

Carlos winced. "I didn't know the details."

After a minute, I said, "I tried to kill him."

"A cop?"

I nodded. "Sanya and Butters stopped me. I told him to get out of town."

"Did he?"

"He probably ran for the border," I said. "I don't know. I haven't heard about him. I haven't gone looking."

"Christ," he said calmly. "No wonder you've got your mojo in a knot."

I frowned at him.

"Drakul kills half of our squad from the war," Ramirez said. "That guy kills Murphy. Your hometown is in shambles. And when you moved back into your old place, it's not your place anymore. And you got this thing with Lady Raith going; that's got to be fucking with you. Plus, Ilyana and everyone who is cheering her on ready to send the Blackstaff after you. You're trying to take care of people whose homes were destroyed." He shook his head. "Fighting ghouls and whatnot. Harry, you need to balance some scales. You need a damned vacation. A year at a monastery. Something."

"Yeah," I said. "Well. I'm not going to get it."

He grunted. "You look like you're in shape."

"Only thing keeping me sane," I said. "Assuming it is. I think it is."

"Depends," Ramirez drawled. "Did you threaten to defenestrate my partner just before I came up here?"

"No," I said defensively. "There are no windows up here."

He barked out a laugh.

"She touched me," I said. "Looking for black magic."

He sighed. "Well. That's what Wardens do."

"It's not what guests do."

"God, Dresden," he said. "You don't make things easier."

"And here we've all had it so smooth and gentle lately."

Ramirez sighed. "Look, I shouldn't be telling you this," he said, "but you know we have spirits and other informants who alert us when black magic is used in most major cities."

"Sure," I said.

"Chicago's been pinging the net," he said. "That's why Ilyana checked your aura."

"Fuck," I said quietly.

He tilted his head and eyed me.

I held up a hand to him. "How bad?"

"Not much," he admitted. "If it had been you, enough for an excuse."

"You sending a team?"

"I don't know yet," he said. "Am I?"

"Give me a little time," I said. "Maybe I can put a lid on it. Without beheading anyone." I swallowed and barely managed to say, "There's been enough blood spilled in my town."

He stared at me for a long moment. Then he shrugged a shoulder. "I'm the regional commander, but there are a lot of eyes on this. You could have a hundred Wardens or the Blackstaff himself at your door if something goes south. And there wouldn't be a thing I could do about it. I hope you know what you're doing, Harry."

"Yeah," I said. "I hope so, too."

Chapter
Twenty-One

Bear!" screamed Maggie as she came pelting out Michael's door toward us, wearing a Sunday dress. "Dad!"

I scooped her up and tossed her in the air and caught her again and started tickling her on the way down. She let out a squealing peal of giggles.

Mouse came rushing up in Maggie's wake, bounding in stiff-legged excited leaps in a circle around us. He threw himself against Bear's legs, all but knocking even her massive form down, and then barreled into me the second I'd set Maggie down on the Carpenters' leaf-strewn front lawn. I went down laughing, with the huge grey dog nuzzling my face while his great tail swooshed back and forth. Maggie shouted something about an atomic elbow and then threw herself onto the pile.

And.

Oh.

My.

God.

That felt good.

It was like stepping out into the sun after a long, cold night.

There are moments in your life that are perfect. You know they won't last long, you know they're rare, you know that they might not ever come again. If you pay attention, you can feel those moments happening to you.

I sank my teeth into it. I inhaled every scent, felt every burst of laughter rise out of my stomach, filed away every single sound of Maggie's delight, of Mouse's whuffling affection, of the crinkle of late autumn leaves under us, felt the crisp cold of the oncoming winter bite affectionately at exposed skin. I wrestled my dog and my little girl and filed that moment away in my heart and my head, because I knew I'd need moments like this one—both now and in the future.

And I felt something ease in my chest and belly.

"Okay, okay!" I burst out finally, with a little over three hundred pounds of love essentially pinning me to the ground. "I yield! Don't crush me!"

Mouse chuffed cheerfully, gave my face a couple of truly viscous kisses, and rose off of me. Maggie didn't. She just grabbed onto my chest and hugged me. I got to my feet and she didn't stop, clinging to me like a limpet. So I just carried her inside that way, with Mouse walking happily with his shoulder pressed against my leg, looking up at us with a huge doggy smile on his face.

I looked up onto the house's porch to see Michael and Molly standing there waiting for us. Both of them were smiling widely, and Molly was holding her father's hand.

And that was how we started Thanksgiving at the Carpenter house.

Michael's wife, Charity, puts on a feast for Thanksgiving, let me tell you. If I hadn't been losing so much weight, I'd have had to unbutton my pants. Not everyone was there. Matthew had become a volunteer nurse for Doctors Without Borders and was in South America. Alicia had gotten engaged and was spending the holiday with her fiancé's family.

I still remembered them as a bunch of kids spilling out of a minivan.

And that would happen with Maggie, too. None of us own our children. We have a little while to hold them in trust, before we turn them over to the adults we've been waiting a couple of decades to meet. I needed to start arranging more time with her.

After the meal and some football (Michael had temporarily mounted a TV outside the living room's picture window, and the house's threshold, so that my magic wouldn't screw up the big game), I went outside to the expansive front porch to sit down.

Michael, wrapped in a cardigan against the evening chill, joined me and passed me a cup of hot coffee. We sat together in companionable silence for a while, rocking on separate chairs.

"You really don't get cold, do you?" Michael noted.

I was wearing jeans and a T-shirt in forty degrees with a little breeze. "Not so much," I said.

"How are you handling the mantle these days?"

"Same as always. Lots of exercise, first thing. Meditation. As long as I do that, it's not much different than feeling like a teenager, only with more perspective."

He raised both eyebrows. "That's an image."

I shrugged.

"The beard suits you," he said.

"Covers up the new scars."

"Ghoul wounds always scar up heavy," he agreed. "You look worried."

I stared at the coffee for a bit. "I got ninety-nine problems and a bi—"

He coughed and gave me a look.

"Woman," I corrected myself, "are several of them."

"Mab, Lara Raith, and Justine," he said.

I exhaled agreement and sipped coffee. "Mab wants me to settle up with King Etri. But he wants Thomas's head. I can't think of a way to make that work."

"The svartalves have very Old Nordic sensibilities," he said. "Perhaps he would accept a weregild?"

"For the life of a trusted retainer of about seven centuries? I don't have that kind of money. And besides, Etri probably makes Scrooge McDuck look like Bob Cratchit. He's not interested in wealth."

"There are some things money can't buy," he noted. "You've made things like that happen before."

"Maybe," I said warily. "But I don't know what he wants. I suppose I could offer him favors three, but God only knows how that could end up."

"Indeed," Michael said. He pursed his lips. "Perhaps you need an emissary. This is a conflict between signatories of the Unseelie Accords, after all."

I arched an eyebrow. "Mab made it pretty clear that it was my personal problem. And I'm not Council anymore. Without her support, I can't make a claim."

"Perhaps a personal mediator, then," he said diffidently.

I frowned. "What are you saying, exactly?"

"I have fought both for and against the svartalves over the years," he said. "I wouldn't say that we are friends, but there is mutual respect. Molly increased my standing with them when she saved Etri and his family. I could talk to him on your behalf."

I scowled. "You're not going to get all Messianic about it, are you? People have sacrificed enough for me."

"A Knight of the Cross can often be called upon to make such choices when they are needful," he said. "But as you may have noticed, I am no longer a Knight of the Cross. I have many things to look forward to with my children, and grandchildren. I fully intend to be there to enjoy them. But that doesn't mean I can't have a civil conversation on behalf of my best friend."

The coffee made me choke up a little. "Thank you," I said quietly. "But I got me into this. I've got to be the one to get me out. Besides. Even if you could get terms from Etri . . . Thomas is dying."

Michael frowned and leaned closer.

"It's his Hunger," I said. "It's the spirit that is attached to him. It's what gives the White Court their abilities. Thomas's Hunger went berserk when the svartalves beat him within an inch of his life taking him prisoner. His body poured all the Hunger's energy into saving his life. It's starving. He won't be able to control himself when it comes out, which means . . ."

"Someone would have to die to save him," Michael said quietly.

"Might not be enough," I said. "He might kill them and die anyway. And he doesn't want someone else to pay the price for him. I've got him in a kind of suspended animation, but it's only buying him time, not solving anything. He . . . doesn't have much hope."

"And neither do you," Michael said quietly.

I closed my eyes and tried to focus on how warm the coffee cup felt in my hands. "I don't even know where to start."

Michael pursed his lips and sat back in the rocker. He went back and forth for a while, thinking.

"A friend of mine," he said, "once told me that when you didn't know what to do next, you gather more information."

I eyed him.

"Huh," I said.

"I mean, what do we really know about the White Court?" Michael asked. "Some, probably not all, of what they can do. How they feed. How they generally operate. We do know that it's possible for them to detach from their Hunger."

"Sure," I said. "If their first time is the sex of true love, which practically never happens, and which couldn't help Thomas."

"Yet we know it is possible. A slim chance is infinitely higher than no chance at all," Michael said firmly. "Miracles happen, Harry. You've seen them. You've done them."

Something bitter and snarky started to come out of my mouth but died partway.

Because he was right.

Michael was right.

I needed more information about the White Court, about Hungers, about the svartalves in general and Etri in particular, if I wanted to sort this mess out.

Assuming there was a viable way to do so. I pretty much always approached problems knowing that I was capable, knowing that I was strong, knowing that I could do some good. There was a fundamental arrogance in that—necessary, maybe, but arrogant all the same. That arrogance had cost Murphy her life. I had dismissed the terrified Rudolph as no real threat, on the scale of things we'd been dealing with that evening.

But Death doesn't grade on a curve.

It is perhaps the only force in the universe that is always impartial, always fair, always equitable. Death comes for all of us. We all end up with the same outcome, eventually. I had forgotten that.

"You're carrying an awful lot of weight, brother," Michael said gently. "Grief is good and right when you lose people you care about. Love. But sooner or later, you're going to have to let go of them and move on."

In my head, the dice rattled on a Monopoly board.

"You're saying I need closure," I said.

"Not quite the same thing as letting go," he said softly.

I licked my lips and stared down at the cup. "My magic failed me against the ghouls. It works well enough in practice. But when the storm came . . . it just dried up on me. Some people have told me they think it's because I have some kind of death wish."

"What do you think?" Michael asked.

"I don't know," I said. "Maybe. I haven't felt this bad . . . ever. Not even when the Reds turned Susan."

"Perhaps that's what you need to let go of most," Michael said.

"What's that?"

"Being so angry at yourself," he said. "Harry, you can do things. More than most of the planet. You can change things. Preserve them. You can challenge beings of tremendous power. Help people everywhere you go." He thumped his fist lightly against my shoulder. "But you're still just a man. You're going to make mistakes. You're going to be wrong sometimes. Sometimes you will fail. And even if you do everything right, sometimes you will still fail to live up to your standards—not because you made a bad choice, but because you are a human being. You can only work with what you know when you are in the moment, and we can't know everything all the time. That's just how life is."

I didn't look up at him.

"Your self-anger is nothing less than you demanding of yourself perfection, Harry. I know it's hard to hear me from way up on the mountaintop of hubris beneath that standard. But as I am your friend, by the living God and on my children's souls, brother, I swear to you this truth: You deserve better than what you've been giving yourself."

To my wizard's senses, the air shivered with the power behind my best friend's oath.

He meant it.

And between the two of us, I probably wasn't the one with the clearest perspective at the moment.

I was quiet while the coffee chilled.

Michael waited. He let half an hour pass in calm and patience.

"I don't know how to do that," I whispered finally.

"I don't know how to tell you," he answered easily. "But between the two of us, perhaps we can figure it out."

Rapid footsteps thudded in the house's entry hall, and the front door and storm door opened in rapid succession. Daniel strode out onto the porch and directly toward us, his footsteps swift and purposeful.

"We just got a call from Father Forthill," he said, his expression strained. "There's a problem. He's asking for you, Harry."

Chapter

Twenty-Two

I heard the screams coming from inside St. Mary of the Angels by the time we were ten feet from the door.

St. Mary's was less a building than an edifice. Taking up a whole city block, the church was famous for its architecture and artistry. To me, it had always looked like someone from a different age had popped into the middle of the city and decided to show everyone how it was done back in the day. The building exuded a sense of solidity, permanence, and order—things I'd never found myself taking comfort in when I'd visited before.

But there was something inside me that ached for them now.

The screams kind of put me off, though. They were high-pitched, desperate, animalistic. I couldn't tell if it was a woman or a man making them. I recognized agony. Recognized it in my soul. And for a second, I was overcome by a sense of pure panic, by dread, by a desire to go find a dark, quiet room and shut myself inside. I had plenty of pain already, thank you, and the wounded part of me wanted nothing to do with more.

But I closed my eyes and took a slow breath, as I'd been practicing daily. Then I did it again, forcing myself to slow my breathing, my heart rate, separating myself from the terror I felt deep in my bones. I visualized myself from a bird's-eye view, noting the panic I was feeling without letting it overwhelm me, and embraced reason as best I could.

Someone was hurting.

Father Forthill thought I could help.

This wasn't about me. This was about the poor soul in agony.

I nodded as my thoughts stabilized and opened my eyes again. Michael and I exchanged a look, his concerned, mine a lopsided smile of reassurance. He'd put on an insulated flannel shirt and a leather vest against the cold. He leaned on his cane and frowned at me for a moment, and then at the church.

"Yeah," I said quietly. "What the hell?"

The door opened before we could step up to it, and Father Forthill appeared there, looking ragged and tired. The old priest managed a faint smile and gave us a quick nod. "Michael. Harry. Thank you for coming. This way, please."

I went in, and as I did, I could sense the quiet power of decades of faith that permeated the building—and it had been roused and was stirring. That was unusual. It took the presence of real evil to bring the power of holy ground out of the earth and stones, and that meant that whatever was happening inside, it was capital-B Bad.

Michael tilted his head at the same time I was sorting through the energies around me, and his grey eyes brightened and went hard. His jaw flexed a couple of times, and his grip on the cane shifted, as though he had begun to seize the shaft of it like the handle of a sword.

Forthill led us to the entrance to the chapel, and as he did the screams weakened and trailed off.

"It's Robert," he said quietly. "He's a member of the Brotherhood of St. Brigid. One of the Brotherhood is a doctor, but he has no idea what's causing the problem. We had him in my quarters, but he was getting worse, and Doctor Brazell feared cardiac arrest. We took him into the chapel on the way to carrying him toward a car to take him to the hospital, and the moment we carried him in, he was given grace and relief for a few moments at a time. It seems to be going in cycles, but we judged it too great a risk to move him and put him in continual agony again. Hospitals are already overloaded, and I feel certain this is not a medical problem."

Forthill opened the door, and we followed him into the chapel. There were a dozen men wearing St. Brigid's cross standing in the nave, while a middle-aged man knelt over a panting, grunting, sweating younger man who lay on a narrow cot's mattress in the sanctuary—presumably Dr. Brazell and Robert, respectively.

The moment I looked at the victim, I felt the nauseating, greasy feel of black magic swirling around the poor bastard, and I was pretty sure I knew what was happening to him.

Because I'd seen it before.

I walked over to the victim and spared a nod for the elaborate altar and painted cupola above it, because I didn't want to show any disrespect and because I didn't think a full genuflection would be appropriate for someone not of the faith. The last time I'd dealt with this curse it had been difficult enough. I didn't need to make myself work uphill to handle it again.

"Doctor Brazell?" I said quietly.

He was a pretty average guy. Grizzled hair, silvering beard, thirty or forty pounds overweight, with thick forearms and capable-looking hands in a polo shirt and slacks. His eyes looked haunted, but he offered his hand.

I shook it. "Harry Dresden," I said. "Wizard. What can you tell me?"

"It started at sundown," Brazell said. He was holding on to Robert's hand. The stricken man was breathing as if he'd just run a marathon at high elevation, covered in sweat, and his eyes were sunken and closed. I wasn't sure he knew what was going on. "He was on a ghoul patrol in the ruins," Brazell continued, his voice bitter, "and he just pitched over and started screaming. He's barely said an intelligible word, even in his pain-free moments. I tried a dose of tramadol, but it did absolutely nothing for him."

"I doubt it did nothing," I said. "If I'm right, it just isn't the right kind of medicine. I need you to let go of his hand for a moment, please."

"Why?" Brazell asked.

"Because you're clearly empathetic, and if you're touching him it's going to have an effect on his aura. I need a clean read."

"Holy Mary," Brazell spat. "His *aura*?" He looked up at Michael and Forthill.

"Do it," Michael said gently.

Brazell looked down at Robert and then at me, and then slowly put his hand down. The victim shuddered and trembled, still gasping.

I put my left hand down to hover over Robert, less than an inch from touching his throat. He was fever hot. Then I closed my eyes and opened my wizard's senses. That same greasy roil of black magic bubbled out hungrily, swirling around my hand, threatening to make me retch in pure reaction. I fought my stomach back down and slowly moved my hand down his body, over each chakra, each energy center, and focused my attention completely on what I could feel.

Every few inches, I passed another line of black magic, as if something had coiled around his body like a snake. I took a deep breath, pressed my hand closer, and could feel the phantom sensation of needle-sharp barbs pressing against my skin.

Oh yeah.

I had seen this before. And I didn't need to use my Sight to identify it this time.

"Michael," I said quietly, "we're going to need fire. At least the size of a big campfire. The holier the better."

"Holy oil," Michael said at once.

"My room, in the ready cabinet," Forthill said, nodding. "And the old pews are in storage in the basement." He turned to the other members of the Brotherhood gathered in the nave and said, "Gentlemen, I need your help, please. If you would follow me."

They all but leapt up to do so. Forthill led them out, and Michael touched my shoulder and limped away as quickly as he could, back toward Forthill's quarters.

I looked up to find Brazell staring at me. "You . . . you know what's going on?"

"Seen it before," I said. "Maybe fifteen years ago."

"What's happening?"

"It's a curse," I said. "Someone used black magic to send pain directly into his nervous system. If you could see it, it would look like a coil of barbed wire wrapped around him."

"Black magic." Brazell frowned. "Is that why he . . . he got a little better when he came in here?"

"Belief can be a powerful positive force," I said. "And black magic like this is as negative as it gets. At its core, the people of your faith believe in redemption, mercy, and compassion. Looks like Someone thought your man needed a little relief until help got here."

"God," Brazell said slowly.

"That's above my pay grade," I said. "I only do religion when it's work adjacent. But it doesn't surprise me that bringing him in here helped."

"Before last summer," Dr. Brazell said, "I would have just assumed you were incurably foolish. Or insane."

"Heh," I said. "Jury's still out on the latter."

Brazell almost smiled. He looked at me intently. "Can you help him?"

The last time I'd used my magic under pressure, it hadn't gone so well. "I've handled this before. I hope so, yeah."

"What happens if you fail?" Brazell asked.

"If it works the same way it did last time, I'll end up like him." I swallowed. I mean, if there was some part of me that thought I deserved to suffer, who was to say it wouldn't take the opportunity to torment me in one of the most hideous ways I'd ever seen?

"What can I do?" Brazell asked.

"Stand by for aftercare," I said quietly. "He might well need a hospital after this. You a believer?"

"More and more, the past few months," he said.

"Then pray," I said.

"Will it help?"

"Maybe. Probably, even. And I don't see how it can hurt."

"Robert is a good man," Brazell said. "A wife. Two small children. God will help him, won't He?"

"Near as I can figure from observation, Doc," I said, "the Almighty mostly seems to be willing to make sure you get a fighting chance when evil supernatural forces stack the deck against you."

"How so?"

"Like maybe by making sure Robert got enough of a respite to survive until I got here." I settled back onto my knees and toes, resting my hands on my thighs and beginning to order my thoughts. "Maybe that's why they say He helps those who help themselves. But talk to the padre. Faith isn't really in my wheelhouse."

Brazell stared at me for a second and then said, "I spent the first half of my life learning so that I could help people," he said. "I recognize knowledge when I see it. What do you need?"

"Some quiet. And a little luck."

Brazell frowned in thought. Then he put his hand in his pocket, pulled out a ring of car keys, and detached an old rabbit's foot that dangled from it. He offered it to me, his expression serious.

I didn't laugh. Personal totems aren't a joke.

"Thank you," I said, and accepted it.

Michael and the Brotherhood of St. Brigid were back in maybe ten minutes. They set up what looked like a big shallow bowl that proved to be a large round shield. They braced it in place with three blocks of wood, and then Michael began to direct the building of a fire.

"Remember Mickey Malone?" I asked him.

"Back when we fought Leonid Kravos. I remember you told me about him," Michael said.

"I'm pretty sure this is the same curse."

Michael frowned. "The one Kravos threw on him?"

"Yeah," I said. "Maybe his Book of Shadows survived him. Or one of his cult lackeys walked away with more knowledge than I'd thought he'd give out. This is more intense than the one on Mickey, though. By a good way."

"That doesn't sound good," Michael said.

"The city's a darker place," I said. "Makes it easier to draw on black magic."

Forthill frowned at me and said, "You're saying this is mortal magic?"

"Probably," I said. "Yeah."

"Who would . . . why would anyone do such a thing?" Forthill asked, his voice bewildered. "The Brotherhood has been convened to protect everyone."

"Maybe we can find out," I said. "After."

Robert had begun to sweat. He was twitching and twisting in discomfort, and it was rapidly getting worse. I wanted to move before he started screaming again. I wasn't sure what that would do to my focus.

"Wizard," Dr. Brazell said urgently. "He's going into the seizure again."

"Fire," I said to Michael. "Get it going."

"Start," he said. He took a plain bottle with a plug held in by a wire rig around the neck. "I'll have it ready."

Forthill suddenly blinked and looked up at the highly decorated, intricately painted ceiling of the chapel. "Oh," he said. "Oh my. The canon and the bishop aren't going to be happy about this."

"If they'd stayed in town when things got bad, they could complain," I consoled him.

"But the smoke," Forthill said plaintively.

"We'll put it out the moment we don't need it anymore," Michael assured him.

I turned to Dr. Brazell and said, "He's going to thrash around. Last guy I did this to had to be handcuffed to the bed. Hold him down if you have to."

"Got it," the burly doctor said.

I nodded, closed my eyes, and held out both hands over poor Robert as he started to groan.

I picked up on the black magic immediately, winding and binding him in pain and misery. I took a deep breath, stabilizing my thoughts and the images in my head I was using to combat the dark spell, and suddenly snapped my hands down as if seizing a snake behind its head before it could bite me.

I felt the curse begin to strain against me, whipping back and forth like a serpent, but I gave it no opportunity to escape. I kept my hands and my thoughts closed around it—and my mind was a hell of a lot stronger than it had been fifteen years ago. Fifteen years of pain and loss, of joy and victory, of steady work and desperate innovation had given my will steel and character that simply had not been possible when I was younger.

The curse was stronger.

But so was I.

I could feel the energy in my hands, see it in imagery in my head, the curse shaped like a coiling line of barbed wire. It struggled against me like a frenzied snake, and I suppressed it with my mind more than my hands. I moved deliberately, extracting one end of the wire from Robert's neck, moving slowly and carefully to avoid damaging his non-material self, whether you wanted to call it his energy field, the flow of his chakras, or his immortal soul. The wire would tear apart his sanity as it left him if I wasn't careful. So I extracted it carefully and began to unwind it from his body with slow, deliberate caution.

Time went away while I focused, eyes closed, wholly and entirely centered on my wizard's senses. I could hear voices talking in the distance, caught a faint whiff of woodsmoke, and with a roll of my hands and arms, I began gathering the writhing tendril of barbed wire into my grasp, feeling the curse lash back and forth, seeking a new victim.

"Michael," I said, my voice strained.

"It's ready," he said.

I took a slow breath. Then with a last slow, firm pull, I withdrew the far end of the barbed wire from Robert's hip, and the thing went mad in my hands. I fought to hold it contained, turning slowly, and opening my eyes to see a fire blazing in the broad shield.

"Get clear!" I snarled, and lurched toward it on my knees, thrusting out my hands and with it the dark curse, sending the dark energy into the purifying fire.

The fire roared up with a hissing scream that sounded even more charming than nails on a chalkboard, and I winced in discomfort as it hit—and then the fire suddenly surged, brightening, burning pure silver-white, and the wail of the dying curse became frantic and then suddenly vanished. The holy flame surged ten feet up, causing the Brotherhood to shield their eyes against the sudden illumination, and then abruptly died down to a very normal, very nonmagical fire that made the shattered wood of the basement pews crackle and pop and produce a considerable cloud of smoke.

I sagged in place, falling forward onto my hands, breathing hard.

Okay, so. It hadn't been a fight, precisely.

But I'd done it.

I breathed out a long, slow sigh of relief.

I heard Michael and Forthill using a large wet blanket to smother the fire, sending out even more gouts of smoke, much to Forthill's chagrin.

I was exhausted, but I started cackling a little. Which is a wizard's prerogative.

Michael and I walked slowly to his truck and got in. We sat quietly for a moment. I wanted nothing so much as to go to bed.

"Harry," he said gently. "The Brotherhood has been attacked by practitioners of magic."

"Yeah. I noticed."

"Poor Robert." Michael sighed. "Is he going to recover?"

"Sure," I said. "Little at a time. He's lucky he's younger. Mickey Malone couldn't do the job anymore after that curse hit him."

Michael frowned. "That's not . . ." He inhaled slowly. "I want to make sure we avoid misunderstandings. That's all."

"I'll look into it," I promised him. I fought off a yawn. "You know. In the morning."

"So will I," he said. "From my end. I'll come visit you in two days. We can compare notes."

"Perfect," I muttered and laid my head against the truck window.

I had dropped off to sleep before we left the church's parking lot.

Chapter

Twenty-Three

The Witch of November came two days after Thanksgiving, rain and sleet and fog and snow all mixed together, as Mab knocked at the castle door.

Will sent the Knights of the Bean on duty out the back door to get an early lunch, which was likely a good idea. Some of the guys had gotten ideas about looking out for me. It was just possible that they might have had a higher-than-average level of snark for some reason, and Mab wasn't the sort to be terribly tolerant of snark.

I had scars and lumps on my skull to prove it.

I came down the stairs from the second floor quickly, with Fitz in tow. "What are you supposed to do?" I asked.

"Keep my mouth shut unless asked a direct question," Fitz repeated dutifully. "Be courteous. Offer nothing, not even thanks. Accept nothing, not even compliments."

"Good," I said. "I'm throwing you into the deep end here, kid. You're probably going to be dealing with Fae in the future, and Mab is pretty much the most dangerous one there is. Follow my rules and keep your eyes open."

I was halfway across the emptied great hall when Bear escorted Mab in from the entry chamber. She was wearing one of those huge fur winter hats and a white fur coat that fell to her white heels. Silver-white hair spilled down her back in a cascade like an abruptly frozen waterfall. Her opaline eyes were thoughtful, her lips the color of frozen mulberries, and when Fitz saw her, he tripped over his own feet and fell.

I paused and offered him a hand up. He had kind of a stunned look on his face.

The Fae have that effect the first time you see them. And the second and the seventy-third. They are inhumanly beautiful. I didn't trip because of my awesome wizardly self-restraint, and because experience had taught me that Mab would look that beautiful even when she was swinging an axe at my skull.

Which she had done.

She was more terrifying than she was lovely.

"It's okay, kid," I said under my breath. "Pretty much what I did the first time I saw one of the Sidhe, too. Remember the rules."

Fitz swallowed, his eyes wide, and nodded mutely.

"Good man."

We finished walking over to Mab and Bear, and I felt Mab's eyes on me the way I would feel the winter wind on my face.

"My Knight," Mab said coolly.

"Queen Mab," I said, and inclined my head.

Fitz was just staring so I elbowed him. He blinked and then emulated me.

"And who is this?" she asked. There was the barest hint of a smile around her eyes.

"This is Fitz," I said. "My apprentice."

Mab arched a silver brow. "Is he capable, or is this another of your charity projects?"

"He set one of the Fomor's heavy troopers on fire during the battle. He's able to use all the basic elements. He's got Council-level potential."

"Interesting," Mab said. Her eyes raked Fitz. "Young man," she said, "there are those among my Court who could teach you the paths of power, if you wish to bargain for the knowledge."

Fitz blinked again and put his eyes firmly on the floor. "Your offer is thoughtful, Queen Mab. But Harry is already doing that."

Mab actually smiled. It was like seeing a cat walk on its hind legs. "Dresden is a capable teacher," she agreed. "But should you find yourself in need of another instructor—and another aegis against the White Council—you have but to call my name three times."

Fitz started to speak, thought better of it, and inclined his head instead.

"You were not so wise when you were his age," Mab noted to me.

"Possibly not even now," I said. "Why are you trying to bogart my apprentice?"

Mab gave me an even look, by which I mean one that told me she regretted not bringing an axe. "It has worked out well for me in the past. Perhaps it will again."

A muscle in my cheek twitched. Molly.

Mab eyed Fitz once more and then said, "I will speak to you alone, my Knight."

I took Mab to the library that Michael's crew had finished only days before. It didn't look like a fancy room in an enchanted castle. It looked more like a school library. Barred windows, lightly stained wooden shelves, which were still largely empty, and several seating areas made of comfortable secondhand couches and easy chairs. Mister had claimed the place even before the workmen had left and was currently sleeping on top of a row of old leather-bound encyclopedias at the outlet of a heating duct from the castle's gas furnace.

Sleet rattled on the windows. The wind gusted and blurred the buildings across the street through the precipitation. I closed the door to the library behind us, and Mab stared out at the worsening storm with a fascinated, sensual expression on her face.

"I do love the first winter storm here," she said quietly. "How it sends so many souls scurrying for shelter. Tests those living without it. We will see who is strong."

"It makes me remember that we still don't have a snow shovel for the walk." I sighed. "I'll have to go out and get one."

Mab made a throaty sound that might have been amusement and turned to eye me. "I suppose a kiss is a beginning, at least."

The memory of Lara's kiss made me feel queasy.

Well.

Also queasy.

"Have I told you how sexy it isn't for you to keep leaning on me like this?" I asked her.

Any amusement her expression might have held vanished. "Half the men in the world would kill you to be in your place," she snapped. "See that it is done."

"And after she turns me into some kind of dopamine zombie, who are you going to replace me with?"

She tilted her head, annoyance replaced by confusion. She frowned, silver brows beetling. "I have told you before that in my calculations, replacing you at this point would be less productive than continuing to use you. Those calculations have not changed. I have no intention of replacing you."

Now *I* got to frown. The Sidhe can do a lot of things, but they can't tell direct lies, much like lawyers and most politicians. Also like them, that rarely slowed them down from practicing deception when they deemed it necessary—but when you got straight, direct, declarative sentences, they were certain to be the truth, or at least a significant part of it.

"Then why are you shoving me at Heroin Barbie?"

Mab's face went blank and her eyes all but glowed. Mister looked up abruptly, took one look at Mab, and silently vanished behind a free-standing bank of bookshelves.

"I am not," she said very quietly, "in the habit of explaining myself to my vassals."

"Ours is not to reason why," I said.

"Precisely," Mab said, biting off the word in crisp syllables. "Be assured, my Knight, that your disobedience in this matter will cause me to take you into my bower while I search out a new candidate."

That sent a cold chill through my guts. The last Knight to visit Mab's bower had been Lloyd Slate, my predecessor. Mab had tortured him to the brink of death. Then nursed him back to health. Then tortured him again. Over and over and over. By the end of it, he'd barely been recognizable as a human being.

"Thought that kind of thing was supposed to wait for the wedding," I said.

Mab made a disgusted sound. "Our tomorrows are more severely limited than you believe. The work must be done, and before it is too late. Lara wields tremendous influence amongst the mortals. Winter must have this alliance."

"What, did you agree that I would boink her instead of signing a treaty?"

Mab smiled slowly. "I believe you recall the nature of our act of conclusion, when you pledged yourself to me."

I swallowed. I'd been through easier battles. I still had dreams about that one. Sometimes flashbacks. Mostly it was a big, terrifying erotic blur.

"You," Mab said, "are my proxy in this negotiation. You must act on it to conclude the bargain."

"You can't do it yourself?" I asked.

Which . . . was an image. One that rapidly expanded in my mind's eye to a short film. Which caught on fire and burned through before it really got anywhere.

"Obviously, or it would already be done," Mab snapped. "You are capable and have a disciplined mind. You have the power of my mantle to draw upon. Close the deal, my Knight. Or I will perforce begin afresh." She walked over to one of the bookshelves, where Lewis's Narnia books stood in a row. She idly began changing the order of them around. "Have you sated Etri's need for vengeance as yet?"

"No," I said. "I'm working on it."

"Good," she said. "I expect the matter to be closed before spring." She gave me a gimlet look. "You met Drakul."

"Looked like a big old stuffed shirt to me," I said.

"I will not fight him," Mab said.

Whoa. That took me aback. It was a second before I said, "You won't?"

She lifted an eyebrow.

"He's . . . more powerful than Winter?" I asked carefully.

"Winter," Mab corrected me frostily, "has no power over him. There would be nothing to gain and much to lose in such a confrontation." Her mouth twitched. "And there are considerations, amongst immortals. I may need him two thousand years from now. Or five thousand. You, at my most optimistic, might give me a few centuries' service. Be mindful of your importance."

I frowned. "Well. I'm probably going to fight him."

"The Winter Knight, throughout history, has engaged in many personal battles that have nothing to do with me. It is in the nature of the role." Her mouth twisted as though the words were bitter on her tongue. "It is one important way in which you are well suited to the mantle. But mark me, my Knight—you are not yet able to carry your battles to the likes of Drakul. If you do so, you court your own ending. And not a pleasant one."

"Like the one you have planned for me," I said bitterly.

"I do not casually cast away useful implements," Mab said calmly. "I take excellent care of the tools with which I work, like any craftsman. When you came to me, your home had burned to the ground, your woman had lied to you about what was most important and all but sentenced you to death by doing so, and you were in the process of leading yourself, and your apprentice, to some vague but undeniably dramatic form of self-immolation. Not only that, but the very White Council you looked to for protection had done little but use and threaten you for years on end." She gestured around her. "Now you are the master of a heavily defended castle that stands where your boarding house once did, capable of protecting you and your offspring. You are engaged to a wealthy, powerful, desirable woman who respects you enough to tell you the truth, and your former apprentice occupies a position of power, which gives her a sense of purpose and has rendered her immortal to boot." Mab looked at me and eyed me up and down. "You are in considerably better personal health and physical shape than when you came to me. And you are free of the White Council of Wizardry, fully capable of charting your own destiny without their constant manipulation and interference. I am many things, wizard, none of them kind. But I am an excellent liege. You have given me your oath and I have returned your faith in kind. Your life has improved in every way, since you swore yourself to my service. I defy you to tell me that it has not."

I opened my mouth to argue and . . .

. . . and just couldn't.

She was right. Or at least she wasn't wrong. Mab wasn't really human. She had been once. She understood some things. She remembered some things. But she didn't feel them anymore. She didn't feel loss.

She didn't miss Murphy.

"You're thinking of Ms. Murphy," Mab said quietly. "You mourn her still."

"Yes," I said.

"She was a warrior born," Mab stated. "She chose to face fear and death as a regular habit. She chose to go into battle. She died there." Her voice grew softer. "She was a woman who knew her mind. That had nothing to do with you, wizard."

"It had something to do with you," I said, even more quietly.

Mab became creepily statue-still. Her eyes glittered.

"The banner of your will," I said quietly. "You sent it out for that battle. You took fear and pain away from those who stood to fight."

"Yes, I did."

"She'd barely been able to walk," I said, my voice growing slowly, volcanically hotter. "She would have stayed somewhere safe if she hadn't been able to move. You made it possible for her to go out and fight that night. Didn't you?"

"I provided the means and opportunity for her to make a choice," Mab said without inflection. "Just as I did for hundreds of other souls who stood to the city's defense. I did nothing to coerce her choosing."

"You *knew* what she would do, given that opportunity," I spat.

"I strongly suspected," Mab said calmly. "She was who she was."

"Did you strongly suspect she would *die* in that battle?" I said. I think I was shouting. My vision was edged with red. "Did you set her up to die, Mab?"

I said her name properly. With intent. I'd heard it from her own lips, after all. A shudder rippled over her, quick but visible, a reaction that had been forced from her, by my words, by my will.

If I'd slapped her in the face, she'd have been less enraged.

Her expression did not change by any movement of muscle or skin, by any reposition of the features of her face. It simply grew bleak, bleak as a pitiless arctic chill settling over stone. There was a crackling sound as frost spread out from her feet in a rapidly accelerating circle. It began climbing the bookshelves and covered the windows, darkening the room. My breath began to plume in front of my mouth in the freezing air.

"A great many mortals died that night," Mab said quietly. "A great many of them gave their lives to limit the civilian casualties, as you well know and remember. All of them took up the defense of this city with my support. All those who died, died in part because I had supported them." She leaned forward, her eyes cold and bright. "Exactly as *you* did, wizard. How many did you lead to their deaths? Do you lie to yourself, tell yourself that none of them had lives, had families, had those who loved them who will miss and mourn them? Just as you mourn her?"

I stared at her, my rage scorching the inside of my belly—while my heart suddenly went cold.

Mab lifted her chin.

The chill in the air eased slightly.

"I did what I did because Ethniu had to be defeated," she said. "Your life was expendable. Ms. Murphy's life was expendable. All the lives of those who fought were expendable. They—you—were expendable because the chaos that would be caused by Ethniu's victory would have drowned all the world in demons and blood. I make such choices because no one else is cold enough and no one else is hard enough. It is only your arrogance and pride that make you believe I would have had the time or attention to spare a thought for you or for Ms. Murphy or for something as fleeting and ephemeral as your emotions when doing so." She inhaled slowly. "What is the phrase? 'Get over yourself.' It was war. She died. You survived. That is the whole of it."

Mab's eyes grew heavy-lidded. She stared at me for a long moment.

I broke the gaze first, looking away from her. I was shaking. I think I was crying.

"The first time one raises the banner of her will," Mab said, speaking very slowly, "it is an unsettling experience. Feeling so much pain. So much death. Being with them in the moment of their passing." She closed her eyes briefly and took a breath. "It pleases me that I was not there with you, my Knight, for your death. But I was there for hers. Felt her fear. Her frustration. Felt how desperately she wanted to tell you what was in her heart. She had the courage to face gods and monsters. But not what was in her own breast."

"She loved me," I whispered.

"Perhaps," Mab agreed. "I was not privy to that part of her. But it would be consistent." She inhaled slowly, and when she spoke again it was in a voice of absolute authority. "We will regard your . . . outburst, with Our name, as an unfortunate aftereffect of your use of a banner of will, and given that it is your period of mourning, and that We were in privy council with you, We will overlook this disrespect." She turned toward the window and said, "If it happens again, wizard, your suffering will be drawn from the darkest caverns of Our imagination, and We will consult with Mother on ways to make it worse."

I felt myself start shaking.

Mab wasn't looking at me, but her cheek rounded, and I could picture the cold smile on her face. Then a frozen gale wind and a blast of snow threw open the nearest window, and Mab was gone.

I stood there in the cold for a while, breathing, shuddering, just feeling the fires cool inside me.

Then I went to find Will to have him get some people into the library with towels.

Frost all over the books. That hadn't been called for.

Chapter
Twenty-Four

The lawyers had decided that Oz Park was, by its very nature, wizard territory. Or at least, that it favored me. So, I had to arrive first for my next date with Lara, on the last of November. I guess negotiations had gotten tense and there had been shouting and thrown documents, food, and beverages.

Things were tough all over.

Or maybe I'd touched on Mab's last remaining nerve ending, and it had been passed down to her people. She mostly used changeling attorneys, half bloods, usually of the Sidhe. They made excellent litigators and negotiators and could navigate tense situations and delicately phrased legal paragraphs with Grishamesque aplomb. But when the Queen of Winter was on edge, so was the rest of the Court. That's just how those things worked out.

I had spent the night pacing my room and muttering out loud to no one.

That was one of the things that told me I was still hurt. That I wasn't healed. I couldn't just sit. I had to get up and move sometimes. I had to pace. And it hurt so much, in my belly and chest and head, that I had to talk to someone. Even if there wasn't anyone there. Just hearing a voice, even if it was mine, even if I was carrying both sides of the conversation, eased something inside.

I kept waiting for that kind of thing to ease up.

To go away.

I just wanted it to stop. Hurting.

"I just need time," I assured myself.

I just needed time.

It was a cold day, with five inches of snow everywhere, after the Witch had arrived. Big wet flakes were coming down. There was a freezing wind off the lake. Tonight, icicles would start forming as the warmth of the day bled out into the night. I was wearing jeans and sneakers and a light jacket. Cold and snow and ice were becoming second nature to me. They gave my brain something to track other than what real pain felt like.

I settled down on my heels at the base of the statue of the Scarecrow, closed my eyes, and waited. Lara made no sound when she approached, but I could . . . feel her coming, through the snow. Just the faintest quiver, or shiver, in the proper time to match slow steps. My nostrils flared, and I caught the faintest hint of expensive perfume, a mix of several scents.

"Nice day for a walk in the park," I said in greeting.

Lara stopped in the snow. She'd been attempting to approach in stealth. "The Scarecrow, eh?"

"I think I can make good arguments for having a certain amount of courage. And a heart." I sighed. "If I only had a brain."

She let out a rueful laugh. "I think we all know that feeling."

"Either that or we're about to," I agreed. I opened my eyes. She stood twenty feet away from me, on the snow over the sidewalk that hadn't been shoveled yet. The trees behind her were thick but almost denuded of leaves. Between them and the steady blur of the snowfall, she seemed the only thing tangible and real in the scene. There was even enough snow to hide the city skyline beyond the park.

It felt like we were alone together. Things had been tough enough in town that people weren't going for casual walks in half a foot of snow. This part of the city was in pretty good shape, and I had seen lights in most of the buildings when I had walked in. Lara's footprints, and mine, were the only ones visible.

Lara wore jeans, a quilted leather coat, and a knitted cap. Her hair had been braided back into a neat tail. Her eyes were sapphire blue, and that and the faint pink shade to her cheeks and nose were the only colors in the grey surroundings.

"It would be very easy," I heard myself say, "to think a lot more about how attractive you are, and a lot less about how dangerous you are."

Lara blinked at that, and her eyebrows went up. She looked thoughtful for a moment and then said, "That may be one of the more flattering things anyone has said to me in at least twenty years."

"I owe you an apology. For my behavior at Halloween. I haven't always done well in situations like that one and . . . The bravado is how I try to compensate. You were well within your rights to be upset. I'll try not to let it happen again."

A little burst of a snicker exploded from her lips as she smiled with one side of her mouth. "Don't make promises you can't keep, Harry," she advised me. "If some terrifying creature shows up in the future and flirts with your fiancée while simultaneously offering to hand you your head, I expect you'll react in exactly the same way."

"Yeah, probably," I said. "But I'll *try*."

She considered that for a moment and then nodded. "That's worth something, isn't it."

"I suppose there's only one way to be sure," I said. "But . . . I'm not really a party person. So that's something you know about me."

She came closer, though without making eye contact, and settled down beside me, in the same posture, both of us facing out in the same direction. "I had been concerned that it was me."

"Being an ass? No, that was me, I promise. You were an excellent host."

She shook her head. "Not that. That your behavior was a reaction to being near me. In my territory. That you were . . . I don't know. Resentful. Frightened." She pursed her lips. "It took me time to realize it, but that was what my father's resentment was about. He was frightened of me. From the beginning. It was what drove several of his more . . . unsavory behaviors."

"How can a sweet Midwestern girl like you resist a man who reminds you of Dad?" I said drily.

I saw her smile in my peripheral vision. "We all face that kind of thing, don't we? Old defense mechanisms that we developed for very good reasons come up at the damnedest times." She turned to face me, her expression serious. "I owe you an apology as well."

I glanced at her and waited.

"The kiss," she said. She looked . . . almost flustered. "Dammit," she muttered, "I have *never* apologized for anything like that before and . . ." She closed her eyes for a moment and I got the impression that she was consulting mental notes. "Part of that was about my past. And a lot of it was about being . . . well. Somewhat intimidated. Partly I did it because your behavior had angered and embarrassed me." She exhaled. "But I should not have done that without talking to you about it first. I'm sorry I did. I should have used my words. And I hope I didn't hurt you."

I studied her face. Lara was a world-class actress and operator. She was a manipulator like few others who walked the earth. She could have been offering me a double dozen artful expressions, all delicately blended together. But she wasn't. She just regarded me and looked . . .

Damn. She looked tired.

"Are you okay?" I asked her.

"No," she said frankly. "My people were on Justine's trail, but something happened to the team. They haven't called in. Riley will let me know what happened in a few hours, when he gets to St. Petersburg. Skavis and Malvora are plotting again. I suspect Father is communicating with them somehow. Which makes him a fool, to move against me. It isn't as if they'd respect him enough to leave him alive after they seize power. And if he's found ways to communicate with them, it's possible he's working with others as well, to undermine me."

"Should I be worried?" I asked.

She frowned a bit and glanced at me.

"Coming after me is coming after you, isn't it?" I asked.

She considered it, exhaling slowly. "I suppose it might be. I hadn't considered that." She shook her head. "I'm not thinking clearly. I haven't slept well in . . . a while now."

Her voice sounded unusually flat. Not like she was doing funny voices or anything, but it lacked its usual vibrance. Physically, she was doing the same thing—slouching. I had always had the impression that no matter how hard you tried, you wouldn't be able to catch Lara in an awkward or unappealing photograph, but today . . .

"You're not wearing any makeup," I noted.

She spread her gloved hands. "At the party, I showed you the part of me that . . . has done some terrible things, in her day. That's one portion of who I am, and I assume it always will be." She focused on me more intensely, her eyes having stolen all the celestial blue from the landscape. "But that's not all I am. For a very long time, I have been working to rise above the . . . the base nature of my heritage. I want you to know that it is a road I will be following."

I stared at her in total silence for a minute.

"That's a big statement," I said.

"It is."

"I hope you realize how big."

"I do."

"It is, of course," I said, "exactly what you should say to get me to like you and lower my guard."

Her teeth showed. "That's the problem with making fools of people," she said. "After a while, they come to expect it even when you're sincere."

"Can you blame me?"

"Not really." She sighed. "There's only one way for you to know for certain. And that will take time."

"I suppose we both have some of that on hand," I said.

"I liked it," Lara said. The words weren't exactly hurried, or stammered, or rushed. Or they wouldn't have been, from anyone else.

"Liked what?" I asked in a neutral tone.

"Kissing you," she said, staring firmly into the distance. "The way you . . . you taste, I suppose."

"You got one bite and haven't slept well since," I said. "Am I right?"

Her mouth firmed into a line. "You aren't entirely wrong."

"Well," I said. I cleared my throat. "I liked it, too. Or at least, a lot better than when we thought we were both going to be blown to kingdom come or torn into little pieces by ur-ghouls."

"My God, you silver-tongued devil," she said levelly.

I felt myself smile.

She noticed. Her own mouth softened, and the corners of her eyes crinkled.

"I have a proposition," I said.

"Really?" she asked. "At the feet of the Scarecrow, of all places?"

"Not that, your pink bits would freeze," I said, feigning annoyance. "This is more . . . an educational opportunity."

"Educational? You can't talk to a woman like that in current year."

Now I felt like there was context I wasn't getting, but I ignored it. "I'm serious. We've done a few little trades. Maybe it's time for a bigger one."

"Interesting," Lara said. "What do you have in mind?"

"I need to know about the White Court," I said. "Where you come from. How it works. What happens when a Hunger gets successfully cut off. Exactly the kind of process Thomas is going through. I need to know everything."

Lara's eyebrows couldn't levitate off the top of her skull, but they tried. "Surely you aren't serious."

"I'm always serious," I deadpanned. "And stop calling me Shirley."

She idly picked up a handful of snow in her glove. "You realize what you're asking me, yes?"

"Me, a wizard, the walking, talking personification of 'knowledge is power,' is asking you to give me power, possibly over you and your whole Court," I said. "And only a few years after I wiped out the Red Court. Every single one of them."

"Well put," Lara said. "Why should I take that kind of chance?"

"Because I won't share what I learn with anyone else. I will only use it to help Thomas. I swear it by my power."

Lara's head rocked back a little as I spoke the quiet oath.

"Okay," she said a moment later, her expression pensive. "What's my cut?"

"This is your cut," I said. "You talk to me, I use it to help me figure out a course of action, then I save Thomas's life. That's what you get."

"What does it cost me?" she asked. "Other than the potential enslavement or destruction of the White Court?"

"I need Etri off my back," I said quietly. "I need your help talking him down."

She replaced the snow from where she'd taken it and began trying fruitlessly to smooth out signs that she had. "That's a tall order. The svartalves may look all Roswell, but they learned their fighting in the fjords. They play by an older set of rules."

"New, old, they're all made to be broken," I said. "I need your help figuring out a way to convince Etri to do it. Otherwise, there's no point in saving Thomas from his Hunger. He'd still have to stay hidden on the island."

"Please tell me what I'm missing here," Lara murmured. "It sounds like I'm going to be doing you favors on both sides of this deal."

"You get Thomas back," I said. "And you smooth over a situation with Etri before it becomes a headache for you, too."

"That's me getting two things that you also want," she said, amused.

"Isn't it great when a deal profits everyone involved?" I asked rhetorically. "Look, I had to get involved in removing a curse and . . . long story short, I liked the work. I'm still not at my best. But things are starting to function again, and by God it felt good to be useful. I want more of that. I want to help Thomas. But I can't do it alone."

"Next time lead with that one," Lara suggested. "It sounds much better than where you try to get me to whitewash your fence for you." She glanced at me, and her smile faded a little. "You're asking for a lot of trust."

"And you're not, Miss Smoochie Face?" I demanded.

"Touché," she acknowledged.

"Which is my point," I said, more earnestly. "I can't say I'm thrilled with the idea of Mab ordering me to marry anybody, but maybe it would be smart to find out if we can work together now, rather than finding out we can't when it's all too late to change."

"If I was really playing you," Lara said, "I'd agree to this right now. Just to get things moving in the direction I want."

"Yeah, you would," I said, and stood up.

I offered her my hand.

She blinked at me for a second. Then she reached up, a little tentatively, took my hand, and came to her feet with my help.

"Let me think this over," she said. "Might take a few days."

"I'd have respected you a little less if it didn't," I answered.

Chapter

Twenty-Five

While I was waiting for Lara to decide, December came to see us, and with it came the old man.

He was built like a bulldog, stocky and strong, wearing overalls and a heavy flannel insulated jacket against the cold. He was about five six, his hair was white, cut in a short buzz that was awfully thin on top, and I knew his forearms still looked ropy and well-muscled despite his age. He was near or over three hundred years old, he was the official clandestine killer of the White Council of Wizardry, and he was my grandfather.

We hadn't really spoken since the battle. Since just after he'd shown me he was willing to kill me.

When the Knights of the Bean showed him into the great hall, I felt Bear tighten up as if a rabid, starving saber-toothed tiger had come to visit. No, check that. She wouldn't have gotten nervous about the saber-tooth.

My grandfather was the sort of man who could pull objects out of space down onto the heads of his enemies. And who had done so. There'd never been a natural predator as dangerous as Ebenezar McCoy.

"Bear," he said, first thing, with a wary smile touching his grave expression. "What the hell are you doing here?"

"Working," Bear replied. "Standard contract."

"Huh," Ebenezar said. "One-Eye let you into the field? Last time that happened there was a world war, as I recall."

"I don't plan them," Bear said. "I just show up for them."

"Does seem to be going that direction." Ebenezar sighed. "Only question is if the mortals are following us or if we're following them."

"I don't get paid for the big questions," Bear said. "Just for keeping hearts beating."

Ebenezar looked from her to me and back again. "I feel better knowing you're on the job," he said. "Obliged to you."

"Thank Lara Raith," Bear said. "She's paying my contract."

"That'll be the day," Ebenezar snorted. "Hoss."

"Sir," I said. "This gonna be a walk and talk?"

"If you don't mind," he said.

"Sure," I said laconically. "Bear, Wizard McCoy and I are going for a walk. Mind the store while I'm gone."

"The city isn't safe," Bear cautioned us. "Especially after dark."

I picked up my wizard's staff from its resting place beside the door. "We'll manage. Don't follow us."

"I won't," she lied.

Bear took her job seriously. She'd be somewhere out of sight behind us. I felt vaguely like a child whose mother was too determined to protect him to give him any freedom. "Bear," I said reproachfully.

She looked back guilelessly.

"This is personal," Ebenezar told her firmly. "I need you to be discreet."

"I will," she promised.

He nodded acceptance and then the old man and I did something we hadn't for a good long while.

We went out for a walk.

We went out of the castle, turned left, and walked down the sidewalks. Some of them were still covered in snow—places where people weren't living at the moment, I supposed. I wondered if the city would ticket them. All things considered, a little snow on the sidewalk seemed like the kind of thing no one would think was important. On the other hand, it might be something over which the city felt it could actually exercise some feeble amount of control, in the face of everything that had happened.

The neighborhoods were quiet, lights of some kind burning in many homes. The old man and I made very little noise as we walked.

I waited for him to speak. I wasn't the one who had acted shamefully.

It took him a quarter of an hour to find words.

"There's history you don't know," he said quietly.

"Hngh," I said, wittily.

"Your mother. And Raith." He spat into the snow after he said the word. "I tried to get her away from him. She wouldn't hear it. She was already . . ."

"Addicted?" I suggested.

He shrugged a shoulder. "Your mother liked to live dangerously. Lord Raith gave her plenty of that."

"Maybe she liked him."

"Maybe it would be hard to tell," he said after several steps. "Even for her. Sometimes you just find your poison. The one that goes right past your reason. Your logic. Your morals. I've seen it plenty, over the years. Sex. Opium. Heroin. Alcohol."

"This is a world that hurts," I said. "Sometimes you get tired of that. You'll take whatever you can get to get away from it for a while."

Ebenezar bowed his head and nodded. "That's true enough. God knows."

"You think my mom found her poison in Lord Raith," I said.

"Yes," he said. "And I'm afraid for you."

I held up a hand and said, "You don't get to talk to me about the future. Not until we've gone over the past."

The old man squinted against the night. It was cold, cold enough that I knew he'd have been settled in his chair by the fire with a book and a mug of hot chocolate if we'd been back at his cabin in Hog Hollow. I barely felt the cold. And when I did, it was pleasant.

"You killed me," I said quietly.

"Not exactly," the old man said. "You were already a step ahead."

"Yeah," I said. "But you didn't know that at the time."

He grimaced. "You're right," he said. "You've gotten stronger and better a lot faster than anyone expected. Even me. I have contingency defenses I never thought you'd push me hard enough to activate. I've been dealing with cornerhounds for several years now. They like to come when I'm asleep. I need reflex-level spells to even the field."

I grunted. "You're saying that the spell that would have killed me was a compliment."

He shrugged a shoulder. "I wouldn't expect to need it for anything but a war-level threat," he admitted. "You fought that duel better than I would have thought possible."

"I'm all grown up, I suppose," I said.

"You're getting there." The old man sighed. "Damn the Merlin."

I frowned. "Why do you say that?"

"For kicking you off the Council," he said irritably. "For leaving you vulnerable to creatures like Mab. Like Lara Raith."

I caught a whiff of lie by omission. He wasn't saying everything.

"Why did you do it?" I asked. "Why'd you come at me like that?"

"I was trying to stop you from throwing everything away for a god-damned vampire," he said. "And . . . some things came back up for me. Ugly things. I don't know if I can explain it to you."

I thought about what I had felt fighting ghouls.

"You don't need to," I said. "You hate the White Court that much?"

"I've had three wives, over the centuries," Ebenezar said. "Three dozen apprentices. A hundred friends." He winced, and his voice creaked. "But just the one child."

I thought of Maggie. I thought of what I would do to protect her. What I *had* done.

I thought of what I would have become if I'd failed.

"She was an adult," I said. "Making her own choices."

"Maybe," he said. "Maybe she wasn't in charge of all of her choices by the time Raith got to her. It's not like there's a test to run."

I thought about what it would feel like, not to know. Never to know. Never to know if he'd failed her, if she'd needed his help, or if he'd been betraying her, ignoring her, disbelieving her.

That would have been one hell of a heavy burden.

"So," I asked him, "if you hated Raith so much, why is he still alive?"

"Because I found out what she did to him before the end," he said list-lessly. "Because I wanted him to die slow. Humiliated. Because I wanted him to suffer. Because he had favors he used to buy off the Council's wrath."

I grunted.

"Why not ask him?" I said.

The old man stopped in his tracks.

"What?"

"Lara doesn't exactly feel overwhelming loyalty to her paterfamilias," I said. "Maybe we get him in a room and ask him. A room with good drains."

He closed his eyes. "I . . . I never spoke to him. I knew that if I stood in front of him, one stray thought and . . ." He flexed his hands into fists and relaxed them again slowly.

I thought about Rudolph.

I thought about him standing in front of me. About what I might do. Had already tried to do.

I clenched my hands into slow fists, too.

"Hoss," Ebenezar said. "All this is . . . Look. I'm sorry. I was trying to stop you from making a mistake and you told me he sired a *child* on her and I . . . things broke loose." He turned to face me. "I lost control. And if you hadn't been one hell of a wizard, I'd have gotten you killed because of it. I'm sorry. It will never happen again."

I faced him squarely and said, "It might."

He tilted his head.

"Thomas is my brother," I said. "My friend. I know you hate the idea of him. But if you raise your hand against him, I swear to God Almighty and by my own power that I will break it off at the wrist. Sir."

He studied my face carefully and then nodded. "I hear you." His jaw clenched a few times and he said, "I got out of line at Etri's place, too. I worry. For Maggie. You lose a child, it . . . it does bad things to you. Maybe my judgment is compromised in that arena."

I was quiet for a long moment.

That had cost him something to say.

I put my hand on his arm and said, "Hell. Maybe you're right, sir. Sometimes I feel like I'm just staying six inches ahead of an avalanche. Guess time will tell."

"Always does," he agreed. His voice was tight. "It always does, Hoss."

"But she's my girl," I said quietly. "And I'll make the calls. Not you. Not anyone else, either."

"That's as it should be," he said. "I'm just . . . accustomed to meddling."

"Well," I said, more lightly. "If you do it again, I'll just have to beat you in another duel."

"Is that what you think happened?"

"Someone once taught me," I said slowly, "that winning a fight and surviving a fight were the same thing."

He snorted. "Suppose I did," he said. He stared out at the night for a moment. "My God, grandson. When you went down, and I thought I'd . . ." He swallowed. Then he looked up at me. "Are we okay?"

"I'm not okay," I said firmly. "I'm more not okay than I've ever been. But you and I. We will be. I'm working on it."

"Ms. Murphy," he said quietly.

It was my turn to fall silent.

"Oh, Hoss," Ebenezar said. "I'm sorry. I know how it feels."

I believed him. I tightened my hand on his arm and bowed my head.

"You're going to be all right," he told me, his rough voice firm. "It takes time. But you'll heal. You'll sleep right again. Food will taste right again."

I huffed out a little laugh.

He did know how it felt.

Standing there in the cold and the darkness, I felt my grandfather stand before me and understand me. As I had begun to understand him.

I could feel the bridge being built between us by that understanding. I could feel something easing out of my shoulders and my belly.

"She was pretty great, wasn't she?" I said quietly.

"Brave as hell," he agreed.

The candlelight in the nearest house blurred.

"I miss her," I said. "So much."

"Oh boy," he said, his voice compassionate.

And at some point, he had his arms around me and I had bent over to hug him back. The damned stubborn old fool.

"Christmas morning," I said. "I need you. Maggie needs you."

"I'll be there," he said. His arms tightened. "I should have been there. So many times."

I'd spent a lot of Christmas mornings alone, after my dad had died.

"You were trying to protect me," I said quietly. "Keep me at a distance from your enemies. I get that."

Get it?

I was doing it.

Oh, I could excuse myself, since the Carpenters had her and were superlative parents whose children had all thrived, in one way or another, and were good friends who would treat her with kindness and patience and love.

But they weren't Maggie's father.

I was.

I had talked pretty big to Blackstaff McCoy about that very subject.

Maybe it was time to start living like it was the truth. Now. Not tomorrow, not at the new semester.

Right now.

I looked up at him and said, "Come with me."

"Where?" he asked.

"The Carpenters' place," I said. "We're going to go get Maggie and move her in."

He peered up at me in the glow of fallen snow and distant light.

"I think you're wrong. But if you've made your call, Hoss," he said, "I'll back your play."

"Thank you, sir," I said gravely.

Chapter
Twenty-Six

December went by in a hectic, happy blur.

There was one more room on the other side of Bear's that had been being used for random storage. We cleaned it out and set it up for Maggie, and I got to spend the next few weeks spending time with my little girl.

Maggie was fascinated with Fitz and his wizard lessons, and she and Mouse would come and watch whenever he and I were working together, which was early morning, morning, and afternoon every day. She found weight lifting and combat lessons mildly interesting, meditation and mental discipline mostly boring, and his practical evocation lessons terribly exciting. But then, something often blew up or got set on fire, so it wasn't like I could say any different.

"You should use 'pew pew pew' for your magic words for those little fireballs," Maggie told Fitz one day after he had done a credible job of mangling the target dummy with slow, careful concentration.

"Hah," he said.

"Hmph," I said.

"Why not?" Maggie asked. "You said the words weren't important as long as they didn't have"—she scrunched up her nose—"intrisic, instinctive meaning."

"Intrinsic," I corrected her, sounding out the word carefully. "It means something is pretty much baked into the cake along with something else so they can't be separated."

"That," she said. "'Pew pew pew' should work."

"It should," Fitz mused, wiping sweat from his brow. He peered at me. "Right?"

"You have your reputation to think of," I told him. "I mean, you can't just go around saying 'pew pew pew' or 'bang' or 'zing.'"

Fitz began to chuckle. "Why not?"

"You're a wizard, man," I told him. "In tune with the primordial forces of the universe. Wielding the leftover energy from Creation itself. Have a little gravitas."

Maggie pointed dual finger guns at the still-smoldering target dummy and said, "Pew pew pew!"

Fitz, tired but merry enough, laughed harder. "Pew pew pew. I mean, yeah, it would work."

"Don't do it," I said. "Look, I have my own issues using badly done Latin, and I got a little bit lucky that my bad Latin is so far off of proper speech. Council meetings are still done in Latin, and I have to speak it sometimes. If I could go back, I'd pick Tuareg or something."

"Why don't you just do it now?" Fitz asked, scrunching up his nose.

"Doesn't work like that," I said. "The neural pathways we're building to run energy through are incredibly specific. If I started switching my words around now, I'd set myself back years and years. Have to learn everything from the ground floor, like you're doing. I mean, I'd probably do it a little faster than you, but not much. This is foundation-level stuff we're dealing with."

"But I could," Fitz mused. "I'm still building up. I could pick 'pew pew pew' or 'kazinga' if I wanted to."

I sighed. "You could. And I wouldn't stop you. But a little piece of my soul would die of shame every time someone heard you."

Mouse chuffed happily and came over to lean against my legs while Fitz laughed at me.

Maggie picked up a tennis ball she had been bouncing for Mouse, tossed it, and bounced it off the target dummy's scorched head. "Kazinga!"

Mouse charged the ball and pounced on it.

*   *   *

Christmas Eve was something special.

We showed up at the Carpenters' place around sundown. I was visited by several different kinds of spirits. Santa came by. Maggie got some great presents. So did I.

Ebenezar appeared at the front door on Christmas morning. Michael welcomed him in. Almost the entire Carpenter clan had made it in, including Daniel's wife, a tiny brunette named Camille who had a baby girl in her arms and another one toddling precariously about, mostly in an attempt to seize Mouse by the tail. Maggie absolutely adored the fact that she was no longer the smallest child in the household and promptly appointed herself the toddler girl's protector, which inevitably brought Michael's youngest son along for the ride: Little Harry and Maggie were still thick as thieves.

They made an odd pairing. Little Harry wasn't quite two years older than Maggie, but at their age, those months were consequential. Maggie was bottom percentile for both height and weight for girls her age. Little Harry had begun to grow, and he was taking after his father and older brothers. His voice honked between boyish tenor and adult baritone at random, especially when he was laughing, which was frequently. He towered over Maggie, though she showed no awareness whatsoever of the difference in their physical sizes.

Murphy would have been proud.

Our two families opened presents together, though most of the gifts were basic products that were still hard to come by in the beleaguered city. Food was consumed. There was a lot of laughter, and a round of traditional Christmas songs. Maggie soaked it all up. My grandfather gave her a red stocking cap he'd knitted himself, and I felt the simple thermal enchantment on it that would keep her comfortably warm in all but the most bitter gales, at least for the first couple of winters. She promptly put it on and then put the red-and-blue scarf I'd crocheted for her with it, and she and young Harry went out to test her new bike on the clean-shoveled driveway in front of Michael's house.

Michael, Ebenezar, and I wound up on the porch, sipping hot cider and watching the children play.

"That's the downside of all this modern infrastructure," Ebenezar was saying. "Maintaining it under normal wear and tear is work enough. Rebuilding after something like last summer . . ." He shook his head. "So many people in so little space."

"It could be a lot worse," Michael said firmly. "The major roads in have been reopened now, and something like a street system is actually functioning. Supplies are getting easier to get hold of. More and more of the water supply is coming back online. My company is working three different sites right now, and we're accelerating. By next summer, we'll be something like the old city again."

"How long until I get those changes I asked for?" I asked.

"Spring," Michael said. "That's the best I can do."

"That should work," I said. "My last check cleared, yeah?"

"It did," he said. "We're good."

Ebenezar lowered his mug. His eyes drifted down the street toward the house where Molly kept an Unseelie action team ready to go in case her family was attacked by purely mundane means. "How are you paying your bills in that place, Hoss?"

"Ill-gotten gains," I said without hesitation. "I should have enough to last until next fall at least."

He looked at me from beneath shaggy grey brows. "Then what?"

"I'm not sure yet," I admitted.

"What kind of investments are you secured in?" he asked.

Which is what he would ask, of course. Wizards live a long time. Not every wizard understands every kind of arcane theory, but they are, every last one of them, versed in the magic of compound interest.

"Ill-gotten gains," I said. "I never had much chance to start a portfolio."

"Mmmph," Ebenezar said, frowning.

Michael glanced at my face and said, "Wizard McCoy, I have to confess, I was mostly stuck at home during the battle. Do you mind if I ask you some questions about it?"

"I'd be honored, Sir Michael," Ebenezar said.

Michael engaged the old man on a review of the battle. The two of them settled down over a small table marked with a chessboard, taking out a number of small objects from pockets or nearby and using them to represent various positions and threats. Michael asked cogent and knowledgeable questions.

I drifted down the porch a way.

I didn't want to hear about the battle.

Molly appeared at my side a few minutes later, smiled warmly at the two men speaking intently over the chessboard, and said, "Hey, Harry."

"Molls. What's Christmas like for the Winter Lady?"

Her eyes sparkled. She was in her human glamour this morning. She looked age-appropriate and weight-appropriate—presumably the way she would have looked if she hadn't gotten dragged into the affairs of wizards and faerie queens. Blond hair, blue eyes, cheeks that were rounded and pink with the winter morning cold. She looked like a kindergarten teacher.

"Oh, I'll visit vassals and bring gifts and word from Mab tonight," she said. "Plus, I sent the troops home to visit their families. Seems like the least I could do."

Part of the Winter Lady's duties was stealing away the children of her vassals to serve in Winter's forces. They'd been building ever since she'd gotten on the job.

"Seems right," I said. "But how are you?"

She looked at me searchingly for a moment, then frowned at the children. Maggie drove her new bike in a wobbly line that ended at a small snowbank and sent her rolling to the snow amid much giggling.

"In a lot of ways, it's like being the big sister to a whole lot of jawas," she said. "It . . . surprised me, how comfortable it felt. Taking charge of that many fae." She shook her head. "The Leanansidhe was getting me ready for this role for a reason." The little chill in the pit of my stomach was echoed in the faint frown around her eyes. "I'm good at this work, Harry. I solve rivalries. Resolve disputes. Help fix problems. I'm everyone's big sister. And they look up to me."

"They give you any trouble?" I asked. The Winter Court could hardly interact with me without making at least a perfunctory effort to eat or kill me. I constantly had to remind them why that was unwise.

"Not after Unalaska," she muttered.

"What?"

She shook her head. "It isn't important. They found out early that I'm not to be trifled with. I haven't had to do much more than drop Mab's name occasionally."

Her expression was remote but unhappy for a moment. Then she saw me looking, smiled, and it was gone. "You look like you've stopped losing weight."

"Yeah," I said. "If I can figure out how to get more sleep, I should be fine."

"Best I can do is thirty-year stretches," she said. "And you might have things to do before that spell came undone."

"Yeah, I don't need to be Van Winkled." Little Harry helped Maggie onto the bike again and tried to talk up her confidence as he helped her get it going once more. I suspected Maggie was throwing it a little. She was an uncommonly well-coordinated child. I think she was indulging young Harry's genuine enjoyment in teaching and supporting her.

She was a hell of a kid.

"Have you decided yet?" Molly asked quietly.

"Decided what?"

"If you want to live or not," she said quietly, bluntly.

I nodded toward Maggie. "She needs me."

She snorted. "Does that dodge work with everyone else? Especially now that she's living with you?"

"Most people get a really nervous look when they get anywhere close to asking me something like that," I said, "and they think better of it."

She bumped my thigh with her hip. "Yeah. But I'm not afraid of you."

I exhaled slowly.

She wasn't.

"Harry," she said. "Do you want to live?"

"I'm trying to remember how," I said quietly. "I'm still in that space where . . . I don't know. I don't think much past the next meal."

"I'm aware," she said wryly. "Especially when you're in close proximity, but anytime I think about you. It's like I get this update about you, from Winter. I get flashes of what you feel like."

I frowned. "Not sure I like that."

"I don't, either," she said. "But if I know, it's a safe bet that Mab knows, too."

That made me feel distinctly uncomfortable. Mab tended to manipulate me with all the subtlety of a swinging axe. But if she had that kind of intimate emotional knowledge of me, she might be operating on more subtle levels, too. Maybe her arm-twisting was mostly a smoke screen for her working me more discreetly.

That I hadn't considered the possibility until now scared me a little. If true, it put me several . . . well, years behind her in my thinking.

"Thanks for the warning," I said quietly.

She nodded. "Sure."

"I feel like it's my fault," I said quietly.

I wasn't talking about Maggie, or the Winter Queen.

Molly's bright eyes studied my profile. "It wasn't you. You were in the midst of war," she said softly. "And Rudolph was supposed to be one of the people you were protecting."

A flash of pure hatred went through me at the name.

Molly saw it.

"You haven't taken vengeance," she said.

"Wouldn't bring her back."

"It might let you move forward," she noted.

"Into becoming what?" I asked. I shook my head. "He left town. That's enough for me. It's got to be."

"You're lying," she said softly.

I mean. I was. I wanted to tear his arms off. I wanted to shove his face into the earth of Murphy's grave and keep pushing until he ran out of air. I wanted to kill him.

But Rudolph wasn't a monster. He was something less than that, and worse: A fool. An idiot. A coward.

I exhaled slowly.

And my pain was not unique. Was not special.

"You haven't let her go," Molly said gently. She was silent for a moment, then seemed to make a decision and took a breath. "I know what that feels like. I've done that. With someone I loved."

I looked down. I couldn't have met her gaze.

"I got very lucky," she said. "He came back. But if he hadn't, I'd have . . . become something I very much would not want to be."

I could feel what she was talking about.

Deep down, there was a part of me that wanted to say *screw it*. That being a decent person was too painful, too harsh, too self-destructive. A part of me that wanted to take my power and use it to start crushing my enemies. Or anyone else who wanted to hold me back. Including me. Especially me.

I closed my eyes.

I said the same thing I said to that part of me every time it stirred: *Not today*.

"There he is," Molly said very quietly, as if she could sense the direction of my thoughts. "Part of what you're feeling is the Winter mantle," she said. "Pure, primal rage. Someone took your mate. The mantle wants them dealt with appropriately. It's adding pressure."

"Fun," I said.

"Mab wants me to tell you to go kill Rudolph. You'll feel better, she says."

"Hah."

Molly swallowed. "She says to tell you the Wild Hunt is at your disposal. That she will lend you her steed."

I paused.

I thought of the howling supernatural tempest that was the Wild Hunt. The pure, primal joy of the hounds' calls. The thunder of hooves. The cries of the riders. And I could let the mantle have me. Be a creature of rage and instinct and fury. Remove that little weasel from the planet. I could ride on Mab's black nightmare unicorn and crush Rudolph's legs beneath its great hooves. Then the Hunt could circle him.

What happened to Rudolph after that would require thirty people to clean up.

"Not today," I said in a quiet, rough voice.

Molly nodded. She put her hand over mine for a moment.

"I know how you feel," she said with gentle emphasis. "I feel it, too. I want him torn apart. But I also want you to be whole. And even more than that, I want you to be Harry."

I stared out at the children playing and began methodically shoving down the vicious, violent feelings trying to claw their way clear of my chest.

Not today. God, not today.

"Yeah," I said. "I want that, too."

But I wasn't sure which I was talking about.

Chapter

Twenty-Seven

It took considerable effort to get the roof to myself at oh God thirty in the morning, but I managed it. Took me two sound-muffling spells and some extreme caution to slip past the sleeping Valkyrie, but the secure communication I had arranged between myself and Lara—notes carried by tiny fae—had specified that she wouldn't show up if anyone else, at all, was present.

So I wound up on the roof of the castle at two o'clock in the morning of New Year's Eve, waiting in stillness and silence. I just sort of sank into the cold of the clear, dangerously chill night and waited. The Winter mantle understood stillness and patience, like all predators. It was pleased to pass the time in quiet.

I waited and soaked up the cold.

There was a whisper in the air, and then Lara, dressed in a long white coat, glided up over the ramparts of the castle at the rear of the building, where she wouldn't be seen by the guards at the front gate. She landed as weightlessly as a bird on one of the merlons, dropping down to a feline crouch with the ease and power of a gymnast. Her eyes were silver-grey in the night, catching light and reflecting it weirdly, even when her face was in shadow.

Lara stared at me with those intent, inhuman glittering eyes for a long moment.

Two predators, facing off.

If Lara wanted to try something underhanded with me—say, seducing me into becoming her devoted sex doll—this would be a prime opportunity for her to do it.

"Welcome," I said to her in a very quiet voice.

Lara inclined her head and prowled down to the roof. I emerged from the patch of shadows I'd been occupying and crossed to the spot where I'd considered pitching Ilyana to the street below. Lara mirrored me, her body and motions tense.

"I've thought about it," she said. "Your . . . offer."

"To be fair," I said, "I more or less demanded it."

The nearly full moon was clear overhead. The silver light bounced off of plenty of snow, making the city glow with that weird frozen illumination of a quiet winter night. It made light spots nearly bright enough to read in, and the shadows darker than Morticia Addams's lingerie drawer.

"You did," she said firmly. "I'm willing to tell you what you want to know, in both of our interests. But I have a demand of my own." She tilted her head at me, shadows showing me first her mouth and then her eyes as she turned. They were the palest possible shade of sapphire. "One you're going to agree with."

"That's where I keep thinking I recognize you from," I said abruptly.

Lara narrowed her eyes.

"Those paintings. From the eighties. Every young yuppie had them in his apartment back then. They lived all over boy basements in the nineties. Narel? Nargle?"

Lara blurted out a quick laugh. "Nagel." She shook her head. "Good eye, actually. Several of my sisters posed for him."

"Did you?" I asked.

Lara sidled a little closer, half of her face coming out of the shadows, and I could see her vulpine smile. "A lady doesn't speak of such things."

"So that is you in that big one. Huh. You're famous."

Another quick laugh, as if she was working not to let too much of it get away from her—and not the throaty chuckle she used at parties. "You know what fame is worth."

"Some people seem willing to die for it."

"Some people are fools," Lara said. "Most people, it sometimes seems."

"Nah," I said. "That's an illusion, explained by my Perfect Idiot Hypothesis."

She lifted a raven-dark brow. "How so?"

"Everyone has a talent, yeah? Something they're naturally good at. It might be something weird and off-putting, or just strange, or something really useful, or something really spectacular that makes them a lot of money. But everyone's got something."

Lara actually spent a moment thinking about that before answering. "I am not one of the elder beings of this world. But I have seen many generations of humans come and go. Yes, I would find that statement to be largely true, by long-term observation."

"Uh-huh," I said. "Here's my hypothesis: Everyone has something they particularly suck at, too. An anti-talent, if you will. Something at which they have the ability to be the Unchosen One."

Lara's eyes wrinkled at the corners. "Go on."

"Well, it explains a lot, doesn't it? You get enough people going, and you're guaranteed to have someone who exactly, perfectly, completely sucks at handling any given situation. Sooner or later, that person is the one with the ball, and of course they screw it up. It's just math. Chance will eventually decide that the Perfect Idiot will wander along to be put into the exact situation they are worst at coping with." I wrinkled up my nose. "There's always a Perfect Idiot, somewhere. I would imagine that, looking in from the outside, it would make humans look quite a bit more stupid than the average member of the species deserves."

"I find it counterproductive to consider life in terms of species and averages," Lara said. "Every individual is its own unique threat. It should be dealt with as it is, not as someone analyzing numbers deems its average."

I studied her profile for a moment. Her eyes were silver, throwing back the winter light like a cat's. "You see everyone you meet as a threat?"

"Everyone you meet is a threat as well," Lara said, her eyes glittering. "You're just too young to see it yet. You still think that society, civilization, law, these imaginary fortresses you've constructed, are something solid. They can vanish in a day. I've seen it. Over and over. Last summer, you saw it, too."

The battle. I leaned on the merlon and said nothing.

"That's what history looks like," Lara said quietly. "There's been an unusually long quiet spell. And sometimes I forget that you're young enough to have grown up in that. That you see a largely peaceful world as normal. It isn't. Peace is easy to lose. Hard to get back." She lifted her head a little, baring the long line of her neck, and inhaled slowly. "And history is on the wind."

"Meaning what?" I asked.

"That it is time to take chances," Lara said, silver eyes glimmering. She wasn't looking anywhere near my face, and I was having trouble looking away from them. I mean, I did. Wizardly mental discipline and whatnot.

But I didn't want to.

"Here it comes," I said, squinting out at the quiet street. If I squinted hard enough, I almost couldn't see the houses that had been burned down during the battle. "What do you want?"

"I want to sort out what it's going to be like between us," Lara said quietly. "Our marriage. Right now."

"I'll expect dinner every evening at six, pipe and slippers at seven . . ."

Lara's mouth twitched at the corners, as her expression visibly wavered between annoyance and amusement. Finally she rolled her eyes and sighed. "I could probably live with that much more comfortably than I'd like to think." She shook her head. "Running the White Court is a ridiculous amount of work. I make difficult or impossible decisions for two hours a day and spend the rest dealing with the consequences of previous decisions. It . . . grinds. A period of routine, quiet, and order could very well prove to be excellent self-care." She gave me a sly sideways look that made my knees feel a little weak. "You should see me in a poodle skirt."

My throat was probably dry because it was so cold. I worked a couple of times and then swallowed.

"I'm serious, Harry," she said in a heavier voice. "How do you want this to work?"

"I get to choose?"

"You're one of the two," she said. "Seems reasonable that you'd have a say in it."

"This is supposed to be a state marriage," I said.

"It is that," she said. "Is that all you want it to be?"

I stared at her. "Given what I've heard from Mab, I thought the plan was for me to be your addict."

Her expression smoothed over into neutrality and her eyes focused into the distance. "I would certainly be comfortable with my part in that role. And you would be treated as close to ethically as the situation could sustain. But frankly, in this matter I don't particularly care what Mab wants. Is that what *you* want?"

It really, really bothered me that it took a long moment before I answered, "Not really."

"Ah," Lara said, bowing her head so that her hair fell forward over her cheeks. "You're tempted. But you have promises to keep."

"And miles to go," I said, nodding. "So, no. And I will totally fight you over it."

Lara nodded and shivered. "I don't suppose it's occurred to you that I might be concerned about you using magic to subjugate me in a similar fashion."

I blinked.

It hadn't.

Lara sighed. "I didn't think so. But it is one of the talents wizards possess, and therefore a possibility I have to bear in mind with you, don't you think?"

"God," I mused. "I'd hate to think of the job I'd do on you if I tried it. My psychomancy is less subtle than most pile drivers. I'd make a mess of you."

"I am, if possible, even more horrified than I was when I first considered the idea," Lara said wryly. "Thank you."

"Welcome."

"Be assured," Lara said, "I am nervous, too."

"Fair enough," I said. "Leaving us where, exactly?"

"In balance?" Lara asked. "Perhaps as allies?"

"Strong word," I said. I narrowed my eyes. "Associates. We share discretionary information. We do one another a kind turn when we can.

We wiggle the line a little for one another when need arises. We exercise reciprocity. And we see where that takes us."

"That sounds like a beginning I can live with," Lara said. "Provided it is understood that we are associates with"—she flashed me a perfectly merry, perfectly wicked smile—"intentions."

The Winter mantle wanted me to tackle her, immediately. I pushed it down and rasped, "Is that a legal term?"

"It is an apt term for our situation. You will find me an excellent associate, Dresden."

"I'm kind of iffy," I said frankly. I paused and added, "Except when everything is on the line."

"I'm well aware of that."

"Good," I said. "We know where we stand."

She nodded. Then her lips pressed together, she nodded as if committing to a course, and said, "The eldest known ancestor of my House was named Laris of Arretium. A sorcerer-king of an Etruscan citadel. He was the man who inadvertently cursed us with the Hunger."

I frowned and turned my body toward her, listening.

"The sorcerer-kings of that day were an elite society," Lara continued. "Always questing for greater power in the dark arts."

I grunted. "The White Council's history class teaches that the Council arose to challenge the sorcerer-kings of the ancient world."

"That is within a reasonable proximity of truth as I know it," she said. "Granted, the rise of the White Council happened in rhythm with the Romans rising against the Etruscan League and was thoroughly mixed with a toxic brew of economics and politics as well as personal dramas by the score. But I am speaking of more than a thousand years before that time. Laris and his circle had been plumbing the depths of the dark arts and they . . . opened a portal to the Outside."

I felt my eyebrows go up.

"A single being got in," Lara continued. "A mad god. The Hunger. The first Hunger. They managed to constrain it, but it began driving the city mad by its mere presence, inflaming every unfulfilled desire of the people who lived there, spreading like a sickness from one to the next.

The other sorcerer-kings fled to the defenses of their own citadels, leaving Laris to face the Hunger alone except for his daughter and apprentice, Thana. They were not strong enough to banish the Outsider, and they could not kill it, but they knew a spell for binding immortal beings indelibly with mortals. Their plan was to contain the Outsider to a mortal shell that would inevitably wither into death, taking the Hunger with it."

I took a moment to do a few mental calculations just to begin to figure out the mix of forces that would be needed for a spell like that, and it made my head spin. Those ancient wizards knew things that the White Council did not let out into the world of wizardry at large today, Hell, which might be just as well, if this story was going the way I thought it was. "How'd that work out for them?"

Lara smirked. "Badly. The Hunger was bound into the prison of Laris's body and will, but it also took possession of him. It did unspeakable things to Thana before she turned the tables and bound Laris in irons for the rest of his natural life." She shifted her weight from one hip to the other, glancing up at me. "The Hunger had the last laugh. The child it sired on her was Sethre, the first of my kind, born knitted in soul to an infant Hunger—a larva of the original dark god. These larvae seek to secure and protect their hosts in order to prolong their own lives—for they are still bound to die with their hosts. Sethre sired many sons and daughters, and they bred more. And so, our kind spread. Some four thousand years later, here we are, all caught up."

I shook my head. "May I ask questions?"

"Of course."

"How long do your kind live?"

"We are biologically immortal, as far as can be determined," Lara said promptly. "However, our . . . appetites generally expose us to greater than average levels of risk. Speaking from a strictly mathematical standpoint, vampires who do not master their appetites generally do not live beyond their second or third century before some violence or mishap befalls them. My father is currently the oldest vampire of the White Court. He says he is two thousand years old, though I have my doubts."

"How old are you?" I asked.

"Harry, I'm shocked."

"Hah," I said. "Talk."

She opened her mouth and then rolled her eyes up a little. "Shall we say more than two centuries and less than three?"

"All right, cradle robber," I said. I frowned. "I don't suppose you have access to these spells your grandcestors used?"

"Harry, it was scores of centuries ago. Little enough remains of that time at all—anywhere. And the White Council took possession of the sorcerer-king's spell books centuries later. If anyone has them, they will."

Oh, they certainly would. At least copies of them. Knowledge of how to create new races of vampires and God only knew what else. The Merlin would have that locked away in the deepest dungeons of the Edinburgh complex, along with every other potential superweapon the entirety of the world's wizard population had been able to lay their hands on over the centuries. I'd never have been able to get to that kind of thing, even when I'd been in the good(ish) graces of the Council.

"How confident are you in the truth of this story?" I asked her.

"It's family history," Lara said. "But it's something close to holy among our kind. I've never had any reason to think it's been doctored."

"Phew," I said, folding my fingers over my nose, thinking.

Lara turned toward me, her expression remote—but I had seen enough clients trying to hold things in that I could tell that she had everything riding on her next question. "Can you use this?" she asked. "To help Thomas with his Hunger?"

Outsiders.

The Hungers were baby Outsiders.

And I was starborn. I still had little idea of what that really meant, but I did know one thing for certain: I had been given power over Outsiders. My magic could affect them when another's could not.

Maybe I wasn't helpless here.

Maybe I could save my brother.

"Maybe," I said slowly. "By God. Maybe." I frowned. "But . . ."

Lara tilted her head. "But what?"

"How would you feel," I asked slowly, "about an experiment? More specifically, about being one."

Lara arched a delicate black brow.

"An experiment with intentions," I corrected myself.

Lara frowned, an expression no less stunning than her smile. "I am fairly sure I already regret this."

"I have some things to prepare," I said, bouncing lightly on my toes. "The New Year's Eve party. Can you arrange for us to have some alone time?"

"Can . . . Harry, please."

"Then do it," I said. I thought through what I'd need, nodding. "I can have it ready by tonight, and we'll see if it works."

"If what works?"

"My idea," I said. "I don't want to say anything else until I have a chance to test it on a . . . live subject. You."

Lara's eyes widened. "I . . . see. Will it be dangerous?"

"Probably? A little?" I guessed. "There's a lot of things I can't predict at all until I learn more. But I haven't had any other ideas as to how to help Thomas, and if this works, I'm going to save his life. You wanted my help for Thomas. This is how you get it."

Lara studied me quietly for a time before she nodded slowly. "Very well. I'll begin working on the Etri problem. Let's see where this goes." She bowed her head. "Sir Harry. Until this evening."

"Ms. Raith," I said, bowing back.

She flexed her legs, leapt weightlessly over the side of the building, and landed below without a sound. Snow was beginning to fall, and her white coat disappeared into it as she walked away.

I stared after Lara for a long moment. I had anticipated a number of possible interactions with her at our meeting, none of which had come anywhere close to the reality. It really forced me to ask the question.

Was Lara playing this straight?

I mean, sure she was a devious, magnificently underhanded operator, but that only meant that she would know that it was certainly the last ploy I would see coming. I mean, I had to assume she was working an angle somewhere. Only a fool wouldn't. But what if she was smart enough to see that her best possible angle was sincerity?

Of all the monsters I knew, Lara was the one with both the brains and the intellectual flexibility to be most likely to pull it off.

"Maybe you could fix her, Harry," I said.

I might possibly have said it with heavy sarcasm—I need to be hit over the head with a shovel to make sure things get through sometimes.

"Maybe instead you should stay alive long enough to save your brother and fix yourself," I added.

Yeah. Good advice, me.

I left the roof, and the warmth of the castle's interior felt like a swamp by comparison to the purity of the winter night. I walked briskly toward my lab.

I had work to do.

Chapter

Twenty-Eight

Lara's New Year's party was being thrown in the first parts of Chicago to be restored—the Gold Coast. It had suffered, since Ethniu the Titan had apparently taken the opportunity to destroy several towers with the Eye of Balor, but the roads had been reopened specifically to begin the cleanup there first.

Collapsed buildings were a mess, especially the ones that had been built more than forty or fifty years ago. The debris was full of toxic materials of one kind or another and cleaning them up was difficult and painstaking. The roads were open, the lights were on, and if not for the missing spaces in the skyline where towers had once stood, one could have mistaken it for Chicago. Or maybe the city was getting better. Maybe I was just being negative about it because I wasn't healing as quickly.

Molly had arranged a deep blue limousine to take me and Bear to the party, which was being held at a hotel called the Drake. When we got out of the limo, in the front of the building, I felt self-conscious in my tux. I'd mostly only worn rentals before. This one had been tailored to me and felt strange. I wore my duster over it. Its pockets were stuffed full of what I'd need for the evening.

"Quit fiddling with the cummerbund," Bear muttered.

"It's an extra belt," I said, adjusting the deep blue cloth. "I don't see the point."

"Lets you fly matching colors, makes slightly overweight people look better," she said.

I opened my mouth to reply as we headed for the front doors and then fell silent as I felt some kind of sensation crawl over the back of my neck, and I snapped my head up to look at the skies above. The lights mostly made me blind, as did the steady fall of moderate, fine snow.

Bear frowned at me. "What is it?"

"Every once in a while, the past few months," I said, "I've felt something overhead."

Bear squinted up at the night sky. She was wearing a silver party dress that clung to her form. She looked good. Solid, confident, and proportionately curved, and her makeup had been applied with skill. Her brown hair was bound back in a tight braid. A rather large clutch purse she carried with her probably contained compact instruments of mayhem. She sniffed the air and said, frowning, "I don't feel anything. You sure?"

"I'm not sure of much lately," I said. The feeling faded and I shrugged my shoulders to prevent a shiver rolling down my spine. "Okay. Ready?"

"Spent a lot of time in your lab today," Bear noted. "How'd your meeting with Lara go last night?"

I paused and squinted up at her.

"Freydis told me Lara slipped out," Bear said. "And when I checked your room, you weren't there."

"Goddammit, Bear," I said, annoyed.

She smiled at me and lifted her eyebrows guilelessly. "I am your bodyguard, not your babysitter. Did I not show the appropriate discretion?"

I gave her a glare that bounced off of her without leaving a mark. Then I sighed. "It . . . went," I said. "We talked. We'll talk some more this evening."

"Hmm," she said, regarding me thoughtfully. She gave the skies one more glance. "That should be interesting," she said, and we walked into the hotel.

This event was a different kind of party than Halloween had been, I noticed. For one, it was at a public venue, and while it wasn't as ritzy as Château Raith, it was maybe an eight on the fancy scale for Chicago. The party itself was less formal and considerably smaller than Halloween had been. The guests were mostly members of House Raith, all but one of them female, and I didn't recognize the rather reedy-looking male member of the Court. He must have been one of Lara's cousins—she only had one brother. The rest of the Raith in attendance were dark-haired, vibrantly attractive women in various flavors of formal attire. I noted a few other visitors from other supernatural nations. LaChaise wasn't there. I didn't see Drakul anywhere. There were a pair of Summer Sidhe in attendance, identifiable by their green-shaded hair. Both of them nodded gravely to me as I came in. I recognized several others from Halloween, and there were a lot of faces I didn't recognize at all. They weren't announcing guests as they arrived this time, either.

Freydis appeared, a slim woman a little taller than average, and approached us as we entered. Her hair was shaven on the sides, bound back in a thick coppery red braid on top. She wore a little black dress that showed off her fair skin and her slender, strong physique. She walked up and braced Bear with a crooked grin.

"Brownhead," she said.

"Freydis," Bear said easily. "How is life with the White Court?"

Freydis rolled her eyes. "Distracting as hell," she said, a faint note of complaint in her voice. "How is it over at wizard castle?"

"Mostly quiet. Can't complain," Bear replied. "You heard anything from Gard?"

"Her client doesn't really come to parties. He's loads of fun."

Bear snorted.

"Dresden," Freydis said. She raked her eyes up and down me leisurely. "You're looking"—she gave me a slow smile—"lean. And hard."

"Gosh," I said. "Thanks."

"Grumpy, though, eh?"

"Been a tough few months," I said.

Her expression sobered and she nodded. "Done those," she said. "You'll get better, bit at a time. Lara's had a last-minute meeting to take care of. There's a side room, if you'd care to wait there for her rather than, you know." She rolled her eyes at the room. "Here."

Not being in a room full of potentially dangerous interactions? Or, worse, awkward conversations I didn't want? "That would be fine," I said.

Freydis showed me to a door that led to a smaller sitting room next to the grand ballroom. There were several comfortable-looking padded leather chairs and couches, though the room was dimly lit. Given that it was a White Court function, it was easy enough to guess why it was here.

Freydis shut the door behind us and said something to Bear in a language I didn't know.

Bear frowned and replied in the same tongue. They exchanged a few phrases and Bear sighed. "Fine," she said finally. "Dresden, can you mind yourself for a few minutes? I need to call my boss."

"I thought I was your boss."

"You're my client. Vadderung is my boss."

"You're still here under guest-right," Freydis assured me. "And I'll be watching the door."

"Sure," I said, and settled down in a chair. "I'll sit here quietly and not touch anything."

Bear looked like she was going to say something, and then shook her head and strode out. Freydis went after her, gave me a quick nod, and shut the door behind them.

The moment I was alone, my thoughts turned dark. Memory started rolling. I rolled the game tape from the night of the battle, when Rudolph had shot Murphy. I'd long ago figured out where I'd made bad choices, but I went over it again. And again. And again.

I was in a deep, dark, brooding funk when the door opened briefly, and the music from the ballroom poured in for a moment.

I looked up, and Lord Raith was standing just inside the door.

I felt my whole body grow tense.

Lord Raith had, at one time, been quite dangerous. My mother had dropped her death curse on him way back in the day, when I was born. She'd rendered him unable to feed on mortal life energy, and he'd carried on ruling the White Court on pure chutzpah. Maybe ten years back, Lara had figured out that he was actually powerless, and she'd . . .

taken steps to neutralize him. These days he ran the White Court in name only. It was more or less an open secret that Lara was the real power in her Court.

He was still dangerous. Every instinct in my body screamed at me that he was.

Raith stepped into the room, pale grey eyes focused on me. He looked a lot like Thomas, but taller and even more marble-statue beautiful. His dark hair was cut short on the sides, longer on top, a style from a decade far removed from the present. He wore an all-white tuxedo, complete with white gloves, and regarded me through half-lidded eyes.

"So," he said quietly after a moment. "You're going to marry my little girl."

"Lara hasn't been yours, or little, for a very long time," I replied.

He spread open the fingers of one hand and rolled his wrist. "Ah. I suppose I have a unique perspective on the matter."

"Uh-huh," I said. "Sure you do."

His eyes narrowed. "Still disrespectful, aren't you?"

"I give respect where it's due," I said without emphasis.

He gave me a slow smile that bared his teeth a little too much. "I'm told you did the Accorded nations great good during the battle."

"Did my part," I said.

"Must have cost you something," he said. "How is that little blonde you were with?"

Something hot and ugly flared in my chest. It must have shown on my face. His smile sharpened.

"Oh, Dresden," Raith murmured in a patently false tone. "Please excuse me. I had no idea."

I took a slow breath. I let myself feel the anger. I let it go through me. I did not set anyone on fire. No matter how good it sounded at the moment.

"Beginning to show signs of maturity," he noted. He cast a glance over his shoulder toward the door. "Did Lara promise to be a nice vampire? Not do a thing to you? It's one of her usual plays. She likes to pretend she's other than what she is."

"And what's that?" I asked.

"A predator," he said calmly.

"Ah," I said. "Like you can't be anymore, huh?"

His pale eyes flickered for a second. A muscle along his fine jawline tensed. "Lara thinks she has her Hunger tamed," he murmured. "It isn't. It can't be. When it needs to be fed, she feeds it. Sooner or later, you'll be food. And I suspect when that happens, she might even be startled by it." He lazily lifted his arms overhead and stretched, a feline movement. "Not that it will matter to you. You'll be just one more buck she's taken."

"Did you have a point you wanted to get to?" I asked. "Or did you just want to blather along until I throw up?"

"Dresden," he purred. "You're here under guest-right. Protected. Much like LaChaise and Drakul were at the Halloween party."

"Didn't see you there," I said, narrowing my eyes.

"I'm sure you didn't," he agreed. "There are all kinds of things you don't seem to notice. Like all children."

That put my hackles up. There was a definite taunting tone in his voice. He was needling me over something and enjoying it. And I had a bad feeling that I should damned well know what it was. But I didn't. And in situations like that, I was beginning, slowly, to realize that the best way to appear to know more than I did was to be silent.

Raith beamed at me, taking it as a small victory. "I just wanted to have a quiet word with my son-in-law-to-be and give you my most sincere wishes for good luck. We're to be family next year, after all. And what else is family for?"

Treachery, deceit, and worse, from what I'd seen of Raith's interactions with his own family. But I suppose my own family's interactions hadn't always been the healthiest and most functional affairs, either. I was working on those.

I just needed time.

The door opened and Freydis came through quickly, her eyes wide, nostrils flared. She took in the situation, body held tense, holding one hand at her side with fingers stiff as if trying to make a sword of her limb.

"Good dog," Raith said calmly, without looking at Freydis. "Though easily distracted, eh?" He smirked at her and glided from the room.

Freydis watched him go, her expression blank. She shuddered as he walked past her. She shut the door behind him and blew out a breath before she looked over at me. "Everything all right?"

"Polite conversation," I said. "Or what passes for one with him."

She shook her head. "Guy makes my skin crawl. Lara wants me to tell you she's done with her meeting with Etri. You'll need to make a few rounds of the party, make small talk. Then she's got the executive suite for your personal meeting. Lucky bastard."

I sat and stared at the closed door to the sitting room as if I could stare at Lord Raith's departing back.

I might not have been operating at my best. But I'd have to be a hell of a lot more out of it than I was not to realize that something was wrong here. He'd come in to tell me something and it wasn't "Good luck." He'd mentioned a couple of my enemies. He'd taken pleasure in doing it.

And he'd picked a night when I needed my attention and focus on something else entirely. What I was about to attempt with Lara carried with it an inherently unknown amount of danger, and I didn't need to be worrying about watching my back while I carried it out.

I took a deep breath. I didn't think I was in any danger from Lord Raith at the moment. This was, after all, a party, and nothing mattered to the White Court as much as appearances. I could focus on his threats later.

I had more immediate ones now.

"Yeah, okay," I said to Freydis. "Take me to Lara."

Chapter
Twenty-Nine

Bear and Freydis kept a discreet distance from Lara and me as we made a few rounds of the ballroom. Lara talked to pretty much everyone. I nodded and gave brief smiles when introduced and otherwise said little. More and more people arrived as the evening got later, the rich and swanky mostly. There were some famous faces there, apparently, but I didn't really recognize them. I did recognize a couple of aldermen, the superintendent of police, and several attorneys from the DA's office, and got introduced to the mayor's senior assistant. None of them really took any notice of me, what with Lara right there, and several other members of the White Court drifting through the room.

The gathering was noticeably more sedate than Halloween had been, by which I meant I didn't see any of the White Court drawing off victims to be fed upon.

It was boring as hell.

Lara wore a deep blue dress matching my cummerbund. It plunged in the back, was slit up high on one side, and looked fabulous, even for her. The Winter mantle wanted me to find out if her skin was as soft and smooth as it looked. I squired her about with her hand on my arm, a cool, light pressure.

We escaped the room around eleven and took an elevator to the top floor. Freydis produced a key card from her dress and opened the door before I'd gotten close enough to screw up the card reader. The two Valkyries took up position on either side of the door to the executive suite after Bear handed me my duster, with the necessary implements in the pockets, and Lara and I went inside.

"Are you sure that's all he said?" Lara was asking me. I'd given her a précis of my conversation with Lord Raith while we rode up in the elevator.

I checked over the conversation in my head. "Yeah, pretty much. Some smug insults, some excuses over them, veiled threats."

She frowned as I shut the door behind us. "That's . . . He hasn't acted like that in a while."

"Like a jerk?" I asked.

"Like he thinks he has teeth," she replied. "Perhaps I should have a chat."

The executive suite was large and tasteful. I felt oddly uncomfortable in the room and after a moment realized it was because of the electric lights. I'd gotten used to lanterns and candles, to longer shadows and dimmer rooms.

Probably said more about me than about the hotel.

"Sounded like standard egotistical villain bluster to me," I said. "Not like I'm gonna believe the guy was giving me a warning out of the goodness of his heart."

"A warning about me," Lara said. She walked over to the wall of glass windows that looked out over the city. The lights only went for a few blocks beyond the hotel. Then darkness. She stared out at the night, or maybe at her ghostly, translucent reflection in the glass. "Do you think he was right?" she asked lightly.

"Do you?" I replied.

She shrugged one alabaster shoulder. "He's had his own philosophy that has guided him. I have mine. They differ. He maintains that his is the more sustainable of the two. I suppose time will tell." She turned to face me. She looked amazing. "Harry? What do you need me to do?"

I realized I'd been staring. I cleared my throat, turned to a dining table, and began unpacking my duster's pockets onto it. "Right, uh. Right. Give me a second here." I forced some order into my thoughts and eyed the short carpet. "Um. You can afford some cleaning or, uh, repair charges, I hope?"

"If we don't burn down the building," she said drily, "it shouldn't pose a challenge."

"No promises." I took up a can of white spray paint and began shaking it to make the steel bead inside rattle. "But good to know."

It took me half an hour to do the layered circle I was going to need. We had to push the furniture out of the way to clear out a spot about twenty feet across. It took an inner and outer circle for what I had in mind, with the space between them lined with sigils of protection and containment. I hadn't done this kind of work in a good long while, and only a single day's preparation and visualization probably hadn't been ideal, either. This was a test run to see how viable my idea was, and didn't have to be done with the same accuracy as the final product. I hoped. Then there was the condition I was in to think about and . . .

. . . and Hell's bells, Lara smelled good.

I forced that out of my head. I had to focus to get this set up. Within the center of the circle, I laid down a figure-eight infinity loop, big enough for someone to stand in either circular side. I laid down five white candles upon the exterior circle, equidistant as I could manage them, then five incense cones centered between them. Then on the table, I set up the stand with the largish tuning fork held upright, and laid down the metal striker beside it. Candles for sight and feel, incense for smell and taste, the fork for sound. The smell of the spray paint was sharp in my nose, and I'd gotten flecks of it all over the pants of the tux and the expensive, shining shoes.

I suppose my magical style was not precisely formal.

Lara watched it all in silence.

"Okay," I said, going over the circle. The runes and sigils were rough but correct—I'd been most careful about those. The circles were even, or at least even enough to the casual eye. Candles and incense were unlit but ready to go. "I think we're just about good."

She arched a raven-dark eyebrow. "Really. I expected it to be . . ."

"Flashier?" I asked.

She frowned. "Well. Less . . . like you'd gotten the things for it at a hardware store."

"I'm not particularly wealthy," I said. "Few more months of running the castle and I'm broke, in fact."

She blinked at me. "You're kidding."

I shrugged. "Never really been a priority."

"I see." She shook her head. "You seem to think little enough of wrecking a hotel room and having me pay for it."

"You going to try to tell me that you've never trashed a hotel room in your time?"

"Hmm," she said. "What will you require of me?"

I stepped into the circle carefully, without touching any of the paint. It hadn't been empowered yet and wasn't active, but I didn't want to smear the lines. Lara took note of my caution and when I gestured for her to join me, she followed my example. I nodded at one side of the infinity loop. "You're going to stand there."

"And do what?"

"Don't step out of it," I said. "Whatever happens, you stand in place."

She pursed her lips, which took me out of the right headspace for a second. "What should I expect to happen?"

"Could hurt," I said. "Or, uh, upset your Hunger."

"Upset it?"

"I'm about to see if I can contain your Hunger without touching the rest of you," I said.

Her eyes widened slightly. "Is that possible?"

"In theory," I said. "Yeah. Of course, the difference between theory and reality is what you aren't aware that you don't know."

She gave me a long look. "What happens if I step out of the circle?"

"Depends," I said.

"Upon?"

"What your Hunger does in reaction. Um, how hard the two of you are stuck together, for lack of a better term. How much energy I've got to pour into this. I'm creating a very specific kind of energy field. I'm going to stretch reality a little here."

A little white showed around her grey eyes. "Is that dangerous?"

"If you don't step out of the circle," I said, "it should be fine."

"In theory?"

"Hmm," I said.

She gave me another look and exhaled through her nose. Then she bent slightly, lifting her feet one at a time, and slipped her heels off. It did interesting things to her calves. "How long will this take?"

"This is just a test run," I said. "Not long."

"You're not going to"—she frowned—"do anything permanent to me?"

"Not really set up for it," I said. "This is a proof-of-concept sort of thing. Modified exorcism. If it's working, I should be able to tell, and we'll back off."

"If?" she asked. "Should? There are more conditionals in that statement than I prefer."

"That's magic for you," I said. "I did say it would probably be dangerous."

"Probably," she muttered. "More conditional statements." She tossed her shoes onto the couch we'd pushed against the wall and delicately stepped into one side of the infinity loop. Her fingernails and toenails, I noted, had been painted a blue that matched the dress.

I stepped out of the circle, checking over everything once more. Then I took a deep breath and irritably removed my tie, opening the shirt at the throat.

"Ready?" I asked.

She took a deep breath and exhaled slowly, her eyes closed. Her toes flexed a little and she folded her arms across her stomach. "Very well."

"Right," I said. "Here we go."

I closed my eyes and took several deep, slow breaths, drawing together my concentration and focus. That came together quicker than I had thought it would. Well. I had been meditating every day lately.

And I'd been doing something close to the inverse of this ritual almost every night for months.

I pushed that thought away, too.

First the circle.

I opened my eyes, pointed my finger at the nearest candle and murmured, *"Flickum bicus."*

A small surge of power flowed out of me to the candle, and flame kindled upon its wick and flickered to life. I repeated the spell four more times for the candles, then went about again for the incense, giving the last one a little bit of extra power, which spilled over the cone of incense into the circle and brought it to life.

The air hummed with unseen power as the circle became active, jumping up in an invisible screen around Lara. She shivered as it did, gooseflesh erupting across the skin of her upper arms.

"Steady," I murmured. "It's going well so far."

"Okay," she breathed. She opened her eyes and they were paler than they'd been when she shut them.

Oh yeah. The Hunger within her knew something was up.

I began gathering energy. The power of magic comes mainly from an emotional connection to whatever the intention of any given spell happened to be. I was doing this to help my brother. I thought of him, of Thomas. I thought of his wry humor. Of his laughter. Of his courage. He'd stood beside me in extremely hairy situations. I thought of his desperation when last I'd seen him outside of stasis, of how battered he'd been once the svartalves had gotten done with him. Felt my desperation and my anger and my fear rising in time with the memories.

Anger and fear.

I had plenty of that to work with.

But that wasn't all I had. It couldn't be.

I focused on imagining my brother's face. On the loyalty I felt for him.

I loved my brother.

I missed him.

And if anyone was going to help him, it was damned well going to be me.

I felt the energy building up around me, felt goose bumps flood across my own skin, the hairs on the back of my neck rising. I'd forgotten the room's lights. They all went at once, first burning brighter and brighter and then bursting into small clouds of sparks within the bulbs, leaving the room dark but for the candles, and faint traces of excess energy that sparkled off the field of the circle and danced about the paint and sigils in shades of pale green.

I lifted my right hand, the hand that projects energy, and directed my thoughts upon Lara. Upon the thing inside her. I pushed my wizard's senses forward, blending them with the circle, and suddenly I felt it—a slow, twisting roil of nauseating energy, giddying and sickening at the same time. I felt a sudden desire to let out a mad cackle and suppressed it.

I'd felt this energy before.

Outsider. Hidden right there in front of me.

Outsiders were entities that existed in the raw chaos beyond the Outer Gates, the borders of reality. They didn't much believe in coexistence. Lovecraftian horrors, madness distilled into flesh, things so alien that there simply wasn't much of a way to understand them, or what they wanted, or why they did the things they did. I knew they were universally dangerous, universally hostile, and that if they had their way, they'd gleefully tear reality back down into primal chaos, taking every living thing with it.

And I knew that when I talked, they had to listen. When I fought them, they got hurt. When I slung my magic at them, they had to labor to fight against it. I and, presumably, the other starborn.

"Hear me, Hunger," I murmured. The power I'd gathered changed my voice. It was deeper, harder, twisting oddly through the room. "Hear me."

Lara drew in a sharp breath and her eyes became brighter, silvery, reflective. "Oh. Oh, empty night," she breathed. Her skin suddenly glistened with perspiration. "What's happening?"

"You know who I am," I said in the same voice. "You know what I am."

Lara's eyes rolled back and she began to shudder, abdominal muscles clenching randomly, rapidly.

"I have been given power over your kind," I said, voice steady and implacable.

Lara's shoulders twisted, as if trying to escape bindings. She let out a low, tortured groan. The flames of the candles around the circle leapt up to ten times their original height, and the white paint became brighter, giving off its own green-white illumination as the energy of the circle intensified.

I poured more into it, visualizing what I wanted to do. I spread my fingers, gathering the power, and released it, voice set in a tone of absolute authority and command as I said, *"Disparus!"*

Power rushed into the circle.

Lara let out a gasping, strangled scream, body arching, arms flinging out wide as she went up onto her toes.

The incense cones flared with heat, and smoke billowed out, filling the circle.

I felt the power take hold. I felt it surround her, her skin going whiter, glittering swaths of green-gold light spiraling around its surface.

"Disparus!" I called, feeling the resistance, feeling the Hunger suddenly struggling wildly against the spell. *"Disparus!"*

And with a sudden implosion, the smoke of the incense condensed, swirling into the other side of the infinity loop, filling into the sudden form of a being of pale white flesh, almost faceless, hairless, sexless, all lean muscle, a mirror of Lara's form. I could feel it struggling against the spell, and I had to keep my will against that force as if pushing up a heavy weight.

But I'd been doing that a lot lately, too.

The Hunger solidified, traces of energy flooding across the infinity loop, misty strands of light that bound it to Lara's pained form, the two moving as one, shuddering precisely in time with each other, still bound—but separated.

I stared, focused upon the strands between the two of them. I pressed against one of them with my will and felt it begin to give way.

Hell's bells.

It worked.

It could be done.

Lara and the Hunger opened their mouths and screamed. It came out a double sound, precisely in time, one voice human, agonized, one utterly alien, hair-raising.

I eased the focus of my will against the resistance of the Hunger. Slowly, I closed the fingers of my right hand, letting the magical energy fade as gradually and gently as I could. I could feel the strain of the spell translating to my physical body, felt myself beginning to shake.

As the resistance faded, the pale form of Hunger began to dissipate, to become smoke again, flowing across the strands of energy back to Lara's body. I began to redirect the energy of the spell, sending the magic all flowing toward Lara, taking the Hunger with it. The flames of the candles began to die down again, as smoke swirled around Lara, the Outsider resuming its place within her, vanishing from the other side of the loop.

Lara let out another gasp, eyes flying open suddenly a deep, rich blue. As I closed my hand, tying off the energy of the spell, letting it come to a close, exhaustion hit me in a wave and I staggered. I dropped to a knee and slapped my hand across the nearest point of the circle, feeling the magic break and disperse.

Lara dropped to her knees, blue eyes unfocused, covered in sweat. She let out an unmistakable moan of pleasure and exhaustion. She fell forward onto her hands and then crumpled over onto her side, curling into a fetal position, body quivering with random spasms.

I slumped onto my ass, head bowed forward, just trying to slow my breathing. The candles sank down to pinpoints and went out.

We both stayed like that as, outside, fireworks began.

When I looked up, only the fireworks and the lights outside let me see anything at all.

Lara was staring at me in something between horror and awe.

"Did . . ." She swallowed. "Did it work?"

I nodded my head slowly. "Yeah," I said quietly. I had to work not to stare at Lara. I wasn't yet clear on everything that had happened just now—that would take some thought and review. But the basic concept had been proved. I could separate Thomas from his Hunger. "Yeah. We can save him."

"Empty night," she breathed. She shook her head, stunned. "Harry. I'm . . . I'm not Hungry."

Chapter Thirty

Fitz and I stood on the roof a couple of weeks later, looking out at the night. They were repairing things "from the middle out" in the city, but it was slow going—not for any lack of work or effort, but the surge in replacement parts needed for the city's grid had caused a serious logistics chain issue, raised prices, and created bottlenecks. Still, we could almost see the glow of lights from several blocks away.

Fitz shrugged a little deeper into his coat. You could feel the extreme cold of the wind coming off Lake Michigan. I was wearing my duster, because it made me feel a little weird to be out in the cold in a T-shirt when other people were bundled up. I hadn't been doing the regular upkeep on the spells that would protect me, and they were probably getting thinner than I should be comfortable with. Well. It was probably time to start talking to Fitz about how to do static enchantments anyway. I could work on my coat tomorrow and show him how to get started on his own first enchantment. We'd been working on meditating in the cold this evening. Fitz was developing discipline fast.

"So, Maggie is at school all week?" he asked.

"Be back Friday afternoon," I said. "Goes back Monday morning."

"And there's a bunch of supernatural kid types there?"

"Mmmm," I said. "And the Accorded nations agreed to leave the place alone a while back. There's several beings there looking out for the place. Now Mouse is included."

"The dog?"

"Foo dog," I said. "Near as I can figure he's at least half an angel's worth of protection. Good guardian. Kept the svartalves from coming at Maggie in their own damned home, so he's pretty solid. He once got hit by a car, got up, and hit it back."

"Oh, wow. I just thought he was a really good dog."

"He's mostly that." I blew out a breath and watched the wind carry the warmed vapor off. Mist was rolling up from the lake, as it sometimes did. The view from the castle's roof would soon be dim shapes and grey background. "Could be that's the more important, really. Most days, you don't need a ferocious guardian. Hard to think of a day a really good dog wouldn't add to."

"Huh," Fitz said. He squinted at me. "You watched pretty close the first time I met Mouse, I noticed. It was a test."

I shrugged. "Mouse has good instincts for people. He thinks you're okay."

Fitz frowned.

The silence stretched for a long moment, brittle. I was careful to be still. Fitz was still half a wild thing, slow to trust. We'd been working together for months, but while he'd been cooperative and earnest, he hadn't ever really opened up to me. So I was quiet and patient. I let the silence go on.

"I don't know about that," he said quietly, at last. "You know where I came from."

That was important. That he was volunteering something. "You had a tough start," I said. "Me, too."

"You turned out okay, though," he said.

"Don't know about that."

"You got a big house. You got money. You take care of people."

"Yeah," I said. "I guess so. For now. Money might not last too long."

"Oh," he said. He frowned down over the battlements at the town. "Why do you do it?"

"Do what?"

"Whole hero thing," he said. "I mean. Seems like it costs a lot. Not money."

"I don't do the 'hero thing.'" I sighed. "Look. I've got powers other people don't. I'm strong in ways they aren't. When there's something that needs doing, someone in danger, sometimes I'm the only one who can do anything to help. That's when I do . . . what I do."

"People staying here," he countered, "there's other places they could stay. Other people who would feed them." He looked back at me, his young face uncertain, green eyes searching. "But you're doing it."

"They're from the block," I said. "Their homes were burned down in the battle."

"So?"

"So, they stay with me, they have the least disruption." I shrugged. "Seems to me a good man helps those that pass through his life. We all did that, help the folks that the winds of life blow through our own yard, the whole world would do a little better. I try to do that when I can. Right now, I can do more than usual. So I will."

Fitz studied me hard. "Even if other people don't?"

"Other people do," I said firmly. "There's a world of damned decent people out there, quietly doing good stuff. You don't see much of it in the papers, on the news, probably not on the internet. Kindness doesn't sell. Don't mean it isn't there."

"I dunno, man." Fitz sighed. "I got a life of experience says otherwise."

"Streets are a hard place to live," I said. "People got fewer resources. Fewer opportunities to step in without suffering badly for it. But you've seen better the past few years, haven't you?"

"I guess," Fitz said thoughtfully. He looked back out at the city, studying it, as if seeing some things about it for the first time. "Maybe so, yeah."

"It's hard to unlearn things," I said gently. "Skills you need to survive one kind of life are not the same as the skills you need to get out of it to something more solid. And those skills aren't the same as the ones you need to make that life more consistent and better. You're always learning new things."

"Always?" Fitz asked.

"Stop learning, start dying," I said seriously. "Why I'm a big believer in reading. Any kind of reading. Even reading pure wild fiction, you learn about what someone else feels life is like. Get a different perspective than your own."

"Stop learning, start dying," Fitz murmured. He smiled out at the rising mist. It was already making the cars at street level look soft and vague. "I like that."

"It's a little metaphorical," I said. "But largely true. Try to keep growing your whole life, kid. You're the only person on the planet you can really change."

Fitz's mouth took a bitter little twist to one side. "Yeah. Learned that one a few times." He glanced aside at me. "I've been meaning to thank you."

"For what?"

He waved his hand back at the castle. "This. All this."

"Sure," I said.

He nodded awkwardly. "Okay, then."

"You know how you pay me back, right?"

His shoulders tensed a little. "How?"

"One day," I said, "when you're standing where I was, when some kid is standing in front of *you*, needing *your* help, I want you to give it to him."

He frowned more. "What?"

"I don't want to be paid back," I said. "I want you to carry it forward. And you teach that kid the same thing."

Fitz frowned harder. He stared out at the mist, which had made the cars into blurs now, and had swallowed the one-stories across the street. "Why?"

"It's what a good man would do," I said. "It's one way to be one."

Fitz thought about that for a moment. Then he said, "The people from the neighborhood. It's not like you ignore them or anything. But mostly you're just talking at dinner and game night. You don't get real personal."

"Don't have a lot of personal resources," I said.

"With me, you get personal," he said.

I grunted.

"And you had less of them when I first showed up."

I bobbed my head to one side, a noncommittal gesture.

"Why?" he asked.

I thought about the answer for a while. "Because when I was in a similar spot, someone showed up for me. If they hadn't, I'd have had a bad end in not long, I suspect. Didn't want that for you. Didn't want to spend time thinking how I'd let it happen."

"You didn't want to feel guilty?"

"More guilty," I corrected him. "But it's about more than that, too. People ought to get something in the vague neighborhood of a fair shot at life. I had a chance to try to help make that happen for you. And don't forget, you helped me when I was in a bad way, too."

"Bad way?" he said, grinning. "That's what you call being all but dead, huh?"

I grinned. "'Bout the worst I've ever felt, yeah. I was lucky I ran across you."

His mouth twisted in wry amusement. "Haven't ever heard those words said in a good way," he noted.

"Little brother," I said, "I was lucky to have the chance to help you out. Getting back to basics has been helping me, too. Get back on my own feet."

He nodded. The mist crept up the walls and had begun to ooze through the crenels, the spaces between the merlons of the castle wall.

"Can I ask you something?" he asked.

"Sure."

"I hear people talking sometimes," he said. "That foreman for the construction guys. Will. Some of the other folks who come through. They talk about 'she' and 'her' and you and they all know who they're talking about. They get quiet when they do, too, like maybe they don't want someone overhearing them."

"Probably talking about Lara Raith," I said.

"No, they say 'Lara' when they talk about her," he replied.

"Oh," I said.

"Who are they talking about?" he asked.

I was quiet for a moment.

The kid had opened up to me. Just a little.

I had to repay him in the same coin. He had to see me act in good faith.

Even if it cost me something.

Then I said, "Murphy. Karrin Murphy. She died in the battle."

Just said it. Out loud.

That she was dead.

The mist rose and poured over my hands, colder and wetter than the evening air.

"Oh," he said. "I remember her. You two were . . . ?"

"Yeah."

"How?" he asked quietly.

"Shot," I said. "Neck."

"Oh," he said. "I'm sorry."

I shrugged. "She was a fighter. She went out fighting. As dying goes, it was quick."

It was likely the mist that made the distant lights blur in my vision. Sure.

"I miss her," I added. My voice was rough.

Fitz was quiet for a long moment.

But I had showed him what to do. I'd set the example.

"I had an older sister," he said, his voice somehow smaller, younger. "Before you met me. Caught between two gangs. She got hit in the stomach and bled out in an alley." He blinked his eyes several times and couldn't quite stop a tear from falling. "I miss her, too."

I looked aside at him. Blinked a lot.

He was looking up at me, his expression serious. "I mean, if you ever need to talk about it," he said. "I feel you."

I hadn't talked about it much.

Not even in my quarters in the evenings.

She'd been gone for more than six months.

Maybe it was time to do the healthy thing.

Maybe it was time to start letting go.

Maybe it was the best thing for me.

"Maybe another night," I said quietly. "Go get some rest. See you at breakfast."

Chapter
Thirty-One

Two more of the Brotherhood of St. Brigid were cursed over the next week. Messengers arrived at the castle to ask for my help around nine o'clock, each time right when I was about to do my evening ritual. I got my curse-breaking technique down fairly well. The spell to remove it was actually quite similar to the one I'd put together to try on Lara. I could have made it simpler and easier on me if I'd used more props, but the church tends to frown on people spray-painting sigils and runes on their nice chapel floors. Maybe I could get some kind of mat made from some substance that was magically resilient enough to handle multiple infusions of energy.

They came to ask for my help again on Thursday night, and the third victim of the week was Daniel Carpenter.

I handled it.

It wasn't pretty.

By the time I was done, Daniel's jaw had locked down on the roll of leather he'd been biting. His face was blotchy and red, his eyes bloodshot, his body soaked in sweat. He looked up at me as the awareness of something other than pain showed up in his eyes. Michael was sitting on the floor, one leg painfully out to one side, supporting his son's head in his broad, calloused hands. He put his thumbs on the muscles at the base of Daniel's jaws and started rubbing them in circles, urging Daniel to relax, until the younger man could spit the leather out.

Then he just bowed his head, murmured a brief prayer of thanks, looked up at me, and said, "And thank you, Harry."

"Sure," I said, without much panting. Repeating the same spell over and over is a lot like working out a muscle group with a specific exercise. The more you do it, the easier it gets to do. I sat back, tired but not entirely enervated.

Father Forthill sat on the nearest pew, and about a dozen other members of the Brotherhood were hanging about, visibly angry and armed. He nodded to Dr. Brazell, and the man went to Daniel with a stand and an IV kit and got to work giving him saline, replacing lost fluids.

"All right," I said. "This is getting ridiculous now."

"We have to do something," said one of the Brotherhood guys, younger, taller, more muscular, and apparently angrier than the others. "We can't just keep putting up with this. This can't be allowed. These Satanic attacks have to be answered."

"Probably not literally Satanic in nature," I said. "There's a lot of evil out there, kid. Powers and principalities abound."

"It has to be stopped," he snarled, the anger focusing on me. He took a step toward me.

In the shadows under the loft, I saw Bear come silently to her feet.

"Carl," Michael said gently. "Take a deep breath."

"Look what those bastards did to your own son!" Carl snapped. He pointed an accusing finger at me. "For all you know, he was the one that did it!"

"Carl," Father Forthill began.

Bear took a step forward. I flipped one of my palms toward her, a silent command to wait.

Carl snarled and slashed his hand at the air. "Well?" he demanded of me. "Witch. Was it you?"

Michael, still holding his exhausted son's head, gave me a look that pleaded for my patience.

I eyed him, took a deep breath, and stood up slowly, spreading both of my hands at my sides, palms toward Carl. "Carl, I'm as upset by this as anyone."

"You don't look it."

"No. Because I'm setting it aside so that I can think clearly about solutions."

"There needs to be a solution," Carl snarled.

"No kidding. Which is why I'm setting my anger aside. And why you should, too."

"Convenient, the guy solving the problem wants us to not get upset about the problem, so he can keep doing it!"

"Yeah, I like going out in the freezing cold at night in a dangerous city for zero pay instead of staying home in my room and getting sleep. Come on, man. Think."

Carl stared hard at me. Then he whipped about and stalked out of the chapel. About half of the members of the Brotherhood followed him out.

Bear turned to watch them go. The big Valkyrie's expression was unreadable.

"This gonna be a problem?" I asked aloud after a moment.

Forthill stared after the departed men for a moment, frowning. "They're afraid. Perhaps they're right to be."

"Sure," I said. "And when people get scared, they often go kinda nuts. Do irrational things. Sometimes if there isn't an obvious source of their fear, they pick something and pour it all out on that. Carl there looks like maybe he's ready to pick anything close enough to pound on."

Forthill rubbed his cheek with one hand, his expression worried. "I'll speak to him."

My mouth twisted with a fraction of the hot bitterness I felt in my stomach. "That'll work. He looks like a reasoned-discourse kinda guy."

"Harry," Michael chided me gently.

I took another breath through my nose, closed my eyes, and exhaled slowly. That had come out a lot harsher than I'd meant it. "Yeah, okay. Might be true, but it wasn't called for."

One of the Brotherhood offered me a bottle of water, and I took it gratefully. I drank half of it, thinking.

See, the thing was, Carl wasn't wrong. That spell was as nasty a little working of black magic as I had ever run across. Pure nerve pain from every nerve, nonstop. If the curse wasn't broken, it could definitely kill someone over the course of days, and there weren't a whole ton of people in town who could stop it.

I could. Possibly Morty could get an angle on it, if he would be willing to try—his ectomancy was a niche form of magic, but within it he was as powerful as anyone on the White Council, and this spell was spirit-world adjacent. Maybe the Ordo Lebes, a crew of low-powered practitioners who got a lot done by working in teams, could break the curse, too.

Of course, this was not a chump-level curse.

Which meant that, barring newcomers to town I wasn't aware of, the list of suspects was the same as the list of potential helpers.

And black magic left . . . stains. A residue. It could be sensed.

It could be tracked.

And if it built up enough, the Wardens would get wind of it. They'd start prowling Chicago, which was the last thing I needed.

"Michael," I said quietly. "Where was Daniel when the curse hit him?"

"I don't know," he said. "I was at home and got the call to come here."

"On patrol, after sundown," Forthill supplied. "Over by McAnally's."

My stomach twisted a little.

Over by the bazaar.

Where some of the magical crowd had gotten roughed up by normies.

I traded another look with Michael, whose face had become grimmer and more lined at the words. Michael had been around the block. He knew about magic. And people. He could see it the same way I could.

"We don't know yet," I said.

"About anything," he agreed. "We need to know more. Father, can you be more specific about where the men were when all the attacks happened?"

"I can," volunteered one of the Brotherhood guys.

"Bear," I called. "Get the car. I need to check something out."

We stopped at all of the sites where members of the Brotherhood had been attacked. The oldest one barely held a trace of dark magic. It got progressively stronger as we went to the more recent ones. Daniel had collapsed several blocks from McAnally's, and we went there last.

I got out of the Munstermobile's passenger side, since Bear had insisted on driving. She barely fit in the driver's seat but managed the old hearse smoothly and confidently. She'd been driving since, well, cars, and had taken all the extreme-driving training she could, so it was just possible she was better at it than me.

We pulled up to the spot where Daniel had been cursed, and I got out, wrapping my duster around me more by reflex than because I needed it against the cold. I closed my eyes for a moment and focused upon my wizard's senses, reaching out, opening myself up to the flowing energy of magic in the immediate area.

It was a creepy area. The lights weren't back yet. The buildings were almost entirely businesses, and none of them were open late. Only the lights from the Munstermobile made it possible to navigate safely. Abandoned cars lined the street. Trash had piled up where the wind had swirled it. Eerily, there wasn't a person in sight. A manhole cover had vanished from an entrance to the sewers, and I had a very clear and loud intuition that it hadn't been done by human beings. Seemed like an excellent area to find supernatural trouble after dark, which is probably why the Brotherhood had been here in force.

I gave the open manhole as much room as I could while I walked by it and paced down the street until I hit a spot of sidewalk that put up a phantom resistance to my moving forward, like a spot of deep, soft, stinking mud. Though there wasn't a physical stench, my body reacted as if there had been, as the nauseating sensation of the residue of black magic washed over me.

Images flickered through my mind as I stood there, as they had at the other points. I caught a flash of Daniel's voice letting out a hoarse cry, and the perspective of the street shifted in my mind as I felt the sensation of him pitching abruptly over onto his side.

I leaned on my staff to help keep my balance and fought to close down my extraordinary senses. I took a moment to catch my breath as the sense of dark power faded. As I had at the other attack points, I took a natural beeswax votive candle out of my duster's pocket, put it down in the center of the patch of dark energy, drew a chalk circle about it while focusing on my intention, and lit the candle with a murmured spell. Then I stepped back and waited.

The candle flickered to life, yellow and bright, and then after a moment burned down to a low point of purplish flame, exactly as it had at the other locations.

Bear came up beside me and looked at the candle. "Well?" she asked.

"They're all from the same source," I said quietly. "Same color, same energy."

"So, a person," Bear mused.

"Or the same group of people," I said, nodding. "Map?"

Bear handed me a paper street map of Chicago we'd been using. I unfolded it, took a pencil out of my pocket, and marked the latest location.

"How far can you throw a curse like this?" Bear asked.

I shook my head. "Not really a specialty of mine," I replied. "Line of sight would be pretty straightforward."

"But seems unlikely," Bear said.

"It does," I said. "Curses can take a while. If they used a focus like a recent lock of hair or blood from the victim, they'd have been able to hit them from anywhere on the continent, theoretically."

"Theoretically?"

"In practice, there's lots of things that get in the way," I said. "Degrade how much energy gets through. Running water like rivers and streams. Certain kinds of stone, especially if they're piled up into mountains. Barriers of thresholds around homes can get in the way. Storms, which are generators of energy themselves. Probably other things I'm not aware of, too."

"These sites are all within about a one-mile radius," she noted.

I looked at the map. "Yeah. They are."

"So maybe whoever is doing it doesn't have the kind of strength it takes to project it very far."

"Maybe," I said, nodding. "Or maybe they're using a poppet or simulacrum to create the link."

"Like a voodoo doll?"

"Exactly like that. You can make one of those with pictures and maybe one of their possessions. Could reach out farther than line of sight, but not as far as if you'd had bits of them in your possession. Weak practitioner, maybe half a mile. Maybe a few more miles if you had help."

Bear grunted.

I took the map and started estimating distances. After a moment I sighed. "Dammit."

"What is it?" Bear asked.

I held the map where she could see it and used the end of the pencil to point at a single block I'd circled. "Here's the block that's most equidistant from all of the attack sites," I said.

She frowned and looked at the map and then back up to me. "That tells us something, too, yes?"

"Yes," I confirmed wearily. I pointed at a corner of the block. "Right there. That's Bock Ordered Books."

Chapter

Thirty-Two

The next night, I brought Maggie back to the castle for the weekend, had dinner with her, got her and Bear set up with a movie courtesy of Bob, and then slipped out quietly and went over to Bock Ordered Books to see if I could catch anyone in the act.

Veils are pretty basic magic, though I have zero innate talent with them. A lot of practice while training Molly, when she'd been my apprentice, meant that I'd become a barely passing student with them, but by the time you added deep shadows, patience, discipline, and a lifetime of practice at moving quietly when necessary, I wasn't going to get spotted by anyone without extraordinary senses.

I set up across from Bock Ordered Books, an unassuming building located on a quiet commercial block, and waited.

Some things had happened to me here. A couple of hooded mystery types called Cowl and Kumori had come at me here once. I hadn't heard from them in a good while, and I hadn't written them off, either. I'd met the purely mental entity Lash here, though it had taken a bit to figure out that she was the reflection of a corruptive fallen angel's personality. She'd died to protect me later on, evidently having been corrupted by basic humanity herself. That had been the last time I'd sighted Cowl, in fact.

That brought up the thought that perhaps the Coins of the Knights of the Blackened Denarius were connected with Cowl somehow, and one of my eyes started twitching.

I brooded over that thought while I soaked up the stillness, my own vision blurred and dimmed from behind the veil that would hide me from sight. The line of thought expanded into increasingly gloomy or ridiculous scenarios, and then people started showing up at the bookstore.

They came in threes, thrice. Nine, a power number for magical workings. They were wary about it, too, all with flashlights sweeping nervously everywhere. That didn't bother me. I was posted up against a wall in front of a giant mound of uncollected trash and wouldn't present any kind of silhouette identifiable as human, with the veil up. I extended my wizard's senses, reaching out for the feel of magic in the air, and got the faintest whiff of malodorous intent coming from them.

Dammit. This was going to be difficult.

The practice of black magic is . . . intoxicating. Sometimes addictive. It's also not fantastic for one's sanity. Usually, low-powered practitioners couldn't really drum up enough dark energy, acting on their own, to suffer particular effects from the use of black magic, so the world was pretty much full of small-time mischief and petty injuries so marginal that it was arguable whether the magic had any effect, or if its subject had simply gotten mildly unlucky.

When they started operating in teams, though, summoning up more serious effects of black magic, it started getting to them. That kind of situation, the genuine intent to harm, coupled with the belief that the practitioners in question could and should inflict that harm, coupled with the addictive nature of the magic and its effects at undermining reason, created . . . an extremely volatile situation, and one not easily or rationally dealt with.

The White Council's Wardens' operations, over the centuries, were primarily handling instances exactly like this one. Sometimes it was one person who had lost it, sometimes a few, sometimes a whole batch. A limited number of Wardens operating under the pressure of an increasing number of talented people being born into larger and larger populations could only afford one solution to the problem: Kill them all and then move on to the next emergency where people were suffering horribly at the hands of others like them. If the Wardens were to protect the mortal populace in any meaningful way from warlocks, those who had given themselves over to the practice of black magic, they had no real alternative.

It was math.

Math can be brutal.

It hadn't given the White Council a particularly kind image among the less powerful talents.

If I'd been operating as a Warden, the playbook would have called for me to blow holes in the walls at multiple points and go in with a dozen other Wardens behind shields, arresting them all and putting to an end by the sword anyone who resisted. Literal swords; it was how Wardens rolled.

But I wasn't a Warden.

The White Council's primary duty was to limit and contain harm and malicious influence from magical practitioners among the mortal population. That duty, arguably necessary, could at times get very, very ugly. And since there were people carrying that duty out, they could screw it up in a million other ways, too.

But I wasn't on the White Council anymore, either.

I knew these people, at least to say hello in passing. I wasn't writing anyone off without making every effort possible to pull them back from the edge.

They needed someone like that.

Or maybe I did.

I gave them a few minutes to chat, and then a few more to prepare for ritual magic. Folks at the low end needed a lot of props and symbols to accomplish curses like this. There might be an animal sacrifice involved, too, near the culmination. I wanted to wait until the curse had started before I disrupted it, and blow their group effort for the evening after they were too tired to go for a round two, but before much power had been built up. Less chance for bad accidents when it went kablooey, that way.

Then someone started using a drum, another common ceremonial feature, and its beats throbbed quietly from the store.

I gave it about five minutes, then dropped the veil and strode across the street. I jammed the end of my staff against the wooden door's dead-bolt lock, focused my will through the staff into the shape of an axe's head, and murmured, *"Forzare!"*

My will wasn't as focused as I would have preferred. Force slammed through the door in an area the size of my fists together and smashed the lock completely out of the wood, but when I twisted the round door-knob, it opened, and I strode into Bock Ordered Books, my spell-armored leather duster rustling against my legs.

"The Wardens!" someone shouted, their voice high and frightened.

I swept my gaze around the store, getting all the information I could in the space of maybe a second. In the reading area, the secondhand sofa and easy chairs had been pushed back against the nearest shelves of books. A circle of salt (I suppose it could have been sugar, but salt is way easier to clean up and doesn't draw bugs) had been poured around a cir-cle of nine people I knew, at least to look at. Five of them were from the Ordo Lebes, middle-aged women (two of whom had been volunteering regularly in the castle). There were also a couple of the old guys who often smoked pipes at Mac's, a morose-looking guy in his thirties beat-ing on a drum beneath one arm, and Artemis Bock, holding a leather-bound journal open in one hand. There was a bloodstained makeshift altar made from an old end table sitting in a plastic tub in the middle of the circle, and a caged chicken sat beside it, looking nervous. A circle of lit votive candles surrounded the circle, every few degrees, probably five for each participant.

"Don't stop! Don't leave the circle!" Bock shouted.

Which went to show that he was an amateur. The ritual they were doing would take a quarter of an hour at least just to pull up the energy they'd need. I strode forward without stopping and kicked a foot through the circle of salt, knocking over a couple of candles as I did.

"No!" someone shouted.

I felt the power of the circle snap and disperse as my foot brushed through the salt. There was a swirl of wind that sent pages rattling all through the store, carrying with it a horrible stench of sulfur and old death. Flames exploded from the candles into twisted shapes and faces, darting in every direction and vanishing into sickly swirls of black, greasy-looking smoke while letting out faint, distant shrieks and wails. A pressure wave washed out from the altar, knocking over the chicken's cage and half the people there, and knocking the cage open. It also sent the tall bookcases on either side slowly tumbling over into their neighbors in a great clatter of wood and falling books.

I mean, there's a reason wizards have labs and libraries and they're in different rooms.

The morose guy stumbled back, dropping the drum and reaching into his jacket pocket. He produced a short-barreled, heavy revolver, maybe a .44, and pointed it at me. I'd been watching for such a move and triggered a couple more charges from the staff. They hit him in the chest, slammed him back into the couch behind him, and knocked it over until it lay against the front of one of the fallen shelves.

The chicken let out a screech and fluttered up into the air and over one of the fallen shelves, careening drunkenly over the other side and out of sight.

I kept the staff gripped like a spear and pointed at them, and I couldn't tell if I was angry or disgusted or just tired.

Greasy, stinking smoke hung over the room, the ugly sensation of black magic coursing about the place, making the air feel as if it had been filled with tiny, sticky particles. I heard the gunman make a soft sound of pain from where he was sprawled senseless on the fallen couch. Several people were panting. One woman was weeping.

"Stars and stones," I said wearily. "Guys? About the time you're taking countermeasures for the number of animal sacrifices you're pulling in your rituals, shouldn't someone be asking if maybe things are going a little too far?"

"This is a private g-gathering," Bock began. His mouth worked for a second; he took a breath, seemed to find his footing, and said, "Get out of my store. Before I call the police."

I fixed Bock with a quiet stare.

He flinched.

"You're lucky," I said quietly. I lowered my staff until one end rested on the floor. "You're all extremely lucky that I'm not the Wardens. If they showed up here, they'd have beheaded half of you already. The others would be being bound up for a fair trial that would find you guilty of the practice of black magic, after which you would be deemed warlocks and also beheaded."

One of the women from the Ordo, I think her name was April, pushed herself slowly to her feet. She had roan-colored hair and long-fingered hands. "What . . . what are you going to do to us?"

"Warn you," I said. "What you're doing isn't acceptable. Quit it."

"Or what?" Bock asked.

"See above, regarding Wardens and decapitation," I said.

"You don't understand," April said. "Some of those men, what they're doing to us—"

"April," I replied in a voice I had to work to make calm. "There are only two paths here. Stop it. Or die. You're already stinking up the whole neighborhood with black magic. It's only a matter of time until it gets the attention of the Wardens and they send a team here to deal with it."

"But they have—"

I slammed the end of my staff on the floor, triggering the release of more force. It let out a rumbling crackling and snapping like thunder and sent splits out through the floorboards of the old building.

Everyone but Bock flinched.

He drew in a breath. He closed the book. Then he straightened his vest and his glasses and walked over to stand in front of me.

"We have a right to defend ourselves," he said quietly.

"By throwing torture spells on people?" I replied. "By practicing outright black magic? There's a difference between taking action to change a situation and indiscriminate violence."

"We have limited options," he snapped. "We don't live in a castle with armed guards. We aren't among the high and mighty. We have to make do with what is at hand." He took a step forward, his expression both pleading and furious. "We came to you. We *asked* for your *help.* You did *nothing.*"

I clenched my jaw and fought down a surge of anger.

Because, well. That was partly true.

I'd been flailing a lot. Barely functioning a lot. Wasn't focused. I'd sent over a few of the Knights of the Bean, part-time. Clearly, they could only deter things when they were there. Otherwise, for me, it had slipped through the cracks.

I rippled my fingers on the quarterstaff, settling my grip.

"Okay," I said quietly. "I'm on it. But this"—I gestured at the room with my staff—"doesn't happen again."

"You don't get to tell us what to do," Bock snapped.

I eyed him.

He was seething. More than he should have been. Working with black magic does that to you. Enhances insecurities. Deepens anxieties. More fear means more anger—fear and anger do bad, bad things to people, even without the magical effects that make you need to exercise power over and over, desperately trying to assuage the ever-growing fear with (admittedly ill-advised) action.

I wasn't going to be able to reason him down.

"The hell I don't," I said, very, very quietly. "If I wanted to, I could have annihilated all of you on the way in. If I wanted you shut down, I could do it in a hundred ways. And if I didn't want to do all the work myself, I could drop a dime on you to the Wardens. You are the one who is in no position to make demands, Bock. That's not saying anything about you or what you're doing. God knows, you wouldn't be the first abused person to react. But the reality is, you're on the edge here, man. I'm trying to make a point. I'm trying to help you."

April came up beside Bock and slipped beneath his arm. Some of the fury faded, and he traded an uncertain glance with her.

"This is already coming back on some of us," she said quietly. "Headaches. Stomachaches. Rashes. The Rule of Three applies."

Ah, ye olde Rule of Three. The belief that the way you use magic comes back to you threefold. Practitioners who blended magic and faith, like most of the Ordo, were big on that one. That wasn't a sentiment I was in a particularly good place to agree with, but I could acknowledge in a general sense that what goes around does seem to come around, given enough time.

Bock frowned at her. Then at me.

"I'm tired of seeing kids get beaten and hurt," he said quietly.

"By the Brotherhood of St. Brigid?" I asked.

He nodded. He described several men. They matched the descriptions of Carl and the guys who had followed him out of St. Mary's chapel the night before. The real problem with any kind of militant order was there always seemed to be a few people in them who were militant first, orderly second.

Maybe they were people who were scared and angry. People who acted to try to assuage their fear. Only to create more things to be afraid of.

Or to be fair, maybe they were just assholes who had sensed an opportunity in extraordinary circumstances to exercise their darker desires and had done so. Knowing humans, likely a mix of both.

Bad times bring out bad things in some people. Sublime things in others.

I described Daniel Carpenter to him. "Any trouble with that guy?"

"No," April said firmly. "He's their leader, yes? When he's there, nothing has gone wrong."

"Well, you lot just about killed him last night," I said quietly. "If I hadn't been around, I'm not sure what would have happened."

"What?" April said, genuinely shocked. She glanced at Bock.

Bock looked back toward where couch guy was groaning. He was sitting up, clutching the wrist that had held the revolver. The blast I'd thrown at him had torn it out of his hand, at the expense of his fingers and wrist. "I . . . was told it was the leader of the ruffians' glove we used . . ." Bock said.

Which confirmed my theory on using personal possessions to link the ritual's energy to the target. "You got it wrong," I said. "And you hit the wrong guy. And if I hadn't been around to put it right, I'm not sure what would have happened to him, or how they would have reacted."

"But . . ." Bock said. He fidgeted with the book. "The journal said the curse only disables. Inconveniences."

"Yeah," I said. "Maybe disables them to an inconvenient death, if they don't get some kind of help," I said. "Can strain their sanity, too. Throwing that much pain at someone."

"My God," Bock said quietly. He traded another look with April. "My God."

"I told you," she said gently. "We couldn't know what would really happen."

"Leonid Kravos was a certifiable psycho," I said quietly. "Bock. Give me the book."

Something hard and ugly flickered through Bock's eyes. "Why?" he demanded. "You're going to burn it, I suppose."

"I'm going to shut it away where people who shouldn't have access to it won't misuse it," I said gently. "You guys are going to turn your talents to cleansing the aura of this space. You need to clean up your mess before the Wardens find it, decide they don't have time to split hairs, and track you all down and end you."

He studied me sidelong, wary. "Why should we?"

"Because it's how you all get away from this dark ritual stuff that is going to make you miserable and eventually kill you."

"So we can be beaten and threatened?" Bock asked tiredly.

"So instead of me cleaning up after you, I can address your problem," I said, and held out my hand.

He stared at my hand for a moment. Traded another look with April.

He passed over the book like he was giving up a winning lottery ticket.

I felt the residue of dark magic all over the damned thing. I didn't know what kind of leather it was bound with, but it wasn't from a cow. I slipped it into my duster's pocket.

"We're putting a lot of trust in you, Dresden," Bock said. He didn't meet my eyes while he did. He just looked tired.

"I know," I said gently. "Your shooter there is going to need medical attention. You don't want to go to a hospital, bring him round the castle in the morning. Doc will be visiting. Won't be any charge." I swept my gaze around the room. No one wanted to meet my eyes except April, who gave me the not-quite-eye-contact gaze of a magical practitioner.

I nodded at her. "You know basic cleansing rituals?"

"Of course," she said. She looked around at the half-wrecked store. "Might take some time."

"Yeah," I said. I nodded to Bock and looked regretfully around the store. The chicken, saved from sacrifice, came walking out of the havoc, made a couple of quiet sounds, and scratched at a fallen book before defecating on it. "Um. Sorry about the mess."

"Just go," Bock said.

I left.

I didn't exactly feel good about it. I'd leaned on them pretty hard.

I mean, for their own good, yeah. I'd been playing pillow fight compared to what the Wardens would have done to them. And it had required leverage and power to get them to even consider changing course.

But I still felt like a bully.

Speaking of which, I would have to have a word with Daniel.

And Carl.

Chapter
Thirty-Three

Daniel and I sat at the base of a building across the street from Mac's place, dressed in layers of mismatched secondhand clothes, and watched the traders in the little bazaar. It was a cold day, but this part of town was still without power and living by the weird values of that temporary between-time of an emergency. Despite the cold, most of the traffic was on foot. There were more people about than usual, even with the reduced population.

Daniel took a sip of hot chocolate from a battered old thermos and watched the people across the street with haggard eyes. He bowed his head and rested it against his wrist for a moment.

"Nice," I said. "You look like an old drunk that way."

"Hah," he muttered.

"You sure you should be out here?" I asked him.

"God's blood," Daniel said quietly. "Given what's been going on, I damned well should be."

He offered me the thermos, and I took some chocolate into my own cup. His hand shook, pouring. After getting out from under the curse, he'd been in rough shape. Probably needed a few more rest days before he hit the gym again.

I sipped some chocolate. The sun was going down, and the air was beginning to bite. I found it pleasant.

Daniel shivered and drank more hot chocolate.

"What I mean is," I said, "are you sure you're up for this?"

"If I'm not, I shouldn't be leading the Brotherhood," he said firmly. His eyes looked past me and locked on something beyond me. "We'll know in a minute."

I didn't lift my head, just my eyes. I could see a group coming down the sidewalk toward the bazaar. I couldn't see faces with my peripheral vision, but it pretty much had to be Carl and crew. I could read in their body language the focus upon the bazaar as they approached, the intention in their tension. They were looking for trouble.

The folks in the bazaar saw them and started scurrying.

Which told me most of what I needed to know, right there.

I glanced aside at Daniel. The young man was looking hard at the members of the Brotherhood people were fleeing from. He was a soldier and had his mother's eyes. He could do a good hard look.

"From this point," he said quietly, "you're an observer from the magical community. I want a witness they'll believe. Don't interfere."

Then he stood up, squared his shoulders, and stalked forward to intercept the group of men.

Whether or not I interfered would depend a great deal on what happened, but what the hell. The kid wanted to solve the problem on his own—which was a right instinct. It would work better if it was an internal thing within the Brotherhood, and since he was their head guy, it was his job to clean house. I'd let Daniel take the lead, see where it went. If things got physical and went bad for him, well. Physically, at least, I was in pretty good shape.

I went after Michael's son, a step behind and to one side, where I could watch his back for him.

Daniel walked straight up to Carl. I couldn't see the kid's face, but when Carl turned from saying something to one of his cronies to see Daniel walking toward him, there was a certain amount of alarm that flashed over his features. He came to an uncertain halt, his four companions almost piling up behind him.

"Carl," Daniel said calmly. "I'd like to speak to you."

"About what?" Carl demanded.

Daniel extended his hand toward the sidewalk past them, an invitation. "We can discuss that privately."

"What's the wizard doing here?" Carl spat.

"He's a witness," Daniel said quietly.

"Then these are my witnesses," Carl said, gesturing back at the men with him.

Daniel's head tilted and he shrugged one shoulder. "Very well. I have reports that you and the men with you have laid hands on your fellow citizens on patrols you have led. Is that true?"

"They aren't like us," Carl said. "They're with that occult crap, is what they are. You saw what came of having them among us. City's been wrecked, hasn't it. Things eating people. Eating *people*. And here they are, bold as brass, selling their occult crap in broad daylight, maybe getting ready to do it to us again. They been striking at us all week, you included. What's gonna stop them?"

"I am," I said.

"Oh, yeah, you," Carl scoffed. He turned back to Daniel. "These attacks can't go unanswered. You know that."

The attacks *were* answers, from where I was standing. But I didn't know everything that had happened. Mileage could vary.

And from the perspective of someone whose belief in the supernatural had suddenly been abruptly reversed in the most traumatic way possible by the Battle of Chicago, yeah. It might be difficult to tell the difference between one terrifying supernatural thing like Ethniu and the city-destroying Eye of Balor, and a curse that would merely torture one to death over days.

Daniel took a slow breath. There was nothing at all yielding in his stance. "Our mandate," he said quietly, "is to protect our families and neighbors from supernatural threats in extraordinary times. It is not to beat and frighten those very same people."

"See?" Carl said, partly over his shoulder. "What they say about his family is right. Maybe they've become a little too friendly with the unnatural."

Daniel went still.

Carl met his eyes and lifted a defiant chin.

"Very well," Daniel said quietly. "I accept your challenge."

Carl blinked. "What?"

"You've defied my authority, Carl," Daniel said. "You've leveled an accusation that could only result in my removal as brother captain as well as blacken my family's name. I accept your challenge to my authority and choose trial by combat, as is my right beneath the Brotherhood's charter." He nodded and started shrugging out of his jackets. "We're going bare-knuckle. I'd strip down a bit if I were you."

"Wait, what?" Carl demanded.

"Would you prefer swords? I don't recommend that. I've studied with my father."

"Jesus," Carl blurted.

"His name is Michael," I pointed out matter-of-factly.

"See," Daniel said, "the way I see it, Carl, you've gotten to thinking that if you're strong enough to do it, you have the right to," he said. "And your actions are a direct challenge to my authority." He got down to a hoodie and pushed up the sleeves. "I'll come toward you. We'll settle this your way." He squared up, fists held loose and lower than I would have. "How about you come tangle with someone your own size?"

"There's one of you," Carl said. "There's five of—"

And before he could say "us," Daniel shuffled up, laid a long right cross through the chin of the guy on Carl's right and dropped him to the ground like a bag of lawn clippings. Then Daniel twisted into a left hook, throwing the punch as much with his hips and legs and abs as his arms, and drilled a shot into Carl's left side that dropped him to the ground with a breathless gasp of pain.

Daniel took a step back, his eyes flashing left and right at the other three. "All right. Who's next?"

Carl made a retching sound on the ground, curling into a fetal position. Liver shot. Ow. I hadn't had the pleasure myself, but Murph had talked about how debilitating they were. Daniel Carpenter was a large man, a soldier, a professional at violence, and evidently a trained boxer. The punches had all been real ones, thrown with his whole body. He wasn't functioning at a hundred percent, but apparently fifty percent plus a sucker-punch approach was more than enough for those two.

Maybe there was a lesson for me in there.

On the other hand, getting away with two quick punches wasn't the same thing as going toe-to-toe with three guys who were ready. I closed one hand into a fist and waited to see what would come next.

The other three men, none of them near Daniel's size, glanced at one another, then showed their palms and took half steps back.

Daniel nodded and lowered his hands. "Fine."

One of the others looked unhappy as he spoke. "Cap," he said quietly, "Carl ain't smart. But he ain't all wrong, either. We can't stand around doing nothing while they're coming at us."

"I'm not here to have a debate with you," Daniel said firmly. "You signed on to work together, which means obeying orders. You men don't come back to this block, ever. You don't rough people up, ever. Anything about that you don't understand?"

The man looked away from Daniel and said, "Naw, Cap."

The guy Daniel had sucker punched stirred and slowly pushed himself to his hands and knees.

"You three take these two back to the chapter house and take care of them," Daniel told the man who was speaking. "I'm not going to have this discussion again. You read me?"

"Yeah, Cap," he said.

The other two fully conscious ones affirmed their agreement on the point as well.

"You guys go on. I'll be there directly. We're going to sit down with my father and Father Forthill and have a long talk in a couple of hours." Daniel walked over to the bazaar, where the little makeshift stalls were empty.

"I apologize for what has happened here in my absence," Daniel said, speaking loudly, so that anyone in the building who was listening or anyone out of sight nearby might hear. He held up a card and then put it down on the ground, weighing it down with a stone. "If there's been harm done, expenses incurred, property damaged, contact me here. I can't make the hurt go away, but perhaps I can make part of it right. It won't happen again."

Then he turned and walked over to me.

Carl's crew were helping him to his feet and beginning to stagger away. I watched them, bemused.

"Not sure your father would have been that, ah, direct," I said. "He'd probably have let them swing first."

Daniel shrugged a shoulder. He'd picked up his discarded jackets and was getting back into them, shivering. "He doesn't feel as terrible as I do. And it was five to one."

"Two," I said.

"I told you not to interfere," Daniel said, his tone either amused or annoyed.

"Did you? Well. I'm getting older. Hearing isn't so good."

"You're a wizard. You live to be a zillion."

"Eh?" I said. "Speak up there, kid."

Daniel cracked a smile and shook his head wearily. "Look. Some things need to get said in other ways for some people to understand it," he said. "Carl's scared. He isn't bright. He might even mean well. But he can only think as far as his knuckles, and there's only so many ways to think about problems and solutions with those. I had to lay it out in terms he would understand on several levels. And do it loud enough the others heard it clearly, too."

"If it matters," I said, "I would only have come in if the conversation hadn't gone the way you planned."

Daniel thought about that one for a second and then nodded, bemused. "It does matter. Thank you. For letting me handle it."

"Sometimes the best way to help somebody is to step back and give them room," I said. "Glad this was one of those times." I paused and added, "'Cause if they'd shot you or bashed your face in, I'd have had to explain to your mother *and* your wife why I let it happen."

Daniel burst out in a quick, low laugh. "You would, wouldn't you." He tilted his head as we began to walk back toward his car. "How'd you know it was the right time for that?"

I put my hand on Daniel's shoulder. "Experience, kid. I've done well trusting Carpenters."

Chapter
Thirty-Four

February came and it wasn't as cold as it might have been. I had been spending a lot of time working on the spell for Thomas. I had proved the concept with Lara on New Year's Eve, but going halfway and backing off wasn't the same as going through the whole process, any more than a quick sketch on a napkin was the same thing as a large oil painting. Magic, like all power, often has unexpected consequences when used. It's easy to call it up, hard to deal with what happens as a result if you haven't employed it with discipline and caution.

Severing the bond between the Hunger and Thomas was the danger point. I had thought my way through it and had realized with a cold little shiver that I was, on a magical level, attempting something that, if done incorrectly, would be a lot like breaking molecular bonds. The amount of eldritch energy that could potentially be released was staggering and could readily consume Thomas or the Hunger, or me, or all of us. There was a very low-order probability that it could chain-react beyond the immediate participants in the spell as well, with results that could be entirely unpredictable. I'd have to do it on the island, where I could have free rein to build the magical equivalent of a vault, clean room, and surgical theater.

I'd have to go to the island and outline to Alfred what I would need. The *Water Beetle* was in harbor land storage at the moment, so it would have to be a trek through the Nevernever to get there. Fun, in the way that I could readily get killed doing it, but I wanted to give Alfred plenty of time. I'd probably need a proper thaw and the boat back in the water to get everything I'd need transported to the site.

Spring, then.

I'd given Fitz the evening off, and he'd promptly gone to the gym to horse around with a couple of the younger Knights of the Bean and several young men who were staying with their families from the neighborhood. They'd worked out a way to throw down the workout pads and play a game somewhere between dodgeball, American football, and Rest-of-the-World football down the long axis of the gym. There was a lot of tackling and kicking the ball with egregious amounts of force. Bruises and minor injuries were common, and the players seemed to regard them as a feature, not a bug.

People get weird when they're cooped up for a while.

I wrapped up my sketched design for a proper major circle for this spell, put it away in a protective sleeve and into a folder, and left it on my lab table. Bob the Skull had helped with it.

I climbed up the stepladder to the lowest floor of the castle and shambled down the hall to my room. Bear, reading a book, glanced up as I walked by her room and I waved good night, before shutting myself in my bedroom, locking the door, and getting out the materials for the summoning ritual, along with a new board game where players cooperatively dealt with urban folklore monsters running about a small town.

Before, I would have said the game was too much like work, but I hadn't been much on the deal-with-monsters train lately.

Maybe she'd feel the same way.

Spells go smoother and faster and more efficiently the more you perform them, and by now this one was second nature. Maybe forty-five seconds, start to finish, closing a circle centered around a SIG Sauer P365 nine-millimeter pistol named Backup, a set of motorcycle keys, and several rough, raw diamonds I once would have considered rocks.

"New game," she noted, a few seconds after I was finished. "Huh. Cooperative? They make cooperative games?"

I opened my eyes. The candles had burned down to blue pinpoints, and like always, it would take a few minutes before I could see her face. "They're mostly playing together against an algorithm, but yeah."

"Okay," she said. She studied me for a moment. "Except you're looking different, aren't you?"

"Shaved," I said. "Haircut. Maggie thought it looked messy."

"Maggie's right, it did," she replied, amused. "Taking care of yourself. Grooming. That's a good thing. Healthy." I vaguely saw her tilt her head. "Something else is on your mind."

The Winter mantle stirred, flickers of anger and need for resolution zinging around my insides.

"Mab thinks I need to get revenge on Rudolph."

"For what?" she asked me.

I felt a flicker of something like shame at the way I felt. "You know for what."

"From where I'm at right now," she said, "it gets less and less relevant to me."

"After what he did to you?!" I demanded.

"From my perspective," she said gently, "he kind of created me. I know you get upset when I say this, but you need to hear it: I'm not quite her, am I?"

"Dammit," I muttered. I stared at the box for the game.

"I don't think I want to play that one," she continued in the same soft voice. "Harry, I understand why you're doing what you're doing. But you can't do this forever. We aren't actually cooperative in all of this."

I didn't look up at her dim form.

"I don't mind helping you," she said. "I'm very, very fond of you, obviously. But I also have very limited agency in this, also obviously."

She let that sit in the air for a long moment of silence.

"Why does Mab think you need revenge?" she asked.

"Said it would make managing the Winter mantle easier."

"You having problems with it?"

"I . . . no. Not so much. I mean, the exercise, the routine, the discipline. And I've gotten better at . . . I dunno. Compartmentalizing? Or maybe figuring out which is the mantle and which is actually me."

"Ah," she said. "So if you're aware that it's the mantle that wants vengeance, why are you even asking me about it?"

"Oh," I said.

"Do you?" she asked. "Is that what you want? To do unto Rudolph as he did unto Murphy?"

I flinched again.

I didn't like it when the shade pointed out that she wasn't . . .

Wasn't . . .

"I . . ." I swallowed. "When it happened. I wanted to crush him. Slow. Painful." The blue pinpoint lights blurred. "And I'd never felt so certain about anything in my life. It was like everything in me was all aligned, pointing in the same direction." I shook my head. "It was like fighting a child. Wasn't a damned thing he could do."

She was sitting in the one chair in the room. She leaned forward, elbows resting on her knees. "Then what happened?"

"Two Knights of the Cross showed up to stop me," I said. "I fought them. My friends. And I lost." I held up the arm that still bore the burn scar from the Sword of Faith. "And the Sword that only smites the wicked did this to me."

"My God," she said. "You're not even Catholic."

I frowned. "Eh?"

She smiled at me. "I suppose we don't have a monopoly on carrying shame, but we're definitely number one." She paused and mused, "We. You'd think I'd not be Catholic anymore given my circumstances. But here we are."

"I'm not ashamed of the fight," I said quietly.

"But you're ashamed of the burn," she said.

"I'm ashamed I failed y . . ." I swallowed and took a deep breath. "Her."

The shade sat back slowly. I could see her face now. Her eyes. Her hair. Exactly like Murph. Her expression was pensive, intent.

"I failed her," I said quietly. "I loved her and I failed her."

"A great many people died that night," the shade said quietly. "Mortals. Supernatural folk. It was a war. And no one was in control of what was happening."

"I *should* have been," I said viciously. "I should have been."

Her eyes glistened with tears. "Oh," she said quietly. "Oh, Harry." She folded her hands and said, "I have all of her memories, you know. I remember that you told her to stay under cover. That she was in no shape to go to war. You did that, didn't you?"

"Yeah," I said.

"But she didn't listen."

"Course she didn't," I said. "You know how she was."

"More than anyone, I suspect." She sighed. "What is it, exactly, you think you should have done?"

"Bonked her on the head and dropped her off at McAnally's," I said.

"One," the shade said, "you're assuming you could have pulled that off. But let's be generous and say you had. What do you think she would have done, after?"

"Been pissed," I choked out.

"Understatement," the shade said, nodding. "You'd have lost her that way, too."

"But she'd *be alive*," I snarled.

The shade stared at me for a long moment. Then she said, "She was too hurt to go out, wasn't she?"

"She was," I said. "Until Mab . . ."

Until Mab had exerted the force of her will. Had reduced the ability of those willing to fight to defend the city to feel fear. Pain. Made them more like Winter, more aggressive, primal, drawing out their combative instincts and sharpening them, the way the Winter mantle did for me.

If Mab hadn't done that . . .

If I hadn't gone and broken Thomas out of his imprisonment . . .

If I hadn't destroyed the Red Court, freeing the Fomor to attack a power vacuum . . .

If I hadn't stood to fight beside the Accorded nations, only to be cast out of the White Council . . .

If Rudolph had had an ounce of personal courage and backbone . . .

The shade watched my face intently. "A lot of things had to come together for all of that to happen," she said. "Some of them were partly in your control. Some of them weren't. It's . . . extremely arrogant for you to take credit for the ones that weren't your fault, Harry. You haven't earned that."

I scowled at the floor.

"I can tell you this much," the shade said simply. "She loved you, though she was afraid to admit it to herself, much less you. She was going to be in that fight, one way or another. She regretted none of her choices. Even at the end. Except that she'd held herself back from you."

I started crying. My shoulders shook.

"We can have conversations like this over and over," the shade said. "But I don't think you're going to get much out of them." She leaned forward. "You need other people for that. People who can put their hand on your shoulder. Tell you things that they see that you can't see for yourself."

"Everyone is under strain," I began.

"Not everyone lost the person they loved," said the shade in a reasonable tone. "You should talk to them. About her. Let them help you remember her." She sighed. "Because you're stuck in your memories, all by yourself. And calling me up almost every night is not going to help you with that. Memories fade. Like pain. Like wounds. Preserve the brightest ones. Talk about them to other people. You're going to find a lot more compassion and understanding than you think." She took a deep breath. "And talk about the worst, too. And let them go."

"I don't want to let go," I said, voice almost pleading. I looked up at her. "Of y . . . of her."

"That's not for you to decide," she said, very softly. "She's gone. That's the truth. There's nothing left to hold on to." She smiled wanly. "Apart from me, I mean."

Shades were not the people who had once lived. They were an imprint, like a footprint in soft ground, a spiritual being made of memories of a life now gone.

"I'm tired," I said, shaking. "Of . . . just, crying. Tears. Fuck, I'm so tired of hurting."

"You need to take steps," she said. "You need to heal. You know what that means."

I shook my head.

"You're getting there," she said encouragingly. "I know you feel terrible still. But you're getting there." She sighed. "I mean what I say. About talking to someone. It will help."

The candles flickered and went out.

And the shade was gone.

I sat on the floor and wept.

After a while, there was a quiet knock at the door, and Bear said, "Dresden?"

It took a moment, but I shambled to my feet, to the door, and opened it.

Bear hovered over me in a long white nightshirt, her expression set in a frown. "Hey. You all right?"

"No," I said quietly. "Not since last summer."

She nodded. "Murphy," she said.

"Feels like my fault," I said.

"Because you survived," she said. "And she didn't."

"At the end . . ." I hesitated and then said, feeling afresh the horror and pain of that night, "Her lips were blue. And she was so pale. Like she was freezing."

"Deep breath," said Bear. "Go on."

I took a deep breath, like when meditating. I felt some of the horror ease. I'd practiced breathing and calming myself so much over the past months.

"I miss her," I said. "And when she went, I . . . I did things I'm not proud of. To friends. And I'm ashamed to talk to anyone about it."

Bear blew out a heavy breath.

Then she said, "Man the fuck up, Dresden."

I blinked. "What?"

"You got hurt," she said. "In a bad situation, you did some things you wish you hadn't. Surprise, surprise, you're human. You make mistakes. You screw things up. That part isn't even a question. Humans do that. Life came along and knocked you onto your ass." She lifted a hand, made a fist, and drove it gently into my shoulder. "It's okay to get knocked down. It's not okay to stay there. That isn't who you are, or who you are meant to be. So gather up your testosterone, think of a wonderful thought, do whatever it is you need to do, and *get back up off the ground.*"

"That's so compassionate," I said.

"Sometimes the most compassionate thing you can do for someone is give them a gentle, firm boot to the ass," she said seriously. "Wake up. Events are in motion. There's not a lot of time. There are massive things on the wind. And we need you. Make things as right as you can and move the fuck on."

I think any night before that, I would have gotten angry. Really, really angry.

But the part of me that was tired of hurting thought that maybe I should consider what she'd said.

I looked at her for a long moment and then nodded slowly.

"Observation to make," Bear said. "More personal than I usually do."

"Go ahead," I said.

"If you weren't a decent person, with a conscience and a soul," she said, "one who genuinely cares about trying to be a good man, you'd never be torturing yourself like this. If anyone else was treating someone the way you've been treating yourself, you'd hat up and take action. Why the hell should it be any different when you are the person being treated badly?"

I blinked a few times at that.

I hadn't ever thought of it that way before.

"So do something about it," Bear said. "Go to sleep. Leg day tomorrow."

"I . . ." I said. "Uh. Yeah." I looked up at her. "Thank you, Bear."

She nodded gravely.

I went to bed, exhausted.

And before I knew it, I'd fallen asleep.

Chapter
Thirty-Five

Lara and I had our February date the week before Valentine's Day.
Which was Thomas's birthday.

We were sitting in a fine restaurant where the menu was all in French on the Near North Side, opening after months of having no power. My French, a relic of my time in the public educational system, is *comme ci, comme ça*, at my very best. I was wearing a casual grey suit with a midnight blue shirt and no tie, because I had decided I wasn't going to bring the garrote to my own assassination, if that's how the evening decided to go. Lara was stunning in a white skirt suit with a midnight blue shirt that matched mine. The place was empty except for us and minimal staff. Lara had called it a soft open.

"*Boeuf* means beef, right?" I asked, peering at the menu. "Is that a steak?"

Lara was watching me with amused pale blue eyes. "Would you mind very much if I ordered for you?"

I narrowed my eyes. "It's not going to be snails, is it?"

Her mouth quirked at the corner. "Don't you enjoy trying new things?"

"As a trend, no," I said. "New things have been a little rough on me, ever since"—I paused, musing—"since my old place burned down, really."

"As I understand it," Lara said, "that's around when you got involved with Mab."

"Probably the least destructive option I had at the time," I said. "And it's also when you arranged for that ship to come by after Chichén Itzá. Saved Molly's life."

She inclined her head slightly. "Wine?"

"Water, for me, but feel free."

"Mmm," she said, her eyes crinkling. "Perhaps I should keep a clear head."

"Hah," I replied. I drew in a breath and considered her. "Okay," I said. "Let's see what happens. I would like it if you ordered for me."

"Excellent," she said. She raised a hand, summoning the waiter instantly, and spoke to him in liquid, native-level French. He replied in the same language, and she said something that made him laugh before he departed.

"Your eyes are paler than usual," I noted.

Lara focused her eyes on me for a moment, with an intensity that I could all but feel on my skin. Then she cleared her throat, looked aside, and picked up her glass of water. "I've not fed since New Year's Eve."

Meaning that she hadn't fed in over a month. Which probably meant something. But I didn't know enough about specifics to understand what, exactly.

"Um," I said. "How does that work, exactly? I mean, is that a long time? Not much time? I've got no idea what the logistics are like."

She took a sip of water and set it aside. "It varies from individual to individual, based mainly on how much discipline and restraint one has developed. For me, absent other factors such as major metropolitan battles, I tend to feed once or twice a week. My sisters on most days. My father"—her face twisted—"would do so as a ritual once a year or so."

I studied her face. "That bothers you," I said. "Why?"

"Waiting so long between feedings essentially guaranteed the subject would die or be rendered a vegetable," Lara said. "Even in his restraint, he is a flawlessly selfish machine."

"Huh," I said. "So, feeding every day is less destructive to the, ah, subject."

"Daily instinctive feedings are smaller bites, if you want to think of it that way," she said. "Though there are few humans who could with-stand that over time without considerable mental damage."

I thought of Halloween and had to work not to squirm. "Do they heal from it?"

"Over time, yes," Lara said. "Some faster than others. The youthful more quickly than otherwise. The healthy more swiftly than the sickly."

"And you get hungry again based on how much supernatural vam-pire stuff you do. Right?"

"Like anything else, when a Hunger is exercised, it requires more sustenance," Lara said. "I find it difficult to . . . maintain a healthy diet, feeding on a daily basis. I am discriminatory in who I will feed upon—they should be physically and mentally healthy. By spreading out my feedings, I am able to remain discriminatory with less risk to a more exclusive pool of subjects."

"But you haven't fed in five weeks," I said. "And your eyes are still blue."

Lara looked down at her glass of water, and her cheeks turned the faintest shade of pink. "Ah. Yes. The . . . energy intake from the spell was . . ." She shook her head a little, searching for words.

"Filling?" I suggested.

"*Vital*," she said. "In the original sense. The sense of being filled with *life*. Like food so rich, you feel stuffed for days . . ." Her voice trailed off and she bit her lip, then covered up the small moment of vulnerability by sipping from her glass of water.

Magic was, in many ways, the raw energy of life, of creation. Wiz-ards had particularly vital life forces as a result of constantly working with such energies. Maybe there was less difference between them than I'd always heard. The White Court fed upon vital life energy. Maybe, given the situation Lara had been in, her Hunger had fed on raw mag-ical power. Or maybe it was about me—the whole starborn thing was still a wild card. Maybe it was my magic, specifically, that the Outsider had been in tune with enough to feed upon.

Lara cleared her throat, inhaled, and composed herself. "Speaking of which, what have you found about helping Thomas?"

I frowned at her for a long moment, then focused my eyes on nothing in particular, thinking. She tilted her head after a moment, and I held up a couple of fingers, asking for time. She folded her hands and focused on me, waiting.

"If what I did for you pacified the Hunger," I said slowly, "it should do the same for Thomas, shouldn't it?"

She blinked. "Was that not the plan?"

"It's trying to kill him," I said. "The plan was to cut it out of him."

Her pale blue eyes widened. "That would . . . He'd . . ."

"Be just a guy," I said quietly.

Lara took a slow breath through her mouth. "Never to feel Hunger again," she said quietly. She shook her head. "How would . . . I can't even imagine how much his life would change. Empty night."

"Change good? Change bad?"

"I suppose that would depend a great deal on one's attitude," she said. Her eyes went distant. "Inari and her husband seem happy. She's had three children."

"Oh yeah?" I asked, finding myself smiling. Man, that case had been a long time ago. "Good for them."

"But she lives a world away," Lara said. "Honestly. I'm not sure you could appreciate it."

"It's like she left the Mafia," I said. "I got kicked out of a gang recently myself."

She blinked at me and gave me a rueful smile. "I suppose you did. You're perceptive for someone so . . ."

"Manly?" I suggested. "Tall? Scarred?"

She laughed. "Young," she said. "From what I've seen, it takes a lifetime to learn to see some things." Her voice went dry. "For some people, more."

"I've had to learn a lot the last few years." I frowned. "Is it possible to, I don't know, force-feed his Hunger?"

Lara considered the question grimly. "It wouldn't be like dealing with mine was. His Hunger is not in the same state of restraint and balance as mine. It is berserk with need and blind to any food but Thomas's life force." She frowned. "And his Hunger is larger and stronger than mine. By a considerable margin."

"How much bigger and stronger are we talking?" I asked.

Lara spread her hands helplessly. "There is no system of weights and measures that applies. If he'd not been with Justine all this time, feeding more or less freely from her, and instead had been forced to develop more discipline and restraint, he'd likely be one of the most powerful of our kind." She sighed. "But he seemed so happy. I couldn't bring myself to do what Father would have done."

"Get rid of Justine," I said.

"Mmmm."

"So we've got no way to know if I can get his Hunger pacified," I said. "I *am* sure I can cut it out. If I'm not exhausted from trying to feed the thing instead."

"A difficult question of balance," Lara said, nodding. She frowned, looking down. "And . . . there is an additional concern."

"Meaning?" I asked.

"It could be," she began slowly, "that this kind of . . . um." She paused, her expression faintly annoyed. "I'm sorry. I find it's very awkward to be discussing these kinds of particulars with someone who isn't in the Court. I haven't felt this way since I was quite young."

"It's been centuries since you felt awkward?" I asked.

She lifted her brows and spread her pale hands. Her nails were silver. "When you . . . fed me, it was intense. As if . . . what I felt before when feeding had been coming through a filter. Or as if I'd been sipping through a tiny straw. And suddenly there were no restraints and . . ." She stared at the table for a moment, her eyes flickering brighter. "It was a formidable experience. I am not sure in his condition that such a thing would be good for him."

"Why do you say that?"

"This process, the transfer of energy, is more complicated than providing someone with food, at the end of the day. If it was a simple transference, I would have been able to help him on the boat on the way to the island."

"Explain it to me," I said quietly. Lara as a cool and remote icon was attractive to a distracting degree. Lara feeling awkward and struggling to communicate made her . . .

Much, much more . . . dangerous.

I should always bear that in mind.

I folded my hands to keep them from doing anything inadvisable.

Lara thought about it for a moment, then said, "Imagine the prisoners from concentration camps in the Second World War. Emaciated. Starving. Dying. Barely living skeletons. You couldn't just drop a five-course meal in front of them after so much time with so little food. The shock to their system could kill them. That's the situation Thomas and his Hunger are in. Even if you could feed them, it might do tremendous harm to Thomas. Or to the Hunger."

"I don't care about his demon," I said. "I care about Thomas. If I gotta pick one over the other, that's easy."

"Thomas's life experience without his Hunger is that of a fourteen-year-old boy," Lara replied intently. "Whatever you think about that symbiosis, it is a significant portion of his life, his philosophy, his method of thought. Cut it out, and you'll be doing something at least as significant as removing his arms or eyes. Do that, and you may be destroying the man you know as well."

I rolled my thumbs over each other and frowned. "Damn," I said quietly.

"This isn't your choice to make," Lara said, after a moment. "Or mine."

"It's Thomas's," I said, nodding. "We'll have to talk to him. Boats are iced in. We'll have to go through the Nevernever to get to the island. Which is going to be dangerous, in ways I can't predict. We'll have to—"

"Go on my helicopter," Lara said firmly. "Which seems simpler."

I blinked. "Um. Yes. Oh." I frowned. "Not sure you want me mixing with a modern helicopter."

Lara looked at me with pale, gorgeous eyes over her glass of water, sensual mouth quirked into a tiny smirk at one corner. "Honestly, Harry. Give me some credit."

The waiter arrived with dinner under silver and swept the covers off of the food with a dramatic flourish.

Steak. And some kind of fancy-spiced potatoes. Some green stuff and some dark brown sauce were spread about decoratively. The scent of it hit my nose and my stomach gurgled with primal enthusiasm.

Lara arched a brow at me over her own fancy fish dish.

"Huh," I said, trying not to stare at the food like a starving wolf, hunger hitting me like after a day at the pool. "When you wanna go?"

"Sooner is better," she said. "After dinner?"

I wondered how I was going to keep the food off my shirt and chin, it smelled so good. "Definitely after."

I had dinner, and then a second steak. I suspected I was sublimating one kind of hunger into another, being in Lara's company the way I was, but I'd probably lost too much weight anyway. Probably wasn't anything to worry about. Probably.

Then Lara got in her car with Freydis and I got in the back of the Munstermobile while Bear drove, and we went down to the Chicago Executive Airport. Freydis spoke to a guard at a gate, and we were waved through, straight out onto some tarmac and over to a hangar where a chopper was being rolled out.

It was a helicopter, technically. It looked like a glass ball and a bunch of metal wire around an engine and a couple of spinning blades.

"What, is this da Vinci's personal chopper?" I asked.

"Please," Lara said. "It's a Bell Sioux. Developed just before the Korean War. Didn't you ever watch that show about the military hospital? You wouldn't believe how much trouble it was getting the pontoon landers installed."

I whistled the opening bars of the *M*A*S*H* theme song. "Going old-school?"

Lara calmly removed her skirt and stepped out of her heels. I blinked, stared for a second at pale, athletic, stunning legs, then cleared my throat and calmly turned away. Freydis hurried over with a pilot's jumpsuit and a pair of boots. Lara stepped into them, fastened and zipped and buckled with calm precision, and then stepped up to the old helicopter.

Bear came over to me with my duster and blasting rod. "She's wearing armor now, and there was a weapon inside it, too," she said quietly, glancing over at Freydis. "Gotta keep things even."

"Yeah, thanks," I said, and slid into the duster. The defensive spells were fresher now, if maybe not up to full strength yet. I didn't yet have quite the same depth and duration of focus as I normally would. The spells on the blasting rod were getting fairly stale. If I had to use it, I'd have to be careful how much power I ran through it or it would shiver apart. I'd have to attend to that soon. I hung it from its tie inside the duster's lining under my left arm, wrapped the coat around me with a flap of heavy leather, and stalked over to the Sioux's passenger side.

Fitting all six feet nine inches of me inside the passenger seat of the helicopter was a brief logistics puzzle, but I got buckled in and shut the door without needing anyone to tell me how to work any of the levers or anything. From enough distance, I might have seemed suave.

Lara ran through her preflight checks, visually ensured that my belt was secure, I think, flashed me a quick smile, and started the thing up. The roaring machine lifted gracefully into the cold winter air, gained altitude, then started forward. Within moments, we were sailing high over the city and out to Lake Michigan.

And then she set course for Demonreach.

In about a quarter of an hour, she frowned and began to turn. I reached out and touched her cool hand with mine. The island itself exerted a subtle influence to turn away those who had no business there, operating on an extremely powerful but subliminal level. Lara could have briefly lost track of her thought and flown away from the island over and over again. I tugged her hand gently the other way, then tapped the side of my head with one finger.

Lara was pretty sharp. She blinked for a moment and then gave me a nod of comprehension, banking the aircraft the other way. I felt it when we flew over the island, and a murmur, a flick of my hand, and a whisper of will was enough to send a subtle green werelight flooding out from the nearest point of the island, spreading over snow and frost, stone and rock, branch and bough, in rippling curls of illumination until the whole of the island was lit in a low, quiet green-gold glow.

She stared down at it, her brow furrowed in concentration, her eyes gleaming more pale. Now that we were over the island proper, it was already putting psychic pressure on her again. She'd been ready for it this time, and her expression was steady.

I directed her down to the landing, where Thomas and I had spent a summer building the Whatsup Dock, from spare wood and blocks of foam and empty barrels. She brought the Sioux down gently onto the water and floating ice beside the dock. This side of the island got steady wind most of the time, and ice formed only thinly. The chopper sank through it, though its pontoon landing gear took up its weight readily enough once it reached the liquid beneath the thin crust.

We tied the Sioux up there and made the hike up the hill to the long stairs down to the tunnels far beneath the island and the lake. We went at a steady pace, without resting, down to the tunnel with Thomas's coffin-sized green crystal.

It took me a few moments of concentration and mental effort in the greenly lit, root-worried tunnels to commune with Alfred, the island's genius loci, and have it access Thomas's crystalline prison cell and begin to rouse my brother from his torpor. The crystal began to glow a bit more brightly, become more translucent, and in a moment I could see my brother's peaceful sleeping expression. Then a faint glowing image formed over his unmoving features, and the image's face twisted up and yawned, then slowly blinked its eyes open.

Thomas's image looked up at me, blinked a few more times, and said, "I thought you were going to leave."

"We did," I said. "It's been a while."

Thomas's handsome face creased into a frown of confusion. "You were just here—" He cut himself off and frowned more deeply. "Oh. Different clothes. You cut your hair."

Somewhere in the vaults of my mind, a sound like a hungry, predatory growl rolled out of the darkness.

Thomas had heard it. His eyes widened.

"It's your Hunger," I said. "We don't have much time. I need you to listen up. Okay?"

"Yeah. Yeah."

I nodded and gave him the short and dirty version of what we had in mind. "So. I think I can get you out of there. The question is whether or not you want the Hunger to come with you."

Thomas stared at me, his expression stunned.

"Lara," he said, looking over at her.

Lara shook her head. "Brother mine, I can't make this choice for you."

Thomas grimaced and nodded. "But . . . you think he can do it? Get rid of my Hunger?"

Lara frowned and hesitated before she answered. "He's confident he can. My . . . instincts say he's right."

"Empty night," Thomas breathed. He shook his head. "Justine. What does she think?"

"Neither of us has been able to locate her," Lara said. "My people caught up to her at one point, but they were ambushed and killed by elements of Russian organized crime."

"She's still out there?" Thomas asked. "The baby. When?"

"Several weeks," she told him. "Gestation runs a little longer for our kind on average. Ten months, give or take. It's a week from your birthday."

Thomas's image twisted its face up in consternation. "Then that thing inside her. It's still got her and the baby in danger."

"Apparently," Lara said quietly.

Thomas was quiet for a long moment.

The Hunger growled again, louder this time, in my mind. Animated. Alert.

"We could be together," he whispered. His eyes were distant. His face tight with pain. "Really together. Just us. If my Hunger was gone, we could have all the kids we wanted. Be in love. Be . . ."

"I know," Lara said gently.

He turned back to me. "When are you going to do it?"

"Depends on you," I said quietly. "You want it gone, I can be ready in a week. You want the thing to come with you, I'll need Lara's cooperation and another month, maybe six weeks."

I glanced at Lara. She nodded firmly at me.

My brother's face turned wistful. His image's eyes grew misty. Then his face smoothed over into an expression of pain so familiar it had become part of his background.

"Plain human Thomas can't help Justine," he said quietly. "Bring my demon out with me."

Chapter

Thirty-Six

Maggie was riding her bike casually around the castle's rooftop in circles the next weekend. Bonea was there, too, the little intellect spirit enjoying the sunshine from the safety of her carved wooden skull, glowing eyelights barely visible. It was my rest day, and Bear and Fitz were in the gym, so Major General Toot-Toot Minimus was pulling guard duty for me and Maggie.

The pixie had continued growing over the past several months, since the battle, as he had so many times before, and was hitched up on his elbows so that he could poke his violet dandelion-fluff head of hair over the lip of one of the crenels in the battlements and eye the calm street below with a melodramatically wary expression. We were waiting for the Winter smiths to deliver his new armor, and he wore clothing that had been meant for small children in several vibrant shades of purple, blue, and pink that clashed distinctly with the little sword he wore belted at his side. He kept his dragonfly wings folded against his back and kicked his feet like a bored child.

"No enemies appear to be attacking, my lord!" he chirped, as he had done regularly every five minutes or so.

"Thanks, Toot," I replied calmly, as I did at every report of my apparent safety.

The day had gotten up to almost fifty degrees, and Maggie had to wear only a light jacket, though the sun was rapidly waning. She idly tested various poses on the bike, standing on one leg, then the other, then holding one leg out behind her.

"We could set up a ramp and then I could try some jumps," she was saying.

"On the roof?" I asked, grinning. "Maybe that's not the best idea."

"From this height to ground level below," Bonnie chimed in a child's voice from the little wooden skull, "in excess of eighty-five percent of falls would prove fatal to a human being!"

"Okay, Bonnie. There's no room anywhere else," Maggie complained. "It doesn't have to be a big ramp. I just want to try it out."

"Ramps are a simple tool known as an inclined plane!" Bonnie burbled. "They are frequently used across the globe!"

"Maybe we can get to a bike park," I said. "Or when it gets a little warmer and there's not so much sand and stuff on the streets, maybe you and Harry can set a ramp up outside the Carpenters' house."

"Hmmph," Maggie said. She swung her legs both over to one side, hopped off the seat, ran a few steps, then remounted the bike without stopping. "Can I do fighting practice with you guys sometime?"

I stared at her as she circled around me for a moment. She looked happy, her cheeks reddened by a light wind. My mind provided me with a picture of her with black eyes and a broken nose, then filled in some missing teeth. I felt sick.

But from a practical standpoint, if I was going to be in her life, she had to start learning some practical things. Like how to defend herself. And when to run.

Toot-Toot glanced over his shoulder at us, giving his muppet-level enthusiastic guard duty a break for a moment. He frowned at Maggie.

"I'll talk to Bear," I said. "She might have some experience with this kind of thing."

Her smile widened as she looked over at me, and my heart went all soft. "Yeah?"

"Yeah."

"I like Bear," she declared.

"Bears exist on every continent on the planet except Antarctica!"

Bonnie sang. "Even though the Greek root for said continent's name, *arktos*, actually means *bear!*"

I blinked over at Bonnie. The little intellect spirit was a repository of vast amounts of information—but she didn't really understand much about the world. It would be a generation or two before she was of much practical use for anything but a trivia night as she slowly learned to apply her knowledge to the real world. "That was an excellent cross-reference, Bonea," I said.

"Yay!" Bonea said, and the little wooden skull wiggled at the praise.

"Yeah, Bonnie's getting better and better at helping me with studies," Maggie said.

"Just you make sure she isn't doing it for you," I told my daughter. "You need to be able to think for yourself. It's one of the most important things you can ever learn to do."

"I know, Dad," Maggie said with a little roll of her eyes. "Mouse wouldn't let me cheat even if I wanted to." She fell quiet and watched me for a couple of circles. "Dad? You okay?"

No, I wasn't. But that wasn't the kind of thing a responsible adult shared with his young child. "Just . . . have things on my mind," I said. The light had gone orange, the shadows of the merlons getting longer. "I'll be okay."

"Like Thomas?" she asked carefully.

"That's one thing," I said. "You still having dinner with Matias's family?"

"Yeah, we're playing games," Maggie said, pleased. She checked her analog watch. "And then you read to me?"

"And then I read to you," I said, nodding.

"'Kay," she said. She braked the bike, parked it, and then got the tarp Michael had made into a weather cover for it. I helped her get it over the bike, and then she jumped up. I caught her, she kissed my cheek, then hopped down, said, "I'll see you in a little bit." Then she took up Bonnie's skull under one arm and ran down from the roof.

I watched her go.

It's strange. Having the care of a child changes everything.

Just everything.

Maybe I should sell the castle. Take all the money left over from the raid of Hades' vault—it was a little over a couple of million bucks in bootleg diamonds I had to sell a little at a time for under market value—and get a place in the middle of nowhere for us until she was more grown-up. Maybe that would be best for her.

Living in Chicago, among so many mortals, meant that ninety-nine percent of the time, any supernatural threat would have to tread very carefully about choosing where and when to come at me. On balance, I had always felt better about living in the city than out in the country, where there were far fewer eyes to see, and where supernatural threats would have a much easier time coming at me.

But maybe the Battle of Chicago had changed that.

I just wanted her to be safe.

But safe . . . is generally an illusion. We live in a world where entropy and a planet full of competing living things, from the microscopic to the very large, will have no compunctions about killing us if we're foolish or unlucky. You aren't safe. I'm not safe. If we do create some measure of safety, it is because we work hard to do it.

Here I was living in a fortress. With my own men-at-arms. With folks who were depending on me. It would take a fairly serious force to threaten me here—which meant anyone who came at me would bring one. And I should have been thinking about that a long time before now.

Maybe my brain was finally coming back online.

I sat down on the ground next to my girl's bike and closed my eyes as the light faded and the night came.

It was time.

Time to start pulling things together.

Time to give myself a break.

I couldn't protect Maggie or anyone else if I was busy trying to tear myself apart.

Karrin wouldn't want that for me. She wouldn't want my grief at her loss to result in harm to me, or anyone in my life.

Because she had cared about me.

Just as I'd cared about her.

And I had to keep going without her.

I let out a long breath.

"I miss you, Murph," I whispered quietly. "I know you can't hear me. But I miss you. I wanted to be with you. I wanted to spend our insane lives together. I hope you're doing things that make you happy."

Tears came. I didn't sob. Just bowed my head and let them fall.

Murphy was gone. But life was still going.

And it was time for me to pick up whatever pieces I could, rebuild the rest, and be alive.

Something eased. Something that had been slowly loosening for a long time. There was a feeling of warmth in my chest and stomach. I felt . . . something strange. A presence. A warmth. I wasn't sure how to quantify it.

I didn't feel alone. For the first time in months, I didn't feel like I was walking through a world of formalities and constructs. I'd been telling myself consciously that I was getting better in an effort to help make it happen.

But now I could feel it.

In the gathering dark, my heart and my brain sat down in the same room and started talking to each other again. There was work to do, and I needed all of me to be on the same page to get it done.

I'd been hurt. But even hurt, I wasn't weak.

I'd suffered loss. But in losing, I hadn't become less.

Pain had subsumed me in fire. But the fire had not destroyed me.

I remained.

Changed, perhaps.

But I remained.

In the face of evil, of the heartless calculations of power, in disaster and destruction and death and chaos, I had screwed up, but I had survived.

Now it was time to learn.

Time to be made stronger by what I had faced.

Time to live.

I sat with that for a long while and *felt* it. Felt it glowing in my chest like a small, bright star. And I liked how it felt.

And being around that kid had been what allowed me to find it.

That was when I felt a subtle thrill of supernatural energy, somewhere in the air above me.

"My lord!" Toot-Toot said in a stage whisper. There was a buzz of his wings in the air, and the little fae was suddenly hovering several feet over my head, his hand on his sword's grip.

"Yeah, Toot, I feel it, too," I growled. I stood up, looked up at the darkened sky, and felt something I hadn't for a while—grumpy, proper wizardly annoyance. I shook out my shield bracelet from my sweater's sleeve and flexed my fists, bringing my focus to my energy rings. "Okay, you!" I shouted up at the sky. "I'm officially tired of this! It's about time you showed yourself, or else leave me the hell alone! It's potpie night and I'm hungry!"

For a moment there was silence, except for the buzz of Toot's wings.

Then there was a flapping, leathery sound, and from the night sky dropped a large form with membranous wings almost twenty feet across. It came gliding down with an aerial grace that was too elegant and precise to be entirely natural and landed on the far side of the roof with a mild thump of something heavy and hard being set gently on stone. The figure dropped into a crouch, wings withdrawing, folding up around it like some kind of dark tent.

From where the being crouched, there was a stir in the air and then pale blue light began to spread through the stones around it, running along faint, ancient knotwork channels carved in the stones. The light spread out from the strange being in a sphere that swept up the merlons behind it and in a circle around where it crouched, slowly illuminating it with increasing clarity.

Steel torches were set in iron sconces on the outside of the merlons every ten feet or so, and they abruptly burst into life, flames burning upon no fuel, wardlights like the ones I'd once used to warn me of magical intruders back in the day. Except apparently Merlin had set the enchantments on these, and more than a dozen centuries later they were still good to go. No idea how that had been done.

Guess they really don't make them like they used to.

"Avaunt, varlet!" Toot-Toot shrilled, and drew his sword from his side. "Avaunt and begone!"

"Toot," I said calmly. "Go get Bear. Now."

Toot flicked a glance around and down at me. "But, my lord!"

I raised my shield bracelet, ready to snap a shield to life or throw a quick strike from the rings as needed. "Now, Major General. That's an order."

Toot made a frustrated sound but suddenly turned into a blur, zipping over the back side of the castle and down, leaving a streak of glowing motes of light in his wake.

I squared off on the intruder and said, "All right, then. Who the hell are you?"

The winged being slowly lifted . . . his, I was somehow sure, head. He had a face like a lion's, if it had been sculpted by someone who had only a messy drawing and a brief description to go on—it was balanced and attractive and more human-looking than it should have been and not at all correct. A mane of dark grey hair grizzled with strands of metallic silver curled wildly down past his shoulders. He was vaguely humanoid, but his arms were longer than human proportions, and he bent forward at the waist like a gorilla, his weight resting on lion-paw feet and upon the knuckles of his close-fisted hands. He might have been made of warm grey granite, if it had been a fluid, living substance.

His eyes were golden brown and very, very human.

The being rose, rolling his broad, heavily muscled shoulders. He carefully, almost fastidiously, tucked his wings back behind him and against his back, until they hung like a long pack down his spine. He straightened his back and fetched me a bow straight out of the Renaissance, sweeping and overblown, one leg forward.

When he spoke, his voice was deep, resonant, melodic. "Wizard Dresden. I bid you good evening."

I stared at the heavily muscled, armored creature warily. "Uh-huh. You couldn't have called ahead?"

The creature tilted his head and blinked its eyes at me. "You invited me, did you not?"

"Hah," I said. I totally had, when I'd told him to come down. The outer defenses of the castle were based upon the foundation of its threshold, the magical energy field around any home. Given all the people living under my roof at the moment, that threshold had been a very, very solid one—and I'd invited the thing right past it. "Hah, heh, hah. I . . . actually did, didn't I?"

Dozens of tiny pinpoints of light had risen around the battlements, the Little Folk, pixies and their like, rising from all around the castle in response to the wardlights being lit. Seconds later, there was a flicker of blue light deep in the stone, and it whirled around the roof as if a child had been waving a laser pointer until it settled on the ground to my left.

"Boss!" Bob the Skull cried. "Intruder! Somehow it got through the outer perimeter!"

I glanced down at the light by my feet.

"Yeah," I said, a bit embarrassed. "I, uh . . . kind of invited it to come down."

Bob made a sputtering, flabbergasted sound.

"You," rumbled the creature, staring hard at Bob. "What is a failed experiment doing here?"

"You!" spat Bob, zipping back and forth in anxious little movements. "Who ordered the uptight anal-retentive burger?"

I frowned down at Bob and then at the creature. "You two have met, I take it."

"Some small number of years ago," rumbled the creature.

"It's been a thousand years at least!" Bob protested. "You're just jealous 'cause Etienne the Enchanter spent more time on me than you!"

"We were not faulty," the creature said. Perhaps very, very slightly smug about it.

"Oh, bite me, Basil!" Bob snapped. "Air spirits rule, gargoyles drool!"

Basil lifted a hand toward his leonine mouth, frowning. He had sharp-looking, thorn-shaped claws on the tips of his fingers. "That is not possible."

"It's an *expression*, you dolt!"

Basil frowned, perplexed. "You do not even have a face."

"Augh!" Bob cried. "It's figurative! Not everything is literal!"

Basil frowned more severely and folded his arms. "After a thousand years, you continue to make no sense," Basil said. "If you serve in this house, it would be useful to your master to make introductions."

"Oh," Bob said. "You're moving in?"

"Indeed," Basil said. He looked around the roof of the castle, at the glowing designs all around him. His expression softened. "I had not thought to return to this place."

"Whoa, whoa, hold your horses, there," I said.

"Don't—" Bob began.

"I see no horses," Basil said seriously, eyes sweeping around the rooftop as he turned.

"Bob," I said plaintively.

"He's a gargoyle," Bob said. "Not like those cheap things Ancient Mai does. Basil here is one of Etienne the Enchanter's master projects— a spirit of earth."

"Like you're a spirit of air?"

"Hey!" Bob said, outraged. "He is *not* like me. He's . . ."

Basil was looking studiously into the middle distance, but he let out a low growl that shook the stone of the roof.

". . . practical," Bob finished tactfully. "He's so practical it can some- times be mistaken for idiocy."

"Yeah," I said. "But what is he doing here?"

"You invited me," Basil said gravely.

I held up a finger toward the gargoyle. "Hey, uh, Basil. Let me talk to Bob for a moment."

"Of course, Wizard Dresden," Basil said.

"Is he a threat?" I asked Bob.

"I mean," Bob said, "he's a security system. So it kinda depends on what you mean by *threat*."

I frowned. "Security?"

"We were created," Basil intoned gravely, "to protect the castle"—he held up one finger—"of a good-hearted wizard"—and he put up the next one. He paused to consider his fingers. "I have found it historically unusual for each to happen concurrently. I have considered the idea that owning a castle does something to a wizard's state of mind."

"Uh," I said, blinking. "How do you know I am a good wizard? I mean, I'm mostly competent, but . . ."

"Not skilled," Basil said firmly. "Good." Standing straight, he was as tall as I was. He took a step forward and pointed his forefinger at my heart. "There." His grey skin wrinkled around his nose as he leaned toward me and sniffed. "Kindness. Hope. Even a little faith." He straightened and met my gaze calmly. "We have been watching you for months. In great pain, you nonetheless make kind choices. Care for others." He turned and paced over to Maggie's covered bicycle, crouching down into an easy animalistic stance. "This was infused with great love for an innocent. A gift for the child?"

I blinked. "Uh. Yeah."

Basil nodded. "We were made to sense benevolence and malevolence. To protect the former from the latter. We are extremely efficient at doing so."

I blinked again. "We?"

"He's part of a set," Bob said petulantly. "Please tell me they aren't all here, Basil."

"I cannot," Basil said firmly. "It would be a falsehood. If Wizard Dresden wishes it, I will call them in."

The door slammed open and Bear appeared, wearing clamshell tactical armor on her torso, carrying the four-bore in one hand. She held a heavy, long-handled war hammer whose head was shaped like a clenched fist with a spiked thumb pointing off the back in the other. She looked around with her eyes a bit wide, focused on the gargoyle, and said, "Everyone all right?"

"Fine," I said slowly. "Uh. This is Basil."

"One of Etienne the Enchanter's guardians," Bear said firmly. "I know of them. Why is it here?"

"I was invited," Basil offered.

"Apparently Basil has been watching me for a while," I noted. "Deciding whether he wanted to, ah, offer his services."

"And you let him in through the defenses without even calling me or knowing if . . ." Bear closed her eyes for a second and then let out a slow breath through her teeth. "Dammit, Dresden. I was eating potpie."

"Hey, I sent for you the second he got here," I said. Then added, "Sorry."

She grimaced and stepped back, relaxing, draping the four-bore over her shoulder more casually. "Basil, eh?" she asked.

He inclined his head to her and turned to face me, his eyes and voice intent. "The world grows darker. Pain and fear spread. Chaos and war have gone running through the earth. A Titan's screams of despair have shaken the firmament. Ancient things stir in their dark lairs. Grand events are gathering speed. The storm is coming. And I, and my brothers, have come to offer our allegiance to you, wizard."

And the gargoyle dropped smoothly to one knee in front of me.

I blinked. I looked at Bear.

The Valkyrie traded a look at me and whistled silently. She stepped close and murmured, "One-Eye tried to recruit them after Etienne passed. They refused him. They've gotten involved here and there over the years."

"He what he says he is?" I asked.

Bear tilted her head and stared hard at the gargoyle, eyes glittering with flecks of color from across the spectrum.

"He's an original," she confirmed, nodding.

"Tell them to pound sand!" Bob snapped. "They're a pain! All they do is stand around and guard all the time and fail to understand jokes!"

"Them?" I asked.

"With your permission, wizard," Basil said calmly.

I frowned and nodded.

Basil lifted his head and let out something that very much sounded like a lion's coughing roar.

In a moment, there was the leathery rustle of membranous wings, and half a dozen more of the things came swooping down, landing on merlons with almost dainty crunching sounds. Apart from the wings, none of them looked alike, and none of them looked like anything natural. Basil was the largest. The others were like stairsteps down, and the smallest, with a bizarre, asymmetrical monkey-like face, was made of some kind of smooth, red-orange living stone and wasn't much larger than Maggie in the body, though it was wiry with muscle. The rest were a menagerie of strange faces, bodies that varied between apelike, birdlike, and anthropomorphic, and were covered in pebbly texture or stony scales. All had eyes that were various colors and almost disturbingly human.

"Basil," Basil said touching his own chest, and then went down the stairsteps in order of height. "Bay. Thyme. Cardamom. Sage. Parsley. And Cinnamon."

"Etienne liked to cook," Bob said sourly.

"The Spice 'Goyles," I said with a straight face.

Bob groaned.

Basil tilted his head to one side like a dog that had heard a new sound. The other gargoyles mirrored him.

"Uh," I said. "You hungry? I mean, what do you guys eat?"

"Stories," Cinnamon piped up in a wobbly, tinny voice. "A new story. Every day."

"Ugh," Bob said, disgusted. "It's less food than maintenance for their limited intellect, Harry. Keeps them centered."

"I suppose I can afford it at least," I said. "And we have the room. Bob, you're sure you know these guys?"

"Yes," Bob said glumly. "Doesn't mean you need to put up with them."

"But they could be useful," I pressed. "Protecting the place?"

Bear nodded firmly.

"I guess, yeah, technically," Bob said sourly.

I pursed my lips, thinking. I could have Mouse check them over and get his take on them, too. He was downstairs in the great hall. With Maggie. And the potpie. But my instincts told me how he would react. Given the way the past few years had gone, I almost didn't want to listen to my own.

But in my chest, the tiny star kept burning.

Hell.

Maybe sometimes, good things happen, too.

Even to me.

"Okay," I said. "For the time being, Basil, you all should consider yourselves my guests, I suppose. We'll talk about what you have in mind."

"Excellent," said the gargoyle. Something, a tension, seemed to ease out of him. There was a faint, sad relief in his tone. "It has been longer than I would like since we have served in a home."

Something told me that the gargoyle's emotions on the subject were considerably less understated than Basil's words.

"We all kind of washed up together here," I told him seriously. "Still making a home of it, I think. And I'm a sucker for strays."

"We did not stray," Basil corrected with quiet conviction. "We deliberately sought you out."

I felt myself smiling lopsidedly. "Right," I said. "You're going to fit in fine."

Chapter
Thirty-Seven

The first protesters showed up at the castle on Tuesday morning.

Will, who had been lifting with me and Fitz that morning, folded his thick forearms on a merlon on the castle's roof and looked across the street, bemused. Half a dozen folks were standing across the street on the sidewalk holding signs. Three of them simply read CHICAGO FOR THE PEOPLE! The other signs said BACK TO NORMAL, END THE MADNESS, and NO OCCULT WEIRDNESS!

"You see this?" Will asked me as I came up.

"Yeah," I said. "Kind of expected something like it, after last summer. Things are getting better. People have more time to think about something other than staying warm and fed. Thought they'd wait until further into the spring, though."

"You kind of have to admire their ethic," Will noted, staring across the street. "It's like twenty-five degrees and windy." Will had been lifting a hell of a lot of weight. Steam rose off his skin. It would be a bit before he cooled off enough to worry. "Not everyone who protests is up for that."

"I suppose," I said. "However, as the resident occult weirdo in chief, I don't like the idea of being prohibited. So we have some disagreement."

"It's just signs," Will said.

"Sure," I said.

Fitz frowned down at the protesters. The kid was still skinny enough that the cold had made him start shivering almost immediately when we came out to observe. "Should we do something?"

"Like what?" I asked.

"I don't know," he said. "Call the cops? Have them go away?"

"Not sure the cops would respond," I mused. "I mean, they're just standing there holding signs. Public sidewalk. They can do that. They're not even on the property."

The stones of the castle rippled like water, and Basil the gargoyle rose through them like a diver being pulled up from the drink. He squinted up at the bright morning sun, wincing a bit, and kept back from the battlements so he wouldn't be easily seen.

"My lord," Basil said seriously. "Shall we shepherd them away?"

"They're permitted by law to do that," I said, waving a hand vaguely at the protesters. "They're not doing anything violent, destroying property or setting things on fire. If they aren't offering direct harm to someone here, we're going to play it just as cool."

"They are not in their own homes, either," Basil said coolly, "but outside of yours, demonstrating their displeasure."

"Eh," I said. "Nobody can make everyone happy." I eyed Basil. "Can't you sense malice and malevolence?"

"Yes, my lord," Basil said.

"You sense any there?"

The gargoyle's leonine face frowned, an expression considerably more intimidating on him than it would have been on most folks I knew. "Humans are always a muddle. Groups of humans even more so. They are afraid."

"Hell, after the Battle of Chicago, that's hardly a surprise," I said. "It's not like it's stupid."

Basil frowned and said, "In a thousand years I have defended seven wizards' castles," he said firmly. "Three ended in the senescence of the wizard in question. Three were attacked and destroyed despite all that could be done by frightened crowds of mortals."

Which . . . seemed a rather grim statistical outlook on my own future. Gulp.

"Was the crowd ever six whole people?" I asked.

Basil frowned. "No. There were more."

"Then we don't start to sweat yet. There's only six of them. And there's a reason the Accords try to keep things low-key where mortals are concerned," I said. "And we're going to continue that unless there's no other choice. Bear is watching from ground level, and they couldn't get by her with a monster truck and a stampeding herd of buffalo. You and your boys stay out of sight, okay?"

Basil inclined his head. "My lord."

"Will," I said, "I want you to let everyone know what the plan is. As long as things are quiet, it's business as usual. Anything gets hostile, they're to retreat and let me know."

"Okay," Will said. "What are you going to do?"

This had the potential to get nasty, certainly. But it would take more than half a dozen normies with cardboard signs to make me start throwing hands, metaphorically speaking. "I'll decide that if it becomes an issue."

"Right," Will said, nodding.

"Fitz," I said. "You come with me."

"Where?" Fitz asked.

"Kitchen," I said. "We're doing a small project."

Half an hour later, Fitz and I came out the front doors, which got the attention of the protesters. Fitz was carrying a folding table. I was dragging a wagon with some stuff in it. Fitz set up the table. I took a sign out of the wagon on a piece of heavy cardboard where I'd used a marker to write FREE HOT CHOCOLATE. ENJOY. And a smiley face, to make it a friendly offer rather than a decree.

Then we set out a box with a couple of stacks of paper cups, and a couple of insulated carafes filled with the hot chocolate Fitz and I had made. Then I taped a plastic trash bag to the table. Then I took a cardboard box of those chemical hand warmers in plastic sleeves and set it next to the cocoa.

I waved at the people across the street, pointed at the sign and the box, and gave them a thumbs-up. Then I poured myself and Fitz a half cup of cocoa, and we stood there sipping it while they stared at us in something between confusion and distaste.

"Oh yeah," Fitz said quietly, after he had a sip. "They look so friendly."

"They went through the Battle of Chicago, too," I said quietly. "And they weren't able to set anyone on fire like we were. They're scared, but at least they're doing something about it. That's healthy. Let them. They aren't hurting anybody."

"What happens when they do?" Fitz asked darkly.

"Burn that bridge when we come to it," I said. "Well. Maybe they're a little nervous about coming over to talk. Smile and wave."

He did, and I did. We got no reaction. We drained the cups, put them in the trash, got the wagon, and went back inside.

I went out as the sun was going down and checked.

The protesters had left with the coming night.

No one had cocoa.

It had taken more than a week to arrange, but I got together for a talk with Michael, Sanya, and Butters at the Carpenters' place one evening. Michael had a firepit in the backyard and we used it, building up a fire and settling on wooden benches around it.

My stomach felt weird as I approached. I didn't want to say some of the things I needed to say. I thought about bailing, making some excuse. But I took a slow breath and made myself walk over to the fire and settle down among men who had, until last summer, always been my friends.

"I tell you the truth, Thailand is beautiful," Sanya was saying in his rumbling low voice and Russian accent. He was a tall and brawny man with deep brown skin and flashing, humorous dark eyes. He wore a big black coat and motorcycle boots. "The beach. The forests. People there are good to animals."

He was assisting Butters, who was walking with the aid of a cane. Butters was a little guy a few inches under average height with a beaky nose. His black haystack of a head of hair had been trimmed down very short, and it made him look even smaller. He had to sit down on the wooden bench slowly and carefully.

"Sounds great," he said to Sanya. "Ow, yeah, okay, thanks."

"This is not a good look for Knights," Sanya said thoughtfully, frowning down at Butters. "But you look much better than when you were in that cast."

"Worst two months ever," Butters groaned in agreement. "Imagine everything below your chest itching all the time, like, every day, and never being able to do anything about it." He set the cane down and raked the fingertips of both hands over his thighs, as if they'd burst into itching hives. "Ugh. But the surgeon said he'd never seen anyone recover so well, much less a guy my age. And the therapist is always shocked when I come in. Everything is going kind of ideally."

"I did that twice, in my time," Michael said affably. He started passing out bottles of Mac's ale. "Reality does tend to function well for those in the direct service of its Creator. Doctors thought it a miracle that I survived the second injury at all, much less walked again."

Butters took up his beer, grinning. "Join the Knights of the Cross: It could be worse."

Sanya burst out in deep, rolling laughter and lifted his bottle. "It could be worse."

"That isn't what . . ." Michael sighed. "All right. Fine. It could be worse."

"Skoal," I said, and we clinked bottles and drank.

"Dresden," Sanya said affably, almost before he'd swallowed his ale. "You look like you have not slept or eaten well in months. Is that succubus devouring your soul?"

I snorted. "I didn't think you were big on the whole concept of souls," I said. "Agnostic guy."

"Soul, life force, anima," Sanya said, waving it off with one hand. "Whatever. Is she eating you?"

"It's complicated," I said.

"I'm watching him," Michael said easily. "He's fine."

I blinked and looked at Michael.

"I have three crews working," Michael said gently. "Normally I rotate between them. But I wanted to make sure your new home was done well."

"And babysit me daily?" I asked.

"Happy coincidence," Michael said, grinning. I made a rude sound, and he laughed. "Hah. I like it. You sound more like you every day."

Sanya snorted. "I was enjoying time on beach with drinks that they sell by the coconut and flew out here to the middle of winter because I hear you need to talk, Dresden," he said. "I wish to know what is this important."

"Yeah," Butters said. He gestured with his bottle. "I mean, you've kinda been a stranger for a while, man."

"Yeah," I said slowly. "Um."

Michael took a drink, gave me a small smile, and nodded encouragingly.

"It's about the battle," I said in a low voice.

Things got quiet, quick.

I checked. Sanya's face was . . . *bleak* isn't the right word, but definitely *distant*. Butters frowned in concentration and his intelligent eyes focused on me through his round glasses, the fire reflected in the lenses.

"When Karrin died," I began.

I choked.

No one talked. The fire crackled.

They waited.

My friends waited on me.

One of the best things you can do for a friend is wait. Sometimes for them to understand something. Sometimes for them to decide on something. But mostly, to give them some quiet. Some space to put thoughts together. Some space to talk.

"When Karrin died," I said finally, focusing on the fire, "I wasn't right. I didn't . . . I didn't act right."

Silence.

Fire popping and crackling.

"I tried to do something terrible," I said after a while. "And when my friends stopped me, I was so angry that I was an absolute asshat about it. And I hurt you both."

"Mainly me," Sanya noted.

"Mainly you," I agreed. "But I made you both have to make a really tough choice. And I tried to hurt you when you were trying to help me. I was wrong to do that. I'm sorry, guys. I wanted to tell you that. And I wanted to thank you for stopping me from . . . well. From killing Rudolph. I would have if you hadn't intervened. And I don't know if I could have handled Maggie's father being a murderer. So, thank you."

Companionable quiet.

Crackle of fire.

"*Bozhe moi*, Dresden," Sanya said finally. "It was war. And you lost her. Terrible time. Terrible place. Terrible decisions go hand in hand, *da*? And we are only men." He swigged some ale. "Though now that I know how dirty you are capable of fighting, I do not think it will happen again."

"It won't," I said firmly, and nodded my head at him more deeply than was customary. "It won't."

"How's the arm?" Butters asked me quietly.

I rolled up my sleeve and showed him the burn from the Sword. It had taken months, but it had healed into an angry red scar. It still hurt when I got tired or upset. Real pain, not the vague staticky sensation the Winter mantle allowed through. "Fine," I said.

Butters winced at the injury and then at my face. "Harry. I mean, you know I didn't want to hurt you, right?"

"I know, man. You did good."

The smaller man gave me a pained smile. He offered his bottle. We clinked and drinked.

More quiet.

More companionable drinking.

My chest easing, so much.

"So," Sanya said, drawing the word out. "Dresden. You and Lara."

"It's political," I said. "Strictly political."

There was a beat.

Then they all started snickering at me. Just snickering.

"Hah hah, guys," I said, feeling the smile stretching over my face.

Because there are two times when you give a man a hard time. First, when you want to start trouble with him. And second, when he's your brother, and you do it because you want him to know that everything is okay.

I was among brothers.

Chapter
Thirty-Eight

It was a few days later, and Lara and Freydis arrived at midnight.

Bear had given the men on the door the night off. Freydis and Bear took up guard positions on the door, the great hall was lit by only a glowing chemical light at each doorway, and I led Lara quickly and quietly through the shadows down to the lower level of the castle, down to the lower hallway where my living quarters were, and where the entrance to the lab waited open.

Lara was dressed down for the evening. Close-fitting jeans, a white sweater, both of which looked excellent. Her hair was pulled back into a simple ponytail, and when she took off the sunglasses, her eyes glittered bright and pale with motes of silver flickering through circles of pale, pale grey. It was like seeing the eyes of a big cat—beautiful and predatory and dangerous. I had to drag my gaze off them.

I'd dressed down, too. Jeans and a black tank top that read YES YOU CAN in big aggressive letters. And it showed off my shoulders and arms, which were very, very defined at this point. That thought only occurred to me when I saw Lara's pale eyes glitter as she glanced at them.

"I met with Etri," she said. "Throwback party last night."

"A whatback party?"

"The host picks a historic protocol from at least a century ago and hosts a party to it exclusively for those old enough to have experienced it in its time."

"Ageist much?" I asked.

She snorted. "You'll understand as you get older. It is sometimes . . . well. Relaxing, not to have the very young teeming about. Throwing insults and threats at other guests, that kind of thing."

"Hah," I said. "What was this one?"

"Northern post–Civil War celebration," she said.

I stopped and blinked down at her. "Huh."

"What?"

"You were there for the Civil War," I mused. "I mean. You just don't come off like someone that old."

Lara smiled. "Well. I do interact with the youth regularly."

"What did Etri say?"

Lara shrugged a shoulder. "He said if I was willing to openly offer an apology for the incident, surrender Thomas to the custody of a neutral third party, return to the process of judgment via an Accorded emissary, with sentencing to follow if his guilt is demonstrated, that he will be willing to consider not setting Svartalfheim into a state of cold war with the White Court."

"Huh," I said. "And how much of that are you willing to do?"

She pressed her lips together. "I can't do any of it, and he knows it. If I admit that the White Court was involved in removing Thomas from custody, it will weaken our stance among the Accorded nations significantly, which would in turn have consequences inside the Court."

"Like what?"

"Challenges would become likely. Most of my people don't mind if one lies, cheats, swindles, and betrays, but they have very firm opinions on the concept of being caught doing it. It's a sign of weakness. That's why the Court would be weakened—I'd be forced to spend time, attention, and resources on maintaining my position. It would limit the sorts of influences and negotiations I could manage with any of the other nations."

"Which Etri can figure out, too," I said.

"I would expect that, yes."

"How'd he seem when he said it?" I asked.

Lara waved a hand. "You know the svartalves," she said. "They show little."

I stopped at the door down to the lab and gave her a look. "Come on. I'm not that dumb."

She gave me a look of consideration and then inclined her head toward me as though I had scored a touch she hadn't expected me to be able to make. "I am fairly sure he spoke with regret." She smiled faintly. "Though I suppose I might have been projecting. Economic and diplomatic pressure from Svartalfheim could prove a heavy burden to bear while maintaining Raith against the other Houses of my Court."

I grunted. "Etri seems a fairly decent sort."

"I would call him perhaps overly direct, but an excellent executor for his people, who are orderly and reasonable."

"That's what I mean," I said. "Wars that could have been avoided aren't reasonable. Etri has got to know you can't deal with this directly and cooperatively. It's going to be easier and safer for you to actually go to war with him than to come out in the open and admit everything."

Lara spread her hands. "I'd expect him to realize that, yes."

"Then why back you into that corner?" I asked. "What's it get him other than a conflict? The svartalves can fight. Doesn't mean they want to."

"If they drop it without extraordinary acts of contrition on my part," Lara said, "then they invite more of the same disrespect from Accorded nations and non-Accorded powers alike."

Hell's bells, that could be true enough. "He can't bend. And he's got to be very clear and aboveboard with everything in this. And because you did sneaky stuff, that's the one place you can't go to meet him. He knows it. So why ask for it?"

Lara frowned at me and tilted her head. "You clearly think you have an insight here. What is it?"

"What if he wants to avoid conflict just as much as we do?" I asked. "But he's signaling that he's unable to meet us partway under the current circumstances?"

She frowned. "I've considered that. I reasoned that he was simply acknowledging the fact that there wasn't a viable diplomatic solution."

"Well, sure. But that doesn't really help us, does it? My way, maybe we can work toward some kind of option."

"Like what?"

I opened my mouth and then closed it helplessly. "I don't know. But maybe we can figure out some way to satisfy both Etri's personal pride and his people's need for respectful treatment that isn't emissaries and diplomats and Accorded neutral ground."

Lara considered that for a moment and then said, "It seems . . . youthfully optimistic, to me."

"Or maybe you're getting jaded and cynical and it's clouding your ability to consider the full range of possibility," I said. "I spoke with Etri on several occasions. I hung out with his people most every day for a good long while. And everything I know about them tells me that they aren't just going to glumly accept the inevitable. Neither am I. And I don't think you're the kind to roll over for fate, either."

Lara's pale eyes glowed brighter, paler, as she studied me for a silent moment.

"No," she said very quietly. "I'm not."

I found myself staring at the motes of silver in her eyes. Her gaze was simply intense and beautiful. I tore my eyes away as things began to get more intimate and instead turned from her to take down an oil lantern from a hook on a nearby wall. I lit it with a gesture and a couple words. Then I lifted the lantern as I descended the ladder into the lab. When I got down, I held up the lantern to light Lara's way down.

She closed the door behind her as she descended, shutting us into the lab together.

"I'll consider what you have to say," she said quietly, turning slightly away from me, looking around the lab as I lit half a dozen candles. "Perhaps there's something to it. And, as you say, it is a course of pursuit that offers at least the possibility of a solution."

"If we can help Thomas," I said. "If we can't, all of this talk about Etri is academic."

Lara turned back to me. Candlelight did incredible things to her face, her mouth, and her eyes. "That's why I'm here," she said. She took a slow breath. "And why I have gone Hungry an additional two weeks while exercising my demon regularly. It has not been an insignificant strain."

"If we're going to try to get Thomas's Hunger fed and reintegrated with him," I said, "I have to know how much energy I'm going to need to pour out. I need you as close to that state as we can arrange so that I can get some kind of gauge for what I'll need for Thomas."

Lara nodded. "Your reasoning is sound." Her tongue, a little paler a pink than a human could have, flicked over her lips. "But you have to understand. If I allow myself to be reduced to that kind of state, I am uncertain how it might influence my behavior."

"Meaning what?" I asked carefully.

Her eyes drew mine again and she said, slow, lips wrapping around the words, "I'm. Very. Hungry. Harry. Any hungrier and I might . . . lose control. Do things to you."

I swallowed. The sound of her voice just slithered into me and made lightning flicker up and down my spine. My heart rate and respiration went up.

"Oh," I choked. "Yeah. I've . . . thought of . . . Okay, look, can you stand in the circle, please?"

Lara let out a throaty chuckle. She drew her eyes away from me only at the last moment, turning and sauntering past me with a languid roll to her step, over toward the circle.

The summoning circle in my lab had been upgraded.

Significantly.

It had been costly as hell to get what I had needed, all that had been left of one of the gym socks of diamonds. Normally, I'd have gone to the svartalves for my crafting, but that wasn't really an option at the moment. Or ever, likely.

A second ring of silver had been placed around the copper one in the floor, and the original had been repaired to a pristine state. I'd used paint of actual gold to lay out the new sigils of containment and warding between the two circles. The candles of rare wax and rarer herbs that burned at five points stood ready. I'd used more paint of gold to lay out the infinity sign in the circle's center. Natural clusters of semiprecious crystals were interspersed between the candles.

Building a greater circle was pricey. Like, supercar-plus-insurance pricey. And I'd gotten enough materials to make two of them.

Lara sidled into one loop of the infinity symbol and turned to look at me. "This is where you want me?"

"Ahem," I said. "Yeah."

"What do you want me to do?"

"Stay put a sec," I said, and went over the circle again, which made the eighth or ninth time I'd done it that day, verifying that everything was clean, clear of any potential debris, and done correctly. I overlaid my drawn plans, careful one-to-one sketches on translucent paper, on each sigil and made sure every single one was exactly right.

Lara stood over me, and I could feel her gaze on me the whole time. I was close enough to smell her—shampoo and scented soap and some subtle, stirring perfume that I suspected was simply her. Part of my brain got distracted by various memories, and my body was into that.

"Okay," I said, rising, tucking my drawings away. If I sounded a little out of breath, it was probably just the nerves of preparing the most complex symbolic structure I'd ever done on my own. Not close proximity to a woman who—

—*to a vampire*, I corrected myself. A succubus. An energy feeder who could leave me a chilly corpse or a drooling vegetable if I forgot what I was dealing with.

I put up the mental defenses almost as a reflex, establishing a barrier around my thoughts and will and pushing away that quivering, almost adolescent excitement that her presence was causing in my body and thoughts alike.

Dammit.

I liked feeling things that weren't loss and grief and regret and fear.

"Okay," I repeated, more firmly. "I'm going to bring up the circle and we'll begin."

"What do you need of me, specifically?" she asked.

I met her eyes and said, "After the circle is up . . . I need you to lose control."

The faint, flirtatious amusement on her face vanished.

"What?" she said after a moment.

I drew in a breath. "Look. It's got to be as difficult as possible to contain your Hunger, just like it will be with Thomas's once he's loose of the crystal. If what you say about his Hunger's relative strength is true, I've got to test this circle out before we do it for real."

She stared hard at me for a long moment. Her chin twitched up and down. "Logical." She licked her lips again. "What is going to stop the Hunger from taking me straight out of this circle and over to you once it's in control?"

"It's like that?" I asked.

"Like being in someone else's dream," she murmured, eyes glittering. "The Hunger will come for you. It will kill you."

"This is a greater circle," I said firmly. "Been working on it most days since New Year's. It should hold just about anything there is. You and your Hunger included."

"Should?"

"We can't know without testing it."

"If it doesn't work," she said, "Mab's going to be rather vexed with me. There will be a great many consequences at play."

I studied her for a moment. Then I said, "Look, you've seen me doing magic in fights, mostly. Lots of blood and thunder stuff. Right?"

"Yes," Lara said, her eyes unblinking.

"I'm fair at that," I said. I pointed at the circle. "This stuff? Slow and careful and tenacious? This is what I am *good* at. It's how I made my bread and butter, and you know how hard it is to be a small entrepreneur in this town. If I wasn't sure this was going to work, we wouldn't be here right now. This is what I do."

Lara lifted her eyebrows, eyes growing more like mirrors. "I adore a confident man." She closed her eyes, suppressing a smile, and slowly reached up a hand to free her hair from its ponytail, letting it fall down past her shoulders.

Damn. That one just doesn't get old.

"Very well," she said. "Tell me when to let go."

I blinked and said, "Right. Stand by."

And I began the spell again, as I had on New Year's Eve, only this time, with the assistance of the deliberately designed material construct, energy flowed remarkably more smoothly and efficiently. I brought candles to life and closed the circle as the clusters of crystals refracted excess energy as light, varied in color, that illuminated the ghostly, curved double wall of the closed greater circle.

Lara tensed on her feet, hands closing into fists, squeezing her eyes tightly shut. Her mouth opened in a gasp as the circle closed, and then she clenched her teeth together, ghostly white against the darker blush of her lips.

"All right," I said, keeping my voice firm as I gathered my will for the spell. "We're ready, Lara."

She nodded jerkily and then arched up onto her toes, her head falling back.

Okay, I know I had just said that I was ready.

But I wasn't ready.

I watched her Hunger take her.

Something changed. Shifted. I couldn't have told you what it was, but every fiber of my being was suddenly sure that I was in mortal danger.

Lara opened her eyes slowly, and they were simply glossy mirrors, silver and bright, reflecting the lab's candlelight in slowly warping images. She tilted her head slightly, looking at me, and the inside of the greater circle abruptly flared with light as a sudden tsunami of smoldering, lustful will flashed forth from Lara toward me, only to splash against the interior of the circle, radiating up like scorching heat waves on a summer road.

Hell's bells. The circle absorbed the supernatural influence, insulating me completely. If it hadn't, I was pretty sure I'd be food for the Hunger by now.

Lara focused upon me and narrowed her eyes. Her balance shifted, but I lifted a hand and made an effort of will, and her foot did not leave the ground. She remained trapped in the loop of the infinity symbol in the circle's center.

She took in her circumstances, her expression unreadable. Then her sensual mouth quirked at one corner and she slowly settled down onto her heels, hips shifting noticeably, hands reaching forward as if ready to spring into a quadrupedal run, mirrored eyes focused expressly upon me. Lara tilted her head and let out a soft, moaning sound, a weirdly quavering thing, while waves of psychic influence continued to pour off of her, lashing around the interior of the circle in dazzling waves of color.

I could feel the energy of the spell vibrate in time with her voice, quivering as it wavered back and forth, and felt a sudden thrum of disorienting sensation flood over me, as if my body had been a guitar string that had suddenly been plucked.

Ah. Ahhhhhhhhh . . . buzzed a voice in my mind. It wasn't a sound, because it never went past those bones in my ears. But I could hear it in my head, and it felt like a slithering ball of slippery tongues writhing about the interior of my skull, pressing at my thoughts. *There it is, the frequency. Now it hears.*

Lara's Hunger swept its silver eyes around the circle. The force of its will slammed against the circle on its other side. Then it turned and picked a new spot, pressing against the energy of the spell, testing for imperfections.

We fed upon it at the celebration, the voice in my head said. Lara bared her teeth in a wide, unnerving smile. *We want more. Come to us, mortal thing.*

The last words struck that chord in my head again, and the Hunger's will surged against my mental defenses. I steadied myself as if against a wave, feeling a surge of naked lust slam against me, wash over me in a full-body frisson—and then it was past, and I still stood before the circle, holding the spell steady, secure in my focus and intent.

I mean, seriously. Investing in a greater circle makes all the difference. If I'd had the means, I'd have done this years ago.

The Hunger's eyes widened. Lara's mouth twisted into a snarl as she slammed her fist out to the side—where it smashed against the circle of light as if it had been a brick wall. The Hunger struck around at several points of the circle, where she could reach, but I'd done my work properly. It held.

The Hunger bared more of Lara's teeth than should have been strictly possible and let out a low, harsh hissing sound.

What does it want? said the slithering voice in my head. *Let me give it whatever it wants. What remains unfulfilled? Let me into the void in you, mortal. Anything you desire.*

It wasn't just words.

It came with pictures. Sensory input.

Things I didn't have senses for. Couldn't understand.

There was a sudden, awful pressure in my head.

"Stop that!" I snapped, and sent a lance of my will forward, against what the Hunger had hurled at me through the connection of the spell.

Lara, crouched low, rocked to one side as if I'd slapped her, and the pressure vanished. She blinked silver mirror eyes wide open and looked shocked. She stared at me for a second and the voice slither-whispered, *Starborn.*

"That's right," I said. "I've got stuff to do and no time for Outsider insanity nonsense. Quit it."

The thing twisted up Lara's face in fury and began to send more psychic force toward me.

I lifted my right hand and sent out another jab of will into the circle.

The Hunger flinched back slightly, mouth agog.

"I said I'm not having it," I growled. "Stand down."

The Hunger grimaced weirdly and then lifted one hand toward me, crouching slightly lower, a gesture of apparent submission that I would be wise not to trust.

Its voice whispered through my head again, sending odd tingles up and down my spine. *What does it wish of me?*

I took a deep breath and lifted my right hand again, fingers spread. With a slow exhale and a far gentler effort of will, I sent more magical energy coursing into the circle, and into the Hunger. For a moment, Lara's face looked shocked—and then the silver eyes glazed over with white, and her head fell slowly back. She let out a mewl like a small, starving animal.

And then raw psychic force seized me like a sudden, treacherous undertow as the Hunger drank in the energy I'd poured into the circle and clawed at my thoughts for more. It was like suddenly experiencing a new axis of gravity, and for a frantic second, I felt myself wobbling, being drawn forward into a silvery daze of sensation. I realized, with a shock like being hit with a bucket of cold water, that the magical connection of channeling energy into Lara's Hunger went both ways, as it frantically tried to draw more energy from me. If I lost focus, lost the spell, the thing could rip my life force out.

And it wouldn't even be in the sexy way.

I held firm against the pull of the Hunger, the construction of the spell giving me all the leverage, while focusing more and more intention upon sending a steady, controlled stream of energy for the Hunger to feed upon. It was famished, and I could feel it devouring what I provided ravenously. Lara's body fell to its side, convulsing.

And this was the test. When a wizard uses magic, we draw it from all around us, yes—but some of it also comes from inside us. That's why we get tired when we keep throwing spells around. It seemed that I could use a stream of magic to feed the Hunger, maybe because some of it was inevitably the life energy of one of the starborn. But the question remained: Could I feed a ravenous Hunger enough magical energy to pacify it? Or would it just keep taking it out of me until there wasn't enough left to keep my nervous system functioning?

I don't know how long I stood there, eyes closed, locked in a psychic push-and-pull with the Hunger. I had to focus so hard upon just keeping myself centered, my intention clear, in the face of the pressure the Hunger exerted on me that there wasn't much brain left over for things like taking notice of the passage of time.

Eventually, I felt the pressure begin to ease. I kept the energy going, feeling that my shoulder was tired from holding my right hand out, that my shirt had gotten soaked with sweat despite the subterranean chill. My legs had locked in place, and my feet ached enough to tell me that I'd been there for a couple of hours, at least. My extended hand felt weak, like it might be about to start shaking.

I opened my eyes slowly.

Lara's eyes rolled back down, unfocused and bluer than sapphires. She was shivering and shuddering on the floor within the circle. I could feel her Hunger subsiding, like a serpent that had swallowed a large meal and begun to sink into torpor.

Stars and stones.

I'd done everything perfectly on a greater circle. I had all the leverage and held every card—even home field advantage. And Lara's Hunger had still come close to doing me in.

Lara gasped and twitched for a few seconds and then began to relax. Her eyes fluttered closed in evident exhaustion.

I closed my right hand and lowered it slowly, gently easing off the flow of energy. As it vanished, Lara made a small, disappointed sound. Then she wrapped her arms around herself, curled into a ball, and fell into what appeared to be desperately needed sleep.

I stood there for a moment, taking deep breaths. I was worn out. It had been a considerable amount of work, but I'd been this bad and worse before, plenty of times. I wouldn't go looking for a battle at the moment or anything, but I'd fought them in worse shape than I was in now, more than once.

If Thomas's Hunger was a challenge on a scale similar to Lara's, then maybe I could actually pull this off. Maybe I could bring my brother back from the brink of death.

And if I couldn't pacify his Hunger, maybe I could still cut it out of him. I'd designed the circle to encompass that function, too.

If I had to do it to save Thomas's life, I would.

I bowed my head and slumped to the floor to sit and rest.

I felt someone's gaze on me after a while, and looked up to find Lara staring at me, the oddest expression on her face, her blue eyes troubled.

"Hey," I said.

Lara blinked several times, smoothing over her expression, and said, "It worked."

"Yeah," I said. "You all right?"

"I'm . . ." She swallowed. "I think I should go." She got her feet beneath her and rose. She swallowed and looked around at the circle. "Harry," she said, voice tense.

I blinked at her reaction but murmured a word, waved a hand, and snuffed out the candles, and the circle's continuity with them. Only the candles on my worktable still lit the lab with a low glow.

Lara stepped carefully out of the circle, murmured, "We'll talk soon," without meeting my eyes, and turned to climb up the stepladder, open the trapdoor, and leave the lab. Her footsteps hurried down the hallway above as she . . .

She fled.

I stared after her for a long while.

What the hell?

Chapter
Thirty-Nine

I went to bed and crashed, exhausted from the energy work, but my mind refused to settle, and I lay there in one of those dozes that drifts freely from thought to dream and back.

Lara's departure had been, frankly, entirely uncharacteristic of her. You could call Lara Raith a lot of names, but *coward* wasn't one of them. Yet at the end of the spell, she'd skedaddled like a cat at a dog show. The look on her face had been as closed as she could manage, but there'd been complicated expressions on it, going by quickly. When she had realized that she was trapped in the circle, it had been something very close to controlled panic.

My mind treated me to the image of her writhing and arching in pleasure as long as we were reviewing Lara. And Hell's bells. Even though my mind had been shielded from influence and even though the greater circle had contained her Hunger's power, just looking at her could have gotten to me in dangerous ways that had little to do with the supernatural and everything to do with primal, fundamental nature.

And, my body reminded me, there'd been very little in the way of fundamental nature in my life lately.

It was far, far too easy to picture things going a different way. Like, maybe if I'd been in the circle with Lara. Sexuality could readily become a source of power and a theater of magical focus, all at once. I mean, sure, standing a safe distance away and projecting energy worked, but if it had been closer . . . more intimate . . .

I tossed and turned. I tried thinking about baseball, but that just meant that imagined-Lara was wearing a Cubs hat and nothing else. I could all but feel her slim, strong, deliciously feminine weight settling over my hips. Her cold, pale hands on my chest. Her hair brushing my face as she leaned down, a shivering exhalation tickling my neck.

"Finally," Mab breathed into my ear. "Well done, my Knight."

Panic shot through me like a bolt of frozen lightning.

I opened my eyes and found the Queen of Air and Darkness straddling my hips. She was wearing a glacial-green gown, off the shoulder, its skirts hiked up around pale, lovely thighs. Her snow-colored hair was down in waves, her eyes bright and electric green, and the look on her face was one of pure, sensual satisfaction.

The Winter mantle howled for release.

"Um," I said.

It was an awkward sort of conversation to be having with your boss. In my present circumstances, extremely so.

Mab smiled down at me benignly.

It was terrifying.

"What did I do?" I asked carefully.

"You have delivered unto me the White Court, of course," Mab murmured. "I cannot think of a Winter Knight who has brought me a finer conquest." She gave me a thoughtful look, and suddenly my body was aflame. I had gone to sleep naked. And she wasn't wearing anything under the gown. I could feel. "Such service demands a reward. What do you desire, my Knight?"

I blinked several times, juggling confusion with . . . some kind of incipient sexual berserker state.

When Mab had taken me as Winter Knight, in a ritual where she'd infused me with the power of the Winter mantle, we'd had sex. I mean, technically, Tab A, Slot B, it had been the act. But with Mab, sex wasn't a storm of passion. It was more like a nation-wrecking, topography-altering hurricane that changes names on maps. Honestly, I couldn't remember much, and I think my sanity was probably safer that way. The idea of more of the same didn't make me excited—it made me flinch from the thought.

(I mean, sure, my body had other ideas, but bodies aren't to be trusted with such choices.)

I swallowed until I got some spit back in my mouth, fighting to think clearly. "Before I answer," I said. "I want to ask questions."

Mab's smirk was slow and wicked. "Wizards." She settled back slightly. I might have jumped a little. "Ask."

"What do you mean I've given you the White Court?" I said carefully.

She tilted her head. "Had you not considered the outcome of your"— her mouth quirked at the corners—"activities with Ms. Raith?"

"What?" I said.

"Thrice she has fed from you, starborn Knight," Mab purred. "Tasted of Winter's power thrice."

My stomach twisted. "Meaning what?"

She stared at me for a moment. "What is magic?"

"Energy left over from the creation of the universe," I said automatically. "Life that hasn't yet found physical expression."

"Yes," she said, drawing out the word. "Life. Raw. Primal. Creation." She shivered and arched the fingers of one hand, drawing her long, opaline nails through the hairs on my chest. I fought not to jump again. "The Hungers are meant to consume the energy inherent in all of creation. That is their purpose. They yearn for it. Lust after it. But because of how they were bound by the ancient sorcerer-king, they can only nibble at tiny, unsatisfying portions that never fill them."

"You're telling me," I said slowly, "that when Lara feeds, her Hunger's been getting unflavored oatmeal."

"And you gave it a taste of ambrosia, starborn," Mab murmured. "As vanishingly few others could. It will want more. Very badly. Regularly. That need will make Ms. Raith . . . pliable."

My eyes widened.

"And that is only the most overt effect it will have on her. One becomes what one consumes, after all. You have fed her Hunger more and better than it has ever known. She has tasted of you, and of Winter. Eaten the food of the Fae. She will become more like both. More and more in accord with you." Mab shivered with an undeniably sensual movement of her body. "You have her. With her comes her Court. And I have you. You have served me very well, my Knight. Name your reward."

I stared at her in horror.

"This whole time," I said low, "you were using me. To enslave someone."

"If all goes well, more than one," Mab murmured. "Lara and her negotiators assumed the language in the bargain about the exercise of control being permissible addressed *her* propensity to control *you*," Mab said serenely. "They even protected its wording, so that it would be certain she would be held free of any retribution should your allies in Winter be upset at her actions." Mab arched a pale brow and looked down at me. "She would have been content to enslave you, my Knight. It is entirely fitting that the tables be turned upon her."

"You used me," I said again, fury making my voice quiet, "to enslave someone."

The Queen of Air and Darkness tilted her head slightly, frowning down at me. "You would never have been able to deceive her if you'd known. Such subtlety is not among your gifts."

"You're right," I growled.

And I punched Mab in her slender throat.

The angle wasn't good and I had no base of leverage from my back, so it didn't crush her windpipe. But her eyes flew wide open and she exhaled in a little choking sound. I seized her by the hair and threw her off the bed to the floor.

"You used me," I snarled, "to do that."

Catlike green eyes flickered to my hands and then up to my face, and her mouth spread into an inhumanly wide smile as she nodded.

I snarled, seized her by the thigh and the front of her gown, picked her up over my head as if she weighed nothing, and flung her across the room into the stone wall. She hit it like a bundle of wet sticks and tumbled down to the top of my dresser, bounced off it, and hit the floor.

"You used me!" I screamed. I stalked across the floor as Mab began to push herself up and brought my heel down on her spine, slamming her back to the floor. She turned her head a little too far around to be natural to stare up at me, green eyes gleaming, her sharp, inhuman smile growing even wider. Blood trickled from a corner of her mouth.

I let out an incoherent cry and raised a clenched fist.

Mab let out a croaking cackle and said, "Yes. Yes. It feels good, does it not?"

. . .

. . .

It did.

Hell's bells.

I froze there, fist raised, ready to drive it down at her smiling face. My body was flooded with adrenaline, limbs singing with the pleasure of tensed muscle about to be used, heart beating steady and hard. I felt afire with rage. I felt certain. I felt so freaking strong.

I felt good. Intensely good.

Insanely good.

Like it had with Rudolph.

"Oh," Mab said, eyes closing. She took a deep breath, and her broken ribs made crackling sounds as they expanded and resettled into their original places. Mab opened her eyes dreamily, rolling her throat, and when she spoke again her voice had returned to normal. "You are coming along quite nicely, my Knight. I approve."

My raised hand started shaking. So did the rest of me.

I reeled back from Mab.

She sat up slowly, laughing a low, satisfied laugh. "Instinct. Fury. Focused aggression. Yes, my Knight. All powerful tools, ones you will need. Excellent." She tilted her head. "Though I would suggest better tactics. Did you think you could beat an immortal to death with your bare hands?"

I looked away from her.

"No," she purred. "You weren't thinking. You gave in to your instincts. And already so protective of Ms. Raith. Also good." She rose, slowly and sinuously, like a cobra. "What is done is done. You *will* control her, my Knight. The alternatives are unthinkable."

I seized the sheets off of my bed. I covered myself.

"I want time to think of my reward," I said, voice hoarse. "I want you to leave."

She was suddenly in my face, faster than I could see.

"Did you think," she hissed, her voice somehow audibly adding capitals to words, "that you would use My mantle to save your child, and then rob Me of My due service? Did you think that in the service of Air and Darkness that you would not be changed? Not bent to My will?" She leaned close and whispered, "The truth becomes more and more obvious, does it not? You are, more and more, bit by bit, a wicked man, in service to a wicked Queen."

I shuddered.

Mab let out another low laugh. "I have had a fine, fine day. Your request for more time to choose is wise. This, too, I wish to encourage. I give you until your wedding."

And with a whisper and a stir of cool air, she was gone.

Leaving me sitting on the cold stone floor under an uneven swath of cotton sheet, legs curled against my chest.

"What have I done?" I whispered.

As a professional wizard, let me tell you—that's one of those phrases you kind of dread saying, with excellent reason.

"You got played," I answered myself.

And so had Lara. She'd extended trust to me.

And, grieving, blindly focused on helping Thomas, needing to keep what I was doing secret, I'd been arrogant enough to proceed with some serious high magic with only bare weeks of research rather than the months or years that were usually recommended. If I'd done that, come at it from enough angles, I might have seen this coming.

But there hadn't been *time.*

My shoulders sagged.

I just needed time.

A wicked man, in service to a wicked Queen.

Mab's voice echoed in my head.

And inside my chest, in that little warm spot that still burned, a quiet voice said, *No. That's not going to happen.*

And I recognized the voice.

Because it was me.

Lies. Mab cannot change who you are.

Right. She could manipulate me, obviously. She could deceive me. But she couldn't change me.

Only I could do that.

And no, that wasn't going to happen. Yeah, maybe I wasn't perfect, but I wasn't going to become her freaking monster, either. And while we were at it, who the hell did she think she was, to deceive me like that? And did she honestly believe that she was going to pull something like that on me and I was going to just sit there twiddling my thumbs?

No. Hell, no.

And if I did it right, maybe I could solve two problems at once.

I needed to talk to Lara.

And Molly.

Chapter
Forty

Molly leaned on the merlon with her arms folded, atop the battlements of the castle, looking down at the protesters across the street.

There were more of them now, and more organized. They spent the top twenty minutes of every hour banging drums and chanting. *No more war and strife, we just want a normal life!* was kind of impossible not to empathize with. Who doesn't want that, at least for their own flavor of "normal"? But by the time they'd gotten to *Ho, ho, hey, hey, culty weirdos go away!* it was getting a little harder not to take it personally.

They were scaring some of the kids.

Molly was wearing jeans and a bomber jacket over a turtleneck. She was looking almost inhumanly lean, and her eyes were glacial blue-green and particularly feline today. She stared out at the protesters, her expression unreadable, and looked like someone who was remembering faces. "Don't you think you'd better do something about this?"

"People got rights," I said firmly.

"Such as the right not to be harassed in their own homes?" Molly suggested.

"Starts getting cold in another few hours," I said. "They'll leave then."

"For now," Molly said. "What about later?"

I sighed. "As long as it's just words, we're fine here."

"Makes you wonder who put them up to it," Molly said.

"Things have been crazy," I said. "People get worked up. They need an outlet." I waved a hand. "Tens of thousands died in the battle. Means a lot of bereaved people. Traumatized people. People whose whole world was yanked out from under them. But they're cut off from the rest of things here, for a while. Could be they're just hurting. Could be there doesn't have to be a villain at work. People get weird at times like this. Maybe it's better to allow for that." The chanting stopped, and the protesters broke up into casual conversations. "There, see?" I said. "Look how happy they look now."

"Hmph," Molly said. "They throw a single egg, vegetable, rock, or firework at this place, and the weather is going to get cold very, very quickly."

And I realized that Molly was being protective. Of me.

I looked aside at her with a lopsided smile.

"Thank you for that," I said.

Molly puffed a breath up from her extended lower lip, blowing some hair away from her eyes, and gave me a somewhat sheepish look. "You've had a tough enough year," she said.

"Yeah," I said. I took a slow breath. "Did you know what Mab was doing?"

Molly went still. She frowned down at the protesters, her expression clouding.

"You did," I said.

"I put it together," she said quietly. "I wanted to tell you. I tried to tell you. But Mab forbade me from communicating with you about it, directly or indirectly. I'm sorry, Harry."

Mab's word was literally law in Winter. If she gave a command to one of her Court, that was that.

I shook my head. "Dammit."

"Harry," Molly said, in a very small voice. "I'm sorry Mab manipulated you like that. I'm sorry I wasn't able to do anything about it."

"I know. I get it. You didn't have a choice."

"You didn't let me finish," she said intently. "I've talked to her quite a bit over the past couple of years. Enough to know that she's scary smart. Have you considered the notion that she might be the one around here with the brains and the perspective that no one else has? She might be trying to look after you. She might even be right."

"There's no 'right' here," I said quietly.

"No? Because I'd rather it was you in control of Lara than the other way around," Molly said quietly. "And I'm grateful that you won't be in her thrall."

I stared at her for a long moment. "You agree with Mab."

"With her strategy, yes," Molly said. "It's practical. Reasonable. It offers one of the only means for containing Lara Raith's increasing influence in the mortal world—the protection of which is Winter's primary task, if you recall." She looked aside at me sadly and then down. "I disagreed with her tactics. I thought she should have communicated with you."

"And you thought I'd have agreed to wholesale abuse of the Third Law because it was practical?" I asked. "That would be all I need. The White Council coming after my head."

Molly grimaced. "The law only applies to mortals. Lara isn't human."

"Wow," I said quietly, "is that so not the point."

She made a dissatisfied noise and waved a hand in acquiescence.

I was quiet for a moment. Then I said, "You know that when Lara understands what has happened, she's going to be furious about it."

"Mab thinks she won't be," Molly said. "At least, not for long."

The protesters started chanting again, well ahead of their usual appointed time. I frowned down at them and then leaned out over the merlon to look up and down the street.

Carlos Ramirez, in a long grey coat, was walking down the street toward the castle. He was too far off to make out his face, but he moved as quickly as he could with his cane, his body tense.

"Speak of the Wardens," Molly said from beside me, "and they shall appear."

We went down to the front door to meet him.

"Harry," Carlos began when I opened the smaller door. Then he saw Molly and froze as if he'd been smacked with a wet fish. "Oh. Um. Lady Molly. Hello."

Molly gave him an awkward smile. "Warden Ramirez. A pleasure to see you."

Ramirez's face twitched, and he turned it into a smile almost instantly. "I trust you've been settling into your new, ah, duties?"

"There's so much travel." Molly sighed. "And you? You're moving well."

Ramirez looked down at himself and shifted a bit uncomfortably, as if he'd had to resist taking a step back from Molly. "I'm . . . really bad at playing nice about this." He sighed. "Another year of really uncomfortable PT and I should be back to full speed."

"I didn't know it would happen," Molly said quickly. "I'd never have . . . I'm sorry."

I frowned and looked back and forth between them. Protesters chanted *hey, hey, ho, ho.*

"My first mission for Winter," Molly clarified. Her cheeks had turned pink. "Carlos was there for something else. We, um. There was a misunderstanding, and he got hurt."

Carlos showed his teeth without precisely smiling. "My own fault. I'll be more cautious in the future."

"Oh," Molly said in a much smaller voice.

He gave her a rueful smile. "My gut says it's for the best. When have you and the Wardens ever gotten along?"

"Hah," she said, without energy. "I suppose that's true."

He nodded. "Harry, I'm here because the Wardens received an anonymous tip about black magic being employed in the city. Ilyana and a team are on the way to Bock Ordered Books right now."

"Dammit," I said. "There's no need for that. It's handled."

Ramirez spread his hands. "It's not my call. Ilyana's been given your old job. I'm back to just handling the western US. Technically, I'm not even supposed to be in the loop for her operations. But I thought you should know."

"You out of here?" I asked him.

He grimaced. "I can't leave if I was never here. And I wasn't." He nodded to me, glanced at Molly, then down, turning it into a small bow toward her. Then he turned and continued walking down the street.

"Bear!" I called after a moment.

The Valkyrie appeared out of the castle. "Yeah?"

"Make sure Fitz knows to stay low. We're going out. Pack for an argument with Wardens. We leave in five minutes."

"Interesting," Molly said. "I think I'll come along."

I arched an eyebrow at her. I glanced in the direction Ramirez had gone.

Molly sniffed delicately, but her glacial eyes glittered. "After all. Everyone knows how I get along with Wardens."

We rolled out in the Munstermobile in minutes and took the flame-painted old hearse to get as close as we could to Bock's place through the maze of partially functioning streets, piled up with mounds of dirty snow, where they had been cleared at all. We had to walk the last few blocks in, and we got to Bock's front door right about the time a group of grey-cloaked Wardens rolled in from the opposite direction. Ilyana's slim, blond form walked with a confident stride in the lead, dressed in close-fit black tactical clothing and a Warden's grey cloak. She made the fifth member of a standard squad who walked behind her, two by two, boots striking the ground in time.

I remembered that sound, from back when I was sixteen. *Tromp, tromp, tromp.* They'd marched me places for my trial after they'd arrested me when I'd killed my old mentor in self-defense. It stirred up old, old fears.

And anger.

I felt it harder and sharper than I ever had before, as if my skin had been peeled off and there was no protection from the memories and the emotions they brought. In my head, the five Wardens turned into bowling pins, and I had to fight to keep from summoning up a sphere of pure kinetic energy and hurling it at them.

I took the same slow, deep breath that I did when meditating, and willed the feelings back. That was the whole point of practicing self-calming with meditation. It worked. The haze of powerful emotion receded, at least enough to let me think clearly.

For me, anyway.

"With me," I said quietly.

"Dresden," Bear asked quietly. "You going to be able to bring any of your game to a real fight?"

By which she meant magic.

And I didn't know the answer to the question.

"Maybe it won't come to that," I said.

Then I started walking toward the Wardens.

Molly fell in just behind me on my right. Bear on my left. And we tromped, too.

Ilyana saw me coming and her ice-blue eyes narrowed. We all came to a halt about ten feet from each other.

"Stand aside, Dresden," Ilyana said firmly. "This is no concern of yours."

"Agree to disagree," I said. "It's been taken care of."

"I'll be the judge of that."

"Not today, you won't."

Her expression didn't overtly change. But I could feel the rage rolling off her. Good Lord. She was boiling.

My own rage leapt up, snarling in answer.

I took another deep breath.

"Look," I said quietly. "Today will go better for everyone if you stand down."

"There are five of us and three of you," Ilyana noted.

"And all eight of us are on a public street, in a town full of people who have recently been traumatized by supernatural violence," I said. "This could go sideways in about a million ways."

Ilyana's pale brows beetled. "The full weight of the White Council is behind us."

Molly stepped up next to me, smiling a little too wide with a few too many teeth. "Oh, darling. Are we having a size contest now?"

Ilyana's cold eyes swept to Molly.

"This city is not recognized territory of the White Council," Molly said. "It is an independent barony. I trust you have a letter of permit from the local Accorded lord to exercise force in his territory?"

Of course she wouldn't. The White Council was used to going where it wanted to go, and for the most part nobody wanted out-of-control warlocks running around their territories, so they'd let the White Council come clean them up for centuries, even before the Accords came into being.

Bear moved suddenly and swept the four-bore out from under her long coat, staring hard at one of the Wardens in the rear rank, one of the older members, a grizzled man with what looked like a dueling scar on his cheek. One of his hands was behind his back. He froze. Then stared hard at Bear.

"Easy," I said quietly, to everyone. "We're just talking right now."

"If you do not carry a letter of permission," Molly continued, "then since Baron Marcone is an Accorded member in good standing, under the Accords, the Winter Court will defend his territory against official incursion from another Accorded nation."

"You expect me to believe you'd start a war," Ilyana snarled, "over a handful of petty warlocks?"

"I've started a war for one soul," I said gently. "You think I won't fight for half a dozen?"

Ilyana blinked, but the older Wardens behind her rocked gently at the statement. They traded uneasy glances, and I could feel their resolve wavering.

"And what makes you think there's only three of us?" Molly asked merrily, her smile getting wider and more unsettling. She walked forward a few slow steps, and while I couldn't see her face, I could see Ilyana swallow in reaction. "Do you honestly think the Winter Lady travels anywhere without an escort detail? Whether you can see them or not."

Molly snapped her fingers, and there came a low round of snickering laughter from an alleyway behind the Wardens, and another across the street. Shadowy figures moved in the latter. Goblins. Which are not at all like the things you may have seen in certain films or games. They are to be feared, and the faces of the more experienced Wardens standing behind Ilyana told me that they knew it.

Ilyana stared up at Molly for a moment. Then her pale face turned scarlet and she drew in a breath.

"Ilyana," the scarred Warden said.

She shot a furious glance over her shoulder, and then glared at Molly, and then at me.

"This will be reported to the Senior Council," she snarled.

"Tell them the Winter Knight sends his greetings," I said.

"This isn't over."

"You know where to find me," I said.

Ilyana snarled again, spun on a heel, stalked through the group of Wardens, and slashed at the air with a hand and a word infused with her will. She opened a Way to the Nevernever, the world of spirit existing beside the natural world, tearing open a seam in the fabric of reality like a band of dim red light, and stepped through it without slowing down.

The Wardens followed her, two of them leaving while two watched us, and then those two bailed as well, vanishing on the open street, in front of God and everybody.

I glanced around. There were maybe a half dozen people in sight. All of them were walking away. Briskly. Scared. And they'd go home and not want to talk to anyone about what they'd seen for fear of being reported as exposed and shipped off to an HBGB treatment center.

Secrets. Fear. Lies. All boiling under the surface.

Fantastic. Just what the town needed.

The alleyways had fallen silent and still again, nothing evident moving in them. "You brought goblins along?" I asked Molly.

She turned slowly back to face us after watching the Wardens go and said, "Did I?"

Molly was hell on wheels with illusion, her absolute specialty of magic. If she wanted to make you see something, or not see it, she could probably arrange to do so. Of course, she could also whistle up an army of angry and dangerous Fae if she needed to and had done so during the battle last year. Which had given today's bluff a solidity most sane people would be reluctant to call.

If it was a bluff.

Maybe she was just running around with a bodyguard of maniacal super-ninjas these days. Hell. I had a seven-foot, four-hundred-pound Valkyrie with a gun the size of a light pole walking next to me.

Times had changed.

The door to Bock Ordered Books opened, the little bell mounted on it jingling.

Artemis Bock came out and walked over to me. As he did, several of the folks from the ritual I'd disrupted appeared, though they lingered near the doorway like rabbits ready to dive back into their warren.

Bock looked past me to where the portal to the Nevernever had faded, leaving a smear of rapidly dissolving ectoplasm on the sidewalk.

"My God," he said. "Those were the Wardens?"

"Yeah."

He swallowed.

"You stopped them," he said.

"Today."

He looked down. His scalp was pink beneath thinning hair.

"Would they have . . . ?"

"Probably," I said.

He folded his arms over his chest and nodded.

"Continue the purification rituals," I said quietly. "And keep your nose clean. Next time I might not hear about it in time."

"Yeah," he said, without looking up. He looked back at his people and then looked up at me for a second. "Thank you. If you need anything . . ."

I sighed impatiently. The anger that was surging around my chest was disappointed the situation had ended without violence.

"Why?" Bock asked me.

"Why what?"

"You came down here. Stood up for us. Why?"

I scowled.

"Someone stood up for me once," I said. "Or I wouldn't be here."

Molly stepped up and got in Bock's face. Her expression wasn't kindly. "He wasn't the only one who stood up for you, Bock," she said. "Winter did as well. And now you are in Winter's debt."

Bock looked up, his eyes wide, face bloodless.

"You people harmed my little brother," Molly snarled.

Bock swallowed and shrank back a little. He had a good idea who the Winter Lady was, and what she might do.

"Molls," I said.

She glanced at me, then rose away from Bock slowly and said, "I suggest you follow the advice of the Winter Knight," she said in a low, hard voice. "Or I may come collect from you sooner and more dearly than otherwise. Am I understood?"

Bock looked down, jerking his head in a quick nod.

"Enough," I said gently. My head twinged with the beginning of a headache, a very vague sensation behind the pain-masking effect of the Winter mantle, though it still managed to be almost as annoying as the real thing. "I bought you a little time today, Bock. Use it wisely."

Bock nodded jerkily. Then he and his folk hurried back inside.

"Well," Molly murmured, after they'd gone. "You and I have just assisted a batch of warlocks in covering up their use of black magic from duly appointed Wardens of the White Council."

"Feels good," I said.

Her face spread into a merry smile. "It does, doesn't it."

"Could be it isn't the best idea," I said. "Black magic. You know what it can do to someone."

She nodded once and spoke in a cool tone. "Which is why I wanted to scare them a bit. Winter's honor is involved in this now. Winter will keep an eye on them."

"It will, huh?"

Molly nodded. Her voice softened slightly, though her eyes stayed hard. "I don't want anything bad to happen to them, either, Harry. But

I don't want them to hurt anyone else like they did Daniel. They aren't playing softball."

I looked back at the door to Bock Ordered Books. Someone reached up and flipped the sign from reading OPEN to CLOSED.

"No," I said quietly. "They're not."

Chapter

Forty-One

"So," I said to the assembled residents of the castle. I was standing in front of them all in the main hall, several days after our confrontation with the Wardens, with the gargoyles lined up motionless as statues behind me. "In conclusion, the gargoyles here are real, yes. They will move and talk and things. They'll also help defend and protect everyone here in the event of danger. I mean, if there's a fire or whatever."

The kids, including Maggie, were all sitting up front. Hands went up like in a classroom.

"Uh," I said. I pointed at a boy who was about ten, one of Matias's kids, whose name was Jorge. "Jorge, yes?"

"Can we climb on them?" he asked brightly.

"Uh," I said. "Maybe treat them like you would teachers at school. They're not really playground equipment."

Jorge took this in with a frown. "Will they give us rides?"

"Only if it's an emergency," I said, "and they need to keep you safe for some reason."

Maggie waved her hand. "Do they turn to stone in daylight? Like in that old show?"

"They're kind of stone all the time," I said. "No, it doesn't work like that."

The kids were all leaning forward curiously.

"Look," I said. "Most of the time they're going to be in the rock of the walls and floor and so on, out of sight, because there's enough people out there who are freaked out about supernatural creatures." I nodded in the direction of the protesters. If you listened hard, you could hear them when they got going. "If the gargoyles come out, it's because I've got them doing something, or because there's some kind of problem or danger. So if one of them shows up and tells you that you need to go to your room or get outside or whatever, just know that they're good guys, and they're on our team."

"They can climb on us," Basil said calmly in his resonant voice. He turned his leonine features to Jorge. "We have a number of graspable outcroppings. We like children, though they often make little sense."

The littlest of the gargoyles, Cinnamon, with the head of a monkey and the body of a cat, nodded vigorously in silence.

Thyme, who had the head of something very like an owl, and the body of something more like a humanoid bear, spoke in a light tenor and a very English accent. "If any of us are to be treated like a teacher, I believe that should be me. If you provide me with the relevant texts, I shall be pleased to offer my services as a tutor for any students here, as well as providing scholarly context from the brightest minds of a number of centuries."

Mouse, who was sitting beside Maggie, made a pleased chuffing sound, wagged his tail, and walked up to sit at Thyme's feet like an eager student.

"Oh," Thyme said. "Yes, certainly, Temple dog. That includes you."

Cardamom, whose head was a boar and whose body was like that of a squat, hugely muscled man, said, "I shall be pleased to officiate in athletic competition and any tourneys here. You will find me completely unbiased in such matters."

Parsley and Sage both had the heads of birds of prey, sort of vaguely, and the bodies of lean and powerful men in loincloths. They spoke in the same voice, at the same time, in eerie stereo. "We clean. We mend. We build. We are glad to help."

Bay shook his hound-dog head and yawned. He had an apelike body that looked like it would be most comfortable in quadrupedal motion, and said, "I like to keep people company."

"Oh," I said. "We're doing introductions, I guess."

Jorge popped to his feet and walked up to Basil. He poked at Basil's leg with one finger and said, "It's warm."

"Yes," Basil said gravely. "We are living stone."

"Do you like tacos?" Jorge asked.

Basil dropped down to one knee so that his eyes were on level with Jorge's. "We are living stone. We do not eat as mortals do."

"Stories!" piped Cinnamon in a chirping voice. "We like stories!"

"Hmm," Jorge said. "Do you know the one about the guy with the lightsaber?"

Every gargoyle there focused suddenly and intently upon Jorge, gathering around, while Basil said, "I am not sure. Will you tell it?"

"Yeah!" Jorge said. "Okay, so there's these robots. Wait, no, first there's a little spaceship, and it's running away from this *huge* bad-guy spaceship!"

I was worried for a minute, that these large supernatural creatures were bunching up around a kid. But as I watched, Jorge started running through the plot of *Star Wars*, and the gargoyles settled in and gathered around, expressions fascinated as they watched the boy's glowing face. He had an audience and he loved it.

Matias walked up to me, his expression bemused.

"Harry," he said.

"How you doing?" I asked him.

"Well," he said. "Last year, my world fell to pieces when those things came here. Creatures, tearing apart the city."

"Yeah," I said. "Lot of that going around."

"Evil things," he said. "Not simply predators. Dark. Evil. Like demons in the Bible."

"More of that going around than any of us would like," I confirmed.

"When the government started talking about HBGB, I wanted to believe them. That I had been poisoned and it had given me hallucinations. But here, day after day, I see things. Things that tell me that the world is not the way I thought it was."

I frowned at that and turned to listen more intently.

"I do not think that is so," he said quietly. "And it frightened me for a long time." He lifted his hands and spread them open. "I saw terrible things happen." He nodded and looked at me. "And I saw good men fight them."

I swallowed and kept listening.

"You and that huge ape came to my home and fought them and saved my family. And you led us to shelter and forced the man who owned this place to let us in. Things from old stories stood with you. And I was terrified." He smiled. "After a while, I realized. If the monsters from the old stories are true, if beings of evil run wild in this world, then it stands to reason that the opposite is true. The old stories are full not only of bad things. But good things, too. Good wizards." He nodded at the gargoyles. "Protectors. The Little Folk we see sometimes. Powers of light that fight the darkness."

I nodded my chin up and down quickly and held back tears. "That's true. I don't know if I'm one of those."

"I do," Matias said calmly. "I have seen you do it. I do not say that it is easy for you. Or anyone. Doing the right thing is sometimes difficult. Sometimes frightening. But I see your little girl's dog is more than just a dog—and he is good. I see Michael Carpenter and he walks like there is always light around him." He clapped a hand on my shoulder. "And I see you, with them gathering around you. I know you lost someone. I know what that looks like. I know you have been going through pain. Grief."

I nodded again.

"Good men hurt. And they heal. And when you heal, when the pain has dwindled, it can make you harder, more bitter, more rigid. Or it can make you more . . . gentle. Understanding. Yes?"

"Gentle . . ." I smiled faintly and shook my head. "Not what I'd call me."

"Then you are wrong," Matias said quietly. "Gentleness is power that chooses to restrain itself. That is under control. Gentleness is someone strong who makes the choice to be careful with that strength. And that is you." He exhaled through his nose and smiled at his son telling stories to things that most people thought were purely imaginary. "That is you."

*   *   *

Later that night, I got out Backup, Murphy's old pistol, and put it on the shrine I used to summon her shade.

Sometimes it's very hard to do the right thing.

I performed the spell that summoned her shade.

"Hey," she said, cheerfully enough. "What'll it be tonight?"

I stared at Karrin's face. The shade looked like she had when I'd last held her, kissed her. Blond hair. Blue eyes. Features that could look cute or tough as needed. Opinionated and smart and stubborn and often wrong but always trying.

"I, um," I said. Tears wet my cheeks.

She tilted her head slightly, eyes warm and suddenly sad, and in complete understanding. She waited for me to speak.

"I just wanted to tell you goodbye," I choked out finally. "I . . . I won't be calling you after tonight."

"Seems about right," she said gently. "I've been waiting for you to get here. Oh, Harry. I'm so sorry. For all the things you never got to say to each other."

"Yeah," I said quietly, and wept a few tears and smiled at her through them.

"You're going to be okay," she said gently.

I nodded and said, "I want to be. I'll get there."

"Things take time," she said.

"Time and sometimes friends," I said.

"Sometimes them, too."

The next day, Mort Lindquist showed up and asked to speak to me. His head was shaved smooth, his suit fit him well, and he'd brought me a couple of beers from McAnally's.

"You knew," I said gently. "You knew I was calling her shade."

"Happens sometimes," he said. "She was kind of trapped around you, even before you started making a conscious effort. Sometimes it takes people time to let go."

"And that's why you brought Fitz to me," I said.

"Fitz needed and needs your help," Mort said. "But if he could keep an eye on things, talk to her shade sometimes, make sure it didn't get unhealthy for either of you while he was getting helped . . ." Mort shrugged. "Two problems sometimes make a solution."

"Damn," I said quietly. "That's . . . some real wizard stuff there, Morty. You've come a long way."

He grinned at me. "We both have."

He passed me a bottle. We clinked them and drank.

Chapter
Forty-Two

Spring sprang a bit early, and by the second week of March we were having cool mornings with warm and pleasant afternoons. The pressure I experienced from the Winter mantle had begun to wane, though it never vanished. It would get even easier after the equinox, until midsummer, and then it would begin to rise again. I'd borne it for a few cycles now. I was beginning to know what to expect.

Lara met me at the botanic gardens, at my request.

The place didn't look like it would in April, but green had come back into the world, and the first insects, and the early flowers, and life was getting about its business again. The gardens are a big place and had been far enough from the fighting to escape any particular damage during the battle. They'd gotten their electricity back—by March, most of the city that hadn't had to contend with collapsed buildings and toxic cleanups had been restored more or less to working order. From walking around the gardens, you wouldn't know that civilization had more or less ground to a halt for so many people. They were pristine and growing and lovely, just the way a garden should be.

Human beings were never meant for constant concrete and steel. It's convenient and economical and in some ways safer—but we were meant for the wilderness. For grass and trees and rocks and rivers. To be among the sights and sounds and smells of life, of things that grow. I got to the meeting an hour early, just so I could spend some time walking in that, even if it was a little curated. To watch the sunlight play with shadows, to hear the wind whispering through long grass and budding branches, *grow, grow, grow.*

Winter always comes to an end. Bad times always come to an end. Spring is the earth's way of reassuring us about that. I could feel the slow stirring of power in that life, gently inexorable as the sun grew warmer, day by day—here much more clearly than I could at the castle.

There weren't many people at the gardens this time of year. The real show wouldn't start for another month or so. I was standing alone by a pond framed by willow trees, their long naked branches studded with leaf-green buds, when I sensed Lara's presence. There wasn't a sound, or a smell, and I hadn't seen her approach. I just knew where she was.

As if she'd been carrying part of me with her and I felt it when she got close.

"It's the smells I like best," I said quietly. I inhaled through my nose. "Earth, and mold and mildew and new green things."

"It's why the White Court is behind so many environmental causes," Lara said, from beside me.

I lifted both eyebrows. "Really?"

"We take the care of the herd as seriously as we can," she said. "At least at the leadership levels. The younger members are too buried in sensation and lack the experience to have reasoned that far forward."

"Sensible," I said. "Maybe a little creepy, but sensible."

"That's my wheelhouse," she said, her tone faint with humor.

I turned to her.

I was wearing jeans, a white tee, and a grey denim jacket. She had on a pale pink sundress with matching sandals and a pale yellow knitted wrap over her shoulders. The pastels shouldn't have worked with her dark hair and pale skin, but they somehow did. They made her blue eyes look electric.

"Do you know what's happened?" I asked her.

Her lips twisted into a small smile. Her expression was unreadable. "I worked it out," she said calmly. "I'm on your hook now. Tables turned."

"I didn't know that's what was happening," I said. "If I'd known, I wouldn't have done it."

Her eyes, her face, neither moved. Thomas got like that sometimes.

He could be more still than anything living. "You did tell me there would be risks."

"Yeah. I didn't realize that was one of them." I shook my head. "I didn't mean to. I'm sorry."

She stared at me for a long time.

"Oh," she said quietly.

"Oh?"

She tilted her head to one side. "You're telling the truth."

I spread open the fingers of one hand. "Yeah."

She smiled faintly. "Oh."

"Oh again?"

"Harry," she said gently, "I don't want to offend you. I honestly don't. But you couldn't have tricked me like that. You didn't get the better of me."

"Mab did," I said.

"There you go," she said.

We both turned to look out at the wind playing on the water. We were both silent for a long time.

"She got the better of both of us," I said.

"And despite my best efforts," she said, "it would seem I really am going to marry someone much like my father."

I winced.

"I'm only talking about you indirectly," she said. "This marriage was always between Mab and me. You were merely her surrogate."

"We'll get you out of it," I said. "I'll figure something out."

"You're going to outwit the Queen of Air and Darkness?" Lara asked, amused. "A creature who has been weaving webs of illusion and deception for centuries upon centuries before either of us was born?"

"No," I said. "But maybe *we* can. I'm not exactly without resources."

Lara folded her arms and inhaled deeply.

"There are factors," she said. Her raven-dark brows beetled into a faint frown.

"Like what?" I asked.

She gave me a long stare. Not a kind one.

"I want to help," I said quietly.

"Your help has been—" She shook her head and cut herself off. She closed her eyes and took a deep, deep breath. "I can accept that you did not intentionally inflict this harm upon me," she said. "But nonetheless. The deed is done."

"Yeah," I said quietly. "She used us both. The question is, what are we going to do about it?"

She opened her eyes again, warily.

"You got out from under your father's control," I said quietly. "And he's a berjillion years old and twisted and sneaky and all that, too. For you, this is just the next challenge."

Something flickered in her eyes.

"And I'm a pretty handy guy to have around in situations like this," I said.

"What's in it for you?" she asked.

"I don't like being used," I said, my voice turning a little hard. "I don't like being manipulated. I don't like it when someone tries to control me. What's in it for me?" I shook my head. "I get to be my own man. I get to be free."

"Idealism," she said, gently chiding, "is foolish."

"Too much of it, maybe," I said. "Too much of anything is foolish. But so is letting people think they can pull your strings. Mab thinks she has you in her pocket. Me, too. We're going to show her she's wrong. But to do that, I've got to understand what I'm up against."

Lara considered me for a long moment and folded her arms.

"I'm going to give you some," she said. "And we will see what you can give in exchange."

"Good place to start," I said.

She frowned for a moment, considering her words.

"What you . . . did to me," she said. She swallowed. "For me. Even thinking about it now, I . . . ache. Want more. My Hunger has never been so, so . . . quiet. Such silence, within." Her eyes went slightly out of focus. "I have lived for centuries and never had so much peace. Such . . ."

"Surcease," I said gently.

Her mouth twisted into a grim little smile. "Precisely. I could return to feeding on mortals but . . . it took me decades of careful feeding, careful restraint, to bring my Hunger into a state of balance. If I fed on them now, after what my demon has tasted, I would not be able to control it. It would seek that peace again. Take and take and take. And it would kill, seek the same satisfaction. Satisfaction that a mortal could not provide—and I would be unable to prevent it from doing so."

"Which would affect you," I said.

"It would likely strip me of reason entirely, either slowly or in a meltdown. It hardly matters. I would be unable to defend my position in the Court, and thus be useless to Mab, who would then either discard me or enslave me completely." She shuddered. "Or worse. I'd just be an animal. Feeding and feeding. This is a very thorough trap. I am reliant upon you not merely for my demon's sustenance, but for my position, power, identity, and life. Which makes me both resent and admire you."

"Oh," I said quietly.

"I am infuriated at the circumstance. At you, for being ignorant, and for meaning well, and for putting a chain about my throat." She shivered. "I considered killing you today."

"If it makes you feel any better," I said, "Mab wanted you to hook me right back. Then she'd have us both wrapped up entirely."

Lara exhaled and nodded. "Yes. She'd have us both, body, mind, and soul."

"But she doesn't," I said. "At least, not yet. And maybe not ever, if I've got anything to say about it. Which I damned well do."

Lara tilted her head, skeptical. "I would very much like to believe that," she said quietly. "Now. I have given you a little knowledge. What do you have to give in return?"

"Thomas," I said firmly.

She frowned. "Meaning what, exactly?"

"I'm getting him out of the mess he's in," I said. "I'm fixing his problem with his demon. And I'm dealing with Etri and the svartalves, too."

"How?"

I inhaled and exhaled deeply. "Mab offered me a boon. I mean to collect."

Lara's eyes widened. "She . . . Oh. For what you did to me."

"Yeah." I sighed. "Mab's . . . Look, she's weird. She deceives, she manipulates, she'll do anything she needs to in order to accomplish her goals. But she also pays her debts. Her obligations go both ways. It's part of what she is. I don't think she has a choice about it."

"You think it can be used against her," Lara said, eyes widening.

"I don't think. I know."

"If you're right," Lara said quietly, "she isn't going to be happy about it."

"Lot of that going around," I said, my voice hard. "She's tough. She'll get over it."

"She's unlikely to simply accept it," Lara said.

"I'm pretty tough, too. I've paid some prices. You know that better than most."

Lara frowned, searching my face.

"May I ask you something?" she said after a moment.

"I guess."

She nodded. "What are you going to do with me?"

I blinked. I opened my mouth. Closed it again.

"We have established that I am at your mercy in a very complete sense," she said, her words only a little clipped with tension. "You could do a great many things with this circumstance. I wish to know what you intend to do with me now that you have me."

Something slipped, in her mask. I didn't think it was intentional.

Lara was afraid.

I turned to her and said, "Do you know what a soulgaze is?"

She looked at me warily. "What little you've said. I've . . . I've read descriptions of them."

"We look into each other's eyes, steady," I said quietly. "And I see you. And you see me. I don't know what you'll see. But it will be the truth. I don't know what I'll see in you. But it will be the truth."

"What do you mean, truth?" she said carefully.

"I'm not sure I can explain it any better than that," I said. "Brains do weird things sometimes. Show you a vision of a person, but it's who they really are, underneath all the lies that we tell other people, or ourselves.

When I saw Thomas, I saw a good man at war with his demon, fighting against it though it caused him great pain. And I saw our mother. It was how I knew."

She frowned. "I always wondered how you found out."

"Well, the picture in your dad's gallery was a clue. But in the end, that's how I knew," I said. "Look. I think we're going to be working together, at least for the foreseeable future. Maybe starting off with some truth under our feet will help." I spread both hands. "What's the worst that's gonna happen? You wind up effectively enslaved?"

That got a short, brief snort of laughter. "Hah." She looked down, frowning. "What do I do?"

I reached out slowly. Cupped her cheek with my right hand. With my left, I drew her right hand up, considerably up, to do the same to me.

"Look into my eyes," I said quietly.

She did. They were intensely blue.

Intensely blue.

Intensely . . .

She drew in a short breath. Her eyes went wide.

And the soulgaze began.

Suddenly, night fell on the gardens, shadows of trees under a bright silver moon. I was standing there alone.

In the darkness, there came a low growl.

I looked up. Down among the shadowy willows along the pond, something moved. Pale, naked skin, entirely hairless. Humanoid, but inhuman, wide silver eyes, prowling on all fours, visible only for an instant between the shadows of the trees. I recognized it. I had seen one like it when I had soulgazed Thomas and during the rituals with Lara. It was a Hunger.

It moved with silence and fascinating grace toward me, passed through the shadows, and blue eyes gleamed from the darkness. When it crawled into another patch of moonlight, it was Lara Raith, naked, lovely, and a thrill of desire, or terror, or hunger, or fury, or something primal and nameless blending all of those together ran down my spine.

Lara wasn't at war with her Hunger. She was intertwined. And she was dangerous.

It came toward me like that, through the shadows beneath the trees. The Hunger, then Lara. The Hunger, then Lara. Closer and closer. Blue eyes, silver eyes, burning with raw, primal need.

She wanted to eat me all up.

And wow.

I wasn't sure but that I wanted it, too.

I tried to take a step back, slipped, and went down, catching myself on my elbows, as she covered the last bit of distance, slithering up my body in a delicious thrill of lust and need and terror, eyes flickering silver and blue until I wasn't sure which of the creatures she was.

Because she wasn't really sure about it herself anymore.

She made a low sound in her throat. Maybe a hungry growl. Maybe a tigress's purr.

Maybe both.

"You wanted to know," I croaked.

The Lara-Hunger paused.

"What I would do with you," I said. "I'm not at all comfortable in this role. But I will treat you as ethically as possible under the circumstances. When you have a need, I'll do my best to meet it. I won't screw you over. I won't lie to you. And in return, I'll expect the same of you."

The creature stared at my eyes, flickering between forms, silver and blue, Lara and demon. Then her mouth descended on mine and my world went silvery with a slow throb of pleasure that spread from my lips and went straight down my throat and—

—and suddenly the soulgaze was over.

We were back in the gardens in the afternoon, cupping each other's face.

We were both trembling.

I let out a gasp and bowed my head, closing my eyes. I felt it as Lara let her head fall back, also gasping for breath.

"Empty night," she breathed, panting. "Oh, empty night."

It took me a minute to recover from the intensity of the experience. Finally, I got my breathing under control and looked up at her.

Lara was just staring at me. We both lowered our hands. She began to slowly shake her head.

"You're unlike anyone I've met," she said quietly. "And I've met a great many."

"It's nice to be weird," I said.

"If you can really do it," she said. "If you can get Thomas out of this. Yes. I'll stand with you."

"And we'll figure out how to shake you loose. Then we'll take on Mab," I said.

She flashed me a sudden, ferocious smile. "Even after that, I can't tell if you're serious or insane."

"No reason it can't be both."

Chapter
Forty-Three

Fitz stood in the practice range in the castle's basement facing off against a cardboard target maybe a week after the soulgaze. This one was a stick figure of a Hollywood vampire, complete with a cloak, Gothic cross medallion, and oversized pointy fangs. A word bubble rose from it reading, "Blah, blah, blah!"

He glanced back at me uncertainly, his features troubled.

"Don't I get a warm-up round?"

"In the real world," I said, standing with my hands behind my back, "you don't get time to warm up. You don't get time to stretch. No one counts to three."

He frowned at me and said, "Yeah. Yeah, I guess so." Then he took a deep breath and turned to face the target. "So, do I have a time limit here or—"

I took Backup out from behind my back and fired down at the target four times, as fast as I could squeeze the trigger. The nine-millimeter weapon was shockingly loud in the confined space.

"Jesus!" Fitz shouted, flinching.

"Now!" I roared. "Do it or die!"

Fitz whirled on the target, face locked in a rictus of concentration, and screamed, *"Fiero! Fiero! Fiero!"* As he spat the words, he slung his hands up from his hips like an old west gunfighter on the draw, and sent several screaming streaks of flame, like balls from a large Roman candle, downrange from his open palms, high-pitched whistling emerging from the spheres that led the streaks, leaving trails of steam in their wakes.

The first projectile missed, the second slammed into the word bubble, but the third went home in the center of the target, right below the Gothic cross, knocking the target back over and setting it furiously ablaze.

I lifted my eyebrows. Wow. Adrenaline seemed to help the kid, rather than shaking his concentration. The spheres had been hot enough to boil the water in the air as they passed through. Call it five hundred, six hundred degrees. One of the angled steel plates at the back of the range briefly showed a ruddy color in a small circle before sinking back into soot-black.

Fitz dropped to his knees, gasping.

I put Backup down on one of the steel tables against the back wall and walked up to stand beside him. Then I dropped down to one knee and put a hand on his shoulder.

"Damn. Took me more than two years to get as far as you have the past few months," I said gently. "You've got a gift, kid. Well done."

He looked up at me, his face earnest and uncertain. He gave me a tentative smile.

I answered him with a grin and squeezed his shoulder. "Well freaking done."

"Engh," he said, panting. He grinned wider. "You jerk. A gun?"

"Gun will kill you just as dead as a spell," I told him. "Or a knife, or a club, or a rock. And when the dancing starts in the real world, you don't get time to wonder what to do. You act or you get taken out. Anyone who knows what you are is going to come down on you fast and all at once."

"Sounds like maybe it would be smart to start the fights," Fitz said. He was struggling to get his breath back.

"Maybe. If you think someone is going to be a problem," I said, "why not just shoot them in the back of the head? Every time?"

He frowned at me.

"It's smart," I said. "You survive. They don't. They don't get a chance to hurt you. Why not do it that way?"

"It's wrong?" he asked. "I don't want to win like that."

I waved a hand. "'Win' doesn't mean anything. There are fights you survive and fights you don't. So why not do it like that?"

He searched my face. Shook his head.

"Because life matters, kid," I said quietly. "Everyone knows that on some level. And whoever you kill might have someone who cares. They think their life matters, too. You go around killing folks, you create more enemies for yourself. More danger. You start killing, it breeds more of it—and you're going to be alive for a very long time. You get a reputation as a killer, folks are way more likely to come at you hard and fast. Maybe with a high-powered rifle from a mile away. Maybe someone pulls a damned satellite out of space onto your head." I sighed. "And it gets to you. You kill people with magic, it sticks to you. Like tar. You remember the guy you burned?"

He looked down and shuddered.

"Exactly. You want a life worth living, don't go starting fights. Just be sure you're the one to finish them."

"You make it sound like I'm going to be some kind of monster," he said softly.

I hunkered down and frowned at the burning target. "Look, kid. You have power. What I want is for you to only use it when it's absolutely necessary. It's best to start thinking about how and why you ought to do that now, rather than after things have gotten out of hand."

"To save my life," he said quietly. "Or someone else's."

"That's the baseline for when it's time to get serious," I said, nodding. "What gets complicated is knowing when you're standing in that place. Learning the signs. Seeing when the balloon is about to go up and doing the smartest thing you can when it does. Violence hardly ever comes out of nowhere."

"That sounds complicated," he said, his voice heavy and serious.

"Yeah," I said. "Right now, you're learning *how* to be dangerous. But it's just as important to know *when* and *why*. We've talked about that a little. We'll do more about that, too."

"Okay," he said, nodding gravely.

I blew out a breath. "Look. There's no easy way to talk about this, so we'll just get right to it. I do dangerous work. It could get me killed. I don't have plans to do it, but that's something real. You get that, right?"

He nodded.

"Anything happens to me," I said, "I've got a number for you to call. It will get you to Carlos Ramirez. He's a Warden with the White Council. You meet with him, alone, and tell him everything. He'll look out for you."

"White Council?" Fitz said skeptically.

"I know," I said. "Look, kid. Organizations can be shady as hell, no matter their intentions. I don't trust them and never have. It's people that can be okay. Ramirez is one of them. He'll look out for you."

"Look out for me how?"

"Get you set up so the Council doesn't declare you a warlock out of hand. Train you. From a talent perspective, the two of you have a lot in common. Hell, he might be a better mentor than me."

"But he's a Council guy," Fitz said.

"Some people work well with more structure. He's one of them. And he's solid."

Fitz nodded uncertainly. "Okay."

"Good man," I said. "You stand up yet?"

He shoved himself unsteadily to his feet.

I got up with him and put my arm around his shoulders as the target smoldered out and lay there smoking. He'd put on ten or fifteen pounds of muscle working out with me since we'd gotten started and gotten physically and mentally tougher, too.

He'd just thrown out about ten times as much power as he had in his early sessions, focused and concentrated and quick. He didn't have my strength, but he had far more natural control and precision.

Fitz was going to be a very dangerous wizard.

Like me. Like Ramirez.

"Hit the showers, kid," I said. "Then meet me in the kitchen. I just got a crate from Mac's, and you've earned the good stuff."

Michael Carpenter was walking me and Will Borden through the renovations to the third and fourth floors. The place still looked like a castle, but when you opened the doors to the rooms, they looked a lot more comfortable and modern.

"Blown insulation between the stone and the drywall," Michael was saying proudly. "Baseboard heating is working, and running the lines through all the stone was a lot of work, let me tell you. Summers won't be a problem, with all that stone between you and the outside. Might need heaters at night anyway."

I shook my head. "And Bob signed off on all the drilling?"

He looked slightly uncomfortable and nodded. "Yes. The spirit assured us he could still operate the castle, though only the bare-bones electrical stuff will survive here. The heaters are very simple. The lighting should be all right. The plumbing won't be an issue, and the boiler we put in the basement is as old-school as they get."

"Hot showers," I murmured, somewhat awed.

He grinned at me. "Well. Yes. You'll need to do preventative maintenance, too."

Will, wearing jeans and an office shirt rolled up to the elbows, waved a clipboard. "I've got a schedule here for you, Harry. Pretty simple stuff, couple of hours a week if you don't let it stack up."

Michael walked us to the doors at the end of one of the long halls running the length of the castle and opened them proudly. "The suite."

I went in slowly, to a sitting room a little larger than the entirety of my old apartment. It was all rich, natural wood panels on the walls, sealed but not stained, bringing out the whorls and knots and imperfections in each board. The floor was stone. Bookshelves had been built in all around three walls, ready to receive. The original fireplace was still there, framed in by new stonework that made it yawn even a little deeper than its makers had intended. There were logs laid upon a grate in it. A tiny flame burned at one spot in them.

"Gas," Michael said, and flicked a switch on the wall.

There was a little whooshing sound, and fire curled up around the logs, which I supposed must have been masonry or ceramic or something.

"Just like magic," I murmured, smiling. Then I frowned. "You couldn't have done this for the price you quoted me."

Michael leaned on his cane, grinning, and shrugged. "The material wasn't as expensive as the labor. I told my people you were my friend and asked them to give whatever extra they'd like to." He scratched his beard with one hand, eyes sparkling. "Honestly, Mouse made a good impression on all of them. Maybe you should thank him."

Will snorted.

The bedroom was smaller, but just as well done. There was a bathroom, too. And a hot shower.

"But I like my basement," I said.

"Nothing stopping you from staying down there," Michael said. "But . . . I was thinking maybe you've been there long enough."

Will pursed his lips thoughtfully and looked at Michael.

"What's wrong with a basement?" I asked.

"Not a thing," he said. "For the man you've been. Maybe the man you're going to be will like it in here, though."

I grunted. "If so, the man I'm going to be will have to walk up a lot more stairs."

Michael laughed. "I thought you needed more exercise lately."

"Hmph," I said. I turned slowly around, looking at the sitting room, imagining a comfy chair or couch in front of the fireplace. Surrounded by books, reading. My cat on my lap.

Mister, my old grey tomcat, came prowling into the room, took one look at the fire, went over to the floor beside it, and stretched out luxuriously. His purr rumbled through the room.

"Huh," I said. "I guess that's settled, then."

Chapter

Forty-Four

I waited until the spring equinox to summon Mab.

It wasn't an insult to do it like that. The equinox marked the beginning of the transfer of the majority of power from the Winter Court of the Fae to Summer, a point of balance. That said, it was still a symbolic handoff—a time for Mab to be focused on consolidating her power through the duration of Winter's nadir, over the summer season. A time for her to be thinking about such things as keeping secure the loyalty and service of her vassals.

I knew there was a major Fae shindig at the equinoxes, where members of Summer, Winter, and Wyld would gather for revels and celebrations. The Fair Folk were big on their seasonal parties, if they weren't fighting at the time, hosted by the youngest queens. Molly was somewhere in the Black Forest for this one. I don't know where the Summer Lady, Sarissa, was hosting. It probably would have been good form for the Winter Knight to have been there, but I wasn't really a party person, and I hadn't ever been to one without my life being threatened, and this year that just didn't sound fun.

Instead, I was up on the roof of the castle at midnight. I'd brought up a table and two chairs, a couple of glasses, a bottle of ice wine, some decent cheese, homemade bread, and some thinly sliced cold steak. I wore one of the suits Molly's staff had provided last year, and I'd spiffed up a bit, trimming my hair and short beard.

The Queen of Air and Darkness probably wasn't going to be happy with me. No reason to show up in sweatpants with crackers and Cheez Whiz on top of it.

I broke a small piece of bread off the round loaf, pinked a fingertip with a pin, put a drop of blood on the bread, and set it on the plate across the table from me. I took a slow breath, closed my eyes for a moment, focused my will into my breath, and murmured, "Mab, Mab, Mab. At your convenience, I would speak with thee."

I felt the rush of power spread out from the words into the night air, faint echoes and distortions bouncing back to me from the enchanted stone of the castle in response.

After that, I waited. Mab's global empire was only a part of the realm she ruled. She had more than a little territory in the Nevernever, too. She could get around it really fast, and she wasn't exactly known as a Chatty Cathy, but there would be a lot of her vassals and clients who would want to speak to her this evening.

Time passed. I waited. The night was cold, flirting with the freezing point, with occasional gusts of wind, rich with chill moisture from Lake Michigan, making it bitter. I'd noticed that my body could sense the freezing point as a subtle thrill of pleasant sensation, now accompanied by a simple sense of relaxation. The night grew deeper and more frigid, and I waited in my seat at the table, just soaking in the cold and the quiet.

I was getting better at that. Waiting.

There's a big difference between being still and doing nothing.

A cold wind blew across my face, making me blink my eyes closed against it for a second, and then Mab stood across the table from me, slim and pale, wearing a white gown, her white hair spilling down her back, a crown of icicles glittering on her head. Her bare arms gleamed in the moonlight, silver sparkling around her wrists and biceps. Her eyes wavered through dark shades of glacial blue and green.

I rose at once.

"My Knight," Mab murmured.

"My Queen," I replied, inclining my head slightly.

She looked me up and down and then regarded the table between us.

"Thou hast gained some measure of discretion," she noted. She tilted her head, staring at me intently. Ah hah. This was a formal and intimate occasion in Mab's view. She tended to use the archaic grammar at such times. "And of self-mastery. Thou dost exert control over thy pain."

"I've been healing," I said.

"As have I," Mab murmured. "Last summer was a difficult time for us all. I greet thee this eve."

I blinked a little at that.

I mean, sure, I'd seen Mab take on an army virtually single-handed, at the absolute lowest point of her seasonal power. I'd seen her impaled upon cold steel. I'd seen her struck down by a Titan.

But . . . it honestly had never occurred to me that she might actually have been affected by her wounds. That the Queen of Air and Darkness might have been hurt. Might have needed time to restore herself.

That she might have needed to hide her pain.

"Welcome," I said. I walked around the table and drew out her chair for her. She settled into it with inhuman grace.

Her eyes focused on the bread with the drop of blood on it, glittering and sharp. But she folded her hands in her lap while I poured out the ice wine, a modest amount for each of us, then seated myself across from her.

I took up my glass as she did.

"To promises kept," she murmured.

"Promises kept," I agreed.

We touched glasses and tasted the ice wine. It was sweet, cold, and strong.

"May I?" I asked, gesturing at the food.

"Yes," Mab said.

I served her out some cheese and meat to go with the bread and served the same to myself.

I took up my bread.

Mab snatched hers and shoved it into her mouth like a starving animal.

It was such an utter reversal of her usual demeanor that my belly jerked in a sudden startled reaction, a thrill of primal fear jolting through me.

She didn't eat the bread with my blood on it. She devoured it, her eyes closed, letting out small sounds of pleasure and satisfaction as she did. She tilted her face to the starry sky when she swallowed. When her eyes opened, they had to roll down, and it took a long breath before they came into focus again.

I gulped. And took a small bite of my bread, chewing it with a dry mouth.

"Small pleasures," she murmured, her voice throaty and rich, "grow more significant over time."

I swallowed and said, "You're right."

She took up a bite of cheese and deliberately wrapped a bit of the thin-sliced steak around it. "Thou dost wish to choose the boon I have granted thee."

"Yes," I said.

"Wealth?" she said, a coy smile on her frozen-mulberry lips. "Influence? An army? Slaves? The perfect lover?"

I blinked again.

She was . . . Stars and stones. She was *joking* with me.

Mab making a joke was perhaps more frightening and disorienting than Mab slamming my head against an elevator wall.

I tried to smile. I think it came out a little sick.

"Thinkest thou I know not thy heart, my Knight? For while I am mortal no longer, yet do I remember what it is to care. To love. To yearn." She took a bite of steak and ate it slowly. "To feel pain for family."

"If you know," I said, "why not just grant it?"

"Of all folk, a wizard should know the importance of the word, imbued with the very breath of thy life."

She had a point.

Words mattered. Even the little ones.

The little ones matter most, in fact.

All of the most powerful words are brief.

"I need to consult with you on something," I said.

Mab tilted her head.

"Lara," I said. "Last summer when she touched me, she was burned. On Halloween, she wasn't. I don't understand why."

Mab stared at me for a long moment. She took a sip of ice wine, considering.

"Twice," she said, "you have loved. And twice death has claimed that love."

I grunted.

"The protection granted from the White Court by love is not a mechanical process. It is an interaction of energy. Where that energy exists, it threatens the White Court. It exists under specific circumstances. When those circumstances have changed, it exists no more."

"You're telling me death defeats love?" I asked dully.

Mab regarded me. "Poetry does not suit you, my Knight. To accept love and give it back in equal measure, one must believe one is worthy of it. By your own judgment of yourself, you have failed. Twice."

There wasn't an actual knife sticking in my heart, but it felt like an argument could have been made. I closed my eyes.

But it made sense. The older I got, the more I realized that most of the things that happen to you in life are your own doing.

But it hurt.

I opened my eyes. Mab was staring at me with the oddest expression, one I couldn't read. Maybe the emotion behind it wasn't something a human could understand. I don't know.

"One day," I said quietly, "I'm going to be free of you."

Free.

Little word.

It hung in the air between us.

Mab's eyes glittered. Her rich lips spread slowly, showing me her pointed canine teeth. "Perhaps," she purred, "but not today."

Difficult to argue with that one.

"Eat," Mab said quietly. "Thou shalt need thy strength, my Knight. One way or another."

Difficult to argue with that one, too.

Besides. Of late, I was hungry most of the time anyway.

"Of course thou art," Mab noted, almost idly. "Thy mind and spirit heal. Thy flesh must follow."

A small, cold thrill went through my belly. Followed by a flash of annoyance.

"Stop that," I said.

Mab . . . Okay, it wasn't a giggle. I refuse to believe that's possible. But it was a low, smug, satisfied sound she made that was technically laughter.

"Am I to take that as the boon thou dost crave?"

Another joke. I scowled at her, and she made the laughing sound again. Instead of answering her, I ate a few bites of steak and cheese.

She watched, her expression relaxed and satisfied. She nibbled a bit more cheese. Sipped a bit more wine. Just two people having dinner.

Hah.

"I want your help with a problem," I said quietly.

"Indeed," Mab said. Her eyes didn't actually get larger, just harder and harder to ignore.

"Thomas," I said. "For my boon, I wish you to grant him every aid at your disposal. This aid will include several aspects: your sincere and genuine cooperation and counsel on how to pacify his Hunger and restore him to health. I want Justine found and returned to him, whole and sane. I want his child safe and secure. And I want his debt to Etri made right, so that he may live in safety from the svartalves."

Mab's huge eyes grew darker, and she shivered so that gooseflesh ran down her arms. "Ahhh," she said gently. "Mab is Mab. Her word is good, and must be. But Mab is neither all-knowing nor all-powerful. This, then, is thy request?"

I took a slow breath. "It is."

"What thou dost wish may be done," she warned, "but not without pain." She leaned forward intently. "Sooth, my Knight. It is within my power to make possible what now is not—but even Mab cannot know all ends. Riches and power, slaves and pleasure, would be far more easily given. This is a road that may wind toward great joy or great sorrow, and I cannot foresee its ending." She drew back, spine straightening, chin lifting, regal in a way that no mortal who has walked the world could ever hope to be. "Knowing this," she said, "is it still thy desire?"

"Thrice said and done," I breathed. "It is."

Mab shuddered. Her exhalation of breath came out in a dense plume of frost. There was a deep crackling sound, and a film of ice spread over the table, the food, the glasses, the surface of the wine. It spread out across the stones of the castle, whose faded runes began to glow with icy blue light.

"So be it," she whispered. "Let the scales be balanced, the debt repaid."

And she was gone.

I sat there alone on the roof of the castle.

If I wasn't so brave and manly, I might have been feeling a sense of horrible dread.

But . . .

Somewhere, deep down, there was also a small, fierce, bright light of hope.

I'm a wizard. And believe me, I know damned well that there aren't any magical solutions in life. Not from spells. Not from Queens of Faerie. As far as I can tell, not even from the Almighty Himself.

Nothing is easy. Nothing is perfect.

But if I'd given my brother his life and his family a fighting chance, maybe that would be enough.

Maybe that's all there ever is.

And if it hurt to do it, well. Only the living felt pain.

My stomach growled.

I ate my food and Mab's share, too. The ice just made it crunchy.

Chapter

Forty-Five

The protests got uglier when it got warmer.

I stood on the roof of the castle, and Bear loomed next to me. Across the street, there were maybe a hundred or hundred and fifty people, and the chanting was going nonstop, in shifts. The signs had gotten angrier, too.

The folks who lived across the street weren't terribly happy about all the ruckus happening in their front yards. They were trying to form a kind of ad hoc homeowners association, and they'd written me asking me to take action to "ameliorate the situation."

I'd spent time and creative effort in my reply, suggesting that they could help me move the castle stone by stone to another location, or that they might contact the protesters themselves, or that they might lodge a complaint with our alderman. They'd tried to go through channels, which always worked so well with supernatural-related conflict. CPD had a car parked down the block to monitor the situation, but if things got ugly, two patrol officers weren't going to be able to do much.

"This is going in one direction," Bear noted calmly to me.

"I know," I said.

I leaned forward as Will came out of the front gate of the castle and walked across the street, smiling. A reception committee of large and unfriendly types, including the former members of the Brothers of St. Brigid that Daniel Carpenter had removed from the organization, and the guy from Bock's ceremonial group with the broken wrist, came forward to meet him.

Will spoke briefly with a couple who appeared to be what passed for the brains of the operation.

"What do you think will happen this time?" Bear asked.

"I think they'll say no to a sit-down," I said. "Again."

She snorted out a breath through her nose. "I think that, too."

"Gotta try," I said.

"Because it's kind," she said.

"Yeah."

Bear shook her head. "I'm from an older world than you, Dresden. The definition of *kind* has changed a lot over time."

"Meaning?"

"Meaning it might have been kinder to run them off when there were only a few of them, when it could have been more easily controlled, and when fewer people might have been hurt. It might have been kinder to draw the boundary a hell of a lot sooner."

"I'm hoping it won't come to that," I said.

"Times change," Bear allowed. "People don't. Anger doesn't. Violence doesn't. Instinct doesn't. What you're seeing here is pure territoriality."

"They're afraid," I said. "They got hurt in the battle. See that couple Will's talking to? I've dug into them a little. They had two little kids. Both were killed."

The memory of a bloodied child's stroller lying on its side, the night of the battle, flashed vividly into my head. My heart pounded harder and I suddenly felt again the terror and rage of that night. I had to take a slow breath and close my eyes for a second, fighting off the remembered emotion. My stomach twisted with nausea, my mouth suddenly watering like I might be about to throw up, and adrenaline zinged into my system.

I bowed my head, breathing slowly and deeply.

"They're in pain," I said quietly after a moment. "Hard to blame them for that. And they haven't gotten violent."

"No," Bear agreed. "Not yet."

The woman of the couple started screaming at Will, turning to the others gathered on the sidewalk, leading them in hard, furious chanting. *No occult, no strife, we just want a normal life!*

Their fury was palpable. The crowd began to roll forward, toward Will, maybe half a step with each repetition of the chant.

I saw Will sigh and spread his hands in a gesture designed to show he meant no harm.

One of the bruisers stepped up.

Will turned to him. I couldn't see the expression on the werewolf's face, but the bruiser could, and his mask of determination faltered a little. He'd lifted a hand, maybe to push Will, but he dropped it again.

Will nodded and said something and then backed calmly away from the crowd. At the midway point of the street, he turned and walked quickly back to the castle. A couple of people started walking after him, but the patrol car down the street abruptly swung into motion, driving through before the protesters gathered momentum, hitting the sirens for a second to send out a warning *whoop, whoop!*

They backed off. Will made it back to the doors without further incident. A moment later, he emerged from the door to the roof and walked over to stand beside Bear and me.

"That went well," I drawled.

Will sighed. "Tell me about it."

"What did they say?"

"That they aren't going to accept anything except everyone in the castle leaving. Everyone. Harry, we're watching a violent mob being born."

"Yes, we are," Bear said matter-of-factly.

I sighed and rubbed at the not-quite-aching spot between my eyebrows.

"They aren't interested in trying to work anything out," Will said. "I can go to the alderman's office again."

"They aren't the only angry protesters in town," I said. "Daley Plaza, Millennium Park, McCormick Place, Navy Pier, Midway—CPD is barely holding things together as it is." I nodded toward the patrol car as it cruised slowly down the street, turned, and parked again, a way off. "That's all they've got available. I've talked to Stallings, too. We're small potatoes here. And we're on our own."

"It's only a matter of time before they start setting things on fire," Bear noted.

"We aren't there yet," I said.

"And if we wait until it goes that far," Bear said, "then you'll have a couple of choices. Neither of them good."

"Stop them," Will said, "or burn." He looked sick. "This isn't good, Harry. What if we give them what they want? Clear everyone out, just for a while, so they can cool off?"

"And go where?" I asked. "Send the people I'm protecting where? The refugee camps out in the suburbs and at the stadiums are overfilled and we've all heard about how bad the conditions there are." I clenched my jaw. "Dammit, the people here are here because they had nowhere else to go. We haven't harmed anyone. And this is my home. I'm not leaving."

Bear shook her head. "Either you flee the territory, or you have to prove yourself strong enough to keep it. You aren't doing you, your people, or any of that mob any favors by refusing to act."

"They've been hurt and scared enough," I said. "That's why this is happening. Adding more to it isn't going to fix anything."

"Standing around while they burn this place to the ground isn't going to fix anything, either, *seidrmadr*," Bear said quietly. "You've got a little more time, I think. But sooner or later, they're going to make you choose."

I clenched my jaw and said nothing.

These were exactly the same people I'd spent my life protecting. The ones who didn't have power like I did. The ones who were afraid of the powers of the night, and right to be.

I wasn't going to raise my hand against them unless I was given no other choice.

"Oh," Will said. "Um. Might as well hear it all at once. We got a letter. The federal HBGB task force wants to come do interviews and test for chemical residue at the castle. We've got to schedule a time for them to come in before the end of May, and if we don't, we might be evicted. Also, if we do, we might be evicted, at least while they clean up hazardous materials."

"Which don't exist." I scowled. "I'm not leaving my home for a government mob, either."

"Yeah," Will said. "Well. You also can't just keep them out, apparently. State and federal lawmakers have given them a pretty broad range of authority. Which is what some of the other protests are about, actually."

I took some more deep breaths. "I am beginning to become annoyed."

Bear snorted.

"Right," I said. "Glass half full. Set it up toward the end of May. Could be we get burned down by then and then we won't have to deal with a government inspection, too."

Will took a notebook out of a pocket and wrote in it. "Heh. Right."

Bear tilted her head slightly, frowned, and then walked down the length of the castle's roof. She leaned into one of the crenels, staring down the street for a moment, then looked over her shoulder at me and called, over the chanting, "Dresden."

"Now what?" I muttered, and Will and I walked down the length of the roof to join her.

Another group of protesters was coming down the street, maybe forty or fifty of them.

"Yippee, more of them," Will said.

I frowned and peered for a moment. I recognized those people. Artemis Bock was at the front of the group, walking purposefully. His inner circle was gathered around him, and a bunch of the others were the crowd from McAnally's. They, too, were carrying signs, though theirs were of a more peaceable nature. Several of them read COEXIST spelled out with a bunch of religious symbology. Some were simply emblazoned with a peace sign. More said HEAL TOGETHER, and one read DO NOT THROW STONES!

"It's worse than more of them," I groaned.

"Counterprotesters," Bear confirmed.

Bock and his people came walking together down the sidewalk, singing some song with a call-and-response about seeing beauty, and filed together down the narrow sidewalk that started about two inches past the walls of the castle, taking up space there and turning to face the protesters across the street, putting themselves between that crowd and the castle.

"Oh God," I said. "They're here to help."

"Um," Will said. "What are we going to do?"

"I guess I'll go talk to them." I sighed.

I hurried down from the roof toward the front gate. It was one thing to stand around being hostile toward a stone castle that you knew was full of armed guards and potentially hostile magical weirdos. It was quite another to have some real live human targets only a few feet away who were specifically there to vex you—and some of these same protesters had already been enjoying bullying Bock's people around during the winter.

A difficult situation had just turned into a powder keg.

Bear and Will stayed with me as I emerged from the castle, which excited the protesters almost immediately. I stomped toward Bock.

"What the hell, Artemis?" I demanded.

He nodded at me. "Dresden. We've been worried about the direction this is going. We wanted them to know that you weren't alone." He looked a little sheepish. "And . . . you know. For you to know it, too."

I tried to scowl at him but . . .

. . . but I couldn't.

It . . . it felt really good that they'd shown up to support me.

"Dammit." I sighed. "Look, man. I can look out for myself just fine. Been doing it for a while."

He traded a handshake with Will, listening to me. "I know, I know. But this is bigger than just you. You know?" He looked across the street as his people formed a couple of ranks across the sidewalk, holding their signs. "I haven't seen open persecution of supernatural folk like this, ever. You're their first target, but if we don't stand together, it's going to spread. There's been people watching my store. Lurking around outside McAnally's."

Oh.

They were scared, too.

It's easier to be scared together with those like you. Easier to bear when you have someone standing beside you. Easier to bear when you were doing something to take action, instead of just waiting around for bad things to happen.

Which . . . was kind of the whole problem. Not just with Chicago, here, today, but with humanity in general.

Sitting with fear and not letting it get to you, letting it make you do things you wouldn't do otherwise, is damned difficult.

"Bock," I said gently, "this could get ugly. The police don't have the manpower to get very involved. And I don't know if I can protect you and your people fast enough if something happens."

He nodded grimly. "I know. I know. But we have to stand together on this. We can't just . . . just wait for them to work themselves up more and more. That is only going to invite them to start actual violence."

"He's not wrong," Bear noted.

"Yes," I said tightly to Bear, "thank you. I have so much help I hardly know what to do with it all."

She lifted her hands and looked nonplussed.

"Argh," I said, putting a hand to my head. "I don't suppose I could just get you all to leave?"

"You didn't leave us to the Wardens," Bock said stubbornly. "And this is a public sidewalk. We have as much right to be here as they do."

"Harry," Will said quietly. "Look."

He gestured across the street.

The protesters had indeed backed off. Not a lot, but they weren't aggressively standing on the edge of the street and screaming. They seemed to be talking mostly among themselves, casting dark and uncertain glances across the asphalt.

"I don't think it's going to last," I noted.

"No, but . . . I mean, they're backing off a little," Will said. "At least for the moment."

"Bock," I said quietly. "Look. If I can't get you to leave, I need to know you and your people aren't going to start anything."

He blinked and looked a little startled. "No. No, of course not. Harry, we don't want anything bad to happen. We just want to show them that our community isn't going to just wait around to be bullied again. That there's more than a few of us and we're standing together."

"Nnnnngh," I said and mopped my face with one hand. "Okay, look. If something does happen, I'm going to have the doors ready to open. You get your people behind the walls if it even looks like things are going to get rowdy. Okay?"

He nodded, smiling at me. "Of course. Of course, thank you."

He took up his own COEXIST sign and joined in with the others, singing about seeing beauty before and behind and all around, and I wanted to scream.

I turned to Bear. "Work with the Knights, huh? Make sure the doors are ready to open for them."

"Strictly speaking," Bear noted calmly, "that's terrible siegecraft on our part. The point of gates is to keep people from coming in too quickly and all at once. That's exactly how you get your castle burned down."

"Do whatever you can to minimize the threat, then," I said. "But make it happen. If things go bad, I want Bock and his people able to get behind the walls."

Bear blew out her breath through her lips, a skeptical sound. "When this goes south, it's going to happen in a hurry."

"If," I said. "If it goes south."

"I'm too old to be that optimistic," she said. "But you're the boss."

I looked across the street for a moment.

There were a lot of hostile gazes over there.

"Do what you can," I told her. I turned to go back inside.

"Harry?" Will asked. "What are you going to do?"

I looked at the counterprotesting crowd and tried to keep the worry from showing on my face. "Whatever I can."

Chapter
Forty-Six

I took the reusable ingredients for the greater circle I'd built in my lab out to the island the next week.

Lara went with me. I'd provided her energy again at my place a few nights before, and she carried half the weight up the hill and down the stairs to the tunnels beneath the island. She wasn't even breathing hard when we got there, though I was.

Her presence was very different, this time. She was wearing stretch jeans, sneakers, and a mostly red plaid flannel shirt over a white tank top. Her hair was under a bandana, held back from her face, and while it made her features look sharper, leaner, I took a lot more notice of the fine lines at the corners of her eyes, particularly when she smiled. She moved with the same liquid grace, but there was none of the sense of electric tension in her I'd almost always seen before. She was relaxed, her voice quiet and without any artifice when she spoke. "Are you sure you're all right for this?"

"Meaning what?" I asked, panting.

"You poured a lot into me the other night," she said calmly. "Are you sure you've rested enough to do this for Thomas?"

"Just haven't been able to do much cardio lately," I said, panting. "Protesters outside, been staying in mostly. I can only run up and down the stairs so many times. Plus, I don't want to spend the time working out on weekends."

"Because your daughter is there," Lara said.

I gave her a look. It might have come out harder than I meant it to. Lara didn't flinch, but she lifted an eyebrow and said, "That's only an observation. Not a threat. I understand about family."

I nodded and said nothing. That came out harder than I meant, too.

Lara looked away and said, "Perhaps we should change the subject."

"No," I said in a quiet, steady monotone. "Let's establish something. You deal with me. You have no connection to her. None. Ever. And if you or anyone in your Court tries to harm her? I. Will. Kill. You. All."

Lara went entirely marble-statue still.

I faced her, meeting her gaze.

She nodded slowly. "If you can."

"So far," I said, "so good. I'm a hundred percent at dealing with entire vampire courts who touched my little girl."

Her mouth curled at one corner, though it didn't touch her eyes. "You're aiming this the wrong way, Dresden."

"Yeah. Maybe," I said. I slid the rucksack off my shoulders, stuck the heels of my hands into the small of my back, and stretched. "Just making things clear."

"Yes," she said, drawing the word out a little with emphasis I might have used myself in her place. "You are. Maybe because you don't want to think about what is on the line today."

A flicker of anger went through me at the words. That happens when people tell you something true that you don't want to hear.

I took a deep breath. "Okay. You're right. Better to be focused on here and now." I took a water bottle from the rucksack and drank it in a single pull. "It'll take me four or five hours to get things laid out. Maybe a little less, maybe more."

"What can I do to help?" Lara asked.

"Can you paint?"

"Will Italian realism do?"

I looked at her blankly. "Um. I mostly just need you to stay inside the lines."

She smiled and it turned a bit impish. "What fun is that?"

"The kind of fun that prevents explosions and a massive cave-in."

"Oh. That." She nodded. "Yes. I can do precision."

"Okay," I said. "Mab will be there."

Lara looked wary. Which I could get. I'd been damned wary of Mab when I'd first been in her service, too. "Why?"

"She's helping."

Lara looked, if anything, more wary. "Why?"

"Because she takes being an ally seriously," I said. "And because I made a deal."

Her eyes narrowed. "You did? You could have asked her for anything. And you asked her to help Thomas?"

I nodded. "I said I would."

She frowned harder and looked down. "Saying is one thing. Doing it is another." She looked away, her eyes focused elsewhere, calculating. "Do you think she will?"

"I think she has to," I said. "It . . . might not be simple. Or pleasant. But I think she'll make something happen when it couldn't have otherwise."

She swallowed. She blinked her eyes several times, soot-black lashes fluttering over deep blue.

"Okay," Lara whispered finally. "Thank you for the warning."

I hesitated. "Are . . . are you okay?"

She shook her head. "We have a job to do. Let's do it."

At my direction, Alfred had prepared a special chamber for the greater circle.

It was a perfect half sphere, fifty feet across, hollowed out of a single enormous green crystal. The entire place pulsed with a living, verdant illumination that took about half an hour to begin becoming vaguely nauseating. I measured to the center of the chamber using a line and some basic trig, marked the center with a dry-erase marker, and with Lara's help outlined the pair of circles via the same means. We painted those in, brought in the anchor crystals and candles, and then marked the positions for each of the containment sigils and runes. Painting those took the longest, and Lara proved to be a hell of a lot better at it than I was. After that, I painted in the infinity symbol, very large this time, at the circle's center.

The whole thing was painstaking, nerve-wracking. Every move had to be considered, every part of the body controlled so that nothing was smeared by a stray foot or knee or bit of clothing. It took every bit of five hours, and by the time we were done, my knees and shoulders and back were protesting through the Winter mantle, my head was fuzzy, and I felt vaguely carsick.

"Okay. Let's take a break," I said. "Get some food, rest our eyes from all the damned green, give the paint a little more time to dry. Then I'll start the checks to make sure we're all set. And I have to let Mab know we're ready."

Lara looked as fresh as she had when we got on the *Water Beetle* that morning. "All right."

I nodded. "Mab," I murmured, putting will into my voice. "Mab. Mab. We're just about ready."

I opened my eyes to find Lara looking at me.

"It's a summoning," I said. "Technically. At the level of power I used, it's more like sending a page."

Lara smiled faintly. "A page? Empty night, Dresden. You really don't use technology, do you?"

"Yeah. No."

We went out into the tunnel outside my new ritual chamber and my stomach felt better almost at once. I opened the rucksack, popped a Coke, slugged most of it away at a swig. It was pretty warm by then, so I covered my mouth and minimized the belch. Lara opened a bottle of water, rolling her eyes and smiling at the same time.

"All that green light, and the translucent walls. Makes me a bit sick," I said.

"Is that what it is?" Lara asked.

I frowned down at the drink.

"You're good at compartmentalizing your fear," she said. "You'd have to be."

"Yeah," I said. "Well."

This was going to be one of the biggest spells of my life. If I screwed it up, Thomas would get hurt. Maybe die.

I wanted my brother back.

I couldn't do anything about Karrin.

I didn't want to lose someone else.

The very thought made me queasy.

I had a sandwich and sipped at the rest of the Coke, and tried to think about the spell, and not what kind of bleak whirlpool might suck me back down if I screwed it up.

Lara nibbled at a sandwich that was probably healthier than mine, watching me with calm, curious eyes.

"I get knocked down a lot," I said. "This time it took me a while to stand back up. Right now . . . I don't know if I could do it again."

She stared at me.

I felt it. A thrill that went through my limbs. The intensity of her gaze was tactile.

"I'm more at peace with my Hunger than I've ever been," Lara said. "In centuries. I can feel myself . . . expanding. It's a freedom I've never allowed myself to so much as dream about." Her eyes flickered lazily, paler for a moment. "But perhaps you shouldn't show me that kind of weakness while we are alone."

I shifted my hips uncomfortably. "Yeah," I said. "Maybe not."

"Besides," she said. "If you have to do it, you will. You're too stubborn for anything else."

"Hey," I said. "Did I ever thank you for saving my ass, the night of the battle? That kick."

She took a bite of her sandwich and smirked. "I do rather wish someone had got that one on camera."

"Ah, everyone would say it was special effects."

"I want to critique my form. It was supposed to cave her head in."

Without a whisper of sound or the faintest hint of warning from my island-specific *intellectus*, Mab was suddenly standing over both of us, resplendent in a deep green robe of something that might have been silk, complete with a hood drawn up over her hair.

"You knocked loose the Eye of Balor," Mab murmured. "Which was the most useful act of the evening. Be content that you did that to a Titan and walked away with your health and sanity."

I choked on the last bite of my sandwich, tried to wash it down with the last bit of the Coke, and wound up mostly making strangling sounds and snorting bits that shouldn't have been there out my nose.

Mab stood over me with a small smirk on her lips. Then she turned her head slowly toward Lara.

Lara swayed where she sat, as if some kind of magnetic force had drawn her toward Mab. Then she squared her shoulders, straightened her back, and made her face a polite mask. You couldn't have read her expression with one of those fancy laser scanners and a panel of body language experts. She inclined her head, slightly, to Mab.

"You understand why?" Mab asked, her voice barely above a whisper.

"Of course," Lara said. "It reduces complications."

"And increases efficiency," Mab noted. She flicked her chin toward me. "My Knight, of course, will attempt chivalry. He is troublesome in that way."

"And if he should succeed?" Lara asked.

Mab smiled faintly. "Perhaps you will choose to remain as a vassal of Winter. You will do well there. Time will tell."

"You would not be angry if he pried me loose of you?" Lara asked.

"I would be vexed," Mab mused. "He is frequently vexing. But only a fool grows angry at a dog for barking, an adder for biting, a scorpion for stinging. It is their nature." She showed her teeth. "I am willing to play the game fairly. I rarely lose."

Lara tilted her head, studying Mab thoughtfully.

I fished some paper napkins out of the bag and cleaned myself up while they talked.

"Is what she says true?" Lara asked.

"She can't speak untruth," I said. "Don't confuse that with an inability to deceive."

"Ah," Lara said. "She didn't say very much that was direct, did she?"

Mab smiled benignly upon me.

"You catch on quick," I said to Lara.

"Lady Raith," Mab said, "I will not deny my Knight his pursuit of folly, even if it threatened such an excellent acquisition as yourself. I am pleased with his defiance, in general. In retrospect, it has yielded me outstanding results."

Lara looked even more thoughtful.

"Blah, blah, blah," I said. "We have a major spell to work."

"Indeed," Mab said. "I have inspected your circle. It seems . . . adequate."

"I think you meant to say *perfect*," I muttered.

Mab sniffed. "I meant to say *adequate*. Though I suppose to you, the terms are, for this working, similar."

"You read the outline of the spell? My notes from the experiments?"

"Mmmm. You do have an exceptional gift for this sort of working, my Knight." She tilted her head. "Shall we begin?"

Chapter
Forty-Seven

I went back into the chamber of the greater circle and went over the sigils again, checking each. I didn't really need to, I supposed, if the design had Mab's seal of approval. But you don't do dangerous magic without covering all your bases, period. So I went around the circle, methodically checking again, each design against its to-scale paper counterpart, one by one, almost in rhythm, ordering my mind for what was to come.

"Lara," I said, when I was done, "Thomas doesn't have the same kind of relationship with his Hunger as you have with yours."

"I'm very aware," she said.

"That's why I want you to observe," I said quietly. "Share any insights you have with me. It could get complicated fast. I might have to make spur-of-the-moment decisions. Your knowledge of them could make a difference."

I caught Mab staring at me hard as I spoke. I frowned at her. She simply kept staring at me for a moment, then curled her lips into a faint expression of approval and gave me a slow nod.

"I can do that," Lara said quietly.

"Mab," I said, "Lara's Hunger was difficult for me to handle. I might need to borrow power to manage Thomas's. I think it would be useful if you stood ready to loan it to me."

"Yes," Mab said, her voice faintly impatient. "I know precisely how

I will be most useful and why you invited me to participate. I have brought all that is necessary."

"Okay," I said. "Time for my ritual clothing."

I went over to my bag and took out a black T-shirt featuring Rock 'Em Sock 'Em Robots across the front, stripped out of my shirt, and put the new one on. I added to that a pair of aviator sunglasses I'd given Thomas a few years back, along with a White Sox baseball cap he'd owned.

Lara looked at me and smiled faintly. "I'm a minority owner of the team, you know," she said.

I glanced at her and sighed. "Of course you are." I took up my wizard's staff, the one I'd carved new from a lightning-struck oak on this very island, looked over the circle once more, and took a slow breath.

"Alfred," I breathed. "Please move my brother's crystal into the circle."

Silence rang around the chamber for the space of a long breath. Then the floor began to rumble as the genius loci of Demonreach reacted to my request. In the center of the circle, in one half of the infinity symbol, a slender column of crystal began to arise from the floor. My brother lay in it, his eyes closed, his face twisted into a rictus of pain, his body tensed into an agonized arch.

"Oh," Lara breathed. "Empty night, Harry. His Hunger. It was tearing into him when you froze it last."

"I know," I said quietly.

"He's in pain," Lara said. "I can feel it from here."

"Yeah," I said. "When I bring him out of the stasis, I'm going to have to act fast."

Mab paced slowly around the exterior of the circle, tilting her head this way and that, staring at my entombed brother. "Power alone will avail you naught, I think, my Knight."

I frowned at her. "Why do you say that?"

"Imagine a beast set upon a child," she said, "its claws and teeth sunk in. Simply tearing it away will rend the child asunder as it is done. Precision is as much needed as power."

"Super," I said. "Great. Right in my wheelhouse. Dammit."

Mab smirked. "In addition," she said, "we have little time. The island's spirit has slowed the passage of time to an intense degree within the stasis crystal but cannot stop it entirely. Your brother's life has been ripped from him very slowly but surely over months. It might be too late already. Had you waited another moon, it certainly would have been." She shook her head. "When he is released, the Hunger will be in the very act of ending his life. In my judgment, you will have seconds. At most."

"Seconds?" I demanded. "Oh, come on."

Mab gave me a frosty smile. "I will not be able to lend you power," she said calmly. "I will have to stretch those seconds to give you more room in which to operate. It will require all of my focus."

"Stretch *time?*" I asked. "You can do that?"

"Theoretically," she mused. "Yes. Though I will admit, it has not been necessary to attempt a working so severe before today."

"Severe? How severe are we talking?" I asked.

"Expect extended consequences," she murmured.

"Ah," I said. "Fantastic. Because I never have enough of those."

"Harry?" Lara said uncertainly.

"Don't worry," I said. "This doesn't change anything. We're still doing this."

Mab glanced at Lara with a kind of wry certainty. "Dogs bark. Scorpions sting. And my Knight pursues his folly."

"Mab," I said, and gestured with my right hand.

The Queen of Air and Darkness inclined her head and took position a step behind me and one to my right.

"Lara," I said, gesturing with my left.

Lara looked uncertain, but she mirrored Mab on the other side.

A single breath can change everything.

I took a slow, deep breath and cleared my mind.

Then I gestured with one hand, murmured, *"Flickum bicus,"* and set the ritual candles and incense alight.

The floor shivered with sudden power as light spread through the anchoring crystals, catching the candlelight and sending it blazing in nearly coherent beams, describing a pentagram between the inner and outer circle.

I took another breath, sent out a murmur of my will, and brought the greater circle to life. The runes began to blaze green-gold, reflected everywhere in the dome of crystal around us, again and again in sharp relief and at varied depths throughout the translucent stone.

I bowed my head, pressed the forefinger of my right hand to the spot between and just above my eyebrows and breathed out to whoever or Whoever might be listening, and said, simply, "Please."

Then I opened my eyes, and with it, my Sight.

The Sight goes by a lot of names—the Third Eye, True Sight, there's a hundred different phrases from a hundred different cultures, but they're all talking about the same thing. Some people can see more of the universe than others, see the supernatural energies that flow through all of reality. When it comes to wizard-level practitioners, the Sight shows you all kinds of things, and there's a lot of overlap with the soulgaze. You can see things that are terrifyingly true, but your brain has a lot of built-in defenses, and as a result sometimes you experience things through the filters your mind throws up to keep you from being harmed—because everything you See is permanent. It stays right there in your head, and time never rubs off the rough edges of the memories. Look at the wrong thing with your Sight and you could quite easily be driven mad, swiftly and permanently.

I was taking a huge risk here. But using my Sight would tell me more about what was happening to Thomas, would let me better understand and direct my power, and I wanted every advantage I could get.

I had braced myself against what I would be looking at, but even so, I reeled at the sheer, overwhelming complexity of the patterns of power that now hummed throughout the circle, the sigils, and the crystalline dome around me. I could see how the anchor crystals both fractured and focused the energy of the circle, the sparkling crackles of small but inevitable energetic inefficiencies, sending stray beams of violet and azure energy that tinged the edges of the green and gold working of the circle.

And, within the crystal imprisoning my brother, I saw the field of deliberate scarlet stasis, sheer, viscous, redshifted time that had been slowed. It dragged at the edges of my brother's image as it struggled to stay connected to the rest of the universe around it, the strain upon the very fabric of reality showing as faint, delicately crazed cracks in the crystal imprisoning him. His pale body was strained, muscles taut against his skin, veins pressed against the surface. He'd been gaunt when I'd passed him to Demonreach's caretaking, his body eating itself to repair the damage that had been inflicted on him at the hands of the vengeful svartalves, and every muscle and tendon showed through his pale skin, while his dark hair hung lank about his head and face. I could read the pain and the terror in his expression and body as easily as any book.

I Saw how much my brother was suffering in that moment.

And I Saw his Hunger.

The demon was huge, towering over him, behind him, within him, a starving mass of bone and emaciated skin straining against lean muscle, pallid as a corpse and terrible and viciously hungry. I could see one of its withered hands clutching his throat, the other wrapped within Thomas's body, encircling his lower spine, while its jaws, sporting something that looked more like serrated ridges than fangs, closed upon one of his shoulders.

"Hear me, Outsider," I said, pouring my will into my voice. The crystal rang with it, the words resounding in sheer, penetrating resonance more than in simple volume. "I forbid thee from doing harm to Thomas Raith. I forbid thee. I forbid thee!"

And on the third repetition, the crystal imprisoning my brother and his demon shattered into light and shrieking sound and a world-weight of pain and savage need thundered down upon me, all at once. The demon's silver eyes whipped toward me, met mine, and through the perception of my Sight I could feel myself, my true, core self, drawn forward, into the circle, into a maelstrom of sheer havoc and terror as the demon lunged toward me, leaving my physical body standing at the circle's edge, splitting my awareness into two places at once. I could See my energetic form from the perspective of my physical body and feel both of them acting at the same time, doubling the disorientation of all that sensory input.

So I had that going for me.

Simultaneously, Mab began a low chant in a tongue that was all harsh, guttural vowels and throaty consonants. Even as she did, everything blurred, edges fading to weirdly translucent lines, shading everything into the color of a bloody sunset.

I've often experienced the perception of time slowing in moments of crisis.

This was the first time I felt the real thing.

It hurt.

The air turned thick. Hauling in a breath became the labor of what felt like half an hour. My heart pressed against my chest, and when it beat, it thundered against the walls of my rib cage like someone striking a huge drum.

My physical body began to raise my right hand, sending out energy.

My spiritual body, though . . . that was moving just fine.

I closed the distance to the enormous Hunger, half a foot taller than me, planting my feet, twisting at the hips, pushing through my legs, and throwing my right fist forward in a strike that brushed past the chin of Thomas's physical body and slammed into the space where the Hunger's nose should have been in a right cross that would have dropped a big man into a boneless heap.

The impact sent a ripple of red light in a languid wave that washed over the Hunger's empty face and simultaneously up my forearm and biceps to my shoulder. Its head rocked back and then whipped toward me, silver eyes blazing. The muscles in its forearms knotted, huge hands squeezing, and Thomas let out a slow gasp of pure agony.

I felt my energy-form seize the Hunger's arms, plunging *through* Thomas's body to do it, my fingers crushing down on the emaciated thing's wrists, digging in hard, forcing the grip to loosen.

"I forbid thee!" I thundered from my physical body. I was repeating it over and over, at least in intention, but my lips moved like they were trapped in amber, every motion and sound dragged from them over the course of a small eon.

The Hunger's silver eyes widened in sudden shock as I crushed its grip into looseness. Then I set my teeth, leveraging my whole body in the motion, and slowly forced its hands away from my brother.

"That's right, big guy," I snarled from lips without physical form. "You aren't the Hulk here."

And I started dragging the Hunger over toward the other side of the infinity symbol carved within the circle.

But its huge eyes whirled and spun in a mad silver-on-silver spiral, and its voice slithered into my head like cold oil. *I know thee, wizard. I have fought by thy side again and again.*

"Thomas did that," I spat. "That was never you."

The Hunger's lips split into a too-wide grin. *Didst thou never question his love of danger? His desire for violence? His skill at battle? Never was that of his own heart. That was me. Ever, 'twas me.*

And with the words, the Hunger twisted, its strength snaking sinuously, reversing, and suddenly I was fighting for my life as one of its huge hands surged against everything I could do and began to close around *my* throat.

"Thomas!" screamed Lara, the sound ringing out painfully slow in the red light.

My eyes flicked toward him. His body was falling, slowly, pale eyes rolled back in his head. He was falling to the floor like a crash test dummy, boneless and helpless.

"You're killing him!" I snarled to the Hunger. Its long fingers closed on my throat and began to tighten like a constrictor, patient and powerful and lithe. A chill went through me, and suddenly my voice was cut off.

Child who thinks it understands, the Hunger's voice purred in my head. *He has already surrendered to the inevitable. I but claim the life he has yielded to the void. The life in which I made him vital, strong. Yet before I snuff out that final spark, I can devour more, if you would force it upon me.*

Its other hand twisted from my weakening grip, sinking into the flesh of my spiritual form, closing around the energy point, the chakra of my heart.

I gasped, from both physical and spiritual bodies, and suddenly the red light blurred to orange and then yellow, and then the green of the crystalline chamber, and time flowed normally again.

Thomas hit the floor like a dead fish.

My heart and my belly twisted in absolute terror.

I felt the strength going out of me, felt the demon tearing it away from me, drinking the energy of my life like blood. I felt my knees buckle.

"Dresden!" Lara snapped. She lunged in front of me as my balance wavered, hands on my shoulders, bracing me up. "Dresden, what's happening?"

I felt the cold spreading through my body, and it wasn't pleasant at all. It was ugly, nauseating, mindlessly malicious, devouring, a cold like must exist in space, ripping from me everything it touched, unable to be truly satiated.

I tried to answer Lara, but it was like my lungs and throat had turned to ice.

I could feel myself dying. Sound faded. My vision grew dimmer.

Yes, the Hunger growled, in my head. *Now you understand. Empty Night. The end of all motion, all joy, all passion, all fear, all pain. The end of all. The absolute, perfect, unblemished silence. Empty Night, wizard.*

And it tightened its grip upon me.

And the cold became everything.

Chapter
Forty-Eight

Empty Night.

The mindless, heedless, reckless end of all thought and light and life.

No wonder the White Court used it as a curse.

It was the first time I'd felt that one, too, felt it as a tangible, real thing, chewing into me from a mad Outsider, its claws twisting, fangs clamping, to rake at my spiritual self.

But it also got worse.

My spiritual self was stuck there. I mean, the whole point of the greater circle was to contain beings physically and spiritually. Simultaneous eye contact with my Sight wide open had drawn my essence, my spirit, maybe my soul even, into the circle with the Hunger.

Now it was a cage match.

I wasn't getting out until it was over.

My physical body was sagging and would have fallen without Lara's support.

"What's happening?" she demanded of Mab. "What is happening?"

Mab's voice came coolly through the chilly chamber. "He has successfully detached the demon from your brother's physical form," she said. Her breathing slightly labored? As much as I liked to think of myself as a rebel to the forms of the White Council, I didn't lightly break the Laws of Magic, and I'd never, ever screwed with time. Neither had anyone I ever knew. I had no idea how heavy a lift it was—but I knew how powerful Mab was, and if it had taxed her, I was pretty sure I wouldn't be messing with that one anytime soon.

"What does that mean?" Lara snapped.

"Your Hunger exists in a state of balance," Mab said, with about as much excitement as an announcer at a golf tournament. "Your brother's demon is quite mad. Dresden contends with it. It seeks to devour him utterly."

"What can we do to help?"

"Nothing," Mab said. "Nothing whatsoever. This is up to him." The Queen of Air and Darkness paused, and then added, absently, "Also, your brother's heart is failing. He is dying."

Lara's head snapped around, her expression horrified. "Thomas?"

And the whole time they talked, the cold became increasingly vicious, increasingly bitter, taking up more and more and more of my consciousness.

The Hunger rose over me, growing stronger by the second, the cold growing deeper, forcing me to bend backwards before its rising power. I was entwined with it, with its thoughts, with its pain and desperate emptiness, a personification of the void itself. I knew that it would devour the energy of my spirit without a second thought, and when it was finished with me it would take whatever was left of my brother, even if doing so meant its own destruction. The thing was simply that focused upon devouring all that it could reach.

The cold of it threatened to drown me. And the most horrible part of it was that . . .

I thought about it.

I'd been through a lot. Hurt a lot. Lost a lot. The pain of the burdens I bore had only grown, year after year. I could have ended that pain. Could have let go. Could have found the ultimate end of suffering. Part of me thought about it. Thought about letting that emptiness consume me. Thought about letting the cold take me and feeling nothing, not pain, not doubt, not uncertainty, not shame, not grief—not ever again.

And all I had to do was not fight.

I thought about it.

But I had promises to keep.

And then I started giggling.

I mean, seriously. Me. Not fighting.

That would be something suspiciously close to sensible, and that had never been my style.

I opened my eyes and met the Hunger's silver ones and felt my lips spread into a wolfish smile.

It stared back at me, eagerness and hate and madness in its swirling silver eyes.

"Stupid bastard," I snarled. "Using cold? On the Winter Knight? You should read more."

The Hunger's inhuman face twisted in something between frustration, pure confusion—and fear.

And when I saw that, the Winter mantle surged up within me. It didn't know about family or love or sacrifice—but it knew all about fear. All about how to respond to weakness. And this demon, hungry and mad as it might have been, was *weak*.

The cold that rose in me was something else entirely. Not the emptiness of nothing, but the savage cold of a world at war with the night. The cold of January. Where if chill winds sucked the warmth from the marrow, it was because elsewhere in the world was sunshine and light giving them energy. Where living waters, kissed by the life-giving sun, rose into the air to come slashing back down as crystalline snow. Where creatures lived in hunger and terror knowing full well that they had prepared themselves for this time, and had every intention of surviving it, of seeing life return to the world, of feeling the heat of summer upon their skin and seeing their offspring gamboling through green days.

Winter wasn't Empty Night.

It was the war against it.

The wisdom and the will required to fight it.

The strength to stand fast, even when all was dark and seemed hopeless, holding to the truth that ahead were better days.

My physical body slammed my staff down onto the green crystal floor of the chamber, and the earth itself shook around me. The lightning-blasted oak of the tree from Demonreach connected me to the island, to the life within it, in the earth, rising to the waters surrounding it and to the spring sun shining down. I drew upon that warmth, upon the power flowing through the island, and when the walls of the summoning chamber began to glow with sunlight, the Hunger howled in sudden terror and confusion, tearing its hands from me, lifting them to shield its mirrored eyes from the light.

And my spiritual body drove forward, planting a shoulder in the thing's gut, half lifting it from the floor and slamming it down firmly into the other half of the infinity symbol. Fury and wild exultation filled me with strength, with the tingling exhilaration of hot blood flowing against the cold of night.

This fight was about more than me and my pain. It was about more than me and my fear. It was even about more than my brother and his life.

It was about denying death. Denying despair. Denying the Empty Night.

Maybe, on a long enough scale, that cold and darkness was inevitable. Maybe no matter what any of us did, one day the universe would settle into unbroken silence, eternal darkness, endless nothing.

But not today.

"Not today!" I bellowed, and slammed my staff on the floor again, and far above me from a clear blue sky, a bolt of lightning as big around as a tree trunk slammed into the stones around the entrance, coursed down through the earth, leaving a streak of green-gold glowing runes carved into the stones by the same man who had built the island and the castle alike, old Merlin's craft and will, and blazed through the crystalline walls with the sheer, fiery power of the living world.

That was power enough to have incinerated my physical form. But my spiritual body was more than up to handling it. I gathered it up, heat and fire and pure spinning energy whirling through uncounted trillions of wandering ions, by very definition a tide of positive energy, and sent it coruscating up through the crystal, up through the spirit-body of the Hunger, whirling through it and around it in a matrix, savage and vital and scalding and nourishing all at once. The thing fell to its knees, covering its head with its arms, curling down in agony.

I was dimly aware of Lara falling away from me, shielding her eyes from the light. Mab remained standing where she had been, wild light playing across her face, her eyes wide as any axe murderer's, her smile spreading out more than should have been possible as she watched me at the center of a veritable thunderstorm of energy, as she watched me contend with my foe.

I could have killed it then. I could have destroyed the demon, the Outsider, utterly. I could have freed my brother from its foul touch forever.

But in the Sight of my physical body, I could still see the blurring connection it had to Thomas. I could see the blur in the air between the Hunger and my brother, could see his faltering breaths, the utter exhaustion of his body. To tear asunder that connection would be to leave his spirit torn and ragged, like separating conjoined twins with two teams of wild horses. The kind of skill required to do that and leave his mind and spirit intact and ready to survive was beyond me. The Winter mantle howled for me to do exactly that, to send my enemy screaming back into the void whence it came.

But I fought against that savagery and mastered it. Because at the end of the day, the demon had been right. At Thomas's will, it had fought beside me, time after time. And if it was mad with the need to devour, it was because it had also labored to keep my brother alive when he had been so savagely beaten.

Whether the Hunger realized it or not, we were fighting side by side again.

I couldn't kill it simply for the sense of satisfaction it would give me.

Both my forms lifted my right hands and began to feed the wild, vital magic of life to the demon.

The thing let out a sudden quavering paean of raw need, spreading its arms wide in supplication and embrace at once, and as it did, its mirrorlike eyes, still panicked, flickered over to my brother's still—utterly still—form.

"Oh, no, you don't, you meathead," I panted. "I haven't walked through the wastes of war and death and my own soul to lose you now."

And with a flick of my hand, I redirected a fraction of the energy I was sending into the demon and hit Thomas with a miniature lightning bolt.

Thunder rumbled through the crystalline chamber, making the walls ring like an enormous bell.

My brother's body arched up into a bow—and the Hunger let out a desperate shriek, arching in time with him.

"Thomas!" I screamed. "Wake up!"

Mab's voice rose in a wild cackle like ten times ten thousand violins shrieking in dissonance all at once.

"Demonreach!" she shrieked, raising bare white arms as the sleeves of her green robe slid down from them. "Bring forth my gifts!"

My head whipped around toward her.

Gifts. From the Queen of Air and Darkness.

What fresh hell was this?

The floor of the chamber rippled again, and from it rose what at first looked like a large crystal of glacier-blue stone.

And then I realized that it wasn't stone.

It was ice. The agonizing true ice of the heart of Winter.

And bound upon its surface, and partly within it, was a very, very pregnant Justine.

She looked awful. She looked as if she hadn't eaten healthily or enough for months and hadn't cleaned herself properly for weeks. She'd shaved her glorious dark hair to a brief stubble. Her skin was blotchy, oily, her face was far too lean and twisted in agony, and a cage of translucent ice that reminded me of those Hannibal Lecter movie masks bound her face with her head tilted back at a painful angle. She was bent back into a spread-eagled bow, gravid belly outthrust, and encased in ice to her upper arms and to her knees.

And there was nothing I could do. It was all I could do to hold the Hunger in place, prevent it from devouring me, while simultaneously trying to ease its starvation and keep Thomas's heart beating. If I turned my attention from that, even for a moment, it might all fly apart.

"Hear me, Raith!" Mab's voice rang out. She drew from her belt a bronze knife.

A knife I remembered, from a Red Court ball long, long ago. Medea's bodkin.

"I have your haunted love!" Mab caroled. "I have your unborn son! And if you do not arise, I swear by stars and stones that I will end both lives in a single stroke!"

Chapter
Forty-Nine

The hardest part of holding together ritual magic is maintaining a balance. Most of magic as practiced by wizards comes from our humanity—our emotions, specifically. But it has to be shaped and controlled with rigid intellect, with raw focus, concentration, directed intent, and will. The state of balance between those two portions of the mind could feel like a lot of things and could be described in a lot of different ways.

But Mab had just seriously harshed my wizard mellow.

I felt the ritual magic begin to intensify, like a spinning wheel beginning to wobble, becoming more forceful and more unpredictable. Wild sparks exploded out from the anchor crystals around the circle in a myriad of colors, blindingly bright.

Lara let out a cry, shielding her eyes with one hand. "Harry?"

"Mab!" I shouted, my words emerging from my lips tortured and groaning, as though I was straining under a heavy weight. "What the hell are you doing?"

I saw her smile, far too wide, her eyes flickering through the color spectrum in mad glee. "Why, being kind, my Knight. As you requested."

And she turned toward Justine, raising the knife over her head.

"Empty night," Lara breathed.

And blurred toward Mab at approximately the speed of an arrow from a bow.

Mab was her match.

She seized one of Lara's arms with her free hand without so much as looking, as if the Queen of Air and Darkness had seen this movie before and already knew exactly where Lara would be. She spun and flung Lara across about a quarter of the summoning chamber, to send her tumbling along the outside of the rounded walls. Lara spun over and over, front and back slamming against green crystal, and landed thirty feet later, stunned.

Then slowly Mab turned, and step by step, inch by inch, approached the bound Justine with that mad, too-wide smile.

I struggled to keep the ritual together, focusing my thoughts on what *should* be happening instead of what actually was. "Alfred!" I screamed.

And Demonreach, the genius loci of the island, rose from the crystal, ten feet of massive, cloaked, humanoid fury. Eyes of green-gold lightning blazed deep within the hood. The ground shook. Cracks appeared in the crystalline walls. The cloak flared back, away from Mab as though a gale of invisible, intangible wind emanated from the Winter Queen. The body beneath, which I had never before seen, was composed of stone and winding oak roots, of earthen muscle and sinews of green leaf and long grass.

"QUEEN OF WINTER," boomed Demonreach's voice from within the depths of the hood, "THOU SHALT CEASE THY ACTION."

The spirit slammed a gnarled-root fist to the ground, cracks spreading through the crystal, and beneath Mab's feet there was a sharp report, like a rifle, and more roots exploded up, winding around the ankles and calves of the Winter Queen, halting her in her tracks.

Mab threw back her head, let out a cackle that chilled the blood of even the Winter Knight, and turned her whirling-color mad eyes to me. "Oh, my Knight," Mab tittered. "Didst thou *actually* think thou couldst draw a bigger gun than *me*?"

Then there was a sound like thunder, and a rift wide enough to drive a Volkswagen through tore open in the roof at the entrance to the summoning chamber, and a black-clad form streaked through the newly created opening, to land hard enough to send a series of spiderweb cracks spinning out through the crystalline floor between Demonreach and Mab.

It straightened slowly, a hunched, elderly, feminine figure that was nonetheless at least half a foot taller than me, shrouded in thick overlapping garments of tattered black. Thick white hair was pulled back into a close braid. She shrugged a shoulder and a heavy cleaver with a black handle hung heavily in her withered old hand.

She smiled.

Green light gleamed from iron teeth.

And in my Sight, I saw the edges of a hundred thousand tales of horror and dread. People, even children, devoured whole, popped into soup, baked alive in ovens, chopped and minced into pies. I saw the faces of countless folk gasping out their last breaths, freezing to death in the cold, lying helpless as they were devoured, still alive, by wolves and worse in the bleak and desolate places of the world. I saw the merciless resolve of nature's darkest face, the hideous and passionless power of the avalanche, the horrible absolutism of dark, cold water rising to drown everything upon the shore with entire and final equity. I saw the wreckage of mortal remains upon countless battlefields, birds and insects and hungry things devouring the carrion. The stench of dead and rotting flesh rose through my nostrils directly into my thoughts, meat writhing with maggots and worms, and presiding over all of it a constant, calm, precise presence that forced me to turn my eyes away before they saw something even worse.

"Spirit," rasped Mother Winter. Her voice was the sound of dead leaves in the wind, of scale rasping upon scale, of insectile chitin skittering along bleaching bone. "Stand not between the Queens of Winter and their promises."

I felt my jaw drop open.

Hell's bells.

Mab's boss.

The Crone Queen of the Winter Court, here in the mortal world.

It hadn't happened for centuries.

Crystals of ice began to spread over and *through* the verdant stone of the summoning chamber, fracturing the green light into dozens and dozens of glacial shades. The temperature plummeted from the steady fifty degrees underground to deep-freeze levels in seconds. The ice spread to the roots wrapping around Mab's calves, and with a gleeful kick of each leg, she shattered them like so much brittle frost—and continued toward the trapped Justine.

"Don't!" I screamed.

Mab whirled toward me. "This is what thou didst *ask* for, my Knight!" she snarled. "To defy the doom of choices made! A doom that cannot be undone without further choice!" She pointed the knife at Thomas. "His," she spat, and then the knife stabbed at me. "And thine!"

I stared in horror as she turned back toward the column of ice.

And my brother made the weakest, softest sound of pain.

I turned back to Thomas. He still lay where he had fallen, but his eyes were open and focused upon the tableau. Tears filled them. His face was twisted with pain. With exhaustion.

Hell's bells. I knew those eyes.

I knew what was behind them.

I'd stared down at them in glasses of booze and my shaving mirror for months.

His head started to fall.

Mab's spectral eyes settled on a shade of cold blue ice, and she turned toward Justine, raising Medea's bodkin.

Hell's bells.

I clenched my teeth, focused upon my physical body—and lifted my eyes to lock gazes with my brother's demon.

The pale thing trapped in the circle felt my eyes and met them with willing hunger as it drank and drank from the steady current of power I'd been feeding into it.

And everything stopped. Mab froze in place in the act of raising her knife. Mother Winter, her hand outstretched in a gesture of forbiddance at Demonreach, froze in place. The genius loci's cloak rustled to a stop where it stood. Lara, pushing herself back toward her feet, locked into position, triceps flexed.

"Let's talk," I said quietly, from my energetic body's lips.

Interesting, replied the Hunger. *You make mouth noises and I hear the intent behind them.*

"Yeah, I'm full of surprises," I said. "We need to come to an understanding."

The Hunger was as frozen as my physical form was, but its mirror eyes gleamed. *I want to devour you. All. Everyone.*

"Sure, I get that," I said. "You got an empty you can't fill. But tell me. Suppose you did that. You got to eat me and everyone else on this rock. Then what?"

Confusion entered its tone. *What?*

"Suppose you get everything you want," I said. "You get to eat the whole damned world. You're still going to be trying to fill that empty place. Only there's going to be nothing left to put in there, is there?"

The Hunger dwelled on that for a moment. *Ah,* it said at last. *Linear time. The feeding ends those lines.*

"Right," I said. "Exactly. And when it does, what is going to be left for a Hunger to nibble on? Forever and ever and ever?"

Its thin lips quivered, ever so slowly peeling back from pale teeth. *That is the nature of the Empty Night.*

"Sure," I said. "But think about it. Wouldn't you rather spend more linear time feeding?"

It seemed to dwell on that for a moment.

"Work with me," I said. "Do it my way. And yeah, maybe you don't get to gobble up everything all at once. But you get to keep feeding. And feeding. And feeding."

Yes, came the hideous, hissing answer.

"Right, okay, follow along," I said. "What happens if Thomas dies? You don't get to eat then, either, do you?"

Again, the thing considered, as though it had encountered an entirely new thought it had to wrap its mind around. I could sense its attention shift to Thomas's battered body.

My portal closes. I am consigned to the Outside once more.

"Not much to eat there, is there?" I noted.

There is emptiness. Hunger. The tone of the voice shrank. *Nothing else.*

"But you could stay here, yeah?" I took a breath and put gentle emphasis on the next words. "For as long as you can keep Thomas alive."

It simply stared at me in silence. I had to hurry this along. I was getting tired. Feeding this thing was as different from satisfying Lara's

Hunger as feeding a finely bred racing greyhound and a friggin' elephant.

I wish to continue feeding, came the answer from the thing, finally. *To feed and feed and feed. For centuries and centuries of your time. The Empty Night will come. But I wish to take my pleasure of the mortal realms until then.*

"Sure," I said. "Why burn down the candy store when you can keep getting more treats? Good," I said. "That's a human concept, called sustainability. I mean, we're still working on it, but this conversation is going really well."

I could hear the hysterical giggle bubbling out of my voice. I was in direct mental contact with a Lovecraftian horror. Which probably wouldn't be recommended by the American Medical Association. I could feel things shredding inside my head as the Hunger continued to draw energy out of me. I'd be racking up insanity points with every single exchange with the thing.

"So, here's the deal," I said. "I'm going to put you and Thomas back together. And you're going to help him."

This portal is failing, the Hunger said, with faint contempt. *Body, mind, and spirit. Hollowed out. Ruined.*

"He's human," I said. "He can be renewed. I've seen it. I've done it. And you and I are going to fight together again. To heal him. And you get to keep on feeding."

The Hunger's eyes flickered and shimmered, mirrors shining more brightly, and I could see my body, clenching my staff, struggling to stay upright in one, and Thomas, eyes beginning to roll back in his head, in the other.

"I mean, what are your options?" I demanded. "He goes, you go. He stays, you stay. What do you say?"

And time almost stopped. Everything depended on this. There's a rule that applies to just about everything there is: You are what you eat. You eat healthy, you are healthy. You eat junk, sooner or later, you're living in junk. This Outsider was a primal spirit of pure, devouring hunger.

But it had been feeding on humanity. For years. Humans are weird and complicated and contradictory, but they pretty much all operate under the same drive as every other living thing on the planet.

Survival.

The desire to live. Grow. Reproduce. Protect offspring. Pure, animal, instinct-level drives that sometimes let us do incredible things, go beyond the boundaries we normally face, defy darkness, despair, self-destruction—sometimes even death itself.

If there was some kind of malevolent will driving the Outsiders, it might have made a mistake with the Hungers.

Because ultimately, they needed mortals in order to exist.

And the more of us they ate, the more like us they would become.

The Hunger's attention focused even more intently upon Thomas.

Done, it purred.

I closed my eyes, especially the third one, breaking the mental connection. Withdrew back entirely into my physical form.

Exhaustion hammered into me, weariness as thorough and nauseating as anything I had ever experienced. I staggered forward to a knee, my head spinning. Dropped my staff. Started crawling for the nearest edge of the greater circle.

And then my arms failed, too weak to keep holding me up, and I dropped onto my face on the green crystal.

My body didn't want to do it, but I forced it to extend one arm, slapping my palm down on the stone floor. I dragged myself a few inches closer to the circle's edge. And I did it again. And again. My whole world became that single, driving purpose. Get closer. And closer. While my strength faded.

And then Lara was there, blood slightly too pale to be human on her lower lip, one eye swollen from her impact with the chamber's walls, hauling me up and getting a shoulder under mine.

"What do I do?" she demanded.

"Circle," I gasped. "Get me to it."

Lara dragged me the last six feet without hesitation, and I summoned up enough of my will to slam my hand down across the outside of the circle, shattering its containment.

There was a howl of energy unleashed, a wild torrent of wind. The expensive ritual candles were consumed utterly in a flash of flame that whirled and spilled up into the green crystal ceiling in a column of blazing light, disappearing into the stone with a thunderclap of cracking rock and a rattle of falling bits of broken crystal. The white shape of the demon on one side of the infinity symbol vanished, blurring back toward Thomas's fallen, still form.

I didn't know what was going on anywhere else. I didn't have the energy to care.

"Thomas!" I sputtered.

Lara dragged me to him, set me down briskly but not roughly, flipped my brother onto his back, and felt for a pulse.

"Hunger is back in him, healing," I gasped.

"No pulse," Lara reported harshly. "He isn't breathing."

"Buy him time," I said. "CPR."

Before I'd finished saying it, Lara was checking his airway, tilting back his head, and started going to work on him, pinching his nose shut, sealing her mouth on his, exhaling heavily, then leaning back up and placing the stacked heels of her hands in the center of his chest. She did twenty or thirty solid compressions, then began again at giving him more breath.

CPR is physically demanding to do. Like, really, *really* demanding. You have to be in shape yourself to breathe and pump blood for two. You have to push not quite hard enough to break ribs, but hard enough to compress the heart and lungs beneath them and get blood oxidized and moving. For a minute, then two, then three, Lara kept it up like a machine.

Mab's voice rang from the stone walls, sharp and clear, "Thomas Raith! Choose! Live *for* them or die *with* them!"

Tears started from my brother's eyes.

He didn't move, didn't draw breath, but he could hear. He was exhausted and broken and dying, but he could still hear her.

"Thomas," I said. "It's me, man. It's me." I collapsed beside my brother and forced myself to place my right hand on the crown of his head while Lara kept working. God, I wanted to collapse. I wanted to sleep.

But not yet.

"Thomas," I breathed, gathering up the scraps of my will, focusing them together, reaching out to make the mental connection with my dying brother. "Thomas," I repeated. "Thomas."

I felt a dizzying sensation as I reached out to bridge the space between Thomas's mind and my own and found myself in near darkness, lit from above as if by a single, distant star, upon a surface of cold black stone. Steady, rhythmic thunder came from some unimaginable distance. Then a faint rush of warm wind.

Lara.

Thomas lay beneath me on his back, naked, wracked, withered. Tears streamed from his unfocused, deep blue eyes.

"Harry," he said softly. "I'm so sorry."

"Don't be sorry, man," I said. I knelt next to him, sliding a hand beneath his head and tilting his face toward mine. "Don't be."

"I just wanted to protect her. Protect the baby," he said. "I should have come to you. Now it's too late. Even if we get out of today, Etri will hunt us down."

"Thomas," I said, gently and warmly. "You knob. You sack of blunt instruments. You crayon-chewing pretty boy. Even you can't be airhead enough to think you're the only one in this fight."

I leaned down and put my forehead against his.

"Remember," I breathed.

And I brought up my memories of my brother and me. The first time I'd met him, dressed as a goddamned butterfly. Our time living together in my tiny basement apartment, the frustrations and the laughter and the arguments and the peace. I shared with him my memories of him with Justine, their joy in each other, their quiet love, the peaceful home they shared. I called up my memories of him and me building the Whatsup Dock on Demonreach, listening to an ancient AM/FM radio while eating chips and sandwiches for lunch while we cooled our feet in the waters of Lake Michigan and randomly pushed each other into the water during the labor.

And then I brought out the real magic.

I showed him his courage, his heroism, from my point of view, battling literal forces of darkness with sword and pistol and courage and skill, laughter on his lips and a snarling smile on his face. I showed him what I saw when I looked at him, a man of deep bravery and conviction, who fought demons within and without with equal courage. I showed him his strength, his courage, his kindness to me and to my Maggie. I showed him who he was in my eyes. The one I depended on. The one I could always go to for help. My brother the hero. My brother.

My *brother.*

"Thomas," I said, and the sheer will in my voice made the empty space shake. "This isn't your time. This isn't your place. This isn't your end.

"Get up," I breathed.

He started to twitch, convulse, his chest spasming, spine and abs flexing weakly.

"Get up," I called quietly.

His mouth gaped open and closed again like a landed fish.

Like he was trying to remember how to breathe.

"Get up!" I cried.

There was a sudden rush of wind, then a torrent, then a gale, and I was suddenly back on the floor of the summoning chamber on Demonreach, my hand coming off of Thomas's head as his body arched into a bow and he gasped and thrashed and began dragging in ragged breaths.

"Thomas!" Lara cried.

His eyes flew open, blue, then light blue, then pale grey. His withered skin smoothed. Ragged hair grew lustrous. Pale muscle swelled slightly over his bony frame as he kept breathing, as his Hunger translated the energy I'd fed it into physical restoration. He gasped, still starving-thin, though he looked less like something out of a World War II film, opened his eyes, and looked wildly around, barely strong enough to move his head, trying to focus his gaze.

"Harry?" he gasped. "Lara?"

"Here," we both said at the same time.

Lara's eyes were filled with tears. They spilled down her cheeks. Her voice throbbed with intensity. "You stupid, romantic, ridiculous boy," she said. She cupped his face between her hands. "You scared the hell out of me. You've given me so many headaches. I should strangle you."

And then she leaned down and clasped him close to her, sobbing.

"Wow," Thomas croaked weakly. He lifted an arm and patted Lara's back clumsily. He met my eyes and smiled, mostly with his eyes, as I took his hand. "With family like this, who needs enemies, right?"

I laughed. Harder than I should have. And with the laughter, I felt some of my weariness fall away. I felt strength coming back into me. I felt my chest heave and draw in a deep, clean breath and felt tears blur my eyes for a moment, and then clear my vision.

I put a fist on the ground. Levered a knee under me. Shoved myself up to my feet.

And then I faced the Queens of Winter.

Chapter
Fifty

Mab and Mother Winter both stood facing me, standing between me and the column of true ice that held Justine's bound form. Alfred loomed in the background behind them, his cloak composed once more, green-gold eyes glowing softly within the depths of the hood.

The queens' expressions were unreadable.

Mab looked at Mother Winter and cocked an eyebrow.

The crone's seamed, lined face was axe-shaped, cheekbones standing out starkly from skin that, while wrinkled, in no way looked soft. Like a rhinoceros. Her eyes were pale, pale green, rheumy and piercing. She stared at me for a long, long moment before she said, grudgingly, to Mab, "Tears. Laughter. He's still soft."

Mab's frozen mulberry lips spread into a slow, wide, wide smile. "Give me time."

The crone snorted. "He's far too mortal."

"That shall change," Mab murmured, bouncing the bronze knife against one silk-covered thigh. "By and by."

There was a soft sound of movement, and Thomas, held up by Lara, appeared at my side. He was shaking and could hardly stand. He fixed a sunken, steady gaze on Mab and Mother Winter and said, to me, "Okay. Let's do this. You want the pretty one or the one with the fake teeth?"

"Thomas," Lara said severely. She faced Mab and said, "Please excuse this behavior."

"He but attempts to protect mate and offspring," Mab said. "This behavior is simple but should not be discouraged."

"It was a fake-out," I said. Then I blinked slowly. "You . . . The one thing you can't do is directly kill mortals. That's why you have a Knight."

Mab smirked.

"You lied," I whispered.

"Is that what you think?" Mab replied, lips curling. "You haven't considered the technicalities."

"Technicalities?"

"The woman bears not one but three lives within her at the moment. The child's Hunger, of course—and the entity possessing her. I could have struck at either, and the other lives lost would have been mere . . . What is the mortal phrase?" She smiled more widely. "Collateral damage. The cost of war."

"You . . ." Thomas said and surged forward. Well, he sort of leaned forward. Lara sighed, let him go, and he fell.

"Oops," Lara said wearily. She looked at Thomas and said, "If you'd asked me for help instead of riding off to start a war with Etri on your own, Thomas, none of this might have been necessary." Then she stepped between him and Mab and said, "That said, he's one of mine." She pointed at Justine. "So is she. So is her child. If I'm to be one of yours, I expect your support in helping and protecting them."

Mab lifted her chin, her eyes narrowing. "Do you?"

"It's what I expect of myself. I ask no more of you."

Mab's frosty gaze turned to me. "And you, my Knight? What do you expect of the Queen of Air and Darkness?"

I stepped up beside Lara.

"I expect you to use your reason," I said. "The entire point of signing the White Court on is to build alliances. You can't do that by being an absolute asshat to the people whose support you need."

Mother Winter's gimlet eyes swiveled to me, and her gnarled old fingers rippled along the handle of their cleaver, securing their grip. "An absolute what?"

Mab glanced aside at the crone. "I told you I was willing to tolerate much of his insouciance."

"For this weak, sentimental fool?"

"Do not be deceived by his demeanor as others have," Mab said. "Ethniu lies bound within these very caverns because of him. He has mastered the island yet remains unmoved by its temptations. And already, in his youth, he has overcome the resistance of not one, but *two* Outsiders and bound their allegiance to him while yet he suffers the psychic wounds of bearing a banner of will and leading others to their deaths."

"Ethniu was a spoiled little princess," spat Mother Winter. "And Hungers are among the least of those Outside with whom he must contend. If this is the strongest the mortal world can offer, then perhaps this cycle will be its last."

"Perhaps it will," Mab agreed. "But that is not for you to decide. Nor me." She tilted her head and stared at me unnervingly. "Note that he stands ready to do battle against us both, though he knows it hopeless."

"That merely indicates his stupidity," spat Mother Winter.

"Stupidity," Mab mused. "Courage. The only difference is the outcome."

"Pah," the crone said. She lifted a weathered, age-spotted hand and drew her hood back up over her face. "He comes of a line of thieves."

"But daring ones," Mab mused. "Effective ones."

"Okay," I said, "we're at a point where either one of you needs to talk more about what's coming or both of you need to shut up."

A startled silence fell over both Queens of Winter.

Then Mother Winter hobbled closer. It was a painful-looking movement, as though her back, leg, and hip all put her in agony to walk. She let out a low, growling sound and loomed over me.

"Tell me, young bantam," she said, and her rough voice was very soft, very smooth, something that could haunt a man for a lifetime. "Have you begun to dream the dreams yet?"

"What dr—" I began.

And quicker than thought, she reached out with her open palm and struck my forehead.

It wasn't the force of the blow that knocked me flat. It was a vast, echoing explosion that happened nowhere except between my ears.

Imagine both ears popping, along with your jaw, along with the dizzying sensation you get when you suddenly *stop* spinning around, all happening at once. Now multiply it by several million. I couldn't tell which way was down, even though I could feel the cold, cracked crystal floor of the chamber beneath me.

"*Mother!*" Mab said sharply, though her voice sounded distant and frail. "How *dare* you!"

"The loom does not stop weaving because a single thread feels strain," hissed the crone. Her voice came from somewhere overhead, clear and strong. "The arrow of time flies swift. The hour draws near. Subtlety is a luxury that can no longer be afforded. The ancient ways and ancient drives and ancient pains draw nearer by the hour. And this young thing must be readied for them—or broken, and another weapon chosen."

The gleaming eyes in the recesses of her hood swerved to Thomas and then Lara. "These younger days," she said with contempt. "Our options grow more fragile, more dependent, more helpless with every passing cycle."

Mab's voice turned colder. "Long have you been absent from the mortal world," she snarled. "Long has it been left to my keeping, my wit, my will. This is *my* seat of power. This is *my* responsibility. It is *not* yours and well you know it. Any further interference will result in challenge, crone."

There was a second long silence. And then Mother Winter let out a low, long cackle. "And you," she said. "For all your cleverness, for all your stratagems, for all your webs and plans—do you really think you can challenge *me?*"

Mab lifted her chin.

And then she squared off on Mother Winter.

"*Arise, my Knight,*" called the Queen of Air and Darkness. "*Arise! ARISE!*" She said it in a voice that blew away my disorientation like a dunk in cold water. Ice filled my chest and my guts and my head like the deepest heart of winter, bringing with it the memories of screams of war, of the howls of wolves, of shrieks of pain and bloodlust and battle madness, as if every single fight I'd been through, every victory I'd won, every ounce of struggle and pain and triumph I'd ever felt, had been focused into a single, blindingly intense emotion.

And I came to my feet, teeth clenched, muttering a word that sent my staff hurtling into my hand, ready to throw down with Mother Winter herself.

"Alfred," I growled. "Prepare a cell for our guest."

Demonreach's eyes flared. Again, the ground shook. Chips of fractured crystal fell from the opening in the ceiling.

Mother Winter went completely still.

Lara glanced aside at me, her eyes wide. She glanced down at the fallen Thomas and then back, letting me know her plan: She would get him clear before she came in herself.

I nodded my chin almost imperceptibly.

"Consider where you are," Mab said coldly. "Consider what you face."

The crone's voice came out in a bare whisper. "You would really dare this? Now?"

Mab lifted her chin as the air grew colder and a crown of ice formed upon her head, snow falling from it about her hair and her green gown. "I will do and dare whatever I must to protect this world. From whatever threatens it. Including *you*."

And I stepped up next to Mab. I felt like hell. But I felt even more like kicking someone's ass, and I honestly didn't much care whose it was.

"I'm with you," I said to Mab.

The crone's eyes swiveled toward me. I felt their weight like crushing black rock.

"Have you any idea," she whispered, "what horrors I could summon? What pain I could bring forth? Think you that you have suffered agonies in one little battle? When over the eons I have fought thousands upon thousands, back unto the dawn of Creation itself?"

I started calling Soulfire into my thoughts and will, and the runes in my staff suddenly flared with light, pure light, the echoes of the First Light, when darkness was on the face of the deep.

The crone hissed. She didn't exactly flinch from the light. But she lowered her head until her hood shielded her eyes.

"Everyone talks a big game," I said, "but at some point, I stopped caring how much bigger they are than me. I've been punching out of my weight class my whole life. You wanna go? Here I am. Let's go."

No one moved.

The air crackled with tension.

Then something creepy happened.

Mother Winter started to cackle. It was a dry, raspy sound. The sound of sandpaper on skin. The sound of broken glass scraping away at leather. The sound of dried stalks of grain falling before a scythe. It sent aches, real pain like I was no longer used to feeling, running through my joints and limbs, cramps and arthritis and ague all at once, and I had to fight to stay standing straight.

"Bold," Mother Winter muttered. "Bold."

She turned to Mab and swept into a stiff, somehow mocking bow.

"Perhaps," she croaked, "he will do after all."

And there was a rushing sound as Mother Winter vanished. Just imploded. The air collapsed in on the space where she'd been like thunder, making us all stagger, making my ears pop, and drawing a cold, earthy, uneasy wind down from the tunnels above us leading to the surface, echoing weirdly like the cawing of a thousand crows.

Mab let out a slow exhalation, her breath pluming into the kind of thick condensation you'd normally see from liquid nitrogen. As she did, pain and cold alike faded from my body, leaving only weariness in their place.

"Honestly," Mab said, her voice rather startlingly human. "I don't understand why Mother feels such a need to be so dramatic."

I turned my head to her slowly and started to say something. But I must have been growing as a person or something. Because I took a deep breath instead and shut my mouth.

Lara helped Thomas sit up, rested her forehead briefly against his, and then rose to face Mab and me. She nodded past us, to where Justine was still bound to the column of ice. "Now what?"

The Queen of Air and Darkness's mouth curled up at one corner. "Fear not, Lady Lara. You are quite correct in your assessment of our situation and in demanding your rights and my obligations be respected. Thomas Raith is under my protection from those powers outside our alliance. So is the woman, Justine. As is the child. I will safeguard all of their interests as I would those of my own."

I must be growing even more, because I thought it might be impolitic to point out that Mab's idea of safeguarding her own daughter's interests had included asking me to assassinate her and standing by doing nothing while she died, precisely because Maeve had been compromised by Outsider influence.

But I decided it would be a discussion to have with Lara later.

Thomas was staring at Justine, his expression absolutely ragged with grief and worry.

"That's not her," he said quietly. "That thing. It's still got her."

Mab turned rather sharply to Thomas, an eyebrow raised. "You can sense this? How?"

Thomas glared at Mab and then looked at me.

I nodded to him.

He took a deep breath. "Her . . . her energy. Her energy. I don't know how else to phrase it. I know it. It's part of me. And I can't *feel* her."

Mab made a thoughtful noise, tapping Medea's bodkin against her cheek. "The enemy spirit, then, is suppressing the woman severely. Generally, it prefers to remain a subtle and unsensed influence. Mmmm. It must have known that you sensed a change and was thus forced to move more aggressively. Interesting. A very limited means of forewarning, then. And one fraught with perils of its own. Yet it might be useful . . ."

"What are you going to do to her?" Thomas said.

Mab turned and considered the bound woman.

Justine's dark eyes blazed with fury and something else for which there might not have been a name, and her naked body strained, wiry muscles standing out. There was a groaning sound, followed by several sharp cracklings, and shatter shards spread briefly across the pillar of ice, only to crackle more and vanish as if the ice was healing, seconds later.

Mab's voice snapped with contempt as she spoke to the thing within her. "Thou hast caused me problems enough, twisted little deceiver. Already has Mab vanquished thee once. From thirteen puppets you are now twelve. So it shall be again, and you shall be eleven."

A muffled, raw, hideous sound came from Justine's throat, though she was gagged with ice. Her eyes were wild, so bloodshot that the whites had all but vanished.

"With enough agony, carefully applied," Mab said calmly, "the woman's mind will eventually be unable to contain the spirit." She held up the knife before Justine's eyes. "And the very vessel in which it attempted to enter *my* Court will trap it before it can flee. At which point I will consign it to as much torment and desolation and confinement as *my* imagination can devise." She stepped up close to Justine. "Already you feel the part of you imprisoned, and what it suffers. I will double that and more, thing. You think yourself untouchable. How *dare* you strike at the world in *my* charge?"

Justine again made that raw sound of inhuman fury.

Mab's slow smile was crueler than anything I had ever seen.

And I've seen some things.

"Harry," Thomas said, voice tight, desperate. "She's going to torture Justine."

"Necessary," Mab said, voice hard. "I did it to my own handmaiden. My friend of many centuries. It is the only way." She turned back to us and faced Thomas calmly. "But know this. When it is done, the memory of her torment will be excised. Calmly. Precisely. She will remember nothing of her possession, or her necessary treatment. It will be a door in her mind that is closed, barred, and locked—and which must remain that way to preserve her sanity. You cannot bring it to her mind, by word or deed. She must not dig at the wound or it will once more rip wide open, and she will be torn asunder."

The thing inside Justine screamed in fury again.

Thomas flinched at the sound. "But . . . I . . . how am I going to . . . There is a blood feud with Etri . . ."

Justine—*Justine*; there was a palpable difference in the voice, even to my ears—let out a scream of utter pain, high-pitched and desperately tired. Her body bowed, gravid belly rippling, and a sudden rush of fluid burst into steam in the air.

"Justine!" Thomas cried, suddenly surging to his feet.

"The child comes," Mab said briskly. "As must balance. My Knight, have I your permission to summon aid to this place for the purpose of assisting in a safe birthing?"

And a horrible thought hit me.

The Outsiders had been trying to crack into Demonreach for a while now. I assumed because they wanted to release the horrors that lay imprisoned in its tunnels.

But what if they'd gotten to Mab, the way they had to the Leanansidhe?

What if she was about to trick me into letting more of them in?

Paranoid?

Yes, definitely. But I was up against beings that deserved paranoia. Nemesis was an absolute nightmare of corrupt influence that could be in more than one place at a time, could infest almost anyone.

"Harry?" Thomas asked, his voice desperate.

Oh yeah. This could be a setup.

I felt myself start to panic. To sink back into those dark places where I'd been living the past year.

I began to clench my teeth.

Justine screamed again in pain, her eyes beseeching.

"Harry!" Thomas cried.

I felt a hand on my shoulder.

I turned to see Lara staring at me. Her expression said it all. She didn't understand my hesitation. But she knew it wouldn't be happening without good reason. She gave me a small nod.

I closed my eyes.

I took a slow, deep breath.

Mab was a nightmare herself. The queen of every dark and horrible storybook tale ever told.

But she was Mab. Always and absolutely.

I didn't like her.

But I trusted her.

I respected her.

If Mab had fallen, we were all screwed anyway.

And if I couldn't extend trust for the sake of saving an innocent child and its mother, what was left that was worth fighting for?

"You have my permission to bring needed aid for Justine and the child," I said quietly.

Mab gave me the kind of look that a teacher might reserve for a slow student who had finally begun to show understanding, and I had the uneasy feeling that she was way too aware of everything that had just run through my head.

"Excellent," she said in a crisp tone. Then she drew in her own breath, bowed her head, and murmured, *"Let scales be balanced and life preserved, that infant may wail and justice be served."*

From the same opening torn by Mother Winter came a sudden sigh of wind, and the scent of fresh earth and new grass. Light grew, a sudden shaft of what looked like sunlight, pouring down from above, somehow, through thousands of feet of earth and stone, setting the crystalline chamber aglow, and I had to squint my eyes against the sudden brightness. Music, like the faintest of wind chimes, if the wind had organized itself for a gentle symphony, filled the chamber.

And then my eyes adjusted, and in the center of the shaft of light was a tall, kindly-looking old woman, her silver hair long, her seamed face wrinkled and grandmotherly, her eyes the blue of a clear springtime sky.

Mother Summer. The Crone Queen of her Court.

Mab turned to her and flourished a deep, courtly curtsy.

Mother Summer quirked a small, wary smile and inclined her head in reply. "Winter Queen."

"Mother Summer," Mab said. "I'm sure my mother gave you the details."

"She wrecked the cottage," Mother Summer said mildly, amused, "and threw her cleaver through the window. I haven't seen her that worked up in ages. I think it was probably good for her to finally get out."

Justine screamed again, writhing.

Mother Summer's eyes went to the bound woman with gentle compassion. "Oh. Poor thing. She's in a very bad way."

And then she turned to me. "I am not capable of interfering directly with mortal matters of my own accord, wizard," she said in a gentle voice. "Only mortal will can allow me that freedom of action, and I am a guest in your demesne. It is no small thing to bring a new life into the world. Is this what you wish?"

"Help them," I said gently. "Help them both. Please."

She smiled, beatifically, and it felt like stepping into a beam of warm sunlight after coming out of a plunge into a cold lake.

"So be it," she said.

The delivery didn't take as long as I thought it would. Or maybe I was just so tired that I couldn't keep track. Either way, it didn't seem like very long before Mother Summer, ably assisted by Queen Mab, finished their work. Thomas and Justine's son let out his first thin little wail from the cradle of Mother Summer's arms.

Mother Summer sang gently to the babe, wrapping him up in white cloth drawn from nowhere, smiling benignly down on him.

"May the days of thy childhood be filled with happiness, wisdom, and peace, child," she murmured, and kissed his dark-haired head. She looked up at Mab and said, "Must it now be thus?"

Mab gestured toward the exhausted but still breathing Justine— who slowly lifted her eyes. The pain in them was gone. What was left was cold. Reptilian. A stare of pure hatred.

Nemesis had resumed control.

"There is more work that must be done if her life is to be saved," Mab said quietly. "This is all the kindness that remains to her now."

Mother Summer sighed. "And the child?"

"That was a matter of mortal will," Mab said quietly. "Balance must be restored. Neither of us has power over that."

And Mab held out her arms.

Mother Summer's expression firmed. "A moment. Let him hold his child."

Mab lowered her arms and bowed her head.

My stomach sank.

Because I realized what was coming.

What had to come next.

What I had asked for.

Mother Summer rose, slowly and carefully, looking down upon the child and singing softly to him, and brought him to Thomas.

"I give you this time," Mother Summer said, "to give him your blessing."

Thomas had recovered somewhat in the intervening time. He took the child uncertainly, as if fearing the baby might simply explode if he did something incorrectly. Lara was beside him, showing him how to support the baby's head and body.

Thomas stared down at the child, weeping openly.

"My God," he breathed. "Harry . . . look at him."

He looked like a newborn. His face was all squished, there was some weird stuff on his scalp, his body still wanted to curl, and he looked odd and a little ugly and beautiful beyond the power of words to describe.

And I realized that I had a nephew.

I had more family.

I swallowed a lot. And blinked a lot. I didn't cry, what with how manly I am. But the kid got blurry. Probably some kind of vampire thing.

I put my hand on my brother's shoulder and we just looked down at the kid.

Thomas swallowed. And looked up at Mab.

"I don't get to keep him," he said quietly. "Do I?"

Mab's face . . . couldn't show compassion. But it could have been a lot more remote. "I have been tasked with restoring balance between the White Court and the svartalves," she said quietly. "You have taken a life. You must give one in return. This is the old way."

"I won't let you take him to have Etri harm him," Thomas said.

"I swear this to you," Mab replied, something suspiciously like reassurance in her voice. "He will be raised as one of Etri's own family. As a prince of his people. Treasured and protected and taught their ways. And when it is his time, to deal with his own Hunger, Etri will permit him contact with your House, to be taught what is needed of your ways."

"If the child was . . . with me . . ." Thomas said. "With us. Justine . . . she'd never be able to heal from what has to happen to her."

"Yes," Mab confirmed.

"I'll never be able to talk to her about him," Thomas said. "Never be able to share how much I miss . . . Because it would hurt her, too."

"Yes," Mab said gently. "The pain you have given, coming back unto you. Balance."

Thomas heaved several breaths in and out, shuddering. Ugly crying.

Lara slid her arm around his shoulders and leaned her head on his.

"And you're doing this," Thomas said, voice anguished, "because of Harry."

"I wanted to save you," I said softly. "All of you. From all of it."

Thomas bowed his head over his infant son and shook.

"My son," he breathed in a whisper, gasping between sobs. "I will always love you. And when you need me most, I will be there. I swear it."

A shiver went through me.

Words have power.

Words are magic.

And I felt a tiny shudder of Doom go running over my skin.

"Let it be done swiftly," Mab murmured, holding out her arms. "I have much work to do if I am to save Justine, and it must begin soon."

Thomas curled around the baby for one more moment.

Then, slowly, as if every movement was pain, he held out his arms.

And the Queen of Air and Darkness stole my brother's child.

Chapter
Fifty-One

It had been two weeks since I saved Thomas, Justine, and their son, and I still felt fairly crappy about the whole thing.

I'd taken to doing my meditating out on the roof at sunrise as the spring mornings got warmer. Fitz joined me every morning, as did Mouse on weekends. For Mouse, meditation looked like him curling up in a sunbeam and taking a nap next to me, but he gave off such an aura of peace and contentment when he did it that I figured he had to be helping.

Bear hung around while I did, always wary, never obvious about it. The massive Valkyrie had tried to convince me, at first, that sitting completely still with my eyes closed on a roof when there were a lot of places that I could be shot from was a bad idea, and on a technical level she was absolutely right. But you can't go through life hiding in a cave. You've gotta get out in the sun, or you aren't living. Just surviving.

Anyway. I was just wrapping up and doing a few stretches, not yoga, and Thomas, in a denim jacket, tank top, and workout pants, came out of the doorway to the roof and stepped into the sun, squinting. It was early yet. The protesters and counterprotesters wouldn't start showing up for another half an hour or so. Mouse lifted his head at once and started thumping his tail on the stone floor.

I lurched up from what an ignorant person would have thought was a pigeon pose.

"Hey, guys," I said to Fitz and Bear. "I'll meet you in the kitchen for breakfast."

I'd given Fitz the very brief rundown on Thomas. "That's him, huh?"

"Yeah."

"Cool." He pushed himself up with the lightness and ease of youth and said, to Bear, "You ready to do coffee yet?"

"My God," Bear said. "Why would anyone drink that bitter nonsense when there's already hot chocolate?"

Fitz shook his head grimly as they headed for the stairs. "Damn. Even with the biker boots, sometimes you only rise to cool adjacent, Bear."

"Guess I'll just have to lose a couple seconds' worth of sleep over the lack of your approval, then," Bear said easily.

Thomas frowned after the pair of them and then glanced at me. "Valkyrie?"

"And new apprentice," I said. "So far, Council doesn't know about him."

He shook his head. "Damn. I missed a lot."

"I know how you feel. Exactly."

He considered that for a moment and then grunted. "When you were dead for a while."

"Not much fun, is it?"

"No."

He walked over to me, and then past me, and leaned on one of the crenels and looked out over the city. "Town's all weird now. I went walking."

"Yeah," I said. "After you got, uh, hospitalized, a lot happened."

"Lara's been filling me in," he said, tone still neutral.

He looked a lot better. Like, all the way better. He seemed to have added on his usual effortless muscle tone, and his face was all planes and jawline and perfect cheekbones. His eyes were a deep blue. His hair looked like a magazine cover again. Had any women walked by, they'd have given him extra looks.

But his eyes were just desolate.

"You've been feeding," I said quietly.

He nodded. "Lara's herd has been neglected, apparently. She's been helping me . . . manage my Hunger. But it will take time."

A year ago, that comment probably would have disturbed me. Now I just thought it was probably necessary to keep anyone from dying.

I didn't know if that meant I'd been corrupted on some level or if I'd just learned things. I wondered where the difference between those things lay. If there was a difference. There probably was. Maybe I'd need to be a lot smarter to know exactly where it was. Which meant I should probably be very, very careful.

In this case, it helped me understand my brother and his pain and troubles better.

I'd take it.

"How you handling the change in diet?"

He smiled bleakly. "You've been learning, huh?"

"Yeah. Looks like."

Thomas shook his head. "It's weird. Lara likes classical musicians. I keep finding myself listening to new music. Having a lot of confusing dreams. I don't sleep peacefully anymore. When I sleep."

"Yeah. I know how that one goes, too."

Thomas stiffened and said, "I'm not here for your sympathy."

I was quiet for a moment. Then I said, "Right. Sorry."

"I'm not here for your apologies, either," Thomas said. "When will Justine be back?"

"I don't know," I said.

He turned to me, his face a remote mask. "Not good enough. Not even close."

I spread my hands. "Look. I can guess. But I can't even promise it will be close."

"And you've already done so much," Thomas said, his voice bitter.

I took a deep breath.

I recognized that voice, too. Thomas was hurting. Hurting in ways I didn't know about in addition to some that I did. He'd always had what were probably unconscious issues of self-loathing, about being a vampire, about the lives he'd taken. He was in enough pain that I could cut him some slack. Pretty much whatever slack he needed. He'd probably feel differently over time, as he healed.

"Okay," I said calmly. "Well. When Mab had the Leanansidhe under, uh, treatment, she was missing for a good long while. At the very least a year or two. But it could be longer or shorter than that, based on how fast time was running in Arctis Tor compared to the mortal world. But Lea is also a supernatural being and extremely strong-willed and tough-minded. Disciplined. Trained in sorcery, psychic battle, all kinds of stuff I probably don't even know about. She had mental defenses that had to be broken down over a really long time to kick Nemesis out of her."

Thomas stared at me. "With Justine," he said, "it might not take as long. Is that what you mean?"

"Maybe not," I said, shrugging. "Maybe it will. I don't know. I've tried calling Mab but she isn't answering. I assume she's busy. I don't want to bump her elbow while she's doing psychic surgery."

"She's a monster," Thomas said.

"Yeah."

"She has *Justine*," Thomas snarled.

"Yeah," I said calmly, "and she might be her only hope. I looked for Justine for the whole year, every week, and I couldn't find her. Me. And I'm good at finding people. Lara looked for the whole year, with the whole power of her organization and influence, and she didn't do any better. But Mab found her. Captured her without killing her. Brought your son into the world in good health. And is now working to save Justine. Mab's a monster. But she can do things no one else can do."

"What did it cost?" Thomas demanded.

I told him. About Lara. About the influence Winter now had on her. That I now had on her.

Thomas stared at me for a long moment. Then he said, "Empty fucking night." He swallowed. "If the White Court finds out about this, they'll tear her to pieces fighting for who takes over."

"Then don't tell them," I said.

He bowed his head.

"Harry," he said, "you and I . . . You've made choices for me. For the people I love."

"I know," I said.

"I think . . ." he said slowly, and very quietly, ". . . that . . . it would be best . . . if we didn't speak for a while."

I swallowed.

My chest hurt.

I felt hurt. I felt angry. Stars and stones, I had done my best. I had been falling to bits and had still done my best to do whatever I could. I hadn't been thinking at my clearest, and Mab had taken advantage of that, but I had tried. So hard.

Deep breath.

All of that was true. But right now, it wasn't about me.

Sometimes, when you care about someone, the only thing you can do to help them is give them space. Time. And be ready to talk when they are. Thomas was hurting, lost, disoriented in adjusting to a new life.

I knew how that felt.

And I loved my brother.

I wanted to help him. But you can't help someone who doesn't want it yet.

"I get it," I said quietly. "I see it. When you're ready, I'll be here."

"A lot," he said, bitter again, "will depend on how things turn out. With my son. With Justine. With Lara. With my people."

I braced myself, forced myself to keep my voice as calm and kind as I could. "Thomas," I said. "I did everything I could."

"You sure as hell did, Harry," he said, voice broken.

Then he shook his head and left.

Mouse watched him go and made a soft, mournful sound. Then he rose and padded over to me and leaned against me, laying his head against my stomach, dark eyes looking up at my face.

I put my hand on his head and said, "I know, buddy. I know. He just needs time."

And that was the last I saw of my brother for a while.

Mouse, Bear, Maggie, and I were in the gym. Maggie had begun doing gymnastics when she was small and had kept it up here and there after her original foster family had been massacred and she'd gone on her own healing journey in the Carpenter home. She liked to practice her basic tumbling, and Bear and I often set up the mats for her to work on when she was in on the weekends.

She went by me doing lazy-looking cartwheels. Bear had assured me that making it look that easy meant that my girl had real skill. I was probably feeling irrationally proud of her and figured that I was probably being a good father by doing so.

"So, he didn't even say hello to me while he was here?" Maggie asked, as she went by in circles.

"I know, kid. I'm sorry. Thomas is hurting a lot right now."

"But I made him pancakes," she said. She came to her feet at the far end of the mat and crouched down to sink her hands into Mouse's fur. That was the kind of thing she did when she was feeling her own demons haunting her.

Mouse came up on his forefeet and leaned his giant shaggy head gently on her shoulder, and she put her arms around him.

"I could make him more pancakes?" she asked, without looking up.

"You know what?" I said. "Give him a little time to rest up, and I'll let him know you want to make him pancakes. Maybe you and he can have a nice breakfast morning sometime soon."

She looked back at me uncertainly. "You think he'd like that?"

"Can't think why he wouldn't," I said, more confidently than I felt. "Hey, how is Bonea doing?"

Maggie turned to face me, settling down, though she kept an arm around Mouse. "Oh, you know. She's the smartest person I know and the dumbest person I know at the same time." She frowned. "Is that mean? To say that?"

"Well," I said, "you might be able to phrase it a little less harshly. But I can see how it's basically true. She's still kind of a baby."

"Oh my God." Maggie sighed. "Yeah, she wants little-kid stuff on YouTube, all the time, and then she won't stop asking me questions about why things don't match up to Newtonian physics."

"It's going to take several years for her to start putting things together," I said. "Bob said he was almost forty before he really started understanding the world. But he's over a thousand now, and I gotta be honest, he still only gets so much, you know? It's not his fault. He just has a very different life than someone like you or me."

Maggie frowned. "How?"

"He doesn't have a body," I said. "Doesn't age. Doesn't feel things or experience them the way we do. He doesn't understand as much about pain, or fear, or being tired, or being hungry. He's kind of . . . like Bugs Bunny, you know?"

"Who?" Maggie said.

I sighed and felt old. "A cartoon character whose antics are seen as much less appropriate for children lately."

"Oh right. *What's up, doc?* That guy?"

"That's the one," I said.

She frowned. "So even though Bonea knows everything, she doesn't know anything."

"Exactly," I said. "And it's going to take her a long time to learn. And some things she won't ever get."

"She's a big help when I'm studying sometimes," Maggie said. "Like, she can check my work in a second and a half."

"Sure," I said. "She has access to a lot of information. Just remember that she's unaware of a *lot* of things, too. So the information she does have has to be weighed carefully against what you know, what makes sense, all kinds of stuff like that. Don't rely solely on Bonea, even though she really does want to help, and really does mean well. Look in lots of places. When you look for what's true, the truth tends to line up over and over, and that's a good place to start. After that, it gets a lot dicier."

"That's . . . confusing," Maggie said.

"Welcome to the world, kid," I said gently.

"My teachers just tell me to follow the textbook."

"You're young. That's probably not a bad way to start."

"And it gets less confusing?" she said hopefully.

I thought about that one for a minute. "The confusing part gets less scary," I said. "Mostly, the answer to lots of questions in your life is going to be 'I don't know.' Don't be afraid to say that, ever, especially to yourself. Then you're free to go look for answers. Sometimes they're hard to find. There's a lot of easy answers and they often aren't very good ones. But it's okay to not know things."

Maggie frowned over that for a minute. "Not on exams."

I laughed. "That's just practice for the grown-up stuff. They make it a little easier for you guys."

Maggie blew out a breath from her lower lip, puffing her hair out of her eyes as she eyed me dubiously. Then she said, "Okay."

"How about you, Mouse?" I asked. "You still enjoying school?"

"*Woof,*" Mouse said firmly, thumping his tail on the floor.

"I got him a pencil he can hold in his mouth so he can hit the arrow keys, and he reads books on my laptop," Maggie said proudly. "He's reading Narnia now."

Mouse's tail thumped on the floor eagerly.

Bear suddenly came on alert from where she'd been leaning on the wall, her bulk balanced.

A moment later, Kyle, one of the Knights of the Bean, showed up. Food had become more frequent and of better quality, and the folk in the castle had been looking less scrawny and more leanly healthy. He nodded to Bear as she came to meet him and handed her a square black envelope. Bear took it, sniffed it, shook it while she listened, and then passed a hand over it muttering something.

She scowled down at it suspiciously and then came over to me.

"Kyle says the folks outside are starting to get rowdy," she said quietly. "And a courier delivered this a few minutes ago." She offered me the black envelope.

I took it, frowning. In bright gold ink on the front side, it simply read in a neat, almost artistic hand, *H. Dresden.*

I closed my eyes for a moment, examining it with my supernatural senses, and found nothing. Apparently, it was just paper and ink.

There was a wax seal on the back. I broke it and opened the envelope. Inside was a single black card, unfolded. There was more writing:

It is my sincere hope that you enjoy your evening.

—Drakul

I flipped the card and showed it to Bear.

Her eyes widened, then narrowed.

"A warning," I said.

"Apparently," the Valkyrie agreed.

"How long until sundown?"

Bear drew out a pocket watch, the kind with gears and springs. "Less than half an hour."

I started to snap orders, then took a moment to think.

Then I said, "Maggie, I want you and Mouse downstairs in my old room."

"Dad?" she asked, her tone nervous. "What's going on?"

"Bad guys," I growled.

I'd had a long damned day. And the Winter mantle rose around me like a coat of cold air.

Someone was coming here?

Looking for trouble?

In *my* house?

With *my daughter* here?

"Mouse," I said, voice hard, "raise the alarm. I want all civilians alerted and moved into the lowest level of the castle."

Mouse huffed out a growling affirmation, rising to his feet. He guided Maggie's hand to his collar with gentle teeth and then started trotting for the door.

"Make sure she gets secured," I told Bear, "then arm up and meet me on the roof."

"Got it," Bear said, and stomped rapidly off with Mouse and my daughter. I heard Mouse begin to bark in steady cadence. The Temple dog's power shook the stones of the castle, harmonizing with the energy of the threshold that had been built around the place by a year of weeping, laughing, and living through crisis.

I heard voices being raised as people heard the sound and were drawn out toward it. Bear began shouting instructions.

I closed my eyes for a moment and then called, "Major General?"

There was a zipping sound, then a whipping sound of larger wings, and Major General Toot-Toot Minimus, all three feet of him in his shining new faemetal armor and his dandelion fluff of lavender hair, came soaring into the room, landed in front of me, and saluted. "Reporting for duty!"

I dropped to a knee in front of him. "I need messengers sent out. Tell these people I need them here by sundown, and to come prepared for a fight. Got it?" I fired off a rapid list of names.

"Yes, my lord!" Toot piped, and his dragonfly wings blurred and carried him out of the gym.

"Basil!" I called.

There was a rippling, rumbling sound in one wall, and the large gargoyle appeared, his lion's head in an expression of sudden wariness. "My lord?"

"I'm expecting danger at sundown. Help the residents into the lowest level and position the Knights to guard the stairwell. Shut and bar the gates. After that, I want you and your people ready to rock."

"We are always rock," Basil intoned seriously. But he vanished into the floor as though sinking suddenly into water.

"Bob!" I called.

A bright blue dot appeared on one stone wall of the gym and tracked rapidly around the room to the wall nearest me like someone shining a large laser pointer. "Yeah, boss?"

"You got a handle on the castle's functions now?"

"Uh . . ." he said. "I think?"

"Get them spun up," I snapped.

The spirit had no need to gulp, but he'd learned enough context to make the noise anyway. "Um. Which ones?"

Bad guys coming here.

To my house.

I felt pure rage rising from my bones.

"All of them," I snarled.

Chapter
Fifty-Two

I came out of my upstairs room, ready to go, and almost tripped and fell over Matias.

The middle-aged father blinked as he looked up at me and swallowed. He looked a hell of a lot paler than he usually did, but beneath his greying beard, his jaw was set in determination, and he was carrying one of the shotguns from Marcone's stash during the battle.

His eyes, though. They looked sick with fear.

Not fear of what was in front of him—but what was already behind him. Fear that piles up in your stomach like thick, acidic mucus. Makes you feel sick. Makes you feel weak. Makes you feel like the ghosts of horrible times past are holding a dance party in your guts, all singing at the same time, *It's happening again! It's happening again! IT'S HAPPENING AGAIN!*

With a little help from an allied Sasquatch, I'd bailed Matias and his family out when they'd been attacked by Huntsmen of the Fomorian forces when the battle began. I remembered the howling sound the blasts from their blood-iron spears made. Their animalistic shrieks as they became more and more frenzied. The smell of death and blood and rotten meat on them. The smoke and fire of burning homes.

But by the time I'd met the Huntsmen, they'd been just one more terrifying thing on a long roster of terrifying things I'd run into. And dealt with.

Matias had been dozing off to a late-night cowboy movie while his wife and children slept in the house behind him.

He nodded briskly at me. "Everyone is on the lowest level. The men are all armed, covering the stairwell, with the children and most of the women in the rooms behind them."

"Most?"

He gave me a rather grim smile. "My wife and some others insisted on learning shotgun."

"Any luck, it won't come to that," I said, and started down the hall for the stairway to the roof. "Get down there with them."

I went several steps before he said, "I . . . I can't."

I stopped and turned to face him.

He struggled several times to swallow, and finally did, croaking out, "I can't just hide. Wait. I can't do that."

"Matias," I said quietly. "You wouldn't be hiding. I don't know what's going to happen. If I can't stop whatever is coming, it might be up to you and the others."

He squared his shoulders and faced me, an ordinary-looking, medium-height man in work pants, an A-frame undershirt, and a green and blue flannel overshirt. "I. Can't. Hide." He shook his head. "I have to stand up. You've done much for us. One of us should be here for you."

"This isn't a bar fight," I said quietly. "Things could get bad."

"I have seen bad," he said quietly.

I took a deep breath.

"Yeah," I said. "You have." I looked down for a moment, thinking. Then I nodded. "Your job," I said, "will be to stick by the entrance to the stairs. Be extra eyes for me. If you see trouble I don't, warn me. If you see me go down, get to the basement and warn them that trouble is coming."

"But—"

"I know what I'm doing. I've done it a long time. You haven't. Anything else and you won't be helping. You'll be dividing my attention. You want to help, I'm good with that. But you'll damned well do it in a way that's actually useful or I'll take that gun away from you and stick you in the room with your kids." I let that hang in the air and said, "Clear enough?"

Matias took an unsteady breath. Then his expression firmed and he jerked his head once in a nod.

I went to him and put a hand on his shoulder. "Good man," I said, and tilted my head toward the stairway. "Let's go."

I strode onto the roof wearing my duster and my shield bracelet, carrying my staff in one hand. My newly restored blasting rod hung on its thong inside the duster. My mother's old silver pentacle necklace with its red stone hung outside my black T-shirt, which read, in simple white text across my chest, FIND OUT.

And I was feeling every bit of the shirt.

I hadn't felt like this in a while.

It felt pretty good.

Bear was up on the roof waiting for me. She probably weighed close to four hundred, and she'd gone up and down the stairs, a lot, and faster than I had. She was wearing her biker leathers, a double-bladed axe on a sling over one shoulder, a big-bore revolver on either hip, either .500s or .45-70s, and carried the four-bore rifle in her hand. In addition, she'd added a round-topped Nordic helmet with a nasal guard, evidently held in place by the braid wound about her head beneath it. The skin on the back of her thick neck looked pale, and she turned to regard me coming across the roof and gave me a sudden, wolfish grin.

"Now, there," she said, "is the *seidrmadr* I've heard about." She glanced past me to Matias, who had quietly emerged with his shotgun. Her eyes raked over him once, paused briefly on his face, and then she gave him a short, sharp nod of greeting and approval. He returned it.

"Good man there," she said quietly as I drew close to her. "Fighter."

"His family is behind him," I said.

She looked at me as if I'd said something childishly obvious. "Pshhh. I've been watching battlefields a long time now, wizard. That's why good men fight."

We took a few steps forward and looked over the castle's battlements.

There must have been a thousand people on the street outside the front gates, and they were loud. Chants were going back and forth. Arms were being waved. There was a lot of screaming, a lot of flushed faces, a lot of inappropriate fingers being flown. Phones were being held up everywhere. There were probably three times as many people on the far side of the street as on the near one.

Here and there, there were people trying to talk, remonstrate, hold things back, moderate things. But there weren't enough of them, and over five minutes, the heat went up observably. Some folks started across the street, and it wasn't really clear which side went first, getting in one another's faces.

"This is going to come to blows pretty soon," Bear said calmly.

"Yeah? How do you know?"

"A person is difficult to predict. The more of them there are, the easier it gets," she said. "Most people need to get a little worked up before they're willing to do violence. They're doing that now. This is going in one direction. Only question is how many minutes it will take to get there."

I narrowed my eyes for a moment. Then let them go a little unfocused, sweeping the crowd again, observing. There was plenty of dramatic movement and noise out there.

Very distracting dramatic movement and noise.

So I started looking for the opposite.

And I spotted them. Little islands of stillness. People who were just quietly standing. Not in the back, but in the middle ranks of the crowds in ones and twos. In the rear on the far side, there were several folks who seemed to be just standing and waiting, not really talking, not even looking interested. All of them were wearing backpacks. I mean, most of the crowd were, so that wasn't in itself odd—but every one of the folks in back biding their time had them on.

I had to lean out over the battlements to look down at the sidewalk below. There were some standers there, too, spaced among the crowd, and as I did I felt a surge of fear and anger out of nowhere.

I suppressed it with a deep breath, leaned back, and frowned, thinking. Closed my eyes. Touched my fingers to the spot between and just above my eyebrows and opened my Sight, giving the street below a quick glance.

The fading daylight made it harder, but I could see the energy swirl-ing among the crowd as their fear and anger grew, red and yellow and orange auras dominating—and centered around the standing figures among the crowd, generating that energy like individual campfires, spaced to spread warmth to as many as possible. At the back on the far side of the street, the people standing and waiting in their backpacks were surrounded by a mad swirl of nauseating color, spinning wildly through the spectrum—utter emotional chaos coupled with their abso-lute stillness in a way no normal human mind could bear. And, among the front lines on both sides, I could see auras of gleeful anticipation, rather than fear, around maybe thirty or forty of the participants, some-thing feral and terribly hungry about them.

I dropped back, gasping, fighting my Sight closed again.

"What?" Bear demanded. "What did you see?"

"They're using human shields," I snarled. "House Malvora of the White Court are fear-eaters. They're working the crowd up, feeding on it, pushing more fear. So the mortals are getting angrier and angrier." I fought to keep from throwing up. "And across the street, the ones with the backpacks. I think they're Renfields. Humans the Black Court have made into their puppets. Plus at least forty ghouls starting the ag-gression."

The shadows were stretching longer and longer, their edges getting softer and more nebulous as the sun went down.

"Od's fucking bodkin," Bear swore. "If you attack them—"

"I'll be killing mortals, and the Council will come after me. Assum-ing I survive."

"They'll try to smash their way in with rioters and ghouls," Bear said. "Timing things for sundown, when the Black Court can be their hammer."

I lifted my head and studied the sky for a moment. Considered the setting sun. The distance to Lake Michigan, no longer icy, but still too cold to swim in.

"We've got to get the people clear," I said quietly. "And we've got to do it fast."

The door slammed open and Fitz came running out onto the roof, wearing biker leathers that hung a little loose on him, because they'd been the closest fit we could find. I'd shown him how to enchant protection sigils into the leather over the past several months, when I'd been refreshing the ones on my duster.

"Harry!" he said. "Basil and the other gargoyles are at the gates, freaking out about evil! And they turned the wood to stone! Straight-up rock!" He paused. "I think you're going to need new hinges."

"We'll file that under 'deal with it later,'" I said.

"Where do you want me?"

I wanted him downstairs with the other kids. But that was my feelings talking. Fitz wasn't a child. And he knew enough to be dangerous. "Stick with Matias," I told him, nodding to the older man. "Watch my back."

"Got it," he said, eyes wide.

"Fifteen minutes until sundown," Bear said, eyeing her pocket watch.

I slammed a fist on the battlement, staring down at the crowd.

Someone, maybe one of the ghouls, maybe not, pointed a finger at me and started shouting, and things got a lot worse, quickly. People started shoving. A woman cried out and went down on her back, striking her head.

And a tall, dark-haired man stepped out from between two of the houses across the street. He took off a baseball cap and a pair of sunglasses and swept me a mocking bow.

Lord Raith.

He gave me a smile that a cat might give a mouse caught out on an open floor. Then he vanished between the houses again.

"Hell's bells," I spat. "That's what's been going on. He's been setting this up for months."

"Who?" Bear said.

"Doesn't matter," I said quietly. "Not relevant. What's done is done. Okay. Okay." I swallowed. I checked my staff. I wasn't sure it could bear the kind of energy I'd need to put through it.

So it would have to go through me.

I wasn't sure I could bear the kind of energy I'd need to use, either. But if I didn't, innocent people were going to die.

Time to wizard up.

I walked to the center of the roof and told everyone, "Stay back from me. You don't want to get too close to this."

"Too close to what?" Fitz called.

"The big time," I said, and rapped my staff on the stones of the roof, sending out a burst of my will along with it.

Green-gold light swept out from the end of the staff in a circle, rolling over the barely visible carvings in the stones, picking out a circle of glowing sigils around me that formed into a magic circle almost at once. I could feel the power congeal around me, feel unseen walls snap up in a cylinder above me—and simultaneously thrust down into the castle and the earth below.

The stones beneath my feet began to vibrate.

"Bob," I said quietly.

The spirit of intellect's voice came, conducted through the stone beneath me, up the length of the dense wood grain of my staff, to buzz in my ear. "Yeah, boss?"

"You got those ley lines called up?"

Merlin's fortress, they had called it, this castle. And it had been built not only to shelter and protect, but to channel magical energy as well. Its layered enchantments gave it a metaphysical mass far beyond the weight of mere stone. Magically speaking, it was made of a superdense substance, like the material of a collapsed star.

And like that material, it had its own kind of gravity.

"It's ready to bring them together," Bob said. "But . . . Harry, are you absolutely sure? You haven't worked with stuff this big before. And even though everything seems to check out, they might not have put this place back together just right, you know? When Marcone brought it here?"

"He had a fallen angel whose province is magic advising him when he did," I noted. "Marcone is a lot of things, but one thing he isn't is incompetent."

I took a deep breath.

A month ago, I wouldn't have even considered this, much less actually tried it.

Either I'd been healing . . . or just getting crazier.

Or both. You know.

Things are rarely monolithic.

"Bring it up to power," I said to Bob.

"Got it, boss," Bob said nervously. I supposed I couldn't blame him. Bob was living in the stone of the castle itself now, and I was about to flood that stone with dangerous amounts of energy.

I closed my eyes, shutting out distractions, the shouts from the crowd. Rocks had begun being thrown, judging from the clack of stone on stone coming from the walls at the castle's front. Screams rose, some of fury, some of pain. I shut those out, too, and sent my senses completely into the stone beneath me.

At first, it was like lying in a dark room, cold enough that I'd lost sensation in my arms and legs. I started pushing with my will, like testing the muscles of my fingers and limbs. I breathed in and out slowly, continuing to apply more will against what faced me, sinking my mind into the weave of magical constructs within the stone.

They were old. Stars and stones, I could feel the age bound within the rock, the slow memory of the witness of millennia passing like days. The rock remembered ice covering the earth and retreating over and over. The rock remembered rain that lasted for hundreds of thousands of years. The rock remembered shocks of impact from stone hurtling through the void and the sweeping wind that followed, spinning off in explosions of myriad hurricanes. The rock remembered eons of molten fire and smoke—all primordial forces that regarded mere flecks of organic matter, like me, the way a mortal would note the passing of a speck of dust in a beam of sunlight.

Dimly, back in my physical body, I felt the stone of the castle begin to shake.

Layer upon layer of memory, of enchantment to enhance that memory, began to envelop me, spreading out over me and pressing down with a heavy, even weight, with a terrible gravity that I knew could have ripped my thoughts to pieces if I allowed it, the superdense supernatural energy showing me that the castle itself had gained its own form of slow and obdurate sentience. I kept focusing harder and harder, sinking myself into that gravity, holding my thoughts together.

As Bob began activating the castle's enchantments, that gravity spread out, drawing toward it flowing rivers of natural magical energy in the earth—ley lines—drawing them toward it like a star being drawn into a black hole, like rivers caught in a massive earthquake suddenly forced to a new course.

I planted myself in the rock and stone. Anchored myself in my thoughts, in myself, as that energy coursed over me in a tidal flood of power, because before those forces, I *was* a speck of dust. But I knew *who* I was.

I was a man.

I was a father.

I was a protector.

I was imperfect and flawed.

I was stubborn as hell.

I was a fighter.

I was a helper.

I was someone who worked every day to be a better man than I'd been the day before.

I was someone who would not stand by doing nothing when there was a clear need for action.

I was a wizard.

I was Harry Blackstone Copperfield Dresden.

The enormous power of the energy of conjoined ley lines flowed over me, and I stood before it like a great tree before a flood, balanced and ready, roots sunk deep into the earth beneath me, swaying slightly before the pressure and then stubbornly pushing back.

Power washed through me. Pure power. Power that could bring a forest erupting up through the streets of Chicago. Power that could level it flat. Power that could destroy those who made me afraid. Power that could warp and bend and break reality itself.

Hell's bells.

In that moment, I knew what it was to be a little-G god.

With power like that, there was no place for fear. No place for anger. No place for passion. No place for outrage. No place for desire.

Only focus.

Only balance.

Only restraint.

Only thought.

Only pure will.

This wasn't like when a Titan had tried to crush my mind. This power wasn't being directed and focused upon me with intent. It was simply power, wild and rushing and as primordial as the first day of Creation.

I bent my will to it, not trying to move that power—God, the very thought was so obviously impossible that I'd have been incinerated if I'd tried. I just tried to redirect a tiny portion of it, to guide it around me.

I shaped the channels in my thoughts, years and years of experience in working with spells, with power formulae, with elemental forces, coming together in a whole. I took that fraction of power, focusing upon it with the forces of Winter, and even with my eyes closed, I could suddenly see the burning white light of Soulfire pouring out of the runes of the staff I held in my left hand.

And then I raised my right hand and sent that energy hurtling into the skies above me, calling, *"Ventas tempestas!"* at the top of my lungs.

My voice rang out, far too loud, and I opened my eyes to see blinding energy of many colors come washing up through me from the rune circle beneath my feet and go lashing into the sky. A crash of thunder loud and close enough to shake my chest smashed the air, and over the course of seconds, the water in the air, now being drawn from the icy depths of the lake, condensed into low, thick, angry storm clouds, lit by a continuous rumble of wildly colored lightning.

The storm boiled up out of absolutely nowhere, not a thousand feet above the street, clouds billowing down and closer, continuous thunder growling and echoing like some enormous and furious beast.

I kept my opened right hand over my head, fingers held in a rigid claw, keeping the energy going, containing the energy I'd unleashed through sheer, unbroken concentration.

"Bob!" I screamed over the fury. "Oz me!"

"On it!" Bob chirped through my staff, his voice in a near panic.

And a second later, I felt my perceptions blur, and my perspective shifted. Suddenly, I felt I was floating about twenty feet above the street outside the front of the castle, and my physical eyes could see that only my head was showing up as an enormous image, bigger than ten men, lightning that echoed the storm above flashing in my eyes.

People screamed. They began retreating to either side of the street, looking up at me in sheer terror. Smartphones were exploding into clouds of sparks on every side.

"All right, people!" I shouted, and my voice was louder than the storm. "I tried to share hot chocolate with you! I tried to be nice! And now you're shedding blood in front of my *home*!" The last word boomed out loud enough to crack the glass of windows all around.

"I have had it!" I thundered on. *"Fulmen! Fulmen! Fulmen!"*

And at each word, bolts of lightning crashed down from the storm above, thundered down into the center of the street, driving the two sides back even farther from each other, sending people to the earth, screaming and covering their ears and heads.

"Pluvias!" I screamed.

And rain, rain barely warmer than ice, rain so thick that you'd have to cover your mouth and nose to breathe, crashed down from the skies above. It smashed into the crowds, driving everyone left standing to their knees, crouching to cover their heads and faces.

And the falling water flowed down, water thick enough to melt through magical energy not grounded in the castle's stone, smothering the fires of fear the Malvora vampires were spreading, bringing sudden, cold clarity to everyone being influenced.

"Nonpluvias!" I called. *"Nontempestas!"*

And like that, the rain stopped. The lightning stopped. The thunder stopped.

The silence was deafening.

The giant floating head of me said, in a voice all the more terrible for its softness, "I'm tired of the disturbance to my home. Tired of you making the good people who live here afraid. So unless you want the next communication from any of your insurance companies to include the words *act of God*, I suggest you all leave in peace. While you can."

There was a long moment of stillness.

And then they scattered, running back down the streets, soaked and shaking, shocked and terrified looks on their faces, fleeing for their lives.

I closed my fist, cutting off the energy, sent it back into the conjunction of the river of ley lines beneath me. The vast projection of my head went with it. Spells backed by *that* much energy wouldn't be of any help to what was coming next. The castle was in a residential neighborhood. It would have been like bringing a howitzer to a fistfight.

For the first time, I looked around and saw the pulsing fire of blue and green and gold energy burning from every inscribed rune in the castle. It lit the streets around it for a couple of blocks at least.

I blew out a breath and disentangled myself from the stone and rock of Merlin's fortress, felt the power fade, felt myself returning to my normal self, felt myself become wholly human again. I felt a little tired, but not as much as I'd thought I would. Most of what I'd done had been a matter of concentration, not drawing energy out of myself, out of my own emotions.

I took a deep breath and looked around.

Fitz was staring at me, his face pale, his eyes wide and bright.

Matias looked like he might be in a state of mild shock.

Bear was watching me steadily, her face inscrutable.

I walked over to the battlements and watched people run.

I felt awful.

That I'd scared them that much. Most of them were just folks.

But if I hadn't, they'd have been right in the middle of it.

Because as the regular mortals fled, what remained was a much smaller crowd. They all just stood their ground as their human shields dispersed. Ghouls, whose faces had grown more gaunt and hungrier as the mortals ran and they began to slide into their true forms. Vampires of House Malvora, mostly men and women with various shades of blond hair and the same pale skin of House Raith. The Renfields, standing solidly exactly as they had been, never moving or changing expression in the pounding rain—their permanently damaged minds every bit as locked into obedience by the power of the Black Court as before.

And sundown came. You couldn't see it under the glowering storm clouds, but it isn't a purely physical event. Instead, you could feel it happen, if you were attuned to the energy. You could feel it like a single toll from some vast bell.

Forms appeared in the darkness, five of them, covered in black clothing, cloaks, hoods. Even from there, I could feel the cold, greasy energy around them, familiar from the battle in the graveyard the previous year.

Black Court elders. Drakul's personal guard. The ones who had killed my friends in the Wardens. Wild Bill. Yoshimo. Chandler.

The Renfields let out soft, eerie, sighing moans as their masters appeared.

"Right," I said, quietly, to Bear. "That makes it simpler."

"You ready for this?" Bear asked.

"Yes," I said simply.

And she shot me a sudden, ferocious smile.

Then I raised my voice and called out over the battlements, "Okay, you evil bastards. You wanna start trouble in my home? Come and get some."

Chapter

Fifty-Three

The last time I'd run into the Black Court elders, they'd come at me without a second's thought—just instant attack, with big and bad-ass sorcery. They were beings with centuries and centuries of power and experience and death and terror behind them.

The coterie had killed two of my friends. Wild Bill and Yoshimo. Drakul had done for Chandler personally.

And between Ramirez and me, we'd killed two of theirs. Didn't know their names, because they hadn't taken time for introductions. They hadn't shown me any respect.

This time they did.

One of them stepped forward and lowered its hood. It had been a female at one time, I thought, though mummified corpses reduce gender considerations to a large degree. It was wearing jewelry that looked like it might have been inspired by ancient Egyptian fashion, definitely somewhere in the Middle East, though historically speaking it was likely an affectation, since Drakul had been a late-fourteenth-century type. I dubbed it Cleopatra anyway. They were doubtless in similar shape.

"Okay, Cleo," I said. "What you got?"

The vampire's eyes glittered with pure malevolence and she raised her right hand, sending a bolt of white-hot flame scorching straight at me.

I narrowed my eyes, focused my will upon the castle's defenses, and otherwise didn't move a single muscle.

The fire streaked toward me—and stopped cold at the line of the battlements. The runes and sigils there burned brightly for a moment, and a faint impression of a wall of blue light appeared in the air between us, immaterial as a phantom and very much real enough to stop the hostile magic in its tracks. The stones of Merlin's fortress absorbed the energy as easily as they stopped the wind.

Cleo lowered its hand, black eyes narrowing. Then it spoke, and its voice was as charming as sandpaper on rusted steel. "Malvora."

I started to say something, and Bear grabbed my collar and jerked me back as a gunshot rang out. I had the flash impression of one of the Malvora moving swiftly, hand extending bearing a long-barreled pistol. Something hissed past my face, close enough to stir some of my hair as I dropped back.

Merlin's fortress had been designed to be impregnable to supernatural forces. Modern firearms hadn't really been a factor in its engineering, and while the stone was damned near impregnable, especially while charged with power like it was at the moment, I couldn't use it to stop bullets from zipping through the air.

"Cover the roof!" someone shouted, and gunfire started ringing out. Bullets zinged through the air and sparked on the castle's stones.

"Get down!" I shouted to Matias and Fitz. The pair of them hadn't reacted as swiftly as they should have, but then they weren't in any direct lines of fire. I was just worried about fragments and weird ricochets. They dropped to a crouch.

Cleo's voice rasped over the gunfire as she shouted, "Forward!"

"Major General!" I shouted.

Toot-Toot came streaking out of the darkness in a sphere of violet light, bobbing and weaving madly through the air, surrounded by a whirling, dizzying cloud of Little Folk in their own spheres. "My lord!" he piped.

"Report!"

"Half the ghouls circle the castle to come from the rear!" he said. "Some of the scary vampires are going with them! The walking corpses send their slaves at the front gates!"

I glanced at Bear. "Explosives, you think?"

"What I would do," Bear confirmed.

"Tell Basil and his people to get back from the entry gate," I snapped to Toot. "Hold them at the inner door."

"My lord!" Toot whistled, pointed, and several of the Little Folk zipped off into the castle, staying low.

"Bob!" I called.

Blue light whirled across the rooftop as the spirit of intellect sped through the enchanted stone of the castle to appear at my side like the splash of an immaterial flashlight. "Here!"

"Show me what's going on," I said, and placed a hand flat to the stone.

There was a dizzying sensation, and my eyes burned as if I were walking through a pall of smoke and began to water. I squinted through it—and could suddenly see *through* the stone of the castle as if it had become as clear as glass.

Toot's report was accurate. Maybe half the ghouls had peeled off to circle to the rear of the castle, and several Malvora vampires, armed with concealable firearms, had gone with them. There was a back door there, but it was built out of the same stone as the rest of the castle, sealed into place with enchantments that made it damned near as tough as the walls around it, and would be too heavily fortified to open without a serious amount of explosives, which they did not appear to have. That crew would have to climb to the roof and try to win entry to the castle from up here. It would take them a moment to get into position, so they were the secondary problem.

At the front gates, seven or eight Renfields were approaching. The gargoyles had indeed transformed the wooden front gate of the castle to a single slab of thick stone that still bore the wood-grain marks of the gate, filling the open area and flush against the castle stone, ruined steel hinges bent and torn. Interestingly, from an academic standpoint, I couldn't see through the newly transformed stone—but I had a good angle from up here and could clearly see the Renfields shuffling forward and dumping their backpacks on the ground in front of the gates.

The ghouls and Malvora in front of the castle had proceeded to the walls, keeping well clear of either side of the gate. The Malvora kept up a suppressive level of gunfire on the battlements, preventing me from standing up and throwing my usual stuff or return gunfire at them. Meanwhile, the Black Court had withdrawn several paces, to the yards on the far side of the street, unnaturally still shadows in their black shrouds, to wait for what came next.

I reported to Bear what I saw as I saw it.

"They're trying to coordinate it," Bear said, as if we were eating sandwiches after pankration practice instead of lying on the stone with bullets going by a foot and a half over our heads. "They'll blow the gate. Black Court goes in on the ground floor. Ghouls and Malvora will come up the walls and come in from the roof, all at once."

"This plan seem kind of simple to you?"

"Simple's good," Bear said. "Less to go wrong. They were counting on having a lot of screaming mortals around to cover them, too."

"Probably work," I admitted, "if I hadn't had warning and it was just me. Major General," I said, "who could make it in time?"

He told me.

"No kidding?" I said. "Where?"

"A block to the north, my lord," he piped.

"Get over to them. Tell them to come in as soon as they hear the front gate go," I said.

"My lord!" Toot snapped and zipped away like an arrow from a bow.

I waved at Fitz and Matias and shouted to them, "There's going to be an explosion! We're going down the stairs not long after! Get into the doorway and hold the stairs!"

Fitz shouted something mostly lost in the gunfire, but Matias, flinching as a ricochet went somewhere near him, held up his thumb in acknowledgment.

"Bob," I said, "I want the energy from the blast contained to just the gates. Absorb as much of it as you can."

"Uh," Bob said. "If I do that, the gates are going to come down."

"That's the idea," I said. "Get to it."

"Will do, boss!" Bob said, and the blue light zipped off through the transparent stone of the castle. As he did, the stone became real and opaque again, and my eyes stopped burning.

Bear was frowning at me. "You want them inside."

"Come on," I said. "They're Black Court. Why do you think I invited them in? 'Come and get some' wasn't an accident."

Bear's frown turned into a fierce grin. "You think you can handle them?"

"Time I get done with them, we'll need a lot of mops," I said darkly. "This is *my* house."

She nodded, understanding. "You want to handle the lightweights first."

"Yep. Scatter the riffraff, then I'll deal with the rest in the main hall."

Bear reached up over her shoulder to flick a snap on her leather strap and take her double-bladed axe down, setting it near at hand. "Sounds fun."

Someone shouted something below. The gunfire abruptly stopped, and I slammed my hands over my ears and opened my mouth. Bear mirrored me.

There was a sound so big that it blew back the branches from the trees across the street, shattered the windows of houses and parked cars, and made everything lighter for a second, as if a wave had come along and lifted me a little up off the stones of the roof. The runes of the castle flared painfully bright. It was followed by the sound of stones rattling, smaller rocks bouncing against enchanted stone, and a cloud of dust and powder billowed out from the front of the castle, filling the already misty air. The resulting mixture condensed almost instantly into a kind of mucky, grimy rain.

Then there was a single, rasping, inhuman howl, instantly echoed by dozens of yowling ghoul battle cries, and my enemies came for me.

Chapter
Fifty-Four

Ghouls are athletic and powerful and tough, but they don't have the kind of strength and grace that allows them a thirty-foot vertical leap.

Freshly fed Malvora vampires do. These had been feeding on the various protesters for hours, and they bounded up through the air with grace and style, all pale skin and blond hair and glittering eyes in the arcane light of the castle's glowing runes, coming from the front and back of the rooftop at more or less the same time.

I'd already gathered my will, and the second I saw the first of them appear, I rose, shield bracelet charged and ready, left arm bearing both the bracelet and my staff held in front of me as I drew back my right hand and flung it forward as if hurling a stone, screaming, *"Ventas servitas!"*

Wind howled forth at my will, swatting Malvora out of the air and driving them back from the castle's walls into wild, tumbling falls. I kept my hand extended, sweeping them back like leaves before a heavy-duty blower.

White Court vampires are faster than striking snakes, and some of them got off shots at me before I could, literally, blow them away. At one point in my career, holding a shield and a wind evocation at the same time would have been a challenge. At one point *this year*, it would have been impossible. If they'd come a month sooner, things might have gone a lot differently.

But I'd just needed time.

And work.

And rest.

And friends.

Healing isn't the work of a moment. I still had a way to go.

But I was better now.

More than that, I'd been teaching.

I was *better* now.

My shield rippled with blue-green light as bullets hit it, and I tried to hold it angled so the shots would reflect as directly upward as possible. Any projectile can be pulled down by gravity, but a lead hailstone was way less dangerous and less likely to harm bystanders than a bullet bouncing directly into a home. I held the shield, focused the wind like a vast broom, and sent Malvora vampires flying.

I could have used fire but, you know. Alliance with Lara's Court and all. It would probably be less of a headache for her in the aftermath if I didn't slaughter them wholesale.

"Watch your six!" Bear snapped.

Someone hit me in the lower back with a heavy stick, maybe a .45 round slamming into my spell-armored leather duster. I sucked in a breath, staggered, but kept the wind spell going, spinning to begin sweeping the back side of the castle of incoming Malvora—but like I said, White Court vamps are fast as hell. Another shot hit my duster over my left thigh before I could get started, and in my peripheral vision I saw half a dozen vampires come sailing up, weapons training on me.

Bear stepped in front of me like a human wall, dropping the four-bore and going for her pistols like an old west gunfighter. I heard her guns speaking and a series of heavy slapping sounds as rounds intended for me struck her instead. She sucked in a breath, staggering, and went to one knee, but kept shooting.

"*Fiero, fiero, fiero!*" Fitz shrieked, and blazing bolts of white-hot flame leapt out of the doorway to the stairway down to the third floor of the castle, adding his fire to Bear's. High-pitched shrieks went up from the Malvora. Four of the vampires buckled and staggered when hit by Bear's heavy rounds. Two of them just went up in flames and dove back off the roof, shrieking.

And then the first of the ghouls arrived, clawing its way up the exterior of the castle and hauling itself into the crenel between two merlons and leaping toward me. It had transformed fully, muzzle extended, lips peeled back from rotten-looking fangs, yellow eyes glaring, its skin grey and covered in spiky hairs. The clothing the thing had worn over its upper body hung around its torso in tatters. Its forearms were unnaturally long, its back hunched and powerful, and gangrenous claws extended from its fingertips.

A shotgun boomed, pellets smacking into the low center of the ghoul's chest, staggering it, and buying me a critical second or two.

I don't know if I've made mention of how much I dislike ghouls.

I dropped the wind spell, drew my blasting rod, pointed it at the thing, sent a fraction of my anger coursing down my right arm, and snarled, *"Fuego!"*

The blasting rod flooded with golden light, and a blue-white bolt of something a couple of steps beyond fire slammed into its gaping mouth. The ghoul didn't catch fire so much as its head instantly superheated and exploded like a kernel of gory popcorn. The ghoul crashed to the floor amid glowing runes and sigils, spewing dark, watery blood like the juice from a crushed cockroach, arms and legs still thrashing wildly and randomly, its body having been relieved of its brain so that it couldn't know it was already dead.

More ghouls began to clamber up through the battlements.

Bear's guns clicked empty behind me.

"Fiero!" came Fitz's voice, gasping, sending another, redder bolt of fire at a Malvora, who fell back over the edge of the rooftop to avoid it. Then he gasped, *"Fiero!"* again and nothing much happened.

The kid had talent, but it would take him time to get the kind of sand in his craw that a seasoned battle wizard had earned.

"Stairs!" I said. "Now!"

Bear groaned and staggered to her feet, almost falling. Blood was coming from her mouth, though she was grinning a wide scarlet grin. "One of them had armor-piercing rounds," she gasped. "Had to take them."

"Cheating vampires," I muttered. I got a shoulder under one of her arms and half dragged her with me to the stairway. Matias emerged from the stairs, pumping the shotgun, and fired three times at the nearest ghouls to cover us, his expression focused, impassive, and grim.

"Help Bear down!" I shouted to him and Fitz. The kid was gasping with the efforts of his evocations, but he rose to try to support Bear. The two of them nearly fell down the stairs. Matias, sturdier by several degrees than the kid, less exhausted, and with a lifetime of work behind him, nudged Fitz aside and got into a more leveraged position.

"¡Uno, dos, tres!" he shouted, and on three, he grunted as they went down a stair. "¡Uno, dos, tres!" he called again, and they went down another stair.

I whirled at the top of the staircase.

I found myself facing a dozen ghouls, with more on the way.

And Lara Raith, in close-fit white clothing, came arcing up through the air at the far end of the rooftop, behind the ghouls, bearing a slim, wavy-bladed short sword in either hand. She landed on a merlon in utter silence, a wide, predatory smile curling her lips.

And as she did, the sweet, ringing notes of a shofar soared through the night from somewhere down at street level.

Ghouls screamed, loud and high-pitched like panicked pigs, and clutched at their ears, and I saw two still climbing up who simply fell from the walls, half paralyzed. Others on the way up must have been falling, too.

And two inhumanly loud, bestial voices rose in shrieks of fear and fury and agony down on the street.

Lara's face twisted into a snarl as the sound of the horn washed over her, but it didn't slow her down. She blurred into motion and hit the stunned ghouls from behind, blades flashing. She went for spines and necks, single, supernaturally powerful slashes, and the wavy blades carved their way through bone and flesh like cutting through so much Jell-O. Green-brown-black ghoul gore swept out in smooth arcs.

I brought my blasting rod up, sent a pair of ghouls to the stones, burning and yowling, and by the time I got to the third one, I had to snap the blasting rod up because Lara had gone through the rest and was close enough to catch some of the thermal bloom.

Lara's pale blue eyes were bright as she flashed me a sharp, hard smile. "Fiancé mine," she said. "I hope I'm not late."

"Right on time," I said. I looked at the luckier ghouls, the ones who still had heads. They didn't have the use of their legs and were dragging themselves toward the battlements, ready to face a thirty-foot fall onto concrete rather than remain on the roof with Lara and me.

I saw no reason to allow them to continue drawing breath.

I raised my blasting rod.

Lara's cool hand touched mine, pressing very gently down. "No, wizard. As a favor to me."

I looked sharply at her.

Lara watched the ghouls with cool, calculating eyes. Stray lightning in the storm I'd summoned flickered in the clouds overhead, vague light and rumbling sound, sending shadows dancing oddly across her face. "The fight is out of them. Let them spread word of how they were received here. And of how the Malvora abandoned them to their fate. It will give my cousins in Malvora fewer potential allies and cat's-paws in the future and make my life somewhat easier."

I stared hard at her and then drew in a breath and nodded. "Fine," I said. Then, after a moment: "Thank you."

She took her hand off mine and inclined her head slightly. Then I strode to the battlements to look down at the street in front of the castle.

My allies had arrived.

Waldo Butters, Knight of the Cross, was walking steadily down the street, *Fidelacchius* drawn and in his hand. The glowing blade of the Sword of Faith shone with pure white light, the faint sound of an unseen chorus intoning chords of calm and perfect purity emanating from it, as though the blade itself was a slender opening to a realm of penultimate light. He wore mail beneath the white surcoat of the Knights of the Cross, complete with a red cross over his heart and sports goggles in place of glasses, and the look on his face was grim.

On either side of him marched Daniel Carpenter and Father Forthill. Both of them held up crucifixes before them, and the holy symbols glowed with the silver fire of faith.

Behind them and on their flanks came the forms of Will and the Alphas, four timber wolves in variegated grey and brown fur. They stalked forward with steady purpose, focused, fangs showing, low growls rumbling in their chests.

"My people went in on the other side of the castle," Lara said quietly. "My sisters, Freydis, and Gard."

"I was surprised to hear about Gard," I said. "What's Marcone's bodyguard doing here?"

"Representing his displeasure at the presence of belligerents in his territory," Lara said. "Besides. Valkyries get annoyed when they aren't allowed to take the field from time to time."

We were in time to see the last of the Malvora fleeing, vanishing into the fog and mist. The ghouls were running—or dragging themselves away—as well. They knew better than to try to stand in a fight where a hostile force had arrived on their flank by surprise.

They were being hurried on their way by the angry hornet buzzing of hundreds of the Little Folk, striking them with straight pins and X-Acto knives and razor blades, mostly at faces and eyes. I saw Major General Toot-Toot soaring in among them, directing organized swarms of Little Folk with waves of his sword and shouted commands.

The pixies rarely showed themselves in battle, but when they did, they played hard. Though the ghouls were too resilient to be easily brought down by their little weapons, they still inflicted pain, and the flashing spheres of light swooping everywhere induced confusion, keeping the ghouls from gathering their wits into any kind of organized resistance, turning a retreat into an absolute rout.

Except for the two Black Court vampires and half a dozen Renfields that stood their ground.

One of the Black Court still had its hood covering its face. The other was Cleo. Cleo had one of her arms raised against the light of the Sword of Faith and the glowing crucifixes on either side of it, as though the light burned her eyes unbearably.

As Butters and company approached, Cleo pointed her other hand and screamed, "Kill them!"

The Renfields lunged forward. Renfields are just regular mortals, but they don't feel much in the way of fear and they will keep trying to carry out their orders as long as they're still capable of moving.

There was a blur in the air, and Carlos Ramirez emerged from behind a veil of magical energy off to one side, unseen until that moment. He wasn't wearing his Warden's cloak, though he bore his enchanted Warden's blade in his hand, and I didn't need my Sight to know what he was about to do.

The Wardens' blades were made to cut through enchantment and disrupt magic, and Carlos did a smooth step and sweep with the sword, speaking a single word, and sent a wave of disruptive energy through the air, across the Renfields at more or less head level. The Renfields' minds had been badly disrupted by hostile psychomancy, courtesy of the Black Court, and that disruption had effectively made them into puppets.

Ramirez had just cut the strings.

The Renfields collapsed as a single body, falling limply to the ground, immobile, their expressions confused, eyes open and staring and unfocused.

Cleo shrieked and spun toward Ramirez, unleashing a bolt of white-hot flame from one hand. Carlos, smiling grimly, whirled his rapier in a tight circular parry, caught the flame on its blade, and promptly sent it hurtling back into Cleo like a miniature comet—which is why sorcerers, even very powerful, very experienced ones, hadn't ought to square off on wizards.

The fire smashed into Cleo. The rain I'd called down had soaked her shrouds, and a cloud of steam burst out of her as fire met water. Cleo shrieked, reeling back. Black Court vampires are pretty close to physically indestructible, but heat gets to their eyes, and hers had just been boiled.

Ramirez flicked his sword to his other hand, his expression furious, and threw out his right forefinger, barking another word, and a pale blue beam flashed out toward Cleo, striking her center mass—and simply melted a hole in her as shroud and undead flesh alike fell apart into their component elements. Carlos let out a cry of pure rage, walking forward, dragging the beam across more and more of the vampire's body, melting more and more of it into dust that quickly became a slurry in the misty air, until all that was left was a withered head—eyes burst, mouth gaping, jaws trying to mouth something.

Carlos spat on the head and said, "For my friends."

Then he disintegrated the head, too.

And lifted a murderous gaze to the last vampire there.

The other withdrew a pace at a time as Carlos kept moving forward, and her hood fell back.

It was Mavra. Black Court vampire of old acquaintance. And she was smiling.

She let out a delighted cackle and blurred into motion, avoiding another disintegration beam from Ramirez, and vanished into the mist, leaving only an echo of her rasping laughter behind.

Ramirez looked up at me and nodded, pointing his sword at what was left of the front gates. "Three more!"

"Make sure she doesn't come back!" I said, pointing after Mavra. "I got them."

Then I turned and swept down the stairs.

I got to the bottom of the stairs, rushed down the long hallway to the next set, and went down them. I passed an exhausted Fitz and Matias along the way. Bear was with them, face red, covered in sweat, breathing like a steam engine, but she shoved herself to her feet as if she hadn't been shot several times a few moments before, took Matias's shotgun with a nod, and came lumbering along behind us.

We went down the stairs by the gym into the great hall and found it full of thunder and fury.

The gargoyles had gathered by the entry door. Cinnamon was lying in a heap—a literal heap of broken stone—against the back wall, and as I watched I saw Basil in the doorway, wrestling a Black Court vampire and being forced slowly inward, his lion's face set in an expression of noble determination. Sage tried to step in, only to be struck by a bolt of lightning that snaked through the doorway, driving him back several paces, and a second vampire added its power to the one struggling with Basil, driving the gargoyle back. The others closed in, but they weren't as physically powerful as Basil. Lightning struck again and again, and the third vampire shoved its way in through the doorway.

Excellent. They were all inside.

"Boys!" I snarled. "Get out of the way!"

The gargoyles flew back and away from the entry door, vanishing into the walls, the floor, as though the stone had been no more substantial than water.

I slammed my open right hand against the wall of Merlin's fortress as the three corpses whirled toward me, reorienting after the sudden absence of resistance. There was an instant of frozen silence.

"You should have come on a school night," I said harshly.

And then, at my will, the enchanted, obdurate stone of the second floor, that entire portion of the second floor, tons and tons and tons of rune-etched rock, slammed down more swiftly than a blinking eyelid, like a vast and ancient sledgehammer coming down on three doomed cockroaches.

It was messy as hell.

Black ichor, thick and sticky as tar, sprayed everywhere in a fine mist.

And that was that.

Cleanup was gonna take a lot of mops.

It cost me about five minutes of pure mental effort and some of Bob's help to get the stones of the second floor over the entry to the main hall put back. The heavy enchanted stone drifted slowly up into the air and locked back into place as securely as ever. We'd have to reseal it, but I was pretty sure Michael and I could manage it on our own with maybe a long day's work.

Lara and her folk didn't come inside, but I made something of a show of going out to them outside the gates, after the fighting was done, the enemy in full retreat, and thanking her in front of her family members. Lara's sisters took the mind-melted Renfields with them, and I didn't argue. Once the Black Court got done using their butcher-shop psychomancy on mortals, the victims weren't coming back. Wizards way better than me had tried to help such victims in the past and failed. And if Ramirez hadn't done what he'd done to them, they'd have thrown themselves after their fallen masters in psychotic rages. Unless we'd lost, I supposed, in which case the Black Court would have devoured them before moving on—the usual doom of Renfields.

The White Court's version of hospice care would be kinder than any other fate awaiting them.

Once Toot's scouts reported that the enemy truly was gone, we brought the residents back up from the basement. Maggie came pelting up the stairs alongside Mouse, flung herself at me, and proceeded to climb me until she had her skinny arms around my neck.

I spent a while hugging her while Mouse pranced happily around us, making huffing sounds of pleasure.

"That was so *loud*," Maggie said. "I was scared."

"Me, too, punkin," I said quietly.

"You got the bad guys?" she asked.

"They came to mess with my little girl," I told her. "Wasn't even close."

"Did you cheat?" she asked.

"As much as possible," I said.

"Good," she replied, and squeezed extra tight.

"Urk," I said. "Ack."

She giggled but loosened her grip, and I hugged her some more.

I saw Matias doing exactly the same thing with his wife and kids. We looked at each other, nodded, and went back to our families.

"Fitz!" Maggie cried out as my apprentice walked wearily over to me, while Bear lumbered along behind him. Maggie let go of me with one arm long enough to give him a high five.

"Hey, kid," Fitz said to Maggie, grinning. "Harry. I'm sorry. I didn't last very long."

I shifted Maggie over to one arm and clasped hands with the young man. "You did just fine," I said. "First fight, you kept it together, only hit the bad guys, and helped out when I really needed it. You survived. That means you won."

"Wasn't like I called down a thunderstorm or anything," Fitz said.

Bear burst out in a laugh. She was still flushed and covered in sweat and she looked as if she'd lost ten pounds, but she was moving without pain. "The *seidrmadr*'s been doing this his whole life. He hasn't even been teaching you for a year yet. Give him a break."

Fitz flushed and looked a little embarrassed.

I put my hand on his shoulder. "You made enemies today, kid. Those Malvora you burned. They aren't going to forget it."

Fitz's face darkened slightly. "Then they shouldn't have come to my home looking for trouble, should they? And if they come back, maybe I won't be so nice."

"My man," I said approvingly. He held up his fist, and we bumped knuckles firmly.

Basil and the gargoyles came out of the walls and floor in the aftermath, gathering around little Cinnamon. The monkey-cat little guy was in half a dozen broken pieces, where one of the Black Court had flung him into the castle's wall.

"Mmmm," Basil said, as I approached, still carrying Maggie. "My lord."

"Uh," I said. "Is he . . ."

"He is but injured," Basil intoned seriously. "This isn't too bad, my lord. With your permission, we will gather materials to mend him. There are many mounds of rubble in the city nearby where it can be done."

"Go and be back before dawn," I said. "Should be foggy tonight."

"My lord," Basil said, bowing his head. The gargoyles carefully gathered up Cinnamon's pieces and vanished into the walls.

Ramirez came walking in the front door with Butters and Daniel and the werewolves, still in animal form. Father Forthill and Rabbi Aaronson were with them. The rabbi wore the shofar on a baldric of colorfully woven cloth.

"Rabbi," I said brightly. "I didn't see you during the action."

"Because I'm too old to be fighting," said the elderly man brightly, "and I am not so much a fool as the Catholic, and blowing the horn once was enough work for one night, I think."

"Daniel," I said to the younger man, offering my hand. He shook it, grinning. "Thank you for showing up. Again."

"Glad to, Harry," he said.

Butters grinned and shook my hand as well, and gestured at Ramirez. "I kind of like being the distraction," he said. "Way less cardio involved."

Ramirez smiled. "I haven't really gotten to work with one of the Knights of the Sword before. It was a pleasure, Sir Waldo."

Mouse barked happily and bounded up to Will and the Alphas. There were a great many wagging tails and sniffing noses and canine noises.

"Will," I called. "War council in the gym in ten, okay? See if you can catch Lara before she leaves? I want her in on it. Ask her if she will."

The most muscular of the wolves nodded to me, an eerily out-of-place motion on the lupine form, and ghosted outside.

"You gotta talk to people?" Maggie asked.

"Yeah." I sighed. "You know. Wizard stuff. Sort things out."

"Can we do a movie night after?"

"I'd be a fool to turn down an offer like that," I said.

We gathered in the gym. Me, Lara, Ramirez, Forthill, Will (wearing a bathrobe and carrying a notepad), and Butters. Bear was hanging out nearby with Freydis, who looked more relaxed than I'd ever seen her.

"A helicopter," Lara was telling Butters. "It dropped us off in a park about three miles from here and we ran the rest of the way. My security people followed in cars and they'll take us home. How did you get here in half an hour?"

"We happened to be about a mile off at a B-dubs to watch the fights," Butters said. "Sometimes things just work out."

"You don't really think that, do you?" Lara said, smiling.

Butters grinned. "No, ma'am. Hey, isn't there supposed to be a wedding? How come I haven't gotten my invitation?"

Lara glanced at me. "I spoke with Mab about that. We agreed midwinter would be a better date symbolically. I suppose we'll do invites at the end of the summer."

News to me. But Mab had gotten what she wanted. She tended to be less utterly unyielding once that had happened. "Okay, okay," I said. "Social hour can continue after." I went around and made the introductions, just to be sure everyone knew who everyone else was.

"I thought the White Council wasn't on good terms with you anymore," Lara said, arching an eyebrow at Ramirez.

"I'm not here," he answered calmly. "And I'll be able to prove it later."

"You know," Lara said to me, "I've always liked him."

"I want to figure out what happened," I said to everyone. "I only saw the fight at the front of the castle and up on the roof. What happened back at the rear?"

Freydis raised her hand. "Me and Gard and the goth girls took it to the ghouls and the Malvora. Ghouls put up a pretty good fight. Malvora are a bunch of cowards. Started running the second blood started hitting the ground. Gard says hello, by the way, Dresden. Says to tell you not to think she was there because Marcone likes you."

"Oh no," I said in a dull tone. "Not that. What do we need to be worried about here?"

"How many injured do you have?" Lara asked at once.

"Uh . . ." I scratched at my head. "Bear, you okay?"

Bear shrugged. "Mostly I'd say I'm better than just okay."

"One of the gargoyles got busted up," I said. "Basil says they'll fix him up in a couple of days. What about your people?"

"Two of my sisters were wounded," Lara said. "They'll be more cautious in the future."

Will, who had been ready to start writing things down, said, "That's it?"

I looked around the room and said, cautiously, "Yes."

"Thank God." Forthill sighed.

"A coterie of Black Court ancients," Ramirez mused. "Several dozen White Court with small arms. Fifty or so ghouls. And no one died."

"We had early warning," I said quietly. I took the black envelope out of my pocket and held it up. "If we hadn't, we'd have had a massacre on our hands. Our dead hands."

"May I?" Lara asked. I passed it to her. She opened it and read the note from Drakul, frowning, then passed it down to Ramirez. Everyone looked at it.

"I don't understand," Forthill said quietly. "Why would Drakul do that? It ensured that his forces took total losses."

"Not total," I said quietly. "Mavra got away. She seemed pleased by it all."

Ramirez made a growling sound. "Why does she keep surviving?"

"Because she's intelligent," Lara said calmly. "And she learns from her mistakes. That is what survivors do."

"Which is what we're trying to do right now," I said. "This whole night was one piece of paper away from being a disaster. I don't want to sit here fat and happy and think because the fight went well that it means we're invincible."

"Without casting any accusations," Forthill said delicately, "I feel I must point out that there was a significant presence of Lady Lara's people involved in the attack."

"They are my people," Lara said forthrightly. "If only barely. I knew they were plotting but I didn't know what they had in mind, specifically. In my defense, in the past my intelligence about the other Houses has been a great deal more precise."

"Maybe," I suggested, "they had help from inside Raith."

Lara looked at me and met my eyes for a moment. I could see the calculation happening there. It took her almost an entire second to get it.

"Oh," she said in a flat, unamused voice. "Really."

This was family business, that Lord Raith had been involved. I didn't want to spread it out any further than it had to go.

"Saw it with my own eyes," I said. "A middleman also explains the coordination of different interests."

Lara pursed her lips for a moment, and then her mouth quirked at one corner. "I believe I know how to turn the issue to advantage. It will be addressed."

"It isn't hard to work out why the ghouls wanted trouble with you," Ramirez said in a dry tone.

"Yeah, I'm good with them showing up, no questions," I said. "Question is, why would Drakul send his inner circle here and then blow it all up?"

Butters frowned and raised his hand. "I'm not exactly a schemy kind of guy," he said apologetically. "But when you're working out logic, the first thing you do is make sure the things you're taking as givens are solid. Do we have any way to know Drakul sent them here to kill you?"

I looked around the circle. Everyone was looking at Butters.

"I mean," Butters continued, "what if the point was to get rid of them?"

Lara chewed on her lip. "At Halloween," she said, "Drakul spoke of making his organization leaner."

"And he's still got Wild Bill and Yoshimo," I said quietly. "They aren't chump sorcerers. They're experienced battle wizards."

"And Mavra," Lara said. She nodded several times. "*Cui bono?* Mavra is now the eldest of Drakul's inner circle. She has advanced herself. Drakul's inner circle were of a courtier's mindset. They would never yield their positions or authority for something as pedestrian as practicality. Mavra is more flexible than that. She has done Drakul a service by removing clumsy, blunt instruments."

"Fighting the last war," Will said, frowning.

"What?" I asked.

"There's an aphorism used among military historians," Will said. "Everyone goes into a war prepared to fight like it was the most recent one they were in. But while the big picture of war is the same, the specifics always change. Whoever is best at adapting to those specifics prevails."

I grunted. "World War II, everyone thought naval matters would be decided by battleships," I said quietly. "But the aircraft carrier had come along."

"Exactly," Will said.

"Drakul is preparing for the next war," Ramirez murmured.

The room was quiet for a long moment.

"And he seems to have his eye on you, Dresden," Lara said.

My throat felt a little dry. Probably needed to hydrate.

"Then it's smart for us to start looking sharper, too," I said. "We need to know more. I'll speak to the Winter Lady. She has access to a lot of Winter intelligence. And I can have the Little Folk take a more active role here in town. Will, be as subtle as you can, but I want you to start reaching out through the Paranet. Disappearances or anything that looks like Black Court activity needs to get flagged."

Will nodded, writing. "It isn't going to take long for word of what happened tonight to spread among the Paranetters," he said quietly. "There's going to be a lot of people afraid of you, Harry. But I'll do what I can."

I grimaced and nodded.

"Once I have cleaned house, I'll take a more active role as well," Lara said. "Mortal intelligence services gather more information about the supernatural world than most of our kind suspect. Perhaps that can be turned to our advantage."

"I'll have to move carefully," Ramirez said quietly. "The Council's intelligence is second to none. But I'm already being watched. I'll see what I can find out."

"As, of course, will I," Forthill said. "The church is not what it once was, but we are not wholly blind to the world, yet. Sir Waldo, I'll send whatever word I receive to you through Rabbi Aaronson."

Butters looked around at us and said, brightly, "I'm just happy to be here."

That got a round of muted chuckles and smiles.

"What else?" I said. "What else can we get out of this? I don't want to get caught out again."

Down in the great hall, I could hear raised voices. Matias had begun playing his guitar. People were singing. And I could smell food being prepared. My stomach growled, and I suddenly realized how ravenous I felt. The residents of the castle had been terrified tonight—and now they were going to do something about it.

Celebrate life.

Bear stepped up to me and said, "Hey, *seidrmadr*. I've been in a lot of war councils. This was a productive one. What you do now is take the W. Go see your daughter. Play with your dog. Eat. Have a few beers. Sing a little. Yeah, there's going to be another fight tomorrow. But the day is yours. Act like it. You've done what you can to get your head ready. Now make sure your heart is, too, huh?"

Butters brightened at that. "Hell, yeah!" he said. Then immediately said, "Sorry, Father."

"Don't be," Forthill said, very seriously. "That's a hell of a good idea."

The rest of April was cool and rainy, but May came and went beautifully. We replaced the gates to the castle. Lara and I had a couple of date nights, which is what we decided to call it when we went out to dinner and then back to my place for a ritual transfer of energy.

We were both careful about keeping things cordial and convivial and calm. As if we were going to a yoga class together.

Very, very careful.

The castle was subjected to a government HBGB inspection a couple of weeks later. I toyed with the idea of having Toot and his people and the gargoyles reveal themselves to the team of inspectors, who would then, presumably, have to be worried about exposure to the imaginary toxin themselves, while I wondered aloud if they were all right. But they were only functionaries, dutifully moving around with their chemical strips and sample containers, which couldn't find something that didn't exist—so I just walked them to each floor of the castle and let them do their thing, then bade them farewell.

Didn't mean there wouldn't be trouble with the government down the road—but those particular folks weren't the ones who would bring the trouble. No sense in being mean to them.

Then June came.

The city finally got electricity working on my block again, to the celebration of all. There were nighttime block parties for a solid week, as folks turned on every light they could, played music on their radios, put TVs out in their front yards for movie parties, and generally danced about in happiness at returning to the modern world. More and more cars would go by on the street as parts to fix them finally came in, or new ones replaced old ones. Slowly, the bustle and noise of Chicago began to return.

It did my heart good to see it.

Then came midsummer.

The anniversary of the Battle of Chicago.

And I woke up in the dark place again.

It was like nothing had changed in a year. Nothing at all. My heart felt bleak. My head refused to go anywhere that wasn't horrible. I fumbled my clothing trying to get dressed. Dropped my brush three times before I could get my hair straightened out. Cut myself several times shaving and had to fight off blinding rage.

I thought about Murphy's ritual shrine, which I'd packed away into storage boxes in my small room in the basement. I thought about getting it out. Spending time drinking and playing board games until the storm in my head faded to black.

But instead, I went up to the roof, and sat in the sun and breathed, and after a while, I felt less horrible. Then I went and made myself exercise with Fitz, and by the time I was done with that I felt almost not bad.

And when I got done with that, Michael had come to visit, and he and Maggie, under Mouse's careful observation, had made pancakes, which were waiting for me when I came downstairs.

And that wasn't bad at all.

Pain is a fire. And twelve months isn't long enough to heal from life's most severe burns.

But, if you're willing to work at it, it's enough time to make a damned good start.

Michael and Fitz were on the roof with me and Maggie while we ate ice cream and I taught Fitz how to capture sunlight in a handkerchief. Mouse had lolled out to expose his belly to the sun and fallen asleep. He was snoring gently. Most of the resident families had moved out, but I'd hired Matias on with my dwindling funds to be the castle's caretaker, and he'd brought up planters to the roof, and vegetables were growing everywhere in the abundant sunshine.

"Lay it out over both hands, palms up, to start," I said.

"Why are we doing this again?" Fitz asked.

"Pocket full of sunshine is awfully handy against Black Court vampires," I said, "and plenty of other things that go bump in the night."

Fitz draped the specially prepared handkerchief over his hands and frowned. "Okay. Now what?"

"You ever see *Peter Pan*?"

"I didn't really grow up a Disney kid," Fitz said wryly.

"Heh," I said. "Okay. The basic idea is to gather your will. You focus it into a positive memory. Then as you do, you wrap the memory around the light as you fold the handkerchief closed. The memory will keep it trapped there for as long as you remember it and keep the fold intact, and you can whip it out all of a sudden if you need it."

"That sounds . . . weird," Fitz said.

"Try it," I said.

So Fitz settled down and held the handkerchief out to the sunlight. He closed his eyes, breathed slowly and methodically, and frowned in concentration.

While he did that, Maggie popped open a can of Coke and brought it over to me. She passed it to me, grinning, and I answered her smile as I took it.

Fitz exhaled suddenly and folded the handkerchief closed, clumsily and unevenly. And he dropped it. There was a flash of light, like sunlight bouncing off a ripple in the water. "Stars and stones," he complained, wincing.

"It's okay," I said. "Takes a little practice to put all that together. Try it again."

He did, several more times, to little more success.

"Again," I said calmly.

"In a minute."

"Try again," I said.

"It's so easy," he said, "how about you show me, great and mighty wizard?"

I paused.

See, the thing is . . . you have to be happy to catch sunshine like that. Truly happy. And that isn't something you can pretend your way into.

I took the white handkerchief slowly and spread it out over my hands. I closed my eyes and lifted my hands to the light, feeling the warmth shining down on me. Surrounding me was the smell of green things. Warmth. The gentle snoring of the huge dog sprawled in the sun. Maggie and Michael were playing checkers on a board a few feet away. I could still taste the Coca-Cola in my mouth that my little girl had given me, smiling.

I thought of her smile.

Michael laughed gently at something Maggie said, and I knew just what it would look like and how it would crinkle the corners of his eyes.

I thought of Karrin, and the way her laughter would peal out in silvery tones when I'd said something that genuinely amused her.

And I felt at peace with every one of those memories.

With a whisper of will, I folded the cloth closed.

And felt the warm, steady glow of sunlight inside between my palms.

I opened my eyes, and the tears in them were not at all sad.

"Huh," I said quietly. "How about that."

Which is when I realized that peace and happiness aren't the same thing. Not at all.

Happiness is peace in action.

And peace is happiness at rest.

And neither one has to be perfect to be real.

I carefully folded the handkerchief the rest of the way closed and smiled at Fitz. "Like that." Then I shook out the handkerchief, and a flash of sunlight like the pop of an enormous photo bulb washed over the rooftop. I passed it back to him and said, encouragingly, "Try again."

A car came down the street and stopped in front of the castle. Then a VW horn went *beep-beep*.

Mouse came awake instantly, flipping onto his feet, his tail wagging wildly.

I clambered to my feet and went to the battlements, looking down.

A powder-blue Volkswagen Beetle was parked in front of the castle. It had a fresh paint job and looked to have been restored with a great deal of care and attention.

My brother got out.

He stood beside the car for a moment and then called up, "Hey."

I nodded down to him and said, "Hey."

"I, uh," he said. He frowned. "I was going to give this to you for your birthday last year. But, you know. Everything."

"Oh yeah?" I said.

"I couldn't save much from the original," he said. "Just the steering wheel, really. But I've been working on it with your mechanic, Mike. I thought, you know. It's way better than a hearse."

My brother stared up at me. His face was drawn. There was a quiet yearning there. An ache.

I knew just how he felt.

"We're having ice cream and playing checkers," I called down to Thomas. "You wanna come up?"

He blinked several times. Tried to talk once and stopped, mired down by the weight of things that we hadn't said.

Then he simply nodded.

And I went down to open the door for my brother and hugged him hard.

Acknowledgments

The author (that's me) would like to thank several people critical to this book's completion. First, the readers of the Beta Foo Asylum, who had to tolerate a lot of inconsistent progress for quite a while. My always patient agent, Jenn Jackson, who does much on my behalf, and whom I probably haven't thanked enough. Anne Sowards and the team at Penguin, lovely folks one and all. Brutus and Fenris, my furry boys, who assisted by taking naps in physical contact with me while I worked and getting me out into the sunshine to exercise occasionally.

And the other Jen. She knows why.